"I've always been a big fan of Jane Porter's. She understands the passion of grown-up love and the dark humor of mothering teenagers. What a smart, satisfying novel *She's Gone Country* is."
— Robyn Carr, *New York Times* bestselling author of the Virgin River novels

"A celebration of a woman's indomitable spirit. Suddenly single, juggling motherhood and a journey home, Shey embodies every woman's hopes and dreams. Once again, Jane Porter has written her way into this reader's heart."
— Susan Wiggs, *New York Times* bestselling author

"Richly rewarding." — *Chicago Tribune*

"Strongly plotted, with a heroine who is vulnerable yet resilient . . . engaging." — *The Seattle Times*

Easy on the Eyes

"An irresistible mix of glamour and genuine heart . . . *Easy on the Eyes* sparkles!" — Beth Kendrick, author of *The Pre-nup*

"A smart, sophisticated, fun read with characters you'll fall in love with. Another winning novel by Jane Porter."
— Mia King, national bestselling author of *Good Things* and *Sweet Life*

Mrs. Perfect

"With great warmth and wisdom, in *Mrs. Perfect* Jane Porter creates a richly emotional story about a realistically flawed and wonderfully human hero who only discovers what is important in life when she learns to let go of her quest for perfection."
—*Chicago Tribune*

"Porter's authentic character studies and meditations on what really matters make *Mrs. Perfect* a perfect summer novel."
—*USA Today*

"The witty first-person narration keeps things lively in Porter's latest. Taylor's neurotic fussiness provides both vicarious thrills and laughs before Taylor moves on to self-awareness and a new kind of empowerment . . . a feel-good read."
—*Kirkus Reviews*

Flirting with Forty
Basis for the Lifetime Original Movie

"A terrific read! A wonderful, life- and love-affirming story for women of all ages."
—Jayne Ann Krentz, *New York Times* bestselling author

"Fits the bill as a calorie-free accompaniment for a poolside daiquiri."
—*Publishers Weekly*

Odd Mom Out

"Jane Porter must know firsthand how it feels to not fit in. She nails it poignantly and perfectly in *Odd Mom Out*. This mommy-lit title is far from fluff . . . Sensitive characters and a protagonist who doesn't cave to the in-crowd gives this novel its heft."
—*USA Today*

"[Porter's] musings on balancing work, life, and love ring true."
—*Entertainment Weekly*

"The draining pace of Marta's life comes across convincingly, and Porter's got a knack for getting into the heads of the preteen set; Eva's worries are right on the mark. A poignant critique of mommy cliques and the plight of single parents."
—*Kirkus Reviews*

The Good Woman

JANE PORTER

BERKLEY BOOKS, NEW YORK

BERKLEY BOOKS
Published by the Penguin Group
Penguin Group (USA) Inc.
375 Hudson Street, New York, New York 10014, USA
Penguin Group (Canada), 90 Eglinton Avenue East, Suite 700, Toronto, Ontario M4P 2Y3, Canada
(a division of Pearson Penguin Canada Inc.) • Penguin Books Ltd., 80 Strand, London WC2R 0RL,
England • Penguin Group Ireland, 25 St. Stephen's Green, Dublin 2, Ireland (a division of Penguin
Books Ltd.) • Penguin Group (Australia), 250 Camberwell Road, Camberwell, Victoria 3124, Australia
(a division of Pearson Australia Group Pty. Ltd.) • Penguin Books India Pvt. Ltd., 11 Community
Centre, Panchsheel Park, New Delhi—110 017, India • Penguin Group (NZ), 67 Apollo Drive,
Rosedale, Auckland 0632, New Zealand (a division of Pearson New Zealand Ltd.) • Penguin Books
(South Africa) (Pty.) Ltd., 24 Sturdee Avenue, Rosebank, Johannesburg 2196, South Africa

Penguin Books Ltd., Registered Offices: 80 Strand, London WC2R 0RL, England

This is a work of fiction. Names, characters, places, and incidents either are the product of the author's
imagination or are used fictitiously, and any resemblance to actual persons, living or dead, business
establishments, events, or locales is entirely coincidental. The publisher does not have any control over
and does not assume any responsibility for author or third-party websites or their content.

This book is an original publication of The Berkley Publishing Group.

PUBLISHING HISTORY
Berkey trade paperback edition / September 2012

Library of Congress Cataloging-in-Publication Data

Porter, Jane, date.
The good woman / Jane Porter.
p. cm.
ISBN 978-0-425-25300-7
1. Sisters—Fiction.   2. Married people—Fiction.   3. Families—Fiction.
4. Adultery—Fiction.   5. Wineries—Fiction.   6. Chick lit.   I. Title.
PS3616.O78G66   2012
813'.6—dc23
2011050908

PRINTED IN THE UNITED STATES OF AMERICA

10 9 8 7 6 5 4 3 2 1

For Patricia Lynn Gurney

1934–2011

*So lucky to call you Mom, loyal reader, and good friend.
Thank you for your love, your spirit, your humor,
your quilts, and your beautiful son.*

Acknowledgments

As a native Californian I have always loved California history, in particular San Francisco, with its glittering gold rush years and devastating earthquake and fire of 1906. San Francisco was my father, Tom Porter's, favorite city and three of his four children lived there at one point, my brothers in the Marina and Cow Hollow, and I in Noe Valley. My younger brother, Rob Porter, is raising his children there today with his wife, Andrea Callen, a fifth-generation San Franciscan.

This book, and the entire Brennan Sisters series, was inspired in large part by Andrea's father, Tom Callen, a brawny (and handsome!) firefighter, who is also a devoted family man and fourth-generation San Franciscan. I have long been fascinated by Tom's stories, his passion for his family, his commitment to his city, and his dedication as a fireman. From the first time I met Tom, I knew I had to write a story that would try to capture his courage, his loyalty, and his character—humility with just the right amount of swagger. Tom's a true man's man and every woman's hero. If I've gotten facts wrong, or if my research in some way failed me, it's my fault entirely. And to the firemen of San Francisco (indeed, all firefighters everywhere)—I'm a fan. Thank you.

There are others I must thank, starting with my agent, Karen Solem, for standing by me during change and finding me a home at Berkley Books with the brilliant, gifted editor Cindy Hwang, who shares my passion for great fiction. Thank you, Cindy, for having confidence that I can grow and do new things. You have taken the Brennan Sisters concept and made it so much more.

Thank you to my husband (!!), Ty Gurney, for juggling the kids and our houses and our careers and our lives and making it seem sexy and cool instead of horrifyingly stressful and borderline freaky. I do love you!

Thank you to my author friends—Megan Crane, you're extraordinary. To Lilian Darcy, who should not live in Australia but much, much closer to me. To Barb Dunlop and CJ Carmichael, who have been in the trenches with me from the very beginning, and to Elizabeth Boyle and Liza Palmer, who've always got my back.

Thank you to my "real life" friends Lisa Johnson and Lorrie Hambling for including me on holidays, propping me up when I'm tired, and hugging me when I'm cranky.

Thank you to the amazing women who work with me—Leena Hyat of Author Sound Relations, an angel, and an author's best friend; Jamette Windham, personal assistant, Mac's beloved nanny, and my friend; Kari Andersen, for savvy help with social media and reading drafts of my manuscripts; Farrell Kaufman-Hogenauer, for being a whiz with book tours and publicity; Alaia Davies, for always stepping in when there's a need and being so wonderful you feel like family.

And lastly, thank you to my readers. You inspire me every single day.

One

He was good.

Meg Roberts stood in the open doors of the Dark Horse Winery's tasting room and watched her boss, Chad Hallahan, co-owner of the Napa winery and VP of sales and marketing, work his magic on the women clustered around him. There were quite a few clustered around, too. But when weren't there?

Women loved Chad. They always had. He had charisma. Sex appeal. Warmth. It was the warmth that melted women into puddles of want.

The corner of her mouth lifted slightly as she saw the woman on Chad's right put her hand on his arm and lean toward him. Women always leaned close, too.

She'd worked at the winery for four years now, and in those four years she'd been both amused and intrigued by his effect on women. Initially she'd thought it was his good looks that sent women tumbling to his feet. But over time she'd come to realize it wasn't *how* he looked to them as much as what he did.

He paid attention to women. And he listened to them. Really listened. And then at some point while listening, he'd smile that slow sexy smile that made even sweet little old ladies' hearts race a bit.

He'd smiled that way at Meg in the beginning—with his eyes and his mouth, a smile that had heat and power—until she let him know she was happily married and the mother of three.

She'd been relieved that he got the message and he'd never flirted with her again. Meg was glad. She was. She didn't want to be tempted in any way, by any man who wasn't her husband. And Chad was tempting. Seven years younger than Meg, he was tall, strong, and ruggedly handsome. He also filled out his old Levi's quite nicely, with a small firm butt and muscular thighs.

Maybe that was his secret. That hot bod of his.

Her lips curved again and yet her chest felt tight. She'd hit forty a couple years ago and had begun to feel a little too settled. No wonder Chad's energy was appealing. To be young and hot and so very alive . . .

She watched him nod and smile at the woman on his left, and found herself wishing she was one of the women he was smiling at. Not because she loved him, or wanted him, but because she'd love to have a man look at her as though she was beautiful. Fascinating. An object of desire.

Not that Meg Roberts, aka Mary Margaret Brennan, had ever been the beautiful Brennan sister, or an object of desire. She was the practical, hardworking one. The sister who made sure all the others were dressed, face washed, hair brushed, and by the front door ready for Mass.

A light hand touched her elbow. "Meg, thank you so much for inviting me. I'm glad my schedule opened up so that I could come."

Meg turned toward Amy Chin, the young producer from the Food Network, who'd surprised everybody by showing up tonight.

"I'm glad, too. And I know Craig and Chad are really pleased you showed."

Amy's lips curled as she threw a quick glance in Chad's direction. "They're certainly telegenic, especially that one."

So another one had fallen, Meg thought, checking her own smile. "Chad's very comfortable in front of the camera," she said blandly.

"I think Dark Horse Winery is perfect for a new show we're discussing at the Food Network. I'll be in touch next week?"

"Of course. Anytime."

Then Amy was walking away, out through the Tuscany-inspired front door into the night. Meg watched her brisk, confident walk until she disappeared from sight, and then drew a deep breath, pleased that tonight's party had been such a resounding success.

One hundred and seventy-five guests had attended. Seven members of the media actually showed—two TV stations, two newspapers, three magazines, and one TV producer. The caterers' menu had wowed. The floral arrangements elicited numerous compliments. Her bosses, vintner brothers Chad and Craig Hallahan, couldn't have been happier.

She was happy, too, but in a subdued sort of way. Meg had never reveled in her accomplishments. She put it down to being Irish-American, Catholic, and the oldest of five. She had to succeed. It was expected of her. But then, from the very beginning she'd been the go-to girl in the family. Need something done? Ask Meg. Need someone dependable? Get Meg. Want it done right . . . and quickly? Meg, again.

But being Meg exhausted even Meg at times.

Or maybe that was being forty-two and juggling kids and a career and keeping track of her wonderful, but rather absent-minded husband.

Meg leaned back against the doorframe, hands tucked behind

her, and glanced toward the guests still lingering on the terrace. It was a beautiful, clear night and the flagstone terrace looked picture perfect in the moonlight with its massive weathered trellis covered in grapevines and lit by thousands of tiny white lights.

Many of the guests had driven up from San Francisco for the party. Some were serious foodies, others loved a good party, and others just needed to see and be seen. But tonight no one seemed in a hurry to leave, and Meg wished she were out there by the stone fireplace with its crackling fire and a glass of the new Merlot in her hand. It was a great wine. Craig and Chad had another winner with the Merlot.

"You're looking pensive," said Chad, joining her at the open door.

Meg straightened, and smiled, even as she swiftly smoothed her black cocktail dress. "Am I? Not feeling pensive in the least."

"What are you feeling, then?"

She stood tall. "Happy. Grateful." Her shoulders twisted. "Mostly grateful."

"Grateful for what?"

"My job. The weather. The good turnout." She nodded at the guests out on the terrace. "Everyone seems to be having a really good time."

"How could they not? It's a fantastic party. You outdid yourself once again."

"One day I'll run out of great ideas and you'll replace me, Mr. Hallahan."

"Not likely. You're as important to this winery as Craig or I am."

Not at all true, but still nice to hear, she thought, glancing at Craig where he stood behind the tasting counter. He'd spent the entire evening behind the bar, talking and pouring wine. "I'd offer to take Craig's place back there, but I don't think he'd let me."

Chad grinned as he looked Craig's way. Four years separated

the two brothers, but they looked a lot alike. They were both over six feet, both fair with light eyes. Craig had an inch or so on Chad in height, but Chad carried more muscle. Chad was also a little blonder and a lot more outgoing. Craig might be the president of the winery, with a good head for numbers, but Chad was the face of the winery and people loved him.

"Absolutely not," Chad said, watching Craig open another bottle of the new label. "That's his spot. That big counter keeps him safe. God only knows what would happen if he had to mingle."

"You're terrible."

Chad winked at her. "I know. But why reform? Good girls love bad boys. You keep us in business."

She groaned and rolled her eyes, thankful she was one of the few women in America immune to his charm. With his thick, wavy dark blond hair and deep blue eyes, people frequently mistook him for the actor Bradley Cooper. In truth, Chad was better looking than Bradley Cooper, but Meg would never tell him that. Chad had way too much confidence as it was.

"So how did you get *Wine Spectator, Wine Enthusiast,* and *Food & Wine* to all send writers?" he asked, crossing his arms over his chest, filling the doorway, making the space his.

"I'm a miracle worker," she said lightly, knowing the only miracle was making phone call after phone call to ensure the right people showed tonight. This launch was hugely important, particularly with the current economy. New wineries were opening as fast as others closed and she'd spent months obsessing over every detail for tonight's party, wanting tonight's event to be the biggest splash yet.

"You are," he answered, suddenly serious. "You're a big part of our success, Meg. We wouldn't be where we are now if it weren't for you."

"We wouldn't be here if you didn't make incredible wine."

"But you make us look good."

"That's my job."

"I know." He paused and ran a hand through his thick hair, combing it back from his brow. As long as Meg had known Chad, he'd worn his hair a little longer than was fashionable, simply because he liked it that way. "And as you do your job so well, Craig and I have been talking and we think you should go to London for the trade fair with me—"

"The London Trade Fair in two weeks?"

"Is there any other?" he asked, creases fanning from the corners of his eyes as he smiled, revealing white even teeth. Like Craig, Chad spent hours every day out of doors, bouncing between the office and the vineyards, the cellar and the tasting room. They both drove big trucks, lived in Levi's and cowboy boots, and were happiest when tromping around in muddy fields.

Craig and Chad had grown up in Napa. Their father had been a rancher, and had been determined to keep the land open for cattle, but fifteen years ago, after Craig graduated from UC Davis with a degree in plant science and agricultural management, their father allowed him to convert part of the ranch into vineyards, and when the winery took off, another portion was cultivated.

Their father, Charles, retired just before Meg had started working for the winery, but he still lived on the property in the original 1890 Victorian farmhouse on the valley floor. Today, 75 percent of the ranch was devoted to grapes, but Craig and Chad had promised their father that the rest of the acreage would remain undeveloped.

"No. But I thought you and Craig were going."

"We were, but Craig has changed his mind. He told me a few days ago that he doesn't want to attend this year and hopes you will take his place."

"He didn't say anything to me."

"I asked him not to. I thought you had enough on your plate without trying to make a decision about the show. But he and I both want you to go. We'd cover your flights, hotel, all expenses. What do you think?"

Meg's eyebrows arched. An all-expenses-paid trip to England? Work the prestigious London Trade Fair? Have a chance to put a face to some of the names she's worked with over the years? It sounded fantastic, but it wasn't that easy. She had kids and dogs, and they had homework, sports, ballet, and car pools. And then there was Jack . . . Jack sometimes being as much work, if not more, than the kids . . .

She gave her head a slight shake, dark hair swinging. "It's so soon, Chad."

"I know. And I'm not trying to pressure you, but if you do go, we should organize some buyer dinners. Craig didn't want to when he was going—hates the whole wining and dining scene—but it's your thing and I think it's essential we do some wooing with our key European accounts."

She'd worked closely with Chad on marketing and knew his goals: to double Dark Horse's European sales and make significant inroads in the Chinese market. Meg agreed that Europe was important, but her focus was China, as China's newfound wealth had created a demand for luxury items, including an appreciation for fine wine. Last year American wine imports to China dramatically increased by 138 percent, with 90 percent of that wine coming from California wineries. Unfortunately, Dark Horse wasn't part of that growth, as they weren't known in China.

At least not yet.

But Meg was privately more optimistic at the chance for growth in a newer market than Europe, where Napa wineries—despite achieving a protected name in the EU five years ago—had had little success. Compounding matters was that overall wine consumption in the EU was falling steadily.

"Which of our buyers?" she asked.

"Germany . . . Netherlands. Maybe Russia."

"Yes and yes, and definitely Russia, too," she agreed, aware that Russia was a bright spot with the consumption of fine wine on the rise.

"So you'll come?"

Meg hesitated. She'd love to attend the trade fair, she really would, but the timing was crummy. It was May, and Jack Jr. had baseball games three times a week. Tessa was dancing every day and then there was Gabi and her horse. Just thinking about the kids' hectic schedule made her stomach churn. If she left, who would manage everything while she was gone? Jack loved the kids, but he had no clue as to the work required to keep the family running.

"I don't think it's practical," she said quietly, feeling a flash of resentment for being the one to handle everything at home. There might be two adults in the house, but she was the one responsible for kids, meals, laundry, shopping, holidays, and bills. And it's not as if she didn't have a job.

"I need you, Meg." All banter was gone. Chad's voice had dropped, deepening, his tone earnest. "We make great wines, but nobody in Europe knows it."

"That's why I want you to visit China—"

"Can't think about China when I've got London on the calendar in two weeks."

She exhaled slowly and tucked a strand of straight brown hair behind her ear. She was already heading out of town this weekend, heading to the beach house in Capitola in the morning for the annual Brennan Girls' Getaway. "I'm already gone this weekend. I just don't know if I could leave my family again so soon."

"At least talk it over with Jack. Let him know we really need you there. Obviously I can go to London on my own, but I can't do what I want and need to do without you. You don't just know our wines, you know the business, the European market, and what we're up against."

It was rather heady being wanted . . . needed. It felt good to know she was considered valuable to the winery operations. "I'll talk to Jack," she said, "but I might not have an answer for you until Monday."

It was a thirty-minute drive home through miles of vineyards illuminated only by the huge white moon. The hills rolled and undulated on either side of her. The first Napa wineries were founded in the middle of the nineteenth century, with early pioneer and settler George Yount planting the first grapes in Napa Valley. A few years later, in 1858, John Patchett produced the first commercial harvest, and Charles Krug's wine cellar was established in St. Helena in 1861. By the end of the nineteenth century there were more than 140 wineries in the region. One hundred and fifty years later, Napa Valley is home to more than 450 wineries.

The wineries defined Napa, and Napa helped define California. Meg couldn't imagine one without the other, and she loved being part of the wine industry. It was exciting and interesting, especially working with the Hallahan brothers.

As Meg headed toward Petaluma, she thought about the party, the turnout, the media who'd attended, as well as Chad's invitation to go to London. The invitation to attend the London Wine & Spirits Trade Fair was certainly appealing, but Meg didn't travel for her job. That had been one of her conditions for taking the position. She'd work hard for the winery, but she needed to be home every night with her family to cook dinner, and then later, to tuck the kids into bed.

The kids were older. Gabi was now ten and she was the youngest, but Meg still needed the nightly traditions and rituals. She'd grown up in a family that put family first, and even if her father was at the fire station, the rest of them still sat down at the dining room table every night for a proper meal. Meg wanted the same for her children. Traditions were important. Stability even more so.

Gradually the dark road gave way to the lights of Petaluma,

where Meg was able to jump on 101 North. From Petaluma it was another twenty minutes to home, where she lived in a newer development of big estates in northeast Santa Rosa, each home nestled on two to five acres.

Her house, a six-thousand-square-foot Cape Cod, stood on five acres, which gave the family privacy and a very long driveway. Pulling past the carriage garage into the back, she parked next to Jack's old Saab, a car he'd had since Meg met him in graduate school.

Inside, she locked the mudroom door, set the alarm, and turned off the light over the stove before heading upstairs, where she found Jack still awake, reading in bed.

Jack looked up from his fat sheaf of papers as she entered their bedroom, his dark hair rumpled, his smile welcoming. At forty-seven, Jack was enjoying his career more now than ever. A respected architect specializing in historical preservation and traditional renovation, he was in great demand not just in California but throughout the country. Even in the early years of their marriage Meg had marveled that her husband could be so focused at work and yet so absentminded at home.

"How did it go tonight?" he asked, briefly glancing up from his reading.

"Great."

"Wonderful," he answered, dropping his gaze back to his reading.

Meg hesitated next to the bed, suddenly wanting, needing, more. More of Jack's attention. More curiosity about her night. More questions about the event, and admiration for a job well done.

She swallowed around the lump in her throat. She had worked really hard on the party and suddenly felt depleted. She needed something . . . appreciation . . . validation.

If other men couldn't flirt or make her feel good, she needed her man to flirt.

Or at least look at her.

Meg didn't like the rush of emotion. She wasn't insecure. She rarely craved compliments, but that's exactly what she needed now.

She needed tenderness. Passion. Reassurance that her husband, her partner, still found her appealing and would marry her again, given the chance.

But Jack was lost in his document and she felt foolish hovering in her black cocktail dress next to the bed, waiting to be noticed. That's what girls did at junior high dances. She shouldn't wait for attention in her own bedroom, from her own husband.

She knew Jack loved her. Jack was a caring husband and a devoted father and they had a good marriage. Even after nineteen years of togetherness, two spent dating, seventeen as husband and wife, she loved Jack. Even better, she liked him.

Meg closed the distance between them, pulling her hair aside and presenting her back so he could unzip her dress. "Chad and Craig were so pleased," she said, wondering if her black lace bra would elicit any interest. Jack had once loved black lingerie. "Everyone came. All the media, the writers, the VIP list. It honestly couldn't have gone better."

Zipper down, Jack patted her backside. "That's my girl. I'm proud of you."

A pat on the butt. She might as well be a basketball player being tapped by a coach.

She smiled faintly and, turning around, dropped a kiss on his forehead, the only bit of skin available to her, before stripping her dress off and heading for their adjoining walk-in closet.

The closet was massive, as big as a guest room, and finished in warm rich wood, but far from crammed with clothes.

Neither Meg nor Jack was a clotheshorse. Meg preferred classic pieces in neutrals like black, bone, and navy, while Jack lived in his uniform of creased chinos or faded jeans paired with his favorite worn button-down shirts. Jack liked soft and worn—it killed him to buy new clothes—and if he had his way, they'd still be living in the 1908 farmhouse they spent ten years restoring before Meg refused to go through one more winter in a house without forced air, insulation, or double-paned windows.

In the closet she stepped out of her shoes, unhooked her bra, and struggled out of her Spanx. It was a relief to be free of the snug undergarments and Meg deliberated between her favorite cotton pajamas and a black slinky nightgown. Pajamas were more comfortable, but if she wanted Jack's attention, the slinky nightgown would be better.

"Chad and Craig want me to go to London for the trade show," she said, sliding the satin gown down over her shoulders and then her hips. She emerged from the closet, sucked in her stomach, and passed close to the bed. "Craig thinks I'd do a better job schmoozing in the booth than he would."

"And you would," he answered, head still buried in his papers.

She waited a moment. "I haven't been to London since our fifth anniversary. Can you believe it's been twelve years since then?"

He made a sound, turned a page, continued reading.

Meg disappeared into the equally lavish bath with thick marble counters and creamy Italian marble tiles covering the walls. Beneath the expensive light fixture, the rich, pale stone gleamed like thick fresh cream. Opulent. Decadent. New. Jack hated it. She loved it. Even two years after moving into the house, Meg was still so very glad to be living among pretty things and nice finishes instead of historically accurate and painstakingly renovated surroundings.

Swishing the whitening prerinse wash in her mouth, Meg squeezed whitening toothpaste onto her toothbrush, more vigilant than ever about taking care of her teeth since she was drinking—and selling—more red wine than white.

"They're paying all expenses, but it's in two weeks," she said, spitting out the prerinse to talk. "I'd be there for the eighteenth."

"Okay."

"But, honey, it's your birthday."

"What?"

"I'd be gone on your birthday."

He hesitated only a moment. "No big deal. We'll celebrate when you get home."

But once it had been a big deal. Her toothbrush hovered in midair as she remembered how sacred birthdays and holidays had once been. They were special occasions, events to be celebrated together. "I head to the beach house in the morning, and am just not sure I should be heading away to London days after I get back from the coast." Meg popped the brush into her mouth and began scrubbing.

"Why not? Capitola is a girls' weekend with your mom and sisters. London is business. And I think it's wonderful Craig and Chad want you to go and represent Dark Horse Winery. I think you should do it."

This was one of the things she'd always loved about Jack, Meg thought, leaning over the sink to spit. He had always been supportive of her career, and proud of her success. He never made her feel guilty for working.

Rinsing her mouth, Meg caught a glimpse of her reflection—light brown eyes and brown hair against pale skin. She'd inherited the Brennan square jaw and broad brow and her mother's coloring. Her mother, Marilyn, was half Irish and half Italian and 100 percent strict Catholic. You didn't swear around Mom without saying a Hail Mary or two.

She spit again and paused, inspecting her face, seeing the faint lines at the corners of her eyes and the barely perceptible droop near her mouth. *Forty-two,* she thought. *Where has the time gone?*

Turning off the bathroom light, Meg crawled under the covers on her side of the bed and faced Jack, who was still reading through

his papers. She watched him read, knowing it'd be historical research on a project he'd been hired to do, or wanted to do. Jack
loved his research. Lived for historical accuracy. And that was
something she loved about him. He was so smart. And dedicated
to excellence.

"You really wouldn't mind if I went to London, then?" she
asked, stretching a hand out to touch his chest beneath the covers.
Her hand trailed down his stomach to the waistband of his pajama
pants.

Jack reached under the covers to stop her hand. "Of course not.
Why would I?"

She slowly drew her hand back, telling herself she didn't mind,
that she wasn't being rejected. "The kids are so busy—baseball,
dance, horse stuff."

"We have sitters who already drive them to their after-school
activities."

Meg suppressed a sigh, aware that it wasn't quite that simple.
Someone had to tell those sitters when to come, where to be, and
how to get there. Someone had to greet the sitters and pay them
and talk about homework and meals and possible problems. But
that person wasn't Jack. After nearly sixteen years of parenting, he
still thought babysitters just magically appeared—babysitter storks
dropping them off fully screened, trained, and prepared on the
doorstep. Ha!

Meg smashed the pillow closer to her cheek, watched Jack read.
"I know the college girls can get the kids to where they need to be,
but when they have a game, the kids want us there—"

"And I'll be there." Jack pushed up his reading glasses to the top
of his head, making his hair fluff at his crown and ears. "It's not as
if you're going to be gone for weeks. It's what? Five days? Six?"

"Probably."

He set his papers on the nightstand and leaned over to kiss her forehead. "Meg, the kids are ten, twelve, and fifteen. We can survive a week without you."

She caught his face with her hand and kissed his lips.

Tonight she wanted more. Wanted touch. Connection. She tried to deepen the kiss, but he didn't respond. Her lips went soft against his, but nothing. It was a very married kiss. A very practical, comfortable kiss. And usually it was enough.

She'd learned that it had to be enough.

But tonight . . . tonight she felt alone and lonely.

Oblivious, Jack rolled away to turn off the lamp next to the bed. "Stop worrying so much," he said as their bedroom went black.

But that was the problem, she thought, staring up at the ceiling in the dark. She did worry. She worried constantly, about everything, which was doubly stressful since Jack apparently worried about nothing. Including the fact that they hadn't had sex since . . . since . . . Christmas?

The next morning Meg had hoped to be on the road by nine-thirty so she'd be at the airport well before Sarah's flight landed, but she got a late start after discovering Jack Jr.'s baseball uniform hadn't gotten washed after his Tuesday game.

Grimacing, she pulled the plastic cup from the jockstrap and stripped the belt from the pant loops before throwing the uniform into the washer and returning to the kitchen to scribble last-minute notes for Lindsay, the Friday sitter.

In the note, she reminded Lindsay that Jack Jr.—or JJ for short—had baseball, Gabi went to the stables either today or tomorrow, but not both, and Tessa needed to go to the dance store to pick up new tights and ballet shoes before Saturday's four-hour rehearsal.

Meg chewed on the tip of her pen, wondering what she should

leave out for dinner when her phone rang. It was Jack calling from his office in downtown Santa Rosa, where he worked in an older building (of course) not far from historic Railroad Square.

"How's traffic?" he asked.

"I haven't left yet," she answered, glancing at her wristwatch and feeling a rush of panic, which only heightened her anxiety. Oh God, it was ten. She was late. Really late. "I was trying to figure out dinner—"

"I'll order pizza."

"But JJ's uniform is in the wash. It needs to get moved to the dryer—"

"I'll come home at lunch. Now go, and give your sisters and mom my love."

"You're sure?"

"Yes, Meg."

"I love you."

"I love you, too. See you Sunday. Have fun."

Two

Traffic was light—probably because it was one of those stunningly beautiful days when the red Golden Gate Bridge popped against a wash of blue and green—and Meg made it to South San Francisco in less than an hour.

She was just a few miles north of the airport when she got a text from her youngest sister, Sarah, who was flying in from Tampa Bay via Atlanta, saying she'd landed and was heading to the curb in front of the baggage claim.

Meg spotted Sarah on the curb as she rounded the terminal corner. Tall, slender, and pretty, Sarah had always turned heads as a teenager, but she was even more beautiful at thirty-four. She still wore her hair long, with the addition of artful streaks in the golden-brown color, and managed to keep her body bikini perfect even after two kids with diligent workouts. But then, Sarah, like Meg, was disciplined.

Little wonder that the youngest Brennan had caught Boone Walker's eye ten years ago when he was a first baseman for the

Cincinnati Reds and in the Bay Area for a three-game series against the San Francisco Giants. Sarah had been wary of the baseball groupies in the beginning, but how did one say no to Boone? Six foot four, gorgeous, and ridiculously charismatic, Boone attracted attention wherever he went, even before people knew he was a major-league baseball player.

"How are you doing, hon?" Meg said, leaning across her white Lexus SUV to open the door for Sarah.

Sarah flashed a smile, showing perfect white teeth. She'd had her teeth done a couple years ago, the same year she'd had her boob job, taking her stunning looks to the next level. Meg liked Sarah's teeth. She wasn't sure about the implants.

"Fantastic, now that I'm here," Sarah answered, opening the back door of the Lexus and dropping her suitcase and purse on the floor before climbing into the front passenger seat. "How are you?"

"Good. Hope I didn't keep you waiting long."

Sarah shut her door and buckled her seat belt. "I was out here only a couple minutes and it felt good to stretch my legs. It was a longer flight than usual today. I guess there were pretty strong headwinds."

"Turbulent?" Meg asked, shooting her a quick glance as she merged with airport traffic.

"Very." Sarah rubbed her hands together. "You don't know how happy I am to be here. Can't wait to get to the beach house. I haven't been since our last girls' weekend."

"You weren't there for the Fourth?"

"No. Boone had just gone on the injured reserve list and I didn't want to leave him."

"How is Boone?"

"Great."

"And the kids?"

"Wonderful, except for Ella not wanting me to go."

Meg accelerated, changing lanes, preparing to enter 101 South to San Jose, where they'd take Highway 17 through the mountains to Santa Cruz. "She's only four. It's hard for them at that age for Mom to go."

"I know. And I feel guilty leaving them, but I needed this. Needed some girl time. Adult time. Boone just got back from a ten-day road trip and I'm already sick of being alone with the kids, but we're only five weeks into the season. How am I going to make it until September?"

Meg shot her sister another swift glance as she moved into the far left lane. "Once the kids are out of school, bring them out for the summer. Come stay with us in Santa Rosa for a couple weeks, then head to the beach house for a couple weeks, and then maybe a week at Mom and Dad's. Take advantage of having family around. Kit's out of school in the summer, too. She'd be more than happy to spend time with your two."

"I wish I could. But Boone would really miss Brennan and Ella. He loves them so much."

"He is a great dad," Meg agreed, gripping the steering wheel more tightly, resenting Boone for putting them in this position where they couldn't be real anymore. Where they couldn't discuss Sarah's marriage and life with any degree of honesty.

Two years ago in June, Sarah found out Boone was having an affair. It was with someone he'd met while on the road. He said it was nothing, but *nothing* nearly shattered Sarah. Devastated, she scooped up the kids and flew home to San Francisco. Dad had picked them up at the airport and told Sarah she never had to go back to Boone.

But she did.

She said she loved him too much to leave him, only the damage had been done. The seed of doubt had been planted. Sarah and Boone were together, but Sarah was no longer secure.

It still made Meg furious that Boone would betray Sarah like that. The whole family had loved him, accepted him. He'd become a Brennan, and Brennans didn't stab each other in the back. But when Sarah forgave Boone, she asked her family to do the same. And so for the last two years they'd all played this game of pretending that nothing had happened, and that Boone was a good guy, and their conversations about him, and about Sarah and the kids, were deliberately upbeat and light. Positive. Even when Sarah looked miserable and trapped.

Meg cast Sarah a sideways glance. Like now. Well, maybe not miserable, but fragile, which made Meg wonder about the state of affairs—no pun intended—at home in Tampa Bay. But she couldn't ask, not directly, not without risking alienating Sarah.

Which was ridiculous. Meg was the oldest and she'd always been protective of Sarah, and over the years Sarah had come to her for advice on everything. But now, due to Boone's indiscretions, they couldn't talk?

Utter bullshit. What was the point of being a family if you couldn't share things?

Temper rising, Meg drew a quick breath. "It's supposed to be nice weather this weekend," she said, trying to focus on something other than Sarah and Boone's marriage. "We could even hit seventy."

"*Blistering,*" Sarah said with a wry smile, as she'd spent the last two years in the Southeast with truly sweltering summers.

"It is if you live in chilly Northern California," Meg answered even as her thoughts returned to Boone and her quiet fury. How could he betray Sarah? How could he sleep with other women after Sarah had given up so much for him? For eight years Sarah had followed him across the country, from one major league team to another, through trades and free agency acquisitions. For eight years she'd put her own life on hold to support his dreams. Where was Boone's loyalty? Where was the gratitude?

Sarah grabbed her hair, twisting it into a knot at the back of her head even as her stomach knotted inside her.

She knew what Meg was thinking. Knew Meg was still deeply

angry with Boone, and it took all of her control to pretend to be oblivious, but she wouldn't talk about her marriage with Meg. She wouldn't talk about her marriage with any of her family, except maybe with Kit. Kit wasn't judgmental. But the rest . . . they were far too Irish Catholic. Far too married to shame and guilt.

Shame. And guilt.

Sarah released her hair, letting it tumble across her shoulders. And the terrible thing was, she needed someone to talk to. Needed someone to confide in. She was worried. Scared. Always scared these days. What if Boone fell in love with someone else? What if he found someone he wanted? Someone who was . . . sexier, smarter, more fun?

Her stomach fell, tumbling. She couldn't imagine life without Boone in it. She loved him. Loved him so much that it made her hate herself. Smart women, strong women, left men who cheated. Smart women had more self-respect.

Apparently she had none.

"Do you think people realize how cold and foggy San Francisco is in summer?" she asked, her breath catching, her heart bruised.

"Nope," Meg answered, lips curling up in a tight, forced smile as she shot her sister another calculating glance. "Most people have no clue."

Meg was dying to ask questions, or put in her own two cents, but Sarah wouldn't go there. The weekend with her older sisters and mother was only just beginning and she'd never survive it if she opened her life up for discussion.

And so Sarah talked the entire way, chatting about her kids and Meg's kids, helping kill the time. Traffic was light on the 101 and they reached Santa Cruz in an hour, and then things did bog down a little once they merged with Highway 1.

Antsy that they were now creeping along, Sarah turned on the radio, flipping through the stations until she found the classic rock one that they'd listened to growing up.

Sarah was delighted to discover that the San Jose station was playing hits from the eighties for the entire next hour. She knew the lyrics to all the songs—it was the music her big sisters had listened to while she was growing up—and turning off the air conditioner, she rolled down her window and sang loudly to Toto's "Rosanna."

Meg didn't join in. But then Sarah hadn't expected her to. Meg was a great person—a very honest, honorable person—but she was a little too uptight for her own good.

Turning off the highway, Meg drove through Capitola Village down toward the beach while Sarah belted out the refrain to Foreigner's "Hot Blooded." *Got a fever of 103 . . .*

Meg parked, and glanced at Sarah, waiting for the okay to turn off the engine.

Sarah shook her head, still singing. *Hot blooded . . .*

Hot blooded . . .

Hot—

Meg apparently couldn't wait any longer and turned the engine off. "We're here."

Sarah laughed, amused by Meg's pained expression. Meg had a hard time loosening up and letting go. "Love this place," she exclaimed, throwing open her door.

"I do, too," Meg agreed, stretching as she climbed from behind the wheel.

Their house was one of the Six Sisters on Lawn Way and had been in the family for years. It had belonged to their maternal grandparents, and when they'd died, the house passed to their mother, Marilyn.

After unpacking the car, they carried suitcases and groceries up to the small, narrow two-story beach house they'd gone to for every holiday and school vacation. As Meg looked back, it seemed like everything important in her life had happened here, too: first steps, first words, first kiss, first love.

"Kit's here," Sarah said, spying a pair of pink-and-red floral clogs on the front porch.

It really wasn't much of a house—"doll cottage" was probably more appropriate—but somehow the little house with the covered front porch that faced the sea had always been able to accommodate the sprawling, boisterous Brennans and their boyfriends, husbands, and children.

"She got out of school early," Meg answered, shifting her grip on the case of wine she'd brought from Dark Horse.

Sarah juggled the suitcases to open the front door for Meg. "I'm so glad to be here," she said, glancing toward the sea. "I feel like I'm home."

"Me, too," Meg agreed, carrying the wine into the kitchen while Sarah headed upstairs with the suitcases. The house was a hundred-year-old structure that had been "updated" in the fifties, with nothing being changed since. Although to be fair, the stove had been swapped out in the seventies and a "new" refrigerator from the eighties kept everything cold.

Meg was unpacking the groceries into the white refrigerator when she heard Sarah squeal Kit's name. Meg smiled.

Sarah was the family baby, but thirty-nine-year-old Kit, an English teacher at a Catholic high school in Oakland, was everybody's favorite sister.

It was impossible not to love Kit.

Growing up, Kit was the sister Meg had been closest to, and even now, when Meg needed to talk to someone, she called Kit. Meg couldn't say the same for Kit's fraternal twin, Brianna. Brianna made her crazy. She was just grateful that Brianna, the Brennan family's prodigal daughter, lived in Africa and rarely came home.

Dairy safely stowed in the fridge, Meg followed voices upstairs to the Girls' Bunk Room, where Sarah and Kit were claiming beds.

Sarah had climbed up the ladder to her usual bed—the upper mattress above Meg's—while Kit was sitting cross-legged on her lower bunk, which faced Meg and Sarah's.

Spying Meg, Kit jumped up from her lower bunk to give her a warm, tight hug. "How did it go last night? I've been dying to get all the details. Did everybody show? Were the critics happy? What did Craig and Chad think?"

Kit had met the Hallahans at various winery events over the years, and had, for a brief period, harbored a little crush on Chad. But then, who hadn't? There was something hopelessly seductive about a man who knew how to smile . . .

"It was great," Meg answered. "I don't think there's anything I'd do differently. And you know me, that never happens."

"You must be relieved."

"I am."

Kit grinned. "And now you can relax."

Meg stretched and smiled back. "I fully intend to."

They settled onto their bunks to talk. They discussed traffic and weather and Sarah's daughter, Ella, who had serious mommy-attachment issues at the moment. They talked about Cass, their sister-in-law who couldn't be here this time due to her latest IVF cycle, and how their mother hadn't been here last year.

Sarah turned her head to look across at Kit, who was curled on her side on the opposite lower bunk. "Where is Mom? Does anyone know when she's arriving? I called her cell when I landed, but she didn't answer."

"I don't know when she's planning on coming, just that she'll be here sometime this afternoon." Kit wrapped her arms around her knees. "Have any of you noticed that she's hard to reach lately? Every time I phoned this week, I went straight to her voice mail."

Meg frowned, thinking that wasn't typical behavior for their mom, who always answered the phone, usually on the first or second ring.

"She's not sick again, is she?" Sarah asked uneasily.

Meg looked at Sarah, and then at Kit. "I'm sure she isn't," she said firmly. "She was probably just busy this week . . . doing stuff with Dad . . ." Her voice faded as she pictured Dad driving Mom to another round of doctor's appointments.

For a moment no one said anything and then Kit sat up. "Let's just call her. See where she is. Find out when she's arriving."

Meg nodded. "That's a good idea. And if she's not going to be here till later, let's just go get lunch now. I'm starving."

"Me, too," Sarah agreed.

"So who should call her?" Kit asked.

"Sarah," Meg said, slapping at the lumpy mattress. She never slept well in the Girls' Bunk Room. But years ago, after a couple of cocktails one night, they agreed this was part of the charm of the Girls' Getaway weekend. You could go anywhere for a luxurious hotel room, but you could only come to the beach house for a narrow little bed with a lumpy bumpy mattress covered in nubby sheets.

The beds had become a bonding thing over the years, particularly as the sisters slipped from their twenties into the their thirties and now headed into their forties.

Fortunately, there were other perks to the annual Brennan Girls' Getaway.

The meals without bickering kids.

The nightly happy hour featuring potent blender drinks.

The long sandy beach just across the street.

And sleeping in as late as you wanted. If you could sleep on your bed.

"Why me?" Sarah protested.

"Because you're the baby and you call her every day anyway."

Sarah laughed, shrugged. "Fine, I'll call," she said, sliding off the top bunk to grab her phone.

Kit climbed off her bed and headed to the corner, where she'd stashed her overnight bag. "And I'll throw on a little makeup. Try to make myself presentable. Just in case."

"In case of what?" Meg asked, rolling onto her stomach to watch Kit rifle through her small cosmetics bag.

"In case Prince Charming rides up on his stallion," she answered, unzipping her makeup bag.

"But you have a boyfriend," Meg protested.

"Do I?" Kit retorted, glancing up from her compact mirror, mascara wand in hand. "We've been together ten years, but Richard still hasn't proposed." Her brow furrowed, lips pursing as she contemplated the future. "I'm beginning to wonder if he ever will. What if he doesn't? We've been living together forever—"

"He will," Sarah said confidently. "How could he not? You are absolutely wonderful and beautiful—"

"Not beautiful," Kit interrupted, applying the mascara with a deft hand. "You're beautiful. I'm cute. At least, on a good day, I can be."

Sarah threw her pillow at Kit, just missing her head. "You still are! And Richard's a fool if he doesn't marry you! You'd be such a great wife and mom."

Kit grimaced as she studied her face, checking each faint line and potential wrinkle. "If my ovaries don't shrivel up and die first."

"You still have time," Meg soothed her, even though she was worried. Kit was thirty-nine. She'd moved in with Richard at twenty-eight. If Richard hadn't declared himself yet, Meg doubted he ever would. Years ago she'd been a fan of Richard's. He was an engineer. He was solid, dependable. Financially sound. But Meg wasn't a fan anymore. If he loved Kit, why didn't he propose? Kit was a teacher. She loved kids. She wanted to be a mom. How could Richard not see that? Make a commitment to her?

"I hope so," Kit said, applying a soft coral lip gloss.

"Maybe it's time you gave him an ultimatum?" Sarah suggested. "Step up to the plate, or step down."

Kit cringed. "I don't think I could. It'd be too brutal—"

"To him?" Meg demanded.

"No, to me!" Kit exhaled hard as she snapped the mirror closed. "What if he just left? I'd have nothing. I'd be starting all over—"

"Katherine Elizabeth, listen to yourself!" Sarah interrupted sternly. "You're beautiful and smart and funny and kind. You're a total catch and way too good for Richard and we all know it."

Meg nodded her head. "He's lucky to have you, Kit."

"Yes, he is," a light, mocking voice echoed from the doorway, and a shadow fell across the wooden floor.

For a moment there was utter silence, then Sarah made a gurgling sound and jumped from the top bunk to the floor. "Bree!" she cried, racing across the room to throw her arms around slim Brianna, the family wild child, dressed appropriately in cargo pants and a faded black T-shirt, her long red curls caught up in a ponytail high on the back of her head. "What are you doing here?" Sarah exclaimed, hugging Briana tightly.

"It is the Brennan Girls' Getaway, isn't it?" Brianna answered drily.

As Sarah freed Brianna, Kit moved forward to catch her fraternal twin in a hug. Kit was slightly taller than Brianna, and had always been curvier, too, with more hips and breasts, but Brianna appeared downright gaunt next to her now.

"I can't believe you're here," Kit spluttered, her hair dark auburn against Brianna's riot of bright red curls. "Why didn't you tell us you were coming? How long will you—"

"I love you, too, Kat," Brianna interrupted with a husky laugh, squeezing her back. "And if I told you I was coming, you wouldn't be surprised."

Meg held her breath, stunned. Brianna, here? Brianna at the beach house? For the weekend?

Had Mom known that Brianna was coming? And if so, why hadn't she said something? Warned Meg?

"Shocked, Mags?" Brianna said softly, casually, glancing at her older sister and using the nickname Meg had always hated.

Yes.

It'd been years since Meg and Brianna had been in the same place at the same time. They deliberately avoided each other. Bree and Meg had just never mixed . . . kind of like oil and water . . . and years ago they gave up trying to pretend that just because they were sisters, they'd ever be friends.

Ignoring the tightness in her chest, Meg went to Brianna and gave her an awkward hug. Brianna remained stiff, arms at her sides. Embarrassed and uncomfortable by her sister's unwillingness to meet her halfway, Meg stepped back, arms crossing over her chest. "Did you just arrive today?"

"Yesterday morning." Brianna smothered a yawn before shoving her hands into the deep front pockets of her olive cargo pants, collarbones jutting beneath her pale skin. "I crashed at a friend's. Felt like hell, but after sleeping for sixteen hours straight, I'm almost human again."

"So does Mom know you're here?" Sarah asked, beyond thrilled that her favorite sister had come home for the Girls' Getaway for the first time in years.

Brianna rolled her eyes. "Of course. She was the one who drove me here."

Three

By the time they finally made it out of the house for lunch, it was after two. Grabbing light sweaters, the four Brennan sisters and their mother headed across the street to the Paradise Beach Grille, which had become a favorite years ago with its great food and perfect location right on the water.

From the beginning the Brennan Girls' Getaway revolved around food, drink, talk, and sleep, although not necessarily in that order.

On these weekends they relished their lazy lunches and dinners and no one worried about setting a good example, eating vegetables, watching fats, or eliminating sugar.

No, the weekend wasn't about being good. It was about being real. Honest. But real and honest could be problematic, Meg thought, glancing uneasily at Bree. Real could be confrontational, and honest could be painful, and Meg wasn't interested in either at the moment. She was tired from the party and conflicted about whether she should go to London or stay home, and for these next few days she just wanted to feel good.

Kit looped arms with Meg as they entered the restaurant. "How are things at home?" she whispered.

Meg remembered how Jack had rolled away from her last night, so very oblivious that she might need anything physical from him. That she might need more anything from him. But then, until recently, Meg hadn't needed more. She'd been so good at being self-sufficient. Independent. "Good," she answered. "Hectic. But when isn't it?"

"So everything's all right with Jack?"

Meg shot Kit a quick glance. Had Jack told Kit things weren't good? "Of course. Why?"

"Back in March, when we were in Tahoe, you said that Jack didn't seem very . . . you know . . . into it."

Oh, right. Meg and Kit had been drinking wine after a day of skiing with the family and the wine had loosened Meg's tongue, made her confide things she normally wouldn't say. "We're just in a phase. It's only a phase. We'll soon be out of it."

"Maybe he needs Viagra."

Meg cringed. There were things she could talk about, but her sex life wasn't one of them. "Maybe. But sex isn't everything and I know he loves me. That's what's important." She hoped her brisk tone would close the subject, and it did.

The restaurant was virtually empty at two o'clock on a Friday of a nonholiday weekend and they were given their pick of tables. Sarah chose a table outside next to the railing with an unobstructed view of the wharf and water.

"God, it's good to be back," she said, sinking deeper into her chair after the waiter took their drinks order. She closed her eyes and lifted her face to the sun, the breeze tugging on her long hair. "I miss California."

For a moment no one said anything, each focused on the horizon, the mood mellow, almost serene.

Then Brianna shrugged. "I don't." She'd changed into a long

African-print skirt and a tiny rust-colored T-shirt that left nothing to the imagination. "Everything is so expensive here and people are soulless. They're never happy with what they have. It's always about getting more, buying more. Where's the joy in that?"

Marilyn looked at Brianna hard. "Brianna, are you wearing a bra?"

"I'm telling you how I feel, Mom, and you're asking me if I'm wearing a bra?" Brianna's expression tightened and she arched her back, thrusting out her breasts. "But, no. Never do. Hate bras."

"Not even for work?" Marilyn persisted.

"Nope."

"You can get away with it?" Marilyn asked.

Brianna groaned. "Mom, I work in a remote African village. I'm the only white woman for hundreds of miles. Some of the women I care for don't even cover their breasts. At least I don't go topless. Not that there'd be a lot to see. I don't have big tits—"

"Brianna Sinéad!"

Brianna shrugged. "Sorry, Mom, but it's true. I inherited my girls from you. But I'm not complaining. I've never met a man who—"

"Hey, Mom, have I told you that I love your new hairdo?" Sarah said, distracting her from Brianna's provocative comments.

"It does look great," Kit agreed warmly. "When did you have it done?"

Caught off guard, Marilyn reached up to touch the short, blunt bob. "You like it?"

"Yes," Kit enthused.

"I do, too," Sarah said, sipping her Chardonnay, which had just arrived. "You look good, Mom. *Très chic.*"

"It's not too short?"

"Not at all. That's a great length." Sarah was still studying Marilyn's hair. "And I love that you've decided not to cover the gray. It's a good look for you. Edgy. Modern."

"Because I'm so modern," Marilyn answered, a hint of laughter in her voice.

"Well, you are on Facebook now," Kit said. "We just set you up with an account last week."

Brianna's eyebrows arched. "Facebook, Mom?"

Marilyn's shoulders twisted. "Everybody does it."

Sarah set her wineglass down with a thud. "You're on Facebook and you haven't friended me?"

Marilyn added a packet of Splenda to her iced tea and stirred. "I'm not sure I was going to add you kids."

"*What?*" Meg and Sarah both talked at the same time.

Marilyn colored delicately and reached for her glass. "Well, it's for your friends, isn't it?"

B ack at the house after lunch, Brianna and Mom both went upstairs to take a nap while Sarah, Meg, and Kit headed to the front porch to read.

Meg and Kit talked for a little bit before opening their books. Sarah didn't even bother to open hers, content to just sit with a glass of wine and chill.

It had been a long flight out from Florida. A hard flight. She'd spent most of the five and a half hours worrying about Boone.

But then, all she ever seemed to do was worry about Boone. Was he faithful? Could she trust him? Was he e-mailing or texting or Facebook-messaging someone new?

The worrying made her crazy. Literally. Sarah wasn't herself anymore. Wasn't sure she'd ever be herself again.

She couldn't tell her family that. They'd be up in arms. Again.

Sarah glanced at Meg and Kit, who were both lost in their novels. Meg was reading a sober literary masterpiece and Kit a battered Regency romance. Sarah smiled faintly, thinking the reading material summed up her sisters perfectly. Meg was all about improving the mind and doing the right thing, whereas Kit was a hopeless optimist who could only see the glass as half full.

Sarah looked at her own novel. A legal thriller by Robert Dugoni. She'd bought it at the airport, but so far she hadn't opened it.

Once upon a time Sarah had wanted to be a lawyer. She'd been applying to law schools when she met Boone. She probably would have been better off being a lawyer than a baseball player's wife. She'd have more control. More confidence. Less neurosis.

Her lips curved mockingly. She had no one to blame but herself. She'd seen the looks women gave Boone before they married. She knew women chased him. For some reason she thought she could handle it.

Sarah drained her wine and went inside to the kitchen to refill her glass, her long cotton skirt brushing her legs, enjoying a nice little buzz. It felt good to be here with her family, away from Tampa Bay and baseball and stress.

Opening the refrigerator, Sarah discovered the bottle of Chardonnay was almost empty. She frowned and examined the bottle, thinking that she'd just opened it after lunch. Weird. Was anyone else drinking?

Refilling her glass, she returned to the front porch, leaned against the wooden railing, and gazed out toward the sea. It was a sunny but breezy day and the flags on historic Lawn Way snapped in the wind. There weren't many people down on the beach, but then, school hadn't gotten out yet for the summer. In just six weeks, though, Capitola, a quaint beach town ten miles south of Santa Cruz, would turn into a parking lot with its annual throng of surfers, teenagers, and tourists.

Thank goodness she was here now before the crowds and cars and noise ruined the charm, she thought, sitting back down in the rocking chair she'd claimed years ago as hers. She got enough of the crowds at Boone's games. Even when sitting with the players' wives and girlfriends, she felt overwhelmed.

But this was supposed to be her weekend. She didn't want to think about Boone or his career or what they'd do when he retired. That was still months off. Maybe a year away—or two—if they were lucky.

M eg closed her book as the screen door opened and shut and Mom sat down in her favorite wicker chair, a chair that once was white but now looked tired and rather gray. Mom's hair was disheveled and she unsuccessfully tried to hide a yawn.

"How did you sleep?" Meg asked her.

"I was out." Marilyn yawned again. "Finding it hard to wake up."

"You must have needed it," Kit said, closing her book and tucking her legs under her. "You never nap."

"Haven't been sleeping well this last week. But that did feel good." Marilyn stretched and smiled. "What time is it?"

"Five-thirty," Kit answered, glancing up from her book. "Happy hour." She looked at Meg. "You're doing your famous strawberry margaritas, aren't you?"

"I am," Meg agreed.

"Want help?"

"I got it." Meg dropped a kiss on her Mom's head as she walked past her on the way into the house.

Entering the tiny old-fashioned kitchen, Meg found Brianna already there, removing glasses from a high shelf and placing the blender and tequila on the counter.

Brianna looked at Meg but didn't say anything. Instead she continued setting glasses on the counter.

Meg hesitated, instinct telling her to turn around and walk out, but that seemed so childish. She'd been assigned the Friday happy hour weeks ago when they made plans for the weekend, and she'd make her margaritas.

Going to the refrigerator, Meg moved the bottle of Chardonnay to reach for the carton of ripe Watsonville strawberries she'd bought this afternoon. The bottle was empty. She threw it away, aware that only Sarah had been drinking white wine today, which meant she'd consumed a whole bottle by herself, and that was in addition to the two glasses she'd had at the restaurant at lunch.

Meg had seen Sarah's photographs from the sorority parties she'd attended at UCLA, and Sarah had always looked gorgeous but a little hammered. It was typical of girls in college, and as long as Sarah wasn't drinking and driving, Meg had been okay with it. But she wasn't okay with Sarah's drinking now.

She was drinking heavily. And it wasn't just socially.

Meg had to step around Brianna to get to the sink to rinse the strawberries.

Brianna made a low mocking sound as she made a show of stepping around Meg. "Excuse me," she said, carrying the blue bubbled glasses to the blender on the opposite counter.

Meg stiffened, her stomach suddenly cramping. She didn't need Bree in here, making things harder. "I've got it, Brianna," she said. "I'll take it from here."

"Mom suggested I help."

Meg began to swiftly hull the strawberries. "Well, Mom's not making the margaritas. I am. And I've got it. Thank you."

Brianna didn't go. She just gave Meg a long cynical look. "Still a control freak, aren't you?"

"I'm not a control freak. I like making the margaritas. I'm happy to do it—"

"So am I."

Meg's hands shook as she picked up another strawberry. She

hated this. Hated how Brianna made her feel mean and childish when she wasn't either of those things. "You can do happy hour tomorrow. I'm sure Kit wouldn't mind relinquishing duties."

"Grow up," Brianna muttered under her breath, grabbing a basket of hulled berries and dumping them in the blender.

Paring knife suspended, Meg turned to watch Brianna drown the blender full of ripe berries with tequila. "That's a lot of tequila," she said sharply.

Brianna tipped the bottle, and drenched the berries again. *"Bree."*

"Mags."

"The margaritas will be too strong."

"I know how to make a margarita."

"Yes, but do they have to be that strong? Sarah already has a drinking problem."

Brianna laughed, her fine eyebrows arching higher. "Because she had a couple glasses of wine at lunch?"

"She polished off an entire bottle this afternoon." Meg paused for emphasis. "By herself."

"She's on vacation, away from her kids. If she wants to drink, she can drink."

"I just don't think we should encourage her—"

"Jesus, Mags! Give it up. You're not mother superior."

Meg's mouth tightened at the frequent use of her hated childhood nickname. Mags. Sags. Rags. Lags. *Hags.*

But isn't that what Brianna had always done? Poked fun at her for being ambitious, spiritual, disciplined, while Brianna skated through life, drunk, stoned, turning life into one great big party?

"Some of us have husbands and children, houses and bills," Meg said tightly, annoyed with herself for letting Brianna get under her skin.

"Care to lead us in prayer, Sister Mary Margaret?"

"Don't."

"Why not?"

"It's so sacrilegious."

"You need a sense of humor."

Meg swallowed hard, aware she sounded like she was a cranky seventy-two instead of forty-two. "I have one."

Brianna rolled her eyes and pushed puree on the blender, turning it on.

"I do have one." Meg raised her voice to be heard over the whine of the blender chopping ice. "But it's just not out of control like you."

Brianna shrugged. "I'm not a kid, Mags. I don't get high all the time. I don't park in cars and make out all night anymore. I haven't stolen any of your boyfriends in at least twenty years—"

"You didn't steal any. I gave Jeff to you when I realized that you two were far more compatible than he and I were."

"Is that what you tell yourself?" Brianna asked, choking on a laugh as she stopped the blender.

Meg flushed. "What does that mean?"

Brianna took the lid off, stirred the pink contents of the blender before popping the lid back on. "It means you're the most unhappy person I know."

Meg went hot, then cold, and for a moment she couldn't speak. "You don't even know me! You never come home. You never call. You never remember my kids' birthdays, so I have to make excuses for you."

"It's hard to find birthday cards in the Congo."

"You could shoot them an e-mail. Just a couple lines to let them know you're thinking of them."

"You know I've got a crappy memory. I can't remember anyone's birthday. Hell, I barely know when Christmas is." She smiled grimly, two deep dimples on either side of her mouth. "But then again, I live in Africa and am focused on other things . . . like administering to dying populations."

"Of course you'd bring that up," Meg muttered, shoving her hair behind her ear before rinsing off the paring knife.

"You hate that my work is important. You hate that I've actually become someone important—"

"I don't."

"You totally do. But that's how you've always been. You're the great, responsible, virtuous Mary Margaret and no one else ever measures up to you . . . or God help them if they do."

Meg's cheeks burned, her face hot. "I've never, ever said that!"

"But it's implied in everything you say and do. Meg, the good. Meg, the martyr. Meg, who's stuck—"

"*Stuck?*"

"Settled. Married. *Miserable*." Brianna jabbed the blender's on button.

Meg's hands clenched into fists. "So says the woman who can't commit," she shouted over the blender. "You couldn't even make your marriage work!"

"My marriage? That sixty-day lark when I was nineteen?" Brianna retorted, turning the blender off again.

"Of course it was a lark. You'd never honor a vow, just as you've never kept your word, not even when—" And then Meg, so angry she was trembling from head to toe, fell silent, because she hated remembering the day four-year-old Danielle Jones was found floating facedown in their backyard pool.

If Dad hadn't come home then . . .

If he hadn't been a fireman and known CPR . . .

Meg shuddered. Even though the accident had been twenty-five years ago, it still made her physically ill to remember it.

In the suddenly silent, cramped kitchen, Brianna cocked her head. "What, Meg? Was there something you wanted to say?"

Yes. No. Meg ground her teeth together, unable to even shift blame because Danielle had been *her* responsibility. Mrs. Jones had hired Meg, not Brianna, to watch Danielle, and yet Meg—high school senior, newspaper editor, yearbook editor, student-body president—had been so anxious about getting the photos for Monday's assembly, she'd asked Brianna to watch Danielle while she dashed down to Long's Drugs to pick the slides up.

After a little bit of cajoling Brianna had said yes, promising to keep a close eye on the little girl.

Promising.

Meg was gone less than twenty minutes, but when she returned home it was absolute mayhem. Police cars, ambulances, and fire trucks lined the street, red and blue lights flashing.

She'd thrown her car into park and run through the house to the backyard, where the police were taking a statement from Brianna on the pool deck while the paramedics worked on Danielle.

Her father stood apart from all, his navy shirt plastered to his barrel chest, his pants and boots dripping wet.

She'd never forget his face when he saw her. He was disgusted. She'd failed him. Failed all of them.

"Say it," Brianna said harshly, her hazel eyes too bright in her pale face framed by red curls.

Meg shook her head.

"Say it," Brianna insisted, taking a step forward.

Thank God her father had come home. Thank God Danielle lived. Thank God there had been no brain damage. It took a year, all the way until Meg's freshman year of college, but her parents' insurance company eventually settled out of court with Danielle's family. The tragedy was over. Behind them.

But never forgotten.

"There's nothing to say," Meg said, staring out the small window at the row of houses behind them on historic Lawn Way. Most of them were shuttered. The summer crowds wouldn't descend for another six weeks. Meg liked these quiet spring weekends when the sleepy beach town south of Santa Cruz belonged to them. But even without the crowds, she couldn't relax. She lived with tension. And no amount of Our Fathers or Hail Marys had ever relieved her guilt or shame.

"There's plenty to say," Brianna retorted fiercely. "But you won't say it. You'd rather go through life hating me for a mistake I made at fifteen."

"You were high."

"I was fifteen!"

Meg turned to face her, feeling engulfed by pain. "I have a fifteen-year-old and he knows right from wrong! At fifteen *I* knew right from wrong! At fifteen I knew that life was dangerous and bad things happened if you weren't careful, and except for that one time, I was so damn careful I could barely breathe. But the one time I asked for help, the one time—" She broke off, pressed her knuckles against her mouth. Why did she always lose it around Brianna? How could Brianna reduce her to crazy?

The kitchen door swung open and Sarah peeked in, her long hair scooped up in a ponytail high on the back of her head.

"What's taking so long?" she demanded. "We're dying of thirst out there and need those margaritas pronto!" Her easy smile faded as she saw her sisters' expressions and felt the thick knife of tension. "Oh, no! You're not fighting again, are you? But why? Brianna only just got here today!"

Meg's lips twisted, her insides just as knotted. It was always about Brianna. Brianna gone, Brianna back, Brianna risking life and limb to take care of people the rest of the world forgot.

She grabbed a sponge to keep from saying things she might regret. "No one's fighting, Sarah," she said huskily, willing the tension to go away. "Everything's good. Margaritas are done."

Sarah glanced from Meg to Brianna and back. "Then how come no one is smiling?"

Brianna looked at Meg. "Tell her, Mags."

Meg's stomach fell. "Tell her what?"

"Tell her what you were telling me."

"I don't know what you're talking about."

Brianna's shoulders lifted and fell. "Sister Mary Margaret was concerned about the amount of tequila I was putting in the margaritas, Sarah." She hesitated before adding with a faint smile, "She's worried about your drinking."

Sarah paled. *"What?"*

Brianna grimaced, and Sarah turned on Meg, two bright spots of color high in her cheekbones. "You think I have a problem, Meg?"

Meg wished Brianna had never been born. Life would have been so much better without Bree in it. "I'm just concerned, Sarah. Just wanted to help."

"Help how? By calling me an alcoholic?"

"I never said that. I love you and think—"

"Mind your own damn business!" Sarah interrupted furiously, voice rising as tears filled her eyes. "You're not my mother. My mother is sitting out there on the porch and she can talk to me if she thinks there's a problem, but she hasn't, and she won't, because I don't have a problem. I drink some wine now and then. Big deal."

"You're right. I'm sorry." Meg gulped a breath. Why had she opened her mouth? Why did she constantly try to manage everyone else? Why did she think it was her place to worry? "I was wrong," she added, hating Brianna for rolling her eyes and belittling her apology.

Meg turned on Brianna. "Why do you do that? I'm apologizing and yet you're making fun of me—"

"What's going on?" The kitchen door had swung open and Kit entered the very crowded kitchen. "Mom thinks you're fighting. Tell me you're not fighting."

Meg turned around with a smile fixed to her face, but Kit's perceptive gaze missed nothing. Her eyes—the same clear blue as their father's—narrowed as she scanned her sisters' faces. "You *are* fighting!" she exclaimed, disgust sharpening her voice. "Why? This is supposed to be a fun weekend!"

"Tell that to Mags," Brianna answered. "She's the one so perfect she can go through life judging others. According to her, I'm a drug addict, Sarah's an alcoholic, and God only knows what she thinks of you."

"Easy, Bree, you only just got home, let's not rile everyone up quite yet," Kit said firmly even as she glanced at Meg, eyebrows arched.

Meg shook her head, her teeth grinding ruthlessly into her bottom lip.

Kit gestured toward the front of the house. "We're here to have fun, not fight, and Mom will be really bummed if we're going at it already. She missed last year's getaway. Let's not ruin this year's for her."

"Well said, Saint Katherine Elizabeth, the Peacemaker, and always the voice of reason," Brianna drawled, filling the five thick bubbled glasses grouped on the tile counter. "What would we ever have done without you?"

Meg bit her tongue to keep from speaking. Sarah and Kit remained silent. The kitchen was quiet except for the *glob glob* of blended strawberries and tequila hitting the glass.

Brianna glanced up and saw everyone's tight expression. Smothering a groan, she shoved a frosty glass in Kit's direction, then Sarah's, and finally one to Meg. "It was a joke, you guys. Relax, Kit. You, too, Meg. You guys take yourselves way too seriously."

And then snagging her own margarita glass, she tossed her head and walked out.

She couldn't do this, Meg thought, watching Brianna stroll out of the kitchen as if everyone else was the problem and she was the only sane one in the bunch.

She couldn't spend two and a half days in the same house, in the same bedroom, with Brianna. For a moment Meg considered grabbing her suitcase and heading to the car and just going home, back to Santa Rosa and her family, the one she'd made with Jack. But that was childish. And selfish. Mom was here and her sisters were here and this was supposed to be a fun weekend.

Fun, she silently repeated, bumping through the screen door, following her younger sisters out onto the covered porch, where they had gathered every afternoon at five-thirty for happy hour for the last ten years of get-togethers.

She took the only empty chair, a short white wicker one next to her mother's and leaned back, hating the heaviness inside of her.

But having *fun* wasn't one of Meg's strengths.

Meg was aware that she'd been described as many things in her life—ambitious, talented, intelligent, successful—but never as fun. Not even her three children would call her fun. And Meg was the first to admit that she didn't have a clue how to cut loose anymore.

Even on her rare girls' night out with friends in Santa Rosa, she found herself glancing at her watch and making mental lists of all the things she should be doing instead of sitting with friends chatting over a glass of wine. Laundry. Grocery shopping. Returning calls. Reconciling the checking account. But nowhere on her to-do list was anything to make her laugh or relax or just have fun.

Thinking of home, Meg glanced at her watch. It was a quarter to six and the girls should be home and Jack Jr.'s high school baseball game would be in the last couple innings. She hoped his team was winning. Hoped he was playing well.

"What's Dad doing this weekend?" Kit asked, squeezed onto the small wicker love seat next to Brianna.

"Enjoying his freedom," their mother answered, taking a small sip from her glass. "Playing golf with Uncle Joe this afternoon and then going to a Giants game tomorrow."

Her daughters registered surprise. "A Giants game?" Sarah repeated.

Their father, a forty-year veteran of the San Francisco Fire Department, had played baseball for five years before joining the department, bouncing up and down the minor leagues, but never hitting the big leagues. It remained a sore point with him, as even now he preferred playing baseball to sitting and watching as a fan.

Obviously he did go now and then to one of Boone's games, but that was different. He was there for Boone, to show his support, not to enjoy the sport itself.

Marilyn lifted her shoulders. "Your uncle Joe can get your dad to do anything."

"How is Dad?" Brianna asked, stretching out to prop her legs on the wicker coffee table.

"He's good. Although I get the sense that he's not as happy as he used to be working now that Uncle Joe and Bobby have retired. Your dad loved working with his brothers."

"I miss Dad," Sarah said. "I love him so much." And then she flushed pink when everyone laughed. "*What?* I do."

"We know," Meg said, reaching over to pat Sarah's arm. "You've always been a daddy's girl."

"Hey! I thought *I* was Daddy's little girl," Brianna exclaimed.

Marilyn rolled her eyes. "You're all Daddy's girls. Every single one of you. Whenever you couldn't get what you wanted from me, you raced to your father, as you knew he couldn't say no to your face. I was always the bad guy."

Meg laughed. "Not with Tommy, Mom. You're a pushover where he's concerned."

"Not true!"

"Very true," Kit chimed in. "I wouldn't go so far as to call Tommy your favorite—"

"Oh, I would," Brianna interrupted.

"But you and Tommy were so tight," Kit continued, "he had you Saran Wrapped around his little finger!"

"He did not!"

"He did, and still does," Sarah agreed. "Whatever Tommy wants, Tommy gets. Poor Cass. She doesn't stand a chance with you as a mother-in-law."

"Cass and I get along great!" Marilyn protested, pushing a short graying lock of hair back from her temple.

"Because Cass knows she has to keep you on her good side," Brianna added wickedly. "One word from you and Tommy would have her on the streets."

"That's the most ridiculous thing I've ever heard! You girls are just being silly." Marilyn placed her margarita on the table with a thud. "I've never interfered in their marriage. I've never interfered in any of your marriages or relationships." Her voice wobbled and she looked dangerously close to tears. "I've always said that I raised you to be independent thinkers and it's true. I'm not here to judge you, or criticize you—"

"It's okay." Meg leaned forward, patted her mother on the back. "You're a great mom, and we were teasing you. We know you treat Cass like she's one of us."

"And I invited her this weekend, she's one of the Brennan Girls, too," Marilyn said, still defensive. "But she couldn't come because of the egg retrieval."

"When is the egg retrieval?" Meg asked. "Do they know the day yet?"

"The doctor is monitoring it day by day, but thinks it'll be Sunday or Monday morning."

"But the doctor believes there are viable eggs?" Meg persisted.

"Thinks she should have quite a few healthy eggs to work with."

"Poor Cass," Kit said. "The waiting and wondering is probably making her crazy."

"It's making me crazy and it's not even happening to me," Marilyn answered.

"Well, Cass calls you, Mom, so you know what's going on," Sarah said. "You know how upset Tommy's been about all this."

"It's not her fault," Marilyn said.

"It's no one's fault," Meg replied. "It's just one of those things, but it's been tough on their marriage and I'm beginning to think they need to take a break from all the fertility treatments."

Sarah settled back in her chair. "I heard they are if this round of IVF doesn't work."

Kit frowned. "Did you?"

Sarah nodded. "Tommy said he's over it. Can't do it again. Cass is praying this time works."

For a moment they were silent, thinking about Tommy and Cass's struggle to start a family. They'd been going through procedures for six years to have a baby, including three failed rounds of IVF. They were in the middle of their fourth right now, with the egg retrieval scheduled for the day after tomorrow.

"I hope it works this time." Kit lightly ran her fingertip across her cold glass, smearing the condensation. "Cass will be devastated if Tommy doesn't want to try again."

Marilyn sighed. "You can't blame Tommy. He feels like he's walking on eggshells around Cass."

"I don't," Kit answered, "but poor Cass. Her stomach is black-and-blue from all those hormones they're injecting into her!"

"Never mind the financial expense!" Brianna spoke up, her tone sharp. "What have they spent now? Sixty-five thousand dollars? Seventy?"

"More. But it's their money. They can spend it on whatever they want," Meg said.

Sarah nodded. "It is a lot of money, but I couldn't imagine my life without Brennan and Ella, especially with the amount of time Boone's on the road. I would hate to be all alone while he's traveling."

"And what could be a better use of your money than for starting a family?" Kit asked.

"I totally disagree." Brianna set down her empty glass on the table next to her. "If they really wanted to be parents, they could adopt. There are millions—*millions*—of orphaned children in Africa needing homes. But this isn't about becoming parents, it's about making a replica of yourself—"

"You can't say that, Bree!" Meg interrupted. "You don't know that, and adoption doesn't guarantee a baby."

"Not a baby, no, but a child. But that's not what they want. They want a perfect little white baby—"

"Oh my God!" Meg choked. "Do you ever listen to yourself?"

Brianna shrugged. "Seventy-five thousand dollars could feed a lot of starving *black* children, if anyone cared about African children—"

The rest of what she said was drowned out by everyone talking at once. Sarah was shouting that nearly all of Boone's friends on the team were black. Kit reminded Brianna that she taught kids of all colors. Meg said Brianna loved to be contrary.

But it was their mother who silenced them all by getting up and walking into the house without saying a word.

The girls were quiet as the screen door squeaked closed. For a long moment no one said anything, and the only sound was the muffled roar of the ocean and the forlorn cry of a lone seagull as it flew overhead.

"That's not what we wanted to do," Kit said.

"No," Meg agreed softly.

Sarah sighed, nervously twisting her ponytail around and around. "And it really wasn't much of a happy hour."

Brianna's lips pursed, eyebrows arching, her expression unrepentant. "But it is typical of a Brennan Girls' Getaway. We either love each or want to kill each other . . . there isn't a lot in between."

Four

In the end only Meg and Kit went for the walk, and they climbed the eighty-six stairs to Depot Hill, and strolled along Cliff Avenue with its row of turn-of-the-century homes before heading south along Grand Avenue. It was a familiar walk, one Meg had done since a child with her grandparents, and then with girlfriends, and then with Jack on their first trip to Capitola when they were dating.

Jack had a love affair with the historic houses overlooking the sea. During their engagement they'd walk along Cliff Avenue and point out their favorite houses, and fantasize about which one they'd buy if money were no object and how they'd renovate it.

They had the money now to buy any house on this street, but if they ever moved from Santa Rosa, it wouldn't be to here. If Meg had her way—and the funds—she'd buy some land in Napa. Maybe one day have a winery of her own. She loved Napa. The cycles of sunshine and cool fog. The rural lifestyle. The golden hills marked by vines. Maybe when all the kids were grown, and college done and paid for, she and Jack could talk about their options. Until then, home was Santa Rosa.

"I needed this," Meg said as they paused at the top of the hill, the long lingering rays of sunlight splashing the houses gold. "Needed to clear my head. Get some perspective again."

Kit shot her sister a sympathetic look. "You can't let Brianna get to you."

"You know Bree and I were never close, but she's getting harder and harder to like."

"She has changed," Kit agreed, kicking a pebble onto the side of the road. "Less easygoing. More militant."

"Why do you think?"

"Too many years living in remote places? Not enough civilized company?"

"Not enough food? She's a stick. Looks like she's starving."

Kit's nose wrinkled. "She is really thin."

"Maybe she's sick."

"Do you think so?"

"I don't know. She just seems really brittle. And angry." Meg sighed, shrugged. "Who knows with Bree. I've never been able to figure her out."

Kit snapped her jacket shut against the brisk breeze coming in off the sea. Below them waves tipped by white foam crashed against the base of the cliff. "I used to be close to her. Not so much anymore. I still e-mail her once a week . . . but now she answers once every three or four weeks, and even then, it's just a one-liner, usually a joke about something."

"Mom and Dad want her to come home."

"I know. Mom's been begging her to come home for years."

They fell silent and picked up their pace, walking more briskly along the cliff trail. It was Kit who broke the silence. "I don't know what to do about Richard," she blurted, her gaze fixed on the path in front of them. "It'll be ten years in September since we started dating and yet I don't think we're any closer to getting married and starting a family than we were eight years ago when we moved in together."

Meg glanced at her, saw the tension at Kit's mouth and the worry in her eyes. "Do you still love him?"

"Of course I do! I wouldn't be with him if I didn't."

Meg wasn't so sure about that—Kit avoided conflict like the plague—so she chose her words with care. "So you love him more than your desire to have children?"

"He's said he wanted kids."

"Yes, but you're almost forty. Your biological clock is ticking. And he's a smart man. He has to know that."

"Sarah thinks I need to give him an ultimatum."

"I don't know if you should give him an ultimatum, because that gives him way too much power. So instead of waiting to react, I think you need to act. Move out. Get your own place. Give Richard some space so he misses you and realizes how much he loves you."

"And what if he doesn't miss me? What if he just lets me go?"

Meg reached out to slip her arm through Kit's. "Then wouldn't you rather know now than later?" She squeezed Kit's arm gently. "That way you'd have a chance at meeting someone new, and perfect for you—"

"Richard is perfect," Kit interrupted. "He's so smart. Truly brilliant. He loves to read. He can build computers from scratch. He's got a great career, is very outdoorsy, and he's a talented musician. You've heard him play with his jazz band."

"And I agree, he is talented, and smart, as well as successful. But does he want a family? Is he ready to settle down . . . and with you?"

Kit stiffened and pulled her arm free of Meg's. She jammed her hands into her coat pockets as she faced Meg on the scenic trail. "What does that mean?"

"I'm just not sure he's ready to settle down—"

"But you said 'with you,' as if there was someone else he might want to settle down with."

"I just think after ten years he'd know his mind, and if he was going to marry you, he'd do it. You know, like Beyoncé's song . . . if you liked it, you should have put a ring on it." Meg felt horrible for being so blunt, but Kit needed to hear the truth. Kit was amazing. Good, and lovely, and so very loving. But somewhere along the way she'd turned into an ostrich and had buried her head in the sand. It was great that she only wanted to see the best in people, but she needed to recognize that not everyone was good, or had good motives, and maybe Richard wasn't abusive, but that didn't make him right for her.

"You're going to hate me for saying this, Kit, but you'll never meet Mr. Right if you're living with Mr. Wrong."

Kit turned her face away, expression stony. "I thought you liked Richard."

"I do, but I'd like him a lot better if he'd commit to you. It's time to fish or cut bait. He needs to put a ring on your finger and marry you, or give someone else a chance to scoop you up and give you all the babies you want."

Kit began walking and Meg fell into step beside her. Kit didn't speak to Meg as they traveled the length of Hollister and then turned left onto Escalona. It wasn't until they reached the former St. John's Episcopal Church, Capitola's first church, built in 1898, and now a private residence, that Kit faced Meg. "What if there isn't anyone else out there?" she asked, her voice pitched low and sharp. "What if no one else wants me?"

Meg's chest suddenly felt tender as she drew a breath. Isn't this what they were all afraid of? Being alone? Going through life without someone to share it with?

"But of course someone will want you," Meg answered firmly. "You have to believe in yourself—"

"Easy to do if you're Mary Margaret, with a wonderful husband, three kids, no credit-card debt, and a mansion on five acres!"

"I don't live in a mansion."

"It's over six thousand square feet, isn't it?"

Meg battled her temper. "Have I ever cared about things? Have I ever wanted a big house, extravagant jewelry, fancy cars? No, no, and no. My family has always meant everything to me, whether it's you guys, the Brennans, or my family with Jack. I love family and being part of a family and that's all I want for you, Kit. If you're happy with Richard, great. But I don't think you are, otherwise you wouldn't have asked me what to do about him. I'm sorry if I hurt your feelings, or implied that I was Mary Margaret the Great. I should have realized you didn't really want my honest opinion—"

"I did," Kit interrupted miserably, shifting her weight and looking anywhere but at Meg. "And deep down I knew what you were going to say. But I guess I hoped you'd tell me everything was fine, and that everything would work out the way I wanted without me having to get hurt and be alone."

"You don't have to live alone. You could find a cute apartment, or even a little bungalow, and get a roommate and focus on friends for a while and meeting new people."

"I'm almost forty, Meg. I don't want a roommate."

"I know. You want a family and kids of your own, but you're not going to get it staying with Richard."

Kit's fine brows pulled and her lips pressed into a tight line. For a long moment she said nothing, and then her shoulders lifted and fell. "He says he loves me."

"Then I hope that's enough."

Meg's phone rang, saving Kit from having to answer.

Meg pulled her phone from her pocket, checked the incoming call. None of the kids were supposed to call her during a Brennan Girls' Getaway, but when she saw it was her youngest, ten-year-old

Gabriela, she ignored the long-standing Girls' Getaway rule of no outside calls and answered. "Hi, Gabi, what's up?"

Gabriela, the family drama queen, launched into a tearful tirade. "I hate riding. Hate it! I'm quitting. I'm never going back. Never, ever, ever!"

"What? Why? You love your pony—"

"I do, but I hate Haley Kirkland. I hate her so much."

"She's your best friend," Meg said calmly, aware that Gabi and Haley had a seriously dysfunctional friendship, one that swung wildly between loving and loathing, sometimes from one to the other and then back again within minutes. It'd been this way since they'd met in kindergarten, and Meg had learned to stay out of the conflict, as nothing she said to Gabi ever helped.

"Not anymore," Gabi said fiercely. "I'm done with riding, and I'm selling my stupid helmet and boots on eBay—"

"You're not selling your helmet and boots on eBay," Meg interrupted firmly, torn between laughter and exasperation. How did she end up with a ten-year-old obsessed with eBay? Gabi seemed to think it was something magical . . . miraculous . . . and she spent hours poring over the site, looking for things to buy, imagining what she'd sell if her parents only let her. "And if you want to quit riding you can, but you have to wait until this session ends."

"I'm not going back!"

"Yes, you are. We're not quitters in our family."

"But what about Haley?" Gabi wailed.

"You'll just have to ignore her—"

"I can't! She's awful."

"You're going to have to figure this one out, Gabi, because Haley's your friend, not mine, and you two love to fight—"

"We do not!"

Meg saw Kit's amused expression. The whole family knew that Gabi took work. She had not been an easy baby. And she hadn't become an easy little girl. Meg suspected the teenage years would be a nightmare. "Have you talked to Daddy about this?"

"Yes," Gabi said sullenly.

"And what did he say?"

Gabi didn't immediately answer. And then she let out a little huff. "The same thing you said."

Meg suppressed a smile. It was nice to know that she and Jack were on the same page when it came to the kids. "And does Daddy know you're calling me?"

"No."

Meg's smile deepened. "I didn't think so. Nor would he like it that you're calling me after he already handled this. So hang up. Calm down. And be a good girl."

"I *am* a good girl!"

"Great. Then I'll see you Sunday night." Meg ended the call and, pocketing her phone, turned to Kit, who seemed absolutely delighted by the exchange her sister had just had with her niece.

"She is such a handful," Meg said with a rueful shake of her head. "She's more work than Tessa and JJ combined."

Kit grinned. "Gabi's definitely spirited."

"And does exactly what she wants."

Kit looped her arm through Meg's. "And who else do we know like that?" she asked as they continued walking together.

Meg frowned, trying to picture someone equally demanding and stubborn and argumentative and then gulped. "Bree!"

"Yep. You gave birth to Bree."

"Oh my God."

Kit just laughed.

Dinner was mellow and uneventful. Kit baked the chicken enchilada casserole she'd made the day before while Sarah threw together her "secret" Italian dressing, which everyone knew was really Good Seasons' little seasoning packet mixed with water, oil, and vinegar. Bree set the table and Meg opened a couple bottles of her favorite Dark Horse Merlot, a 2004 vintage. They ate in the cramped dining room by candlelight, and with just the five at the old pine table, it was cozy, but if you'd added a few more, it would have been too much of a squeeze.

"I like eating in here," Sarah said, using her fork to separate the soft corn tortilla from the chicken and then popping just the chicken into her mouth.

"It'd be so much nicer, though, if we had a view," Meg said, topping off wineglasses. "I know you looked at removing the wall that separates the dining room from the living room before you got sick last year, Mom. Now that you're better, can we revisit the idea?"

Kit nodded. "I know a couple of our neighbors have done it with their houses. It's so much nicer to have one big sunny space than little tiny rooms."

"But it's a historic house," Bree answered. "Do you really want to take away the historical integrity?"

Meg groaned and reached for her wine. "You sound just like Jack!"

"But it's a valid point, Meg," Sarah said. "The Six Sisters are historical landmarks. They've been here since—what?—1905?"

"Nineteen-oh-three," Marilyn answered, "and designed by Edward Van Cleeck, the same architect who designed the turn-of-the-century Capitola Hotel, bathhouse, theater, and other buildings . . . most of which aren't here anymore, which makes the Six Sisters even more important to the community."

"But have you seen the neighbors' house?" Meg persisted. "It looks good. And the renovation didn't touch the exterior, just updated the interior—"

"Mom doesn't want an update," Brianna interrupted. "She likes the house this way. It's the house she grew up in. The house we all grew up in."

"Mom's not the only one that doesn't want it changed. I like the house just as it is," Sarah said softly, loving the beach house just as it was, grateful that nothing in the house had changed over the years. The kitchen was the same pale shade of aqua blue. The living room walls were a pale yellow and the large white vinyl couch turned into a sofa bed that creaked when you rolled over on it. The coffee table was a relic from a San Jose flea market, and although the wicker chairs on the porch were routinely spray-painted to spruce them up, the wicker was threadbare and showing its age.

"In a world where nothing seems to stay the same," she added, "it's nice to have something stable . . . familiar."

Sarah craved security. Nothing in her life felt stable right now. During baseball season, Boone belonged to the game, his team, and his performance. And right now he wasn't performing. He was in a slump and not hitting well.

Of course he didn't tell her that. Like many pro players, he was superstitious, and projected positive energy, but underneath all that positivity Sarah knew he had to be concerned about his career. It was never a good thing to be signed to just one-year contracts, and that's all they'd gotten for the past three years. Boone claimed he wasn't worried. He said that at thirty-nine he was as strong as he'd ever been, and smarter at reading pitchers than ever. But designated hitters, even the great ones, were only kept around if they connected with the ball.

Boone wasn't connecting with the ball.

At least he hadn't in the last six games. Which was forever when you were the one bringing your team down.

Meg did the dishes, shooing everyone else out of the kitchen. In the quiet of the kitchen she glanced at her watch—nine-thirty—and made a quick call home to Jack, phone tucked between her shoulder and chin as she scraped plates waiting for him to answer. "How's it going?" she asked, when he picked up after three rings.

"Fine."

She could hear the TV on in the background. "What are you watching?"

"A Disney show with the girls. *Shake It Up* or something like that."

Meg stacked the scraped plates. "Are they both fighting about being CeCe again?"

"No. They both wanted to be Rocky tonight."

"Of course. It's too easy otherwise. So how did you get the argument settled?"

"I just turned off the TV until they stopped yelling."

"In the middle of the show?"

"Caused a few tears."

"But they stopped fighting."

"For a while they were mad at me, but I think we're all okay now."

"Good job, Dad."

"Thanks, Mom."

She smiled, glad she'd married such a nice man. There wasn't a mean bone in his body. "Thanks for taking care of them this weekend so I could come."

"Of course. It's the Brennan Girls' Getaway." He paused, his attention momentarily sidetracked by something happening near him. "So how is it going? Everybody in a good mood or is it hormone central?"

Meg knew he was referring to last year's get-together, which took place two or three weeks after Cass's miscarriage, so Cass was very withdrawn, Kit was in a fight with Richard (and Richard was punishing her by giving her the silent treatment), and Sarah was either PMSing or just in a shitty mood. Meg wondered why she'd even bothered to go, as nobody seemed to want to be there. Thankfully they headed to Margaritaville Saturday night for dinner, where they ordered massive amounts of nachos and pitchers of margaritas. The greasy finger food and alcohol mellowed them out and they began to relax, and talk, and laugh. By the time everybody went home Sunday, they were all close again and in a great mood.

"It's okay," Meg answered. "The usual ups and downs. But there was a surprise when I arrived."

"What was that?"

"Bree. She's here."

"From Africa?"

"Yes." Meg glanced at the closed kitchen door. "And she's still Bree. Hates my guts."

"You've always had a sibling rivalry."

"It's just getting worse, though."

"I'm glad you're there and not me."

Meg's lips twisted. Jack wasn't into family gatherings. Couldn't stand his family. Just barely tolerated hers. But then, his parents' nasty divorce had pretty much obliterated his childhood. "Yeah, I bet you are."

"I imagine your mom is thrilled, though."

"Sarah is, too."

"Well, make the most of it and try not to let Brianna get to you. You're only there a few days."

"You're right. Thank God you're sane. Need it."

"I'll see you Sunday."

"Love you."

"Love you, too."

It was a quarter past midnight and everyone was in bed, but Sarah couldn't sleep. In Florida it would be a quarter past three and she was exhausted. She hadn't slept on the plane. Probably should have, because now she lay awake staring at the ceiling and wondering if Boone was in bed, or on the computer, or on his phone, talking to someone. With her gone, he could talk all night to someone if he wanted to.

The thought made her heart fall and her stomach hurt.

Throwing back the covers, she slipped from her upper bunk, grabbed her purse, and headed outside to sneak a cigarette. No one else in the family smoked—their dad would have a fit if anyone of them had tried—but it was a habit Sarah picked up a couple years ago from one of the other players' wives, and while she didn't smoke a lot, she liked having a cigarette now and then. It calmed her down. Gave her something to do when she needed something to do so she wouldn't go crazy. Like now.

It'd kill her if Boone was cheating again. Absolutely kill her.

And what would she do if he was? Would she leave him this time? Would she demand counseling? Or just make more empty threats?

Because that's what her threats were. Empty. She could no sooner leave Boone than walk away from one of her children. He was family. Her family. And she loved him more than life itself.

Eyes smarting, Sarah drew harder on the cigarette, holding the smoke in her lungs.

But if he was cheating . . . didn't she have to leave him? How could she stay with him without losing what was left of her self-respect?

And yet to actually leave him . . . to pack, go, take the kids from him, that would kill her, too.

The door squeaked open behind her. Sarah exhaled, blowing smoke downward in a thin stream, before glancing over her shoulder.

Kit.

"Can't sleep?" Kit asked, drawing on a sweater as she joined Sarah on the front steps.

"No." Sarah quickly put out her cigarette, and hid the butt with her shoe.

"It's late for you."

"I know. But I never sleep well away from Boone."

"I have some Ambien."

"Better not. I drank enough that I'd worry about mixing wine with pills."

"You've never been much of a drinker."

"Not since college."

"Are you drinking more now?"

"Sometimes. When Boone's not around."

"He doesn't like it?"

Sarah shook her head. "He doesn't drink. And I shouldn't. It packs the pounds on fast."

"How *is* Boone?" Kit asked.

Sarah shot her a swift glance, but Kit's expression revealed nothing—no judgment or anger, no dislike either. But then, Kit was the family peacemaker. She never took sides but ran in circles trying to support everyone. An impossible task, but that was Kit, Queen of All Things Nice and Good.

"Great." Sarah's fingers itched to light up another cigarette. "He just got back from a ten-day road trip." She said nothing for a minute, her brow furrowed as she stared across the lawn toward the beach on the other side of the street. "I hate it when he's gone that long."

"You miss him?"

"Yeah." Sarah's lips twisted. "And I get nervous."

"Of what?"

Silence stretched, and Kit didn't try to fill it, and Sarah didn't speak, couldn't, but then finally managed to shrug. "You know. What's happened before."

Kit chewed on the inside of her lip. "You don't think he's . . . he's . . . you know . . . again. Do you?"

Sarah didn't reply immediately "No. At least I don't think so. But what do I know? I didn't know before. If I hadn't seen that text message, I wouldn't have known anything." She laughed and grabbed her hair, twisting it into a knot on top of her head before letting it all go. "Jesus! I hate this. I do. I hate feeling this way."

"Would you be happier without him?"

"No." Sarah laughed, feeling slightly mad. "I love Boone more now than when I first fell in love. I'm crazy about him. But not feeling secure makes me feel even crazier."

"He knows this?"

"Oh, he knows. He knows I freak if he's out late, or if he doesn't answer his cell, or if he goes out with the guys after a game. He sees me jump every time he gets a text. Knows I look over his shoulder if he gets on Facebook. He hates that I'm so paranoid, but do you blame me?"

"No," Kit answered softly.

"So what do I do?"

"I guess you do what I'm doing . . . you stay as long as you can, and then the day it hurts too much, you gather your strength and walk away."

Kit stayed outside after Sarah went back to bed, sweater bundled tightly around her middle to ward off the cold night air. She needed to take an Ambien because tonight she wouldn't be able to sleep without it. It was hard falling asleep in the Girls' Bunk Room. The beds were too small and lumpy and it was strange sleeping in the same room with all her sisters. It'd been a long time since they were all together like this and it was both good and bad being together. Good to see everyone, but bad with the tension between Meg and Brianna.

Brianna could be such a little shit. And so disrespectful to Meg. That's the thing Kit had never understood. Why be mean to Meg? What did Brianna get out of it? It's not as if Meg went out of her way to annoy her. Meg was just Meg . . . the oldest, the bossiest . . . but there wasn't a mean bone in her body, and the truth was, Meg had always had it harder than the rest of them. Meg had been responsible for them growing up. Because she was the oldest, it had fallen to her to make sure they were dressed for Mass, or had teeth brushed and were in bed for prayers by lights-out. Meg was just in sixth grade or so when Mom and Dad started leaving her in charge when they went out. At eleven Meg was making them dinner and giving baths and helping with homework. Kit had tried to help as much as possible, but Meg was the heavyweight. She knew how to inspire terror and make everyone behave. And if you didn't behave . . . watch out. Once you were in trouble with her, you were in trouble, and there was no bribing Meg, no sweet-talking to get her to change her mind about telling Mom and Dad. She always told Mom and Dad because Meg did the responsible thing.

Kit stretched her legs in front of her and flexed her feet to admire her colorful red floral clogs. She loved her clogs. Her students made fun of them for being dork shoes, but she didn't care if they weren't fashionable. They were comfortable and just looking at them made her happy. And she needed happy right now. She needed something to make her feel good, as Richard certainly wasn't.

She should have ended things with him years ago. Before it got this far. Before she'd spent ten years waiting for the rest of her life to happen.

She'd thought being patient was the right thing to do. She'd thought that being good, and sweet, and helpful, and supportive would make Richard want to keep her, marry her.

But it hadn't.

It'd just made him lazy. He didn't have to do anything because she did everything for him. Cooked, cleaned, shopped, washed. He paid the mortgage on his condo and she did the rest . . . paid the other bills, did the errands, kept things clean and tidy and Richard's stomach full.

And she was lucky if they had sex twice a month. And when it happened, it followed a precise routine: she gave Richard head for a couple minutes while he squeezed one of her breasts and then he climbed on, thrust a few times, and came.

She never came. Never, ever with him. Not even once, although she'd come close (no pun intended) once in the early months of their relationship, back when he still tried to have her orgasm.

The thing was, Kit could come. She just couldn't do it with Richard.

Kit suddenly shivered, chilled by the cold, and the knowledge that unless she did something soon, she'd end up an old maid . . . one of those doting spinster aunts who lavished attention on nieces and nephews because she'd never have children of her own.

Abruptly Kit rose, pressed her sweater closer to her body, and headed back into the house. The idea of climbing the narrow stairs and smashing herself into the narrow bunk bed with the thin hard mattress wasn't particularly appealing, but staying outside and thinking about never having great sex or kids or a man who really loved her was even worse.

Kit locked the front door, switched off the porch light, and quietly climbed the stairs.

She should have left Richard years ago. She should have done something the moment she realized he wasn't her dream guy but just an available guy.

Five

Meg woke early as usual and grabbed clothes from her suitcase before slipping out of the bedroom to dress in the hall, not wanting to wake her sisters. Her head felt heavy and achy and she tried to remember just how many glasses of wine she'd had. Three? Four? Certainly no more than that.

Once dressed in jeans and a black fisherman's jacket, she headed up the street to Mr. Toots to get a latte. A low coastal fog had rolled in during the night and it obscured the water and clung to the village. Meg didn't mind the fog in Napa, but for some reason it tended to depress her here.

Made her miss home. Made her want to be with Jack and the kids.

But she'd be home tomorrow. She'd be back in the thick of things, juggling five things at once. She might as well take advantage of this quiet time while she could.

There weren't a lot of people out and about on the streets, but the coffeehouse was busy, the sunny yellow walls and blue flag-stone floor warming the morning, creating a cheery glow. Coffee in hand, Meg took a seat at one of the tables overlooking the la-goon, the brightly painted stucco homes of Venetian Court, and the long wooden pier. It seemed like she'd been coming to Mr. Toots forever . . . at least since it opened when she was a sophomore in high school. During weekends and holidays she'd sit at one of the tables and scribble furiously in her spiral-bound notebooks, writ-ing articles and pieces for the school paper, feeling intellectually, if not morally, superior to the tan, toned girls on the beach who never read, or scribbled in notebooks, or needed a cover-up for their bi-kinis when they walked through town.

Even at sixteen Meg wouldn't walk through town in a swimsuit without something wrapped around her hips. She hated her hips. They were large, square, and matched her ample chest. As a teen-ager her stomach had been flat, but even then Meg avoided bikinis, favoring one-pieces instead. She'd read in *Cosmo*—must have been the summer before her junior year in high school—that guys liked girls with some mystery, which meant not showing everything. Her shirred navy-and-brown one-pieces definitely didn't show everything.

God, she'd been such a good Catholic girl.

Her lips curved as she sipped from her cup. Growing up had not been easy. She'd felt pressure to succeed from the moment she first learned to walk and talk. Who put the pressure on her? Her mom, dad, Meg herself? She supposed it didn't matter where the pressure came from anymore. It was there, weighing on her like an old itchy winter coat, and if it wasn't weighing her down it was whispering in her head: *Behave, be good, be smart, do it right, don't mess up, don't make a mistake, hurry up, do more, do it faster, do it per-fectly, better than anyone else.*

So exhausting.

Meg was taking another sip from her cup when she spotted a

woman at another table with thin shoulders and a brown knit cap pulled down low, nearly masking bright red hair, and felt a sharp jolt of recognition. Brianna. When had she arrived?

For a moment Meg did nothing, confused and conflicted. And then it struck her as silly to just sit here alone with her sister at another table.

She stood up and carried her coffee to Bree's table. "How long have you been here?" she asked her sister, wondering if she should just sit down at the table or wait for an invitation.

Bree glanced up, her hazel eyes more green than brown in the fluorescent lighting, her cheekbones prominent in her heart-shaped face. "A little bit after you got here."

"You could have joined me."

Bree laughed coolly and leaned back in her chair. "Why?"

It was ridiculous, but for a moment Meg felt ashamed. Raw. As if she were standing here naked in Mr. Toots. Uncomfortable, she swallowed hard, tried to keep her tone light. "Because we're sisters."

Bree laughed again, dimples flashing, eyes glittering. At almost forty she'd come into her own and she was strong, tough, fearless. Cruel.

"What does that mean?" she asked, arching an eyebrow.

"That we're family."

"Oh, because we've got the same gene pool?"

"And because we were raised together in the same house—"

"I don't buy that definition of family. I've created my own family in Likasi, and they're people I care about . . . people I want to be around. And I'm sorry if it's mean," she added, looking Meg in the eye, "but I don't want to be around you. I don't like you."

But she wasn't sorry at all, Meg thought, suppressing all emotion. Brianna seemed to enjoy being hurtful. "That's rough, Brianna."

"But true. At least I have the balls to be honest." Bree smiled and it was glacier cold. "You don't like me either, but you're too much a Goody Two-shoes to say it."

"You're the one that can't let bygones be bygones. I'd like to be a good sister to you, Bree. I'd like to get along."

"Then like me. It's as simple as that."

Meg stood next to the table and tried to like Brianna. She did. She willed love to come, willed herself to feel good emotions, but couldn't. There were no warm and fuzzy associations with Brianna, not anymore, and so she went back, pictured Bree as a little girl with wild red curls and freckles on her nose. Tried to remember the way Bree laughed—it was so mischievous, so naughty—and the mocking you-can't-catch-me smiles she'd throw at Meg as she ran away from her sister when Meg was supposed to be watching her.

It was Brianna's favorite activity.

Make Meg run. Make Meg panic. Because the more upset Meg got, the more Brianna laughed.

"I want to," Meg said huskily.

"But you don't. You can't." She shrugged. "Which is fine with me, as I don't like you either. I'm not into having shallow, judgmental people in my life—"

"I'm not shallow!"

"Whatever," Brianna said dismissively, standing. "But I don't want to talk about this anymore, and especially not at Mr. Toots." Picking up her cup, she walked away from Meg, her black tie-dyed skirt swirling around her legs.

Meg watched as Bree pushed open the glass door to go outside onto the deck and sit down at an empty table with her back to Meg.

For a moment Meg couldn't breathe. For a moment she felt nothing. And then some hot emotion rushed through her—fury, pain, shame, humiliation. But most of all pain because Brianna made her feel insane, absolutely insane, and for a split second Meg longed to chase Brianna down and tear her apart, limb by limb, and then force-feed her those shredded limbs.

She wanted to slap Brianna's self-satisfied smirk off her face.

Wanted to make her suffer the way Meg had suffered all these years, suffering in secret, and silence, burdened by a shame she could never escape. There were still nights she woke up in a sweat, having dreamed yet again of fishing drowned little girls from swimming pools, and when she turned the little girl over, it wasn't four-year-old Danielle Jones, but Gabi. Or Tessa. Or sometimes both when the faces would morph from one to the other and Meg would reel with shock, crying for one daughter and then the other . . .

Maybe Brianna could put the past in the past, but Meg still hated herself, hated the teenage girl she'd been, the one who had been so busy, so ambitious, so driven that she'd taken on too much, stretching herself too thin, putting herself in a position where she had to ask for help.

And to think she'd turned to Bree for that help . . . what a critical error that had been.

Sick on the inside, emotions thick, sharp, heavy, Meg left Mr. Toots and headed for home, numbly walking the short distance back to the row of identical little historic houses. As she walked, she talked to herself, trying to calm herself, trying to suppress the darkness within her, a darkness that had over the years developed sharp teeth, long fangs, and wild red eyes.

You're not a monster, Meg told herself. *You're not evil. You're just a person. A person that made a mistake. And you can't let Bree get to you. She's not worth the heartache. She's not.* Brianna might be a miracle worker overseas, but here at home she inflicted so much pain.

Stomach hurting, emotions still raw, Meg entered the beach house's front door. All was still quiet and dark on the inside, but Meg thought it unlikely that everyone was still asleep. Mom, like Meg, was an early riser, and Sarah was in a different time zone and should be waking soon. Kit, though, would probably sleep as late as she could since it was the weekend and she never seemed to get enough sleep during the school year between grading papers, preparing lessons, and running the required extracurricular activities every teacher had to shoulder.

Meg went to the kitchen to make some toast to try to settle her stomach and was surprised to see Sarah already there, leaning against one counter.

"Morning," Meg said, forcing a smile.

Sarah lifted her head, glanced at her. "Hey," she said woodenly, expression vacant.

Boone, Meg thought. He'd fucked up again. "What's wrong?" she asked, her stomach cramping all over again as she set her paper cup on the counter.

Sarah shook her head, lips compressed.

Meg crossed her arms over her chest. "What's happened?"

Sarah squeezed her eyes closed. "I can't—"

"Sarah."

"It's bad."

"Tell me."

"Mom's cancer is back."

"What?" It was the last thing she'd expected Sarah to say.

Sarah just nodded and Meg stared at her, too horrified to say anything.

Mom had been in remission for the past year, after battling breast cancer twice before. *Twice.* And each time it had been a fight. An out-and-out war.

It couldn't have returned. Couldn't have. Not so soon.

Sarah pushed her long hair behind an ear, revealing the bone structure that fifteen years ago had made her a UCLA calendar girl. "She doesn't know I know." She exhaled in a quick puff. "I heard her and dad talking on the phone this morning. You know the walls are so thin and our bathroom backs up to theirs . . ." Sarah's voice faded and she stared out the back window at the house behind them, where a teenage girl was jumping onto a pink bike.

"It's why Brianna's here," she added after a moment. "Why we're all together this year. Dad flew Brianna home for the weekend so that Mom could spend time with us before she starts chemo next week."

Meg just shook her head, unable to take it all in.

Sarah's voice thickened. "We can't tell Mom we know. We're not supposed to know. She's supposed to tell us when she's ready . . . but how do we pretend not to know?"

"I don't think we can. This is bad. If the cancer's back, and so soon . . ." She shook her head again, unable to complete the thought. "We have to tell Kit and Brianna. They need to know, too."

"But Bree won't be able to keep it a secret—"

"It shouldn't be a secret."

"Mom's going to tell us. That's why we're here. But she wants to just enjoy the weekend first." Sarah turned her head and looked at Meg. "It's not fair. Her hair has finally grown in. She's just starting to play tennis again. She's feeling like herself again."

"It sucks," Meg said softly.

For a moment neither said anything, and then Sarah shrugged. "Maybe we just tell Kit. Because she's the one that helped take care of Mom last time. She should know."

"Okay. And you're right. Bree won't be able to keep it quiet. She's far too confrontational."

"So we just tell Kit."

"Yes."

They stood there, silent, feeling the joy at being in the beach house for the weekend drain away.

Sarah's eyes watered. "Dad's got to be a mess."

"That's probably why he's staying so busy this weekend with Uncle Joe."

Sarah shoved hair back from her face and blinked back tears. "I'm going to go take a shower. Pull myself together. But don't tell Kit until I'm back. Promise?"

"Promise."

And Meg didn't, even though she could think of nothing else when Kit rambled into the kitchen five minutes later, still dressed in her blue plaid cotton pajama pants, T-shirt, and obligatory sweater to fight the morning chill.

"Where is Mom?" she asked between yawns while putting the teakettle on a burner.

"Haven't seen her," Meg answered, buttering yet another slice of sourdough toast and wishing she didn't crave carbs when she was stressed. And she was stressed. The idea that Mom was sick again made her physically ill, which meant that she shouldn't be hungry, but somehow Meg felt ravenous. As if there was a bottomless hole inside of her. And maybe there was. Because Mom was Mom and invincible and she meant absolutely everything to all of them.

Kit opened the chrome step stool that masqueraded as a kitchen stool and sat down to wait for the water to boil. "I sleep so badly here," she said, raking her long hair back from her face as if she could bring some order to the auburn curls. "Maybe we don't change anything structural about the house, but we have to get new beds for our room. I'm too old to sleep in those bunk beds anymore. Can we make a deal that we'll get them swapped out before Fourth of July?"

The Fourth of July was only two months away, but it was always a big deal in their family and everyone who could headed to the beach house for the holiday. Last year Mom wasn't supposed to come—she'd only just wrapped up chemo—but she insisted on traveling down for the day even though the car ride made her ache all over. She was still bald and wore a red-white-and-blue-flag bandanna to cover her naked head.

Meg swallowed around the lump in her throat and cut her slice of toast into tidy quarters. "I think that's a great idea. Do you want to pick out the beds, or should I?"

"I'm terrible with design stuff. If you pick them out, I'll split the cost with you."

Meg nodded but she wasn't picturing bunk beds, or furniture. She was picturing Mom in her chair at the clinic with a bag dripping toxic chemicals into her hour after hour.

"Should we tell Mom?" Kit asked, pulling the kettle off the stove just as it started to whistle.

"What?" Meg looked blankly at her sister.

"Should we tell Mom we're swapping out the bunk beds, or should we just do it?"

For a moment Meg couldn't speak, her throat swelling closed, her heart aching at the thought of Mom hurting again. Suffering more.

"Well?" Kit prompted impatiently.

Meg blinked. "Just do it," she said hoarsely before taking an enormous bite of toast to appease the hollow emptiness inside of her.

"We need to go grocery shopping," Sarah announced a few minutes later, entering the kitchen with wet hair. "Want to come with us, Kit?"

Kit dunked her tea bag in the old blue cup. "We have a fridge packed with food."

"But we need stuff for lunch," Sarah said brightly. "So come with us. We'll be heading out in twenty minutes."

"If you don't mind, I'd rather stay here." Kit dunked the tea bag again. "I just want to chill. And I do have some papers to grade."

Sarah glanced at Meg and then smiled unsteadily. "We could always go for a walk. Down to the beach. See if we can find any shells."

"Okay, now you've got me worried," Kit said, looking from one to the other. "First you have to go grocery shopping, and now you're suggesting collecting shells, two things you hate doing, Sarah." She set the tea bag on the saucer and looked from Sarah to Meg and back again. "What's going on?"

"Nothing," Sarah answered, glancing over her shoulder.

"Then why are you acting like a guilty teenager? Something's going on."

"Something is," Meg said. "And we want to tell you. But not here."

Fifteen minutes later they said good-bye to their mom, who had taken a seat on the porch with her paperback novel, and were crossing the road for the beach when Brianna whistled, flagging them down. Brianna wasn't alone. She was walking with a tall, shaggy-blond-haired guy with a fairly impressive tan.

Brianna made the introductions. "Drew, these are my three sisters, Meg, Kit, and Sarah." She gestured to Drew. "And this is Andrew Lytton. We worked together a couple years ago in Uganda."

"Are you a doctor?" Sarah asked.

"No." Andrew grinned easily, flashing white teeth. "I'm a photographer." He nodded at them and then turned to Brianna and kissed her cheek. "I better run. Let's meet later if you can get away, all right?"

Brianna watched him walk away, his long legs covering the ground quickly, and her lips curved in a faintly wistful smile. "He's still so hot."

"He's Australian?" Meg guessed, thinking that she and Brianna agreed on something for once . . . Andrew Lytton definitely had a sexy vibe.

"English," Bree answered.

"Single?" Sarah asked hopefully, forever trying to marry off her single older sisters.

"No. He's been in a long-term relationship for years." Brianna shrugged. "So where are you all going?"

"To the beach. To collect shells or something," Kit said. "Want to come?"

Sarah and Meg exchanged hasty glances. Brianna saw. "What?" She bristled, standing tall. "You don't want me to come?"

For a moment no one said anything and then Sarah sighed. "No, come. You might as well hear this."

"What?" Brianna asked.

"You're leaving Boone?" Kit guessed.

"No!" Sarah cried, horrified. "No. Boone and I are fine. This is . . . about . . . Mom."

"What's wrong with Mom?" Kit demanded.

Meg put a hand on her shoulder. "Let's wait until we're on the beach—"

Kit's eyes widened. "Her cancer's back." She whispered the three words, but it was enough to silence everyone.

Sarah glanced away. Brianna's jaw jutted. Meg's eyes met Kit's. "Yes."

Kit's mouth moved and yet no sound came out. She drew a breath and then another. "What stage?" she finally managed to ask.

"I don't know—"

"Four," Brianna said. "It's metastasized. It's in her liver and lymph nodes." She saw the way her sisters were looking at her and shrugged. "Mom told me in the car on the way down."

"And you didn't tell us?" Meg demanded furiously.

"Mom asked me not to. She wanted to tell you herself." Her eyes narrowed. "How did you find out?"

"I heard Mom talking to Dad this morning," Sarah said. "The walls are paper thin upstairs," she added defensively.

Kit glanced at each of them. "So do we tell Mom we know?"

"Yes," Meg said.

"No," Brianna retorted. "Absolutely not. This is her weekend.

She gets to break the news to us her way, when she's ready, and not a minute sooner."

The weekend had changed. It was no longer the Brennan Girls' Getaway, where they lolled about, eating and drinking too much, but a weekend of impeccable manners, unfailing politeness, and painfully false cheer.

It was awful. Meg wished she were anywhere but here in this little house pretending to be celebrating life's goodness when, in truth, Mom was dying.

Mom was dying.

Standing at the cutting board, she violently chopped a Fuji apple into slices, slamming the massive butcher knife down again and again, letting the sharp blade bite into the board and the noise echo in the aqua-blue kitchen.

Meg grabbed another apple and whacked it savagely into two.

Damn the cancer and damn Brianna for being told first and for knowing the awful details.

If anyone should have been told first, it should have been Kit. Kit was the one who helped take care of Mom during her last treatment, staying at the house on weekends to give Dad a break and making meals so Dad and Mom would eat. Sarah phoned daily and sent flowers and cards and gifts. Meg visited every week, but rarely stayed overnight. But when she did visit, she tackled laundry and cleaning and did whatever errands were necessary, and there always seemed to be so many. And Brianna . . . what did she do?

Nothing.

But why should she? She lived in Africa and ministered to dying populations.

And now her own mom was dying.

Meg slammed the knife through the half apple, sending a quarter wedge flying across the room. *Jesus.*

"What's wrong, Margaret?"

Meg hadn't heard her mom enter the kitchen and she jerked around, hand flailing, knife waving. She exhaled in a whoosh. "Mom. Don't sneak up on people like that. You scared me."

"I've been standing here quite awhile."

"Do you want some apple?" Meg asked, setting the knife down and crossing the kitchen to retrieve the apple wedge from the floor near the back door. No one ever used the back door, but it had a small window and Meg glanced outside at the beach cruiser leaning against the house. The bike's paint was a bright pink color and it made Meg feel wistful. She could almost imagine being nineteen and riding the bike around town in a cute summer skirt and soft white T-shirt.

"Are you offering me the piece from the floor?" Marilyn answered, pulling out the step stool that Kit had sat on earlier and sitting down in the exact same spot.

"No." Meg's lips twitched as she threw away the wedge. "Would you like one?"

"Do you have any peanut butter?"

Meg smiled, amused. Her kids had taught their grandma to dip apple wedges in peanut butter years ago and now her mom couldn't stand to eat apples without dipping. "I don't. Sorry."

"That's fine. I don't really need it. But tell me, what's going on with you? It feels like you're avoiding me."

Meg put the cored slices on a plate and wiped off the counter. "Of course not." She placed the sponge back on the sink and turned to face her mother. "Why would I do that?"

Marilyn gazed back at Meg serenely, her eyes almost the same brown as Meg's. "I don't know." Sarah was the only other one with brown eyes in the family. The rest had inherited their dad's blue eyes, or in the case of Brianna, hazel green.

But you do know, Meg thought, staring back, trying to see past the surface to what her mother must really be thinking and feeling.

But her mother was so good at masking pain and sadness. In Marilyn Brennan's world everything was good. People were good. God was good.

Meg suddenly wasn't sure how good God was if he'd let Mom's cancer spread to her liver.

"You're upset about something," Marilyn persisted.

Yes, Meg thought, she was, and there were so many things she wanted to say, things that needed to be said . . .

Anger, pain, frustration bubbled up, adding to Meg's sense of helplessness. She couldn't stand being helpless. Couldn't bear to feel out of control. And if Mom's cancer was back—and had spread—then life was wildly out of control.

Tell me, Mom. Tell me it's back. Tell me the prognosis. Tell me the truth.

And then I can tell you how I feel, and how much I need you. But Meg couldn't say it, not any of it, because she and her sisters had committed to this wretched game of pretending not to know . . . pretending to be fine . . .

"I just have a lot on my mind," she said instead, grabbing one of the apple slices and snapping it between her fingers. "I've been asked to go to London to help represent the winery at a trade fair. The Hallahans will cover all costs. But it's soon. We'd leave eight days from now."

"How long would you be gone?"

"The trade fair is only three days, but there is travel time, and we'd have to set up the stand at the exhibition hall and that will take at least a day . . . so six days . . . five if I can get the right flights."

"So why wouldn't you go?"

Meg ticked the reasons off. "Jack. Jack Jr. Tessa. Gabriela."

"They'd survive six days without you, Mary Margaret."

Meg's eyes suddenly smarted. Her mother only used her full name when she wanted to make a point. She was making a point now. Everyone was mortal, everyone was replaceable. "It's just that there's so much going on right now. Ballet rehearsals, riding lessons and clinics, baseball practice and homework. And the homework is insane. We never had this much homework—"

"I'll come stay at the house. You have to go."

"Mom."

"I'm a nurse, Meg, a hospital administrator, a mother of five, grandmother of five, wife of a fireman. I'll manage just fine."

Meg's eyes burned and she grabbed the sponge off the sink and scrubbed at a sticky spot on the counter to hide the hot rush of tears. "Of course you can manage, Mom, but—" Her voice, already husky with emotion, cracked. "But you've got stuff to do."

Marilyn breezily waved her hand. "It can wait. Nothing's more important than family."

Six

Sunday morning they attended Mass at St. Joseph's in Capitola before going for brunch at Shadowbrook Restaurant.

During Mass, Meg did her best to ignore Brianna, focusing instead on praying for Mom, although privately she wondered if God would even hear her prayers, because she didn't go to Him often, having come to accept that God was a lot like her parents and expected her to handle her problems herself. But maybe God wouldn't be opposed to Meg praying for her mother, since her mother was a devout Catholic and prayed often.

In the ladies' room at the restaurant Sarah told Meg that she wished Mom would just break the news about her diagnosis, confessing that she was getting anxious waiting. She needed to talk about it with Mom, and soon. Meg agreed.

But Mom said nothing during brunch, or during the drive home. Back at the beach house she suggested a walk on the beach.

Kit glanced at Meg, eyebrows arching. Maybe now she would tell them.

They rolled up pants and pulled up skirts and walked in the surf away from town. They walked and walked, comfortable at the ocean's edge. The sky was very blue today and fat white clouds sailed serenely overhead like great ocean liners. Meg breathed in the salty air and listened to the waves crash and roll. This stretch of beach was so very familiar. It was *their* beach. It was home.

With the cold water rushing up against her, making her bare feet tingle, Sarah turned her head to look at her mother. Mom looked so calm and composed. As if everything was good and perfect.

And it was a lie. Because if Mom wasn't well, nothing was good or perfect.

The light, cheerful conversation wore on Sarah. She needed to talk with her mother, really talk. Unable to maintain her distance, she moved closer to her mother, slipping her arm through Marilyn's. "You doing okay?" she whispered.

Marilyn nodded, her expression serene. "It's a beautiful day, isn't it?"

Sarah's brows pulled. She hated it when Mom wouldn't let them in, wouldn't let them get close. But Mom didn't like weakness, couldn't accept help. "It is," she agreed huskily.

"Have you talked to the kids?"

"I have. Ella wishes she could come. She says she's a Brennan girl, too."

Marilyn smiled. "She's right. Maybe it's time we included the next generation in our getaways."

Sarah's lips trembled. Mom couldn't have cancer. She just couldn't. Sarah fought the urge to wrap her arms around her mom and hold tight. And cry.

Mom had barely survived the treatment last time. It wasn't fair she'd have to go through it all again so soon. Wasn't fair that her hair would fall out and that she'd get so sick that she couldn't walk or stand without help. That she couldn't go to the bathroom without Dad or Kit helping her. Mom hated being dependent. And weak.

Sarah blinked hard. Her throat ached. Thank God Mom was a fighter. That Mom was tough.

Overwhelmed by love, she slipped her fingers through her mom's and squeezed hard.

Marilyn looked at her, eyebrows lifting slightly with surprise.

"I love you," Sarah whispered, squeezing her fingers again. "I love you so much. You know that, don't you?"

Marilyn's brown eyes searched Sarah's. Her mother was looking for something—Sarah didn't know what—and must have found it, because after a moment she smiled. "I do, Sarah."

"And you know that even though I live on the other side of the country, that I'd be here with you more if I could."

"I know that, too."

Meg heard the quiet interchange between Sarah and Mom and waited for Mom to say something more, to Sarah, to all of them, but she didn't. She simply held Sarah's hand and walked, her face lifted to the sky, letting the sunlight bathe her face. They walked the length of the beach and then back.

Returning to the beach house, they rinsed the sand from their feet with the garden hose and sat down on the porch in their favorite chairs.

Now, surely, Mom would speak, sharing her news, but they sat for ten minutes, and then twenty, and then Mom sat forward in her rocking chair. "It's time to go, I think." She glanced at Brianna, who sat in the wooden rocker. "Are you still getting a ride back with Kit?"

Brianna nodded and tucked one foot behind the other. "Kit's going to drop me off in the city on her way back to Emeryville, but I'll be staying at your house tonight." She looked over at Sarah. "Aren't you staying at Mom and Dad's tonight, too?"

Sarah shook her head. "I'm catching a red-eye home. Want to be able to spend a few days with Boone before his next road trip."

"If everyone has a ride, then I'll go on home," Marilyn said,

standing. "Think I'll stop at the store on the way and pick up ingre-
dients for chicken enchiladas. Tommy loves my enchiladas and that
way Cass won't have to worry about dinner after the procedure."

"Good idea, Mom," Sarah agreed, rising to kiss her.

They all stood and she hugged each of them before retrieving
her overnight bag and purse and keys and starting down the porch
steps for her car.

Meg followed but Marilyn waved her back. "Stay, visit. I'm
fine."

Meg hovered on the stairs, ambivalent. Mom was just leaving
without saying a word about her cancer? Hot emotion rolled
through her. Why wouldn't she talk to them? This wasn't something
Mom should keep secret. It was a burden to be shared with those
who loved you, and wanted to support you. But Mom wasn't letting
any of them in. She was shutting them out. Keeping them at arm's
length.

"Mom!" she called sharply, moving to the top step.

Marilyn turned on the sidewalk and looked back at her. "Yes?"

For a moment Meg wasn't sure she could speak. Her legs felt
weak. Her heart pounded. "You're just going to leave?"

Marilyn's forehead creased.

"You're not going to say anything?" Meg persisted.

Marilyn's chin lifted. "About what, Margaret?"

"Let it go, Mags," Brianna said quietly from behind her.

Meg glanced at Bree from over her shoulder. Bree sat curled in
her chair like a complacent cat. Meg's jaw hardened and she headed
down the stairs, resentment flooding her. Why should Mom confide
in Bree but not the rest of them? What made Brianna so privileged?

"We know, Mom," Meg said thinly, turning her attention back
to her mother. "We know and you're just going to leave without
talking to us about it?"

Marilyn shrugged. "If you know, then there's nothing to discuss."

"But you didn't discuss it with us. You didn't say anything to me, or Kit or Sarah. Just with Brianna. And why just Brianna?"

"She's a nurse."

"So you're not going to tell the rest of us because we're not nurses?"

"I didn't tell you because I didn't think you needed to know right now."

Meg stiffened. "Why not?"

"Because I'm still trying to decide what I'm going to do, and I was waiting to share the news until I knew what I wanted to do."

Footsteps sounded on the porch and then echoed on the pavement as Kit and Sarah joined them. "What do you mean that you haven't decided what you're going to do, Mom?" Kit asked, shielding her eyes from the sun's glare. "Are you thinking about going to a different doctor? Is there an experimental treatment or drug you're considering?"

Marilyn didn't immediately answer. "I'm probably not going to do anything."

There was a moment of stunned silence and Meg knew she'd remember that moment forever. The sound of seagulls crying overhead even as the sun blinded their eyes. The beach house casting long shadows across the lawn. The paperback novel lying facedown on the painted porch steps. And her mother, so calm and serene in the face of death.

Meg's eyes locked on her mother's face. Even in her midsixties, Mom was pretty, her face soft, her brown gaze steady.

She'd made up her mind, Meg thought. Mom knew what she was going to do. And she wasn't going to do anything. She was going to let the cancer take its course.

Suddenly Meg and her sisters were talking at once.

"What do mean, you're not going to get treatment?" Sarah choked.

"Why wouldn't you get treatment, Mom?" Kit demanded.

"We love you, Mom!"

"I know," Marilyn said gently. "I know you love me. But there is no remission anymore. No cure. It's just a matter of time."

"But time is everything," Sarah protested, wrapping her arms around her mother. "We want as much time as we can have with you, and the treatments would buy you time."

"But buying time makes Mom sick," Brianna said quietly, joining them on the grass. "The treatment is too hard on her. Makes her wish she were already dead."

They looked from Brianna to their mother. "But you did get through it, Mom," Sarah said. "It was rough, but you did it."

"Yes, I did it, and I missed every birthday, every holiday, every one of the kids' games and performances because I was too ill from the chemo's side effects." She smiled as if to reassure them, but no one smiled back. "I did everything they told me, was sicker than a dog, and the cancer still spread. It wasn't worth it."

"Mom!" cried Kit, horrified.

"It wasn't," Marilyn repeated. "And if I only have six months, nine months, a year—"

"Six months?" Sarah interrupted.

"Might be nine months, might be a year, but that's probably pushing it," Marilyn added, her tone detached, as if she were speaking of someone else. "But whatever I do have left, I want to enjoy it. And I want to be there with you and your dad and my grandkids instead of lying in a darkened room somewhere wanting to die."

"But, Mom, we need you." Sarah's voice broke. "We can't do this without you."

"But you have to," Marilyn answered, lifting and smoothing Sarah's long hair back from her face. "Eventually we all die."

*   *   *

Meg had planned on taking Sarah back to the airport, but since Sarah's flight wasn't until ten-thirty that evening, Kit offered to drive her to the airport after dinner since she was already taking Brianna to San Francisco and they were planning on spending the rest of the day in Capitola.

Meg said good-bye to her sisters and cried as she drove home. She cried for her mom, cried for her kids, who were going to lose the best grandmother in the world, and then finally, exhausted, she cried for herself because she loved her mom, but it was a complicated love.

Meg had always needed a little more of her mother's time and attention than she got. From the time she was two, there was always another baby on the way, and the babies needed so much more than she did, because she'd become the big girl. She was supposed to be Mother's Little Helper.

But it wasn't just the babies that took Mom's attention. There were the pregnancies that ended in miscarriage and those claimed Mom, too, because that's when her mother would disappear into her room to grieve in private and Meg would stand outside the closed door, forehead pressed to wood, and listen to her mother cry. It was then that Meg had vowed never to do anything that would make her mother cry. She'd be good. She'd be so good that her mother would never be sad again.

It was six by the time Meg arrived home and the sun was hanging lower in the sky, washing the big shingle house with the gold light that comes just before sunset. After parking the car in the garage, she ran a hand through her hair and wiped away all traces of smudged mascara and liner, since it wouldn't do to return home weepy. She was the family rock. She had to keep it together. And she would. That was her job, and it was a job she knew how to do.

Dropping her bags in the mud room, she caught a glimpse of Jack in the back on the patio grilling steaks for dinner while Tessa sprawled on a lounge chair talking to him. His dark hair was rumpled, and he was wearing an old white Grateful Dead T-shirt that had turned gray from years of wear, loose 501s, and his hideous Birkenstocks, but Meg didn't think he'd ever looked better. She stepped onto the patio and he greeted her with a hug and kiss and she stayed there in his arms, absorbing his warmth, grateful for his inherent goodness, his kindness, his patience with her and the kids.

"Thank you," she whispered, breathing in his scent of soap and clean skin.

"Thank you for what?" he asked, tightening his arm around her waist.

"Just being you."

He kissed her, released her, and Meg moved to the lounge chair where Tessa sprawled in white denim short shorts and a pale pink T-shirt that read EAT, SLEEP, DANCE, her long legs crossed delicately at the ankle. She looked like a ballerina even in repose.

Leaning over Tessa, Meg kissed the top of her head, stroked her dark auburn hair. "How did rehearsal go yesterday?"

"My new pointe shoes have given me blisters." Tessa lifted a foot for her mother's inspection, toes pointed. "Look."

This was Tessa's first year on pointe and it had been a difficult transition despite her passion for dance. Examining her daughter's foot, Meg could see that every toe was bloodied, blistered, and bruised. "Ouch," she said, lightly touching one popped blister, glad to see that the blisters were drying, necessary for the skin to heal quickly. "Were you able to dance?"

"I danced. But it hurt so bad. I felt like crying the whole time."

"But you didn't."

Tessa didn't immediately reply. "My eyes did water." She paused. "I hope no one saw. I don't want them to think I can't handle it, because I can. I did."

"How are you padding your toes?"

"The way I always do."

Meg had danced growing up, taking ballet classes at the studio in their neighborhood, just as her sisters had. And while she had loved it, she didn't have the talent. None of them did except for Brianna. Brianna was just naturally gifted and had perfect turnout, exemplary technique, and snared coveted roles in the dance recitals all without trying.

It killed Meg.

Meg attended every class, every rehearsal, and yet never managed to look anything other than solid and sturdy, while elfin Brianna exploded across the dance floor. No one's pirouettes were cleaner, faster. No one's jetés were crisper. No one's jumps higher.

At eleven Brianna played Clara in the local production of *Nutcracker.*

At twelve she became the poster girl for the studio, appearing in their ads and print work.

At thirteen Brianna was invited to attend the San Francisco Ballet School. (She turned the offer down.)

At fourteen she discovered pot and within months was kicked out of class for being stoned. She never danced again.

Meg didn't understand it. She didn't understand how someone, with so much talent, could just walk away from opportunity. Meg wasn't gifted or talented at anything. She just happened to work exhaustingly hard.

And now Meg had a daughter who loved dance, and while she didn't have Meg's solid, wooden form, she didn't have Brianna's explosive technique either. And to make it in dance, you have to be better than good. You have to be brilliant.

Tessa wasn't worried about the odds, though. She dreamed big and took four classes a week, plus rehearsals on weekends, and pictured herself attending the San Francisco Ballet School soon.

Tessa knew she would dramatically increase her odds of getting noticed if she attended SF Ballet School's five-week summer program, and she'd wanted to attend this year, but she wasn't old enough. Next year she would be and Meg had agreed she could audition.

"A little over a month from now SF Ballet School's summer program starts," Tessa said, reminding her mother. "I'm going to be doing it next summer."

"You have to be accepted."

"I will be," Tessa answered, rising from the lounge chair.

Meg had to admire her confidence. And innocence. Tessa hadn't yet learned that sometimes one didn't get what one wanted, despite hard work, and faith. But those lessons would come. Meg just hoped they wouldn't come too soon. She was grateful for the bubble of youth, the protective skin of obliviousness. Her children knew bad things happened, but it was a concept that took place "out there," somewhere in the world. Not near them, and certainly not at home.

Once upon a time Meg had been the same. There was nothing she couldn't do. All she had to do was try. And believe.

And Meg had believed. She'd grown up going to a Catholic school from kindergarten to eighth grade, and every day for eight years they studied religion. Every Friday was a school Mass. Every Sunday she attended Mass with her family. There were nightly prayers and blessings and trips to confession. She was wrapped in the Church, cocooned in faith, and taught to believe that as long as she didn't sin, she was safe. And then she grew up.

You could be as virtuous as you wanted, but bad things still happened.

The door closed behind Tessa and Meg looked at Jack, who was flipping the steaks. They smelled great but Meg had no appetite. She felt drained. "Mom's cancer is back," she said abruptly.

Jack turned and looked at her. She couldn't even meet his gaze. She almost didn't want him to see her, not when the shock was still so new and raw. Her voice shook. "It's metastasized. It's in her liver. Inoperable."

"Oh, honey—"

"She's not going to do any treatment this time," Meg rushed on, afraid that if she didn't say the words quickly, she wouldn't be able to say them at all. "They'll make sure she's comfortable at the end—" Her voice broke, and she fought to regain control. "But that's all she's going to do."

"How much time are they giving her?"

Meg shrugged. "Months? A year? Hard to say." Now she looked at him, really looked at him, and her eyes stung. "How is that possible?"

"I don't know."

She swallowed hard, blinked back tears. "How do we tell the kids? What do we tell the kids?"

"I don't know that either."

Going to bed that night, Meg pressed close to Jack's back, needing his warmth even as he snored on. She felt scared in a way she hadn't felt in years. Scared that she'd fail. Scared that she wouldn't be able to cope. Scared that she couldn't do it anymore . . . this endless juggling of chores and duty and responsibility . . .

Sometimes it was too much.

Sometimes she couldn't breathe.

She'd never admit it, would never tell anyone, not even Kit, but there were times when she felt dead inside. As if she wasn't Meg anymore. As if Meg had gone somewhere—supposedly for a brief respite—but she'd never come back and this other person, this body called Mary Margaret, was going through the motions, keeping it together, until the real Meg came back.

But what if the real Meg never came back?

What if this was all there ever was?

Could she do it? Could she be happy with numb and empty?

Of course she could. She had to be. She was a Brennan, for God's sake. The oldest Brennan girl. It didn't matter if she was tired. She'd push on. Push through. It's what her mother did. It's what she'd do, too.

Shivering, Meg pressed herself even closer to Jack, slipping her legs between his to feel anchored and secure.

Sleepily he reached out and patted her bottom. "You okay?"

She blinked back tears. "Mmm-hmm."

He mumbled something unintelligible and fell back asleep.

She kissed his back, once and again, swallowing hard to keep from crying aloud. She hated herself when she cried. Hated the sadness and fear clawing at her insides. This wasn't a good way to feel. Wasn't the way she wanted to be.

Determined to regain control, Meg forced herself to think about something else, like work, and the London Wine & Spirits Trade Fair. She didn't know if she should go, and yes, the trade fair was important for the winery, but it wouldn't be important to her family. And her priority ought to be her family, especially now with Mom sick again.

But to turn the opportunity down? That didn't feel right either.

Dark Horse Winery depended on her, almost as much as her husband and kids. In a way, the winery had become her family, too. So what was she to do? Go? Stay? Her mind said go. Her heart said stay. Too bad the timing wasn't better.

The next morning, Meg had just dropped Gabi off at school, the last stop on her morning car pool, when her phone rang. It was Kit, and Meg's first thought was that she was calling with news about Cass's egg retrieval. But it was something entirely different. "It's over with Richard," Kit said in a breathless rush. "We ended it last night."

"*What?*"

"I know. Crazy, isn't it?" she said, voice wobbling. "After dropping Sarah off at the airport, I came home and told Richard I needed more. That I wanted to get married and have kids and I hoped he did, too. But he didn't. And so I said it's over."

Meg couldn't believe what she was hearing. Kit had been with Richard for ten years. A decade. How could it be over so abruptly? "Just like that?"

"You were right. You and Sarah. He was never going to marry me."

Meg's heart fell. Kit had played the wild card and she'd lost. "Oh, Kit."

"It's okay." Tears thickened Kit's voice. She sounded far from okay. "Life is really short. Too short to waste with someone who doesn't want you—and let's face it. He didn't. He didn't want to be bothered. And if I ever got sick . . . or had cancer . . . he'd never take care of me. Not the way Dad takes care of Mom."

"Dad adores Mom."

"I know." Kit's voice broke. "I want that, too."

Meg wanted it for Kit as well. Kit deserved every happiness, and a prince of a man, instead of a selfish boor who didn't give a fig for anyone but himself. "So what happens now?"

"I have to move out."

"When?"

"Tonight."

"*Tonight?*"

"It's his place and Richard doesn't want me there anymore."

"He can't give you a few days?" Meg asked incredulously.

"I guess not."

"Oh my God. What an asshole! Do you need help? I can head down after work," Meg offered, scrambling to think of her schedule. JJ had a baseball game and Tessa had dance, but Gabi had nothing. Gabi would need supervision, though. Meg hated to miss another one of JJ's games, but there was no way she could leave Kit to move on her own. She'd been living in the condo for ten years. She had so much there . . . not that Meg had visited their place much. Richard didn't like to socialize with Kit's family much.

"I'm going to stay with Polly tonight, and her boyfriend, Brad, and his friends have offered to help me move after school," Kit answered, referring to her best friend, one of the math teachers at Kit's school. "Most of the furniture is Richard's. I just have a few pieces, and then dishes, and clothes."

"Where will you put your stuff?"

"In Brad's garage. But it's only for a few days. I'm hoping to get a place of my own by this weekend and then Tommy and some of his friends will help me move in."

"Are you sure you don't want my help?"

"Not tonight. But if I haven't found a place by Friday, maybe I can come stay with you guys this weekend?"

"Of course. Anything. Just let me know, okay?"

"I will."

"Love you, Kit Kat."

"Love you, too, Mags."

Meg heard the wobble in Kit's voice and her heart hurt all over again. Kit did not do well with change. She must be feeling like hell right now. "Call me anytime," she said gently.

"I will."

They said good-bye and hung up, and over in Oakland at Memorial High School, Kit covered her face with her hands as she sat stiffly in the chair at her desk at the back of her classroom.

She felt bad. Horrible. And she'd done this to herself, brought this heartbreak on by going home last night from Capitola and giving Richard an ultimatum. Marry her, or it's over.

And of course Richard chose it's over.

She wanted to cry at her folly, wanted to cry for loving and needing someone who didn't need her. Wanted to cry that she'd settled, because she had; she'd chosen the first man who showed interest and then stayed with him, afraid that there would be no one else.

And now there *was* no one.

It horrified her that she was so weak, so dependent on a man. She hadn't been raised to be a coward. And if she was acting out of fear, where was her faith?

Kit wondered if she even had true faith.

She drew a slow breath, feeling like an impostor. She'd been hired at Memorial for her teaching skills, her faith, and her values—and yet she was no role model.

Kit's phone vibrated on her desk. She pulled it toward her. Dad. He was returning her call from earlier. "Morning, Dad," she said, her voice still thick with tears.

"You all right?" he asked.

"Yes. Just wanted to check on Mom. Is she okay?"

"She's a tough girl, Katherine Elizabeth, and I'm proud of her."

Kit's eyes burned. Her father was a big, burly man, a forty-year veteran of the San Francisco Fire Department, and yet their mom had always been the center of his universe. "How long have you known that the cancer's back?"

"Three weeks."

"And you didn't tell us?"

"Mom's had a lot on her plate. There were appointments, biopsies, more consultations. She needed time to focus on herself, figure out the best course of treatment."

"Which is apparently none."

"I respect your mother's decision, and so should you."

"But with proper treatment she could have years."

"If she thought she could get years, she'd do anything, but there wouldn't be years. Months, maybe, but that's it. The cancer has just spread too far, too fast. And so now we focus on the best quality of life she can have. Doing the things she wants to do." His voice roughened. "Giving her the support she needs for this next step."

Kit closed her eyes, held her breath. Her parents had been married for nearly fifty years and she couldn't imagine one without the other. Couldn't imagine what her father would do without their mom. "I can't lose her," she whispered. "It's too soon."

Her father didn't immediately answer, "It wasn't in the plan," he finally said, his voice deep, gravelly, a voice that matched his square jaw and massive forearms.

Her father, Tom Brennan, a sixth-generation Irish-American San Francisco fireman, could trace his genealogy straight back to County Clare, when his great-great-great-grandfather Seamus Brennan headed to America to find his fortune in the gold and silver rushes of California and Nevada. Seamus panned for gold and worked the mines for six dirty, dusty, backbreaking years before accepting that he wasn't going to strike it rich and ended up in the beautiful new city of San Francisco, where he worked in a hotel and part-time as a volunteer fireman. Within five years the volunteer job turned into a permanent job and every generation of Brennans since had at least one son follow in Seamus's footsteps. Kit's brother, Tommy Jr., was a fireman, but he couldn't get a job in the city, so he'd taken one in Oakland.

"How are you doing, Dad?" she asked, her voice softening as she pictured his thick salt-and-pepper hair and intensely blue eyes. Her dad was focused and fearless at work and yet gentle at home. Ever since she was a little girl, she'd idolized her father, adoring his strength and warmth and good humor. He was always laughing, or making others laugh, and she'd been so sure that when she grew up she'd marry a man just like him.

"Not great," he admitted. "But the department's been great about giving me time off. Makes me think it's time I retired."

It was the first time she'd heard him mention retirement. Kit couldn't imagine her father not working, but she understood his desire to be close to Mom now. Time was short. Life was shorter. "When would you do it?"

"Soon. I haven't said anything to your mom yet, but I think she'd be happy. You know how she worries so."

Mom couldn't ever sleep properly when Dad was working. "Yes," she agreed. "And now that Tommy's joined the department she never has any peace of mind."

"I don't sleep that well when Tommy's working either."

"You know the dangers."

"I can't help thinking he's still my boy."

"He is." Her lips curved. "He just happens to be a six-foot-one, thirty-eight-year-old boy." The bell rang overhead, a shrill, loud ring signaling that class would start in five minutes. "I better go, Dad, my kids will be coming in any minute."

"Have a good day, Kit."

"You, too, Dad. And give Mom a big hug from me."

As she hung up, her classroom door opened and sleepy-eyed students began trickling in. Kit sat taller, squared her shoulders, trying to mask her panic and pain.

What had she done?

What had possessed her to confront Richard last night and demand more?

She should have waited. Should have counted to ten, and then one hundred. Should have slept on the impulse, knowing she would feel differently in the morning.

And she did feel differently this morning. She'd wanted to find Richard and fall into his arms and tell him she was sorry. Sorry and wrong and that she was happy with him. Everything was perfect with them. But he wasn't there, and when she tried to phone him, she discovered his phone was off. The phone rang once before sending her to voice mail. Richard never turned his phone off. The only time he did it was when he was angry with her.

The idea of Richard being angry with her made her hurt worse.

And he had been angry last night. He'd been calm. Cool. De-tached. He was sorry she wasn't happy. It was unfortunate. In his mind, things were good and he liked how things were going. But if she needed more, she should go get more. It just wouldn't be with him.

And you can just let me go like that?

Apparently the answer had been yes.

Now he was gone. After ten years living with someone, loving that someone, she was on her own. Starting over.

Seven

After hanging up with Kit, Meg shot Cass a quick text saying that she was thinking of her and praying the retrieval would go well. And then with the text sent, her focus returned to the narrow country road before her. The morning sun was burning off the last misty tendrils of fog that collected in the low-lying pockets at night. Traffic was moving at a good pace today and the grape-covered hills rolled in waves as far as the eye could see.

Meg loved Capitola and the beach house, but she loved the hills and vineyards even more, with all its greens, russets, and golds. She hadn't been raised here—she was a city girl, San Francisco was home—but she couldn't imagine living anywhere but in the wine country now. The hills, the smells, the seasons . . . it was in her blood, part of her.

Meg flipped the sun visor down to block some of the morning glare, and her thoughts shifted to Kit.

Kit had finally given Richard the boot.

Unbelievable.

It must have been a scene, at least on Kit's part. Richard had the cool, detached logic of an engineer, while Kit wore her heart—and it was a big one—on her sleeve. Meg could only imagine what was said last night, and how it was said, and how Richard's decision had hurt Kit. It would have been crushing.

Anger welled up, anger with Richard for not treating Kit better.

Meg knew that Kit was going to have a rough few weeks ahead of her. Between coming to terms with Mom's diagnosis—how did one do that?—and moving into her own place, she was going to be hurting, and there wasn't anything Meg could do about it.

The Dark Horse Winery's administrative offices were tucked in the back of the Tuscany-inspired tasting room and wine shop, which was open seven days a week to the public. The dark, cool, pungent barrel room separated the winery offices from the public tasting room and provided a measure of privacy, but last year, the Hallahans remodeled the building and reworked the office wing, giving it a walled garden and private entrance to allow staff members to focus on administration and business, rather than the comings and goings of tourists and the curious public.

But the walled garden and rustic wooden door couldn't keep the office from smelling like a winery, not with the barrel room immediately next door. But Meg liked the tang of ripe, fermenting grapes, and the damp smell of oak.

"Good morning," she greeted Jennifer, the winery's receptionist, who was already at her desk. "How was your weekend?"

Jennifer had worked for the winery since graduating from St. Mary's College almost two years ago, and she did a little of everything for the winery. There were days when she never left her desk, and then there were other days when she never sat down, too busy walking the winery grounds with event planners, pouring wine in the tasting room, and helping out with the cash register in the wine shop.

"Great," Jen enthused. "Mike and I went to the city for the

weekend. Stayed down by Fisherman's Wharf. Played tourists all weekend long."

Meg suddenly wished she was twenty-three again. She'd travel more. Play more. Enjoy life more. "Where did you eat?"

"Alioto's."

"I love Alioto's. Touristy, but great food and so much fun."

"That's why we went there."

"Did you wear the bib?"

Jennifer laughed. "We both did."

"And did you visit Alcatraz? You said wanted to."

"Yes. Took the whole tour, and Mike bought the T-shirt. Then we visited Ghiradelli Square, and rode the cable car to Union Square. Forgot how fun the city can be."

"I know. The kids love it."

"So how was your weekend? Weren't you at the beach house?"

"I was, and it was nice. But I'm glad it's Monday and I'm back here. My sisters are a lot of work."

"Speaking of work, these are all for you," Jennifer said, handing Meg a stack of mail and phone messages.

At her desk Meg turned on her computer, scanned her calendar, and remembered that the winery grounds were being used for a big wedding this weekend. She made a note to touch base with the wedding planner today to make sure everything was set for Saturday. She also scribbled a reminder to follow up with the Food Network producer, Amy Chin, before writing a series of quick thank-you e-mails to the different food and wine writers who'd attended the launch last Thursday.

Meg was on the fourth thank-you e-mail when Chad knocked lightly on her open door. "You survived your Girls' Getaway?" he asked.

She lifted her head to look at him. The jeans and cowboy boots Chad wore at the winery suited his personality. He was rugged and charming and terribly appealing. "I did," she answered. "It was exhausting—all those women in one little house—but also good to see everyone."

"Everyone's healthy? Happy?"

She thought of her mom, and then Bree. Kit and Sarah. The Brennans were passionate people with strong personalities, and Meg had expected some controversy over the weekend, but Mom's news had devastated them all. "There's stuff happening," she said blandly, glossing over the heartache. She'd never confided in Chad. They didn't have that kind of relationship. "But when isn't there?"

"Any thoughts on London?"

Thoughts on London? Meg suppressed a slightly hysterical giggle, thinking she had plenty of those. They'd kept her awake for half the night. She reached for a pen. Fiddled with it. She was wound so tight that she felt close to tears—*again*—and Meg wasn't a crier. "I want to," she said after a long moment. "I really do."

"Then come."

Chad sounded so calm and reasonable that she looked at him, brow furrowing.

He lifted an eyebrow. "Surely your family can do without you for five days?"

There was something in his tone that gave her pause. Slowed her racing thoughts. Made her realize that perhaps she was being a tad melodramatic. She wasn't her mom. She wasn't dying. Jack and the kids could survive five days without her. "Yes," she said hesitantly.

"Yes, your family could survive without you, or yes, you'll go?"

Meg thought that if Brianna were here right now and privy to this conversation, she would be laughing, mocking Meg and her inflated sense of importance. It wasn't a happy thought, but in this case, Bree just might be right. Meg did have a hard time relinquishing control. Maybe it'd be good for her to take a step back, let her family manage on their own for a few days. Maybe it'd be good for all of them.

"Yes," she said carefully, then added more firmly, "I'd love to go."

"I'll have Jen get on the travel arrangements."

Meg stared at the door after he left and waited for guilt and second thoughts to strike. It was inevitable. She'd turned guilt into an art form.

She waited, tapping the pen. But a moment passed, and then another, and Meg still felt nothing. No panic. No guilt. No second thoughts.

Hmm. Interesting. Apparently her inner voice was too exhausted to be critical.

That was saying something, wasn't it?

M eg worked through her lunch hour to make up for time lost last Friday, and was so engrossed in the project before her that she missed a text from Kit. It wasn't until midafternoon when she the glanced at her phone to see if any of her kids had called that she spotted the text.

Don't think I can do this, it said.

Meg's focus was shattered. She sent Kit an immediate text. *Can you talk?*

Ten minutes later the answer came. *Will call when school is over.*

The phone rang a half hour later. It was Kit. Meg answered, "Bad day, huh?"

"Pretty awful," Kit agreed, her voice hoarse.

"I'm sorry I missed your text. I would have called earlier if I'd seen it."

"Just as well you didn't. I would have lost it completely."

"Find any apartments you like yet?"

"Haven't even started looking. Can't stop crying. The kids were freaked out. Needed to tell them something, so I said my dog died—"

"You don't even have a dog!"

"I certainly don't now." She took a breath, made a hiccuping sound. "What a day. I'm a wreck, Mags. An absolute mess. I don't know how I'm going to get through tomorrow."

"Don't go tomorrow. Call in sick—"

"Can't."

"I need my sick days for Mom." And then Kit was crying hard. For a moment she couldn't speak and then she choked, "Why did I do this? Why did I have to confront him? Why couldn't I just leave everything alone?"

"Because you needed more."

"And now I have nothing!"

"Kit, sweets, if you're having second thoughts, it might not be too late to reconcile."

"What?"

Meg did not want to give her this advice, couldn't stand the thought of Kit crawling back to Richard and pleading for him to give her another chance, but if Kit truly loved him, then Meg couldn't stand in the way. "Maybe you should try to patch things up with Richard."

"I thought you didn't like him."

"This isn't about me. It's about you. And if you're happy with him, that's all that matters."

Kit made a strangled sound. "I was happy, Meg, but he doesn't want me. Said this was the best thing for us."

"So you talked to him today?"

"No. He sent me a text. He won't take my calls."

"The ass," Meg muttered, despising Richard more than ever. He was so cold and indifferent and dull, really truly dull, and Meg had never understood how warm, bubbly Kit could be attracted to him. Richard, with his degree from MIT, had the classic engineer personality—flat, one-dimensional, uninspiring—but he had a great job with some government agency that he couldn't ever talk about and a nice condo in Emeryville with views of the Bay. Meg had always privately believed that Kit had been seduced by the image he projected rather than the actual man. Ten years ago they'd met in a North Beach bar while out with friends. Richard, new to the area, asked for her number and called Kit the next week. Kit hadn't been with anyone else since.

In his defense, Richard wasn't . . . ugly. Six feet tall with a decent build, he had a decent midwestern face, short brown hair, and blue-gray eyes he hid behind tortoise-shell-frame glasses. Kit used to say Richard reminded her of Clark Kent, but Clark Kent had warmth and charm and the ability to turn into a superhero. The only thing Richard turned into was a dick.

"I'm sorry, Kit," Meg added more gently. "I wish he wasn't being such a jerk."

"I just can't believe I wasted so many years with someone who cared so little for me."

"What's done is done. Now just get through the day and call me later."

No sooner had Meg hung up than another text appeared. *Thanx for your text. Retrieval went well. 11 Eggs. Keep fingers crossed that some fertilize! xoxox Cass*

Meg reread the message, her heart trying not to be overwhelmed by life. It was so intense. Such a roller coaster. Up and down and all around. Life and death, babies and cancer, marriage, sisters and broken hearts . . .

How did anyone survive it?

M eg and Chad were to fly to London on Sunday, less than six days away, and Meg had a lot to do first to prepare for the show. She was also in frequent communication with her mother and Kit. Kit was emotional. Mom was surreal.

Mom didn't sound sick. She sounded like someone on a luxurious around-the-world cruise. Everything was lovely. Everything was just perfect. The weather couldn't be better, food was delicious, TV was exciting.

"Looks like quite a few of Cass's eggs fertilized," she said ebulliently, filling Meg in on the latest in Cass and Tommy's fertility saga. "We won't know for sure for another twenty-four to forty-eight hours if the embryos are all growing properly, but odds are that there definitely will be embryos to transfer on Thursday."

"That's great news," Meg agreed. "And Thursday is the transfer day, then?"

"If they go with the conventional three-day transfer. Their doctor had mentioned that maybe this time they should wait until day five, see how the blastocysts have developed, and then pick the best."

"It's got to be tough waiting and hoping."

"Cass is very focused."

"I think you'd have to be," Meg answered, knowing that initially Mom hadn't been pleased when Cass took a leave of absence from her job three months ago to "prepare" for this last IVF cycle. Cass, like their mom, was a nurse, and Marilyn was proud of her daughter-in-law's career, but while Mom worked in administration, Cass worked on the maternity ward as a labor-and-delivery nurse. It was a high-stress position, with many hours spent on her feet, and Cass's newest specialist wanted her to scale back her activities, see an acupuncturist, and start yoga. She had done all three.

"But it's not easy for them to make it on a one-person income," Marilyn added. "Not if they're going to continue with the fertility treatments."

"She'll work again, Mom. It's just temporary."

"I know." She paused. "Speaking of working, did you know that your dad is thinking of retiring?"

Meg was caught off guard. "No."

"Apparently he's quite serious. He told Tommy and Kit. Tommy mentioned it to me when I was at their house last night. I confronted your father about it this morning. He left for work in a huff. But I don't think it's a good idea. Your father needs his work. And he'll need it even more when . . . down the road."

Down the road, meaning when she was gone.

Meg nearly lost her temper just then. She had to bite her tongue hard to keep from shouting at her mother that she needed to go through treatment. That she needed to give them more time. Six months . . . a year . . . it wasn't enough. Not for any of them. "Maybe Dad wants to be with you."

"And he will be, but he doesn't need to be sitting around the house, doing nothing."

"He won't be doing nothing—"

"It's not a good idea," her mom answered brusquely, cutting Meg short. "I know your dad. It won't be good for him."

Meg ground her teeth, hating how they were dancing around the words *cancer* and *death.*

None of them could say it yet. Death, dead, gone. That's what this was all about, but God help them, they had to stay upbeat. Had to be positive and strong.

"Talk to Dad," Mom urged.

"I will, but if Dad's made up his mind, nothing I say will change it. You're the only one Dad listens to."

"But he's not listening to me this time."

"Probably because he shouldn't."

"We'll see," Mom said, sounding breezy again. "I know you have lots to do, so I won't keep you. I'll be there Sunday morning bright and early since Dad and I will be going to the Saturday Mass."

"You don't have to go to Saturday's Mass. My flight's not until early afternoon."

"I know, but you'll want to show me everything, make sure I know what's what."

"You know all this stuff, Mom."

Marilyn hesitated. "But I want to see you, too."

Meg pressed a hand to her eyes, turning everything black. "I wish you'd try one of the new treatments."

"I've had a good life."

Meg couldn't do this anymore. At least not right now. "I'll see you Sunday."

L ater that evening Meg attended JJ's baseball game at the high school and sat in the old wooden bleachers with the other JV moms. Meg loved baseball. She'd grown up watching her younger brother, Tommy, play; her dad had played in the minor leagues; and with a brother-in-law in the majors, baseball had become the official family sport.

Meg had her own reasons for loving baseball, and they had less to do with the crack of the bat connecting with the ball than with the communal aspect. Attending games had become a social outlet. She could go to a game and sit with other women her age and discuss the things mothers of teenage sons discussed: boys and drinking, boys and driving, boys and studying (or lack of), and most troubling of all, teenage boys' belief that they were somehow immortal and could therefore drink and drive and party and be okay.

Meg and Farrell and Laura and the other moms routinely joked about their foolish boys, and rolled their eyes and shook their heads, making light of the worry and danger. But the jokes and rolled eyes were just a facade. Each of them lived with a quiet terror. *Please don't let my son drink and drive and hurt someone. Please don't let him get hurt. Please don't let him become a statistic.*

This afternoon they'd already covered the upcoming prom and the rash of spring parties and had just moved on to discussing the looming SAT and ACT tests, and whether their sons were prepared and if they were good test takers, when cheering erupted all around them, and Laura, who'd been sitting on Meg's right, jumped to her feet and whistled.

"Great play!" she shouted, clapping hard. "Nice. Double play. Inning's over. Let's see if we can get some runs on the board."

Meg glanced at the scoreboard. Montgomery was still up by two. It was now the bottom of the eighth and JJ's team, Maria Carrillo High School's Pumas, were at the top of the batting order, which meant JJ had a chance to do something. He usually batted fourth, so if Trevor, Riley, or Lucas could get on base, he might be able to drive in one or more. JJ liked being the cleanup hitter. Didn't faze him. She clapped with the other parents as the Pumas jogged back to the dugout, hopeful that they could turn things around soon.

"I think this is our last year of baseball," Farrell said, on Meg's left. She was shielding her eyes as she gazed out onto the field. It was late afternoon and the setting sun glazed the grass, gilding the stands with long golden rays of light. It looked pretty from the stands, but the sun would be shining right into the batters' eyes. "Riley said he wants to try out for the lacrosse team next year."

"I didn't know Riley played lacrosse," Laura said, glancing from the field to Farrell as they sat back down.

"He doesn't," Farrell answered. "He attended a lacrosse camp a couple years ago, but he's never been on a team. But he's getting bored by baseball. Too much standing around and waiting."

Laura grimaced. "Cole's frustrated, too, but that's because he's spending more and more time on the bench. He hasn't even been in the game today. I'm beginning to think he won't get any playing time at all."

"I'd miss baseball if JJ quit," Meg confessed, watching Lucas, the shortstop and leadoff hitter, step into the batter's box and looking forward to seeing JJ at the plate. She enjoyed watching her son play ball. From the time JJ picked up his first glove at five, he loved the game and everything about the game. Meg knew he hoped to play in college before getting drafted and going pro, and it was a long shot making it to the majors, but it was hard to discourage him from dreaming big when his uncle Boone had a great career playing ball.

"I miss watching Cole play," Laura said flatly.

Meg felt a twinge of guilt. Cole and JJ had grown up playing baseball together, and until a couple years ago, Cole, like JJ, always made the all-star team. But the boys were older—fifteen and sixteen—and they weren't just bigger, stronger, and faster, they were expected to read pitches better, too. While Cole was still a solid defensive player, his inconsistent performance at bat meant he was seeing less and less playing time. "Cole's a great athlete, a solid player," Meg said.

Laura's lips compressed. "Kevin said that if Cole didn't see more playing time today, he was going to talk to the coach."

Meg and Farrell exchanged swift glances. Approaching a high school coach was never an easy thing, and rarely a good thing.

Laura caught the look. "I can't really control Kevin, and I don't see how it could hurt. Cole barely plays as it is."

Meg worried that Kevin would only alienate the coach. "I know, and I agree, but Coach Devers has a short fuse with parents, and at least Cole is playing—"

"Maybe two innings in a game, while JJ gets to play every game, all game!" Laura exhaled hard, cheeks flushed. "You've no idea what it's like watching your kid sit inning after inning on the bench hoping against hope that he's going to have a chance to play. It's awful. For him, for me. And you've never experienced that, Meg. JJ's a star. Cole used to be. But now Cole gets to watch his best friends play while he sits next to the Gatorade."

Uncomfortable, Meg looked down toward the dugout, where Cole was leaning forward on the railing, spitting sunflower seeds, joking with the other kids. He was smiling now, but she knew he found it hard to be on the bench. And she hadn't meant to upset Laura, and certainly hadn't wanted to draw comparisons between the boys. Cole and JJ had been friends for years and she knew Laura had been taking Cole to the batting cages to work on his hitting and Kevin had begun to look into outside coaching.

"Kevin's just going to be so mad," Laura added after a moment. "I don't know who he's madder at . . . Cole or the coaches."

"Why would he be mad at Cole?" Farrell asked.

"Baseball was Kevin's sport. He played for Arizona State the year they went to the college world series. Kevin has always thought that Cole would play in college like he did. But now it doesn't even look like Cole will make the varsity team next year."

Meg wanted her kids to be successful, but it had to be on their terms. She'd learned that the hard way, having felt so much pressure growing up that she was determined not to push her children hard. If they chose to set big goals, have high standards and goals for themselves, fantastic. If not, she'd love them anyway. "Does Cole want to play in college?"

Laura shrugged. "He did. Before he lost confidence."

"Do you think it's the age?" Farrell asked, sliding on her sunglasses. "They're all changing so much right now, and while Riley hasn't lost confidence, he's definitely bored playing baseball. That's why we're switching to lacrosse."

"It won't be the same without you," Laura said, reaching over Meg to pat Farrell's knee. "You're my baseball buddy."

"What about me?" Meg demanded in mock outrage.

"You're lucky to make it to half the games," Laura answered. "Farrell never misses one."

Meg's jaw dropped. Was Laura serious? "I make it to nearly every game. I've maybe missed three the whole season."

"Five. You missed last Thursday and Friday."

Had Laura really been counting? "I didn't."

"You did. Two games, back-to-back."

Irritated, but realizing that Laura was right, as last Thursday was the winery launch and then Friday was the weekend in Capitola, Meg fell silent. And now she'd miss a game next week with the trip to London. But there was no way she'd make that announcement now. Not when Laura was already in a prickly mood.

Fortunately, Meg was saved from having to say anything as her phone rang. It was Kit.

Meg answered right away. "How are you, Kit?"

"Cloud nine!" Kit sang happily. "I'm buying a house!"

"What? When?"

"Now. This week. It's a lease-to-own, so I can move in this weekend and we'll close in sixty days."

"Seriously?"

"Yes! It's the cutest little house, Meg, you'll love it—1895 Queen Anne in the Highland Park area," she said, referring to one of Oakland's older, working-class neighborhoods. "Mom and Dad are fronting me the down payment. They helped out Tom and Cass when they got married and Dad said that it was silly to make me wait until I married to get a place of my own." She paused for breath. "I'm finally going to have my own place, Meg. Not Richard's or anyone else's. Mine."

"That's wonderful, Kit. I'm so happy for you."

"So do you think you'd mind helping me move in on Saturday? Polly and Brad would but they're heading to a wedding on the Big Island and Tommy's working."

"I'd love to," Meg said, watching JJ take a couple practice swings in the batter's box. She felt butterflies in her middle. JJ needed a big hit now.

"We don't have to move any furniture. Everything is being delivered Friday. Washer, dryer, fridge, furniture. You and I will just unpack boxes and make up the bed and stuff like that."

"Sounds good."

"You don't have to if you're too busy getting ready for London," Kit added.

"I'm not too busy. And how did you know I was going to London?"

"Sarah."

Meg frowned. She hadn't talked to Sarah since Capitola, which meant that Sarah had talked to Mom and Mom had volunteered the information. "I told Mom I didn't think it was a good idea for her to babysit the kids, but she's insisting."

"Brianna thinks it'll tire Mom out too much."

"Brianna knows, too?"

"Apparently Sarah e-mailed Bree about it."

Meg exhaled, seriously annoyed. God, her sisters could be busybodies. "I'm concerned, too, but this is between Mom and me."

"If it's any consolation, Mom's really looking forward to it."

But it wasn't any consolation, Meg thought, irritated that she was even having this conversation with Kit, when she heard the crack of the bat and saw the ball fly out toward the centerfield fence. The ball sailed over the tall green fence. Home run. The stands erupted in cheers.

"Who?" Meg asked Farrell, covering the phone as she jumped to her feet to better see the field.

Farrell was on her feet, too. "Your boy. Three-run homer. JJ might have just won the game for us."

And Meg had just missed it. She'd watched JJ strike out and get thrown out, but had missed his shining moment. How was that fair? "Kit, I got to go. I just missed JJ's home run. I'll call you later, I promise, and congratulations on the house."

Thursday morning the embryo transfer took place. Meg knew all the details because Mom was there to drive Cass home from the fertility center since Tommy had to work. Tommy had tried to get the shift off, but he'd taken the weekend off for Monday's egg retrieval (important, as he was also needed for the sperm collection) and there was no one to cover him.

In the end, Cass said it was better that Mom was there with her since Cass cramped a lot after the procedure—more than she usually did—and Tommy didn't handle pain well. Meg sent flowers, Sarah sent cookies, and Kit popped by with a pot of her homemade chili and corn bread.

It was after two when Meg arrived at Kit's house Saturday afternoon. She had planned on getting there earlier, but traffic for the Oakland A's game had snarled bridges and reduced her speed to a crawl.

Kit had told Meg it was a charming 1895 Queen Anne, but the house needed work along with fresh paint.

"Are you sure this is a safe neighborhood?" Meg asked, standing on the cement walkway and looking at the beige-and-brown house next door with iron bars covering all the windows and doors. The house across the street wasn't much better. It looked like something built in the post–World War II era of practical housing—no-frill stucco, a metal awning over the cement front porch, and a narrow cement pad pretending to be a driveway. "There's no gang activity, if that's what you mean," Kit answered, leaning over one of the scraggly red rosebushes to deadhead a rosehip.

Meg pursed her lips, her gaze returning to the iron bars on the next door house. It wasn't what she meant. She was more worried about burglars and rapists than gangs at this point. "A nice new condo in Emeryville would have been more practical . . . and safer."

"The house was cheaper than nice new condos in Emeryville, and I'm closer to school here. Less commuting." Kit shoved her hands in her back pockets and headed up the front steps to her house. "And look at this," she said, pointing to the trim around the door and then at the window casement. "Look at the architecture. The house has great bones. It just needs love."

Meg's lips pursed. "Jack would love it."

Kit nodded eagerly. "I knew he would. I'm hoping he can give me some suggestions to help me with period detail and paint." She nodded toward the street. "And some of the houses here need work, but it's a good neighborhood. There's no graffiti, no trash, no junk cars sitting on lawns. Every house is neat and tidy. And I love that mine is a hundred and seventeen years old." Kit beamed. "You know how much I love that period in history and literature. Henry James was in the middle of writing his greatest fiction and Edith Wharton—"

"*Kit*," Meg said firmly, interrupting her sister before Kit began discussing authors and their literary themes. "You are aware that half the houses on this street have bars on the windows?"

"Yes, I am. But, Meg, half of them don't." Kit scooped her long hair into a ponytail high on the back of her head and twisted an elastic band around the heavy mass of curls. "But just to be safe, Dad came over yesterday with Uncle Joe and they checked out the house, installed locks on the windows, and put new dead bolts on the door."

"Dad thinks the house is okay?"

"He's helping me buy it. He's excited for me."

"I bet he wishes you were getting a nice new condo in Emeryville."

"He probably does, but he realizes I'm a big girl and can take care of myself." She saw Meg roll her eyes. "Stop it! I'm not Sarah. I've got a job, a very good job, with great benefits, and I'm thrilled to finally be a homeowner. I can restore the house over time, make it my dream house, plant my garden—" Her voice suddenly broke and she looked away, stared at Meg's car where it was parked on the street. "I don't have anything else, Meg. Be happy for me."

Kit looked so vulnerable that Meg's chest hurt. "I'm sorry," she said, hugging Kit. "I know I'm a pain. I shouldn't be such a big sister. I'm happy for you, Kit, I am. I just want you safe."

"I'll be safe."

Meg stepped back, aware that Kit was the least street smart of all of them, but it would accomplish nothing to tell her that. "Now show me the inside. And put me to work!"

Four hours later, Meg had finished unpacking the kitchen and had moved to the living room to deal with the boxes of books and Kit's assorted knickknacks.

"Where do these little doodads go?" she asked Kit, who happened to be passing through the hall on the way to the front door with yet another empty box.

Kit glanced at her collection lining the coffee table. "Aphrodite can go on the bookshelf. The frog next to my bed. The rock is a paperweight for my desk and you can just leave the candles there."

"Why the rock?" Meg asked, examining the smooth peach-and-cream stone. It was bigger than an egg, but similar in shape, and the cream stripe ran right through the middle.

"I found it on a walk years ago and saved it. I just thought it was pretty."

"It is."

Kit pointed to a red lacquer box inside the cardboard box on the living room floor. "And that Chinese box has more rocks. I collect them. And sea glass." She crossed the floor and reached into the moving box for a large glass jar filled with colorful bits of glass. She held the jar up to the light. "Richard hated my collections. Said I'm a hoarder. What an ass."

Meg laughed. "He is an ass. And I like your collections."

"Me, too."

At seven they ordered Chinese takeout and had it delivered. Chopsticks in hand, Meg sat on the floor and leaned against Kit's new couch, upholstered in a blue-and-white ticking fabric, and nodded approvingly.

"It is a darling house, Kit," she said, her gaze moving from the bookshelves to the armchair in the same blue-and-white fabric to the large framed poster of an impressionist seascape hanging on the wall. Fat red pillows sat plump and inviting on the sofa, the red picking up the colors of the painting. "And I love your new furniture. You've got a very cozy little home."

"It is cute, isn't it?" Kit hugged her knees, glanced around, trying to see the living room through Meg's eyes. "I wasn't very confident shopping, but I think I did all right."

"More than all right. This could be something you'd see in a magazine."

"Maybe a budget magazine."

"Accept the compliment! It's great. And your bedroom will be just as pretty when you're done with it."

Kit set aside her empty paper plate. "That's going to be a while. I've run out of money."

"You have a bed, and your old dresser. You can get by with that for now."

"I know. And it's not as if I'm going to be doing any entertaining in the bedroom anytime soon."

"Not immediately no, but you're going to meet someone, Kit, and he'll be the right one, and you'll end up pregnant before you know it."

"Hopefully married before pregnant. I *am* a Catholic schoolteacher."

"That's true. Wouldn't do to get you fired." Meg got to her feet and gave Kit a quick hug. "I better head home. I fly out tomorrow and want to see the kids before they go to bed."

Kit walked Meg to her car and then returned to the house to wave good-bye from the safety of her porch. After Meg pulled away, Kit went inside and locked the front door behind her. Alone in her house, she looked toward the small living room with the new furniture and the large framed reproduction of American impressionist William Merritt Chase's *At the Seaside*.

The painting was one of her favorites, and she'd blown what

was left of her budget on having the poster framed. But the women in the white dresses and the puffy white clouds in the sky, and the colorful yellow- and red-painted umbrellas in the sand made her feel. Made her hope. Kit needed hope. She wasn't feeling very good or strong right now. She was terrified. Terrified of this new life of hers in this new intimidating neighborhood. It wasn't the best neighborhood, but then, it wasn't the worst. She had nice people on either side of her, too. She'd met them when her dad went next door to introduce himself. It had embarrassed her when he did that this week, but he didn't care. He was Irish and a fireman, and family was family and community was community and that's all there was to it.

Kit checked the dead bolt again and then moved to the living room, where she rearranged some of the books Meg had shelved for her. Kit loved her books, and now she could have them out of the boxes and onto shelves. Richard hadn't wanted all her "novels" crowding his place, and even after ten years of living together, the condo had always been his. This house was hers.

Kit moved a D. H. Lawrence novel from the American literature bookcase and placed it on the bookcase for English literature before lightly touching the spines of several books. They weren't new paperbacks, but old hardbacks she'd picked up in used bookstores, thrift shops, and antique shops. The bindings were both leather and fabric, the fabric color faded reds and blues, browns and greens, and they'd sat on other people's shelves long before they'd sat on hers. She liked knowing that others had owned these books before her, that they'd meant something to someone else, too.

And then, fearing she was turning into an eccentric old spinster, one of those dotty aunts who didn't marry or have children of her own, she turned off the living room light and went to bed, hoping she was wrong, because Kit wanted kids and a family and all the things she hadn't yet known.

Eight

Jack had offered to drive Meg to the San Francisco airport. Gabi wanted to go for the ride, too, and Jack said yes. Meg felt mean when she said that Gabi needed to stay home with Grandma, but she needed some alone time with Jack. It never seemed as if they had enough time alone together.

They drove with the windows down since it was a beautiful sunny day. Jack was in a good mood, too.

"Looking forward to the trip?" he asked as they neared San Rafael. In his faded, tattered 501s and his equally faded Grateful Dead T-shirt, he looked rumpled but familiar.

"I am," she said, reaching out to put her hand on his upper thigh. He covered her hand with his.

It felt good, touching. She needed it. Needed it more than she ever had. Life seemed to be careening out of control and it scared her. "What are you going to be doing this week?" she asked, linking her fingers through his.

"Not much. I have a one-day trip to Virginia to meet with some prospective clients about their home."

"You're going away while I'm gone?"

He glanced at her. "Hopefully it's just a one-day turnaround. I'll go out, meet, and come back the same day. And if I can't get back the same day, I'll be home early in the morning."

"But Mom's here."

"Your mom can handle the kids. She said so herself. And we have the sitters after school."

Meg pressed her lips together and looked out the window, holding back her protest. Jack could say what he wanted, but he knew she wouldn't like him heading to the East Coast when her Mom was at the house with the kids. "You didn't even say anything to me," she said flatly.

"I just did."

"Because I asked what you were doing."

"You're making a big deal out of nothing."

"Because I'm worried about Mom."

He removed his hand from hers, put it back on the steering wheel. "I'll cancel my trip. Does that make you feel better?"

She watched the hills go by. It had been a dry spring and they were a faded green, parched for water. She felt equally parched. Her insides hurt, sharp and tight, as if she'd swallowed glass. But it wasn't glass cutting her. It was him. Them. Nothing about them was easy anymore. "No."

"I thought it's what you wanted."

"That's not what I wanted."

"Then what do you want?"

Meg forced her knotted fingers to relax and lie flat against her thigh. She had to stay calm. Had to deflect her anger. Anger wouldn't help. It never did. "To just make it easy for my mom. To be grateful she's helping us out. She's doing us a favor—"

"Doing you a favor. It's your trip, not mine."

"But they're our kids, Jack, not just mine."

"What does that mean?"

"It means that we have three kids who need *you*, Daddy, home helping with homework and driving them to their activities and being there at their performances and games."

"And you don't think I do help?"

She closed her eyes, held back the scream of frustration. Did he help? Significantly? No. He helped the way a babysitter helped. When requested for a short period of time, and then he expected, if not compensation, then gratitude. "I have a job, too, Jack," she said softly, eventually. "I bring in a decent paycheck."

"And I've never said you didn't."

And that was all they said until they reached the airport and Jack pulled up to the curb at the international terminal. "Have a good trip," he said flatly, leaning across to kiss her good-bye.

She forced a smile, and injected warmth into her voice even though on the inside she felt cold. "Have a good week. I'll see you Friday."

Inside the terminal, Meg stood in line at the counter to check her bags to Heathrow with her heart pounding and her hands shaking from too much adrenaline. She hated leaving like this. Hated getting on a plane when she felt so undone. But staying home would solve nothing, she thought, tucking a strand of hair back behind her ear. Jack didn't see, couldn't see, that she needed more from him and she didn't know how to tell him without losing control. And it would kill her to beg for his attention. Kill her to beg for affection. If only she wasn't so proud.

Relieved of her bag, Meg headed through security and walked to the gate. She was still upset, far too emotional, and was glad that

Chad didn't show up for almost another hour, giving herself time to pull herself together.

The flight passed quickly. Meg read and then slept, waking to the clink of dishes and the smell of coffee. A driver was waiting for them at Heathrow, and he ferried them straight to the ExCeL Centre, where the international wine and spirits fair was being held.

Chad had warned her that the venue was vast, and he was right. The "campus," as they called the convention center, was in east London overlooking Victoria Docks and part of a development that included five hotels, apartment buildings, and the sprawling convention space itself.

With luggage still in tow, they set off through the cavernous hall in search of their booth. The hall buzzed with activity, and reaching their assigned space, they discovered the booth was nearly finished being constructed. Chad explained how they'd set up their display. The wines would go here, the glasses there, and they'd take turns behind the counter so neither one was trapped all day.

They left the hall for their hotel. The Crowne Plaza was bustling with arriving exhibitors, visitors, and media. While waiting to check in, Chad spotted several men he knew and he introduced them to Meg—dashing Eduardo Verde, a slim, handsome vintner from Chile, and young, blond Philippe Mourat, a vintner from France—and the four made plans to meet up for dinner later.

As Eduardo and Philippe moved on, Chad looked at Meg. "Are you all right with that? I should have asked you before assuming you'd want to go to dinner."

"Of course."

"Good. I thought maybe you were sorry you'd come."

"Why would I be sorry?"

"You've been quiet. Rather distant."

And suddenly the dull ache was back, and the worries. Worries that she and Jack wouldn't ever be happy again together. Worries that she was gradually growing too tired, too resentful. Meg could take a lot, endure a lot, but she feared she'd almost reached her breaking point.

"There are just some problems at home," she said lightly, hiding the truth, because that's what she did. It's what she'd always done. She never admitted to having needs. Never asked for help. Just tried to manage it all herself. "But it's fine. It will be fine."

"If you want to talk—"

"No! But thank you. I'll see you at dinner?"

They were to dine at the Dockmaster's House, a gourmet Indian restaurant tucked into a stunning Georgian home in the London docklands. The Dockmaster's House was Chad's new favorite restaurant in London with its classical Georgian exterior and its glamorous, contemporary interior. It was the perfect setting for a meal with international vintners and there were five of them that evening, as Philippe had invited a colleague, French vintner Alexandre Huchet.

Meg would have enjoyed dinner more if Huchet hadn't joined them, but she didn't say so. Instead she smiled as he flirted with her throughout dinner. He seemed to think he was God's gift to women, and she was sure there were plenty of women who would welcome his attention. She wasn't one of them.

"You should come work for me," Alexandre said to her as coffee was served. He was leaning forward on the table, closing the distance between them. "I need you, Meg."

Meg gave her head a slight shake. He was outrageous. Ridiculous. Did women really fall for this? "And what would I do for you?" she asked, eyebrows arching.

"Whatever you would like," he answered boldly, his gaze sweeping appreciatively over her thick dark hair, which she'd left loose tonight, before dropping to her breasts.

Meg had felt quietly confident in her chocolate leather pencil skirt and ivory silk blouse but Alexandre's leer left her feeling naked. "I like where I am," she said crisply, leaning back in her chair. "I like what I do."

Alexandre's brown eyes met hers. "You haven't even heard my offer yet."

"No poaching," Chad said. "That's my girl."

"But maybe she'd like to be my girl?" Alexandre retorted, his fingertip suggestively skimming the rim of his wineglass.

Meg found herself staring at his finger as he stroked the glass, wondering if Alexandre was as sensual in bed as he was with the wineglass. Apparently there were men who really enjoyed touching and exploring women's bodies. She hadn't married one of those men. Hers preferred to gently explore blueprints. But such was life.

"Meg?" Chad asked, looking at her.

Would she want to be Alexandre's? She glanced from the Frenchman's finger to his face. His olive jaw was smooth, his eyes dark and intent, his brown hair sleekly styled. He was an attractive man, but she felt absolutely no connection. No chemistry at all. She shook her head, and tried to sound regretful but failed. "No. I'm sorry."

"But how do you know you wouldn't be happier with me?" Alexandre persisted.

"Because I'm a woman, not a girl, and I have a husband and three kids and they wouldn't approve of me commuting to France."

On Tuesday, the opening day of the international wine and spirits trade fair, Meg was irritated that Alexandre was the first person to stop by the Dark Horse Winery booth, determined to continue his onslaught of Gallic charm. She wasn't in the mood to deal with him today, or with any difficult man for that matter. She'd sent Jack a text on arriving yesterday to say she'd landed safely and he responded *K*, as in okay, but that was it.

"Miss me?" Alexandre drawled, leaning on the counter and smiling mysteriously into her eyes.

She felt like poking his eyes out. "No."

"Why not, *chère* Meg?"

Meg's jaw tightened. "Because I'm married."

"Do you miss your husband so terribly much?"

"No."

"So why don't you like me?"

"I don't know you, Alexandre."

"You're terrible at flirting."

"Good. Because I don't like it."

He glanced at Chad, who stood by listening with some amusement to the conversation. "How can a woman not like flirting?" Alexandre demanded. "Flirting makes you feel appreciated and alive. And what woman doesn't want to be complimented?"

"I don't," Meg said crisply, "if it's insincere."

"And who said I was insincere?" Alexandre protested. "I was most sincere. I find you quite attractive, although I confess your attitude is not so attractive today. You are very uptight. Very . . . mmm . . . what is the word? Prudish?"

Meg heard Chad's muffled laugh and she shot him a cool look before turning to Alexandre. "No, it's moral."

"And you think I do not have . . . morals?"

"Not if you're intent on seducing a married woman."

"But a married woman is the best woman to seduce! She isn't looking for marriage and commitment. She only wants fun."

"That's terrible."

"You Americans are still little Puritans. Just because you are married, it doesn't mean you can't flirt and make love and enjoy life. If you will let me, I shall help you enjoy life."

"I will not let you."

"Oh, *non*! I can not accept that. I will not accept that. I will have you." He nodded for emphasis and then walked away.

Meg watched him for a moment before turning toward Chad. "You like this guy?"

Chad grinned, eyes bright with laughter. "I do. But I have a different relationship with him. Alexandre doesn't try to make love to me."

"Lucky," Meg muttered, squaring up the wineglasses on the counter all over again.

At six o'clock the fair closed for the day and Meg and Chad returned to their hotel to shower and dress for dinner. That evening they were hosting a dinner for their German buyers, as Germany was very important to Dark Horse Winery's success, ranking fourth internationally in total wine consumption.

Conversation was lively at dinner, but no one lingered late since it was only the first night of the trade fair. By eleven the remaining guests were on the curb, hailing cabs to return to their hotels.

Wednesday of the London International Wine & Spirits Trade Fair was even busier than Tuesday. Meg spent the entire day on her feet, pouring wine and talking wine, while Chad met with various importers and distributors, taking orders as well as discussing which of his labels would be most successful in particular markets.

While Chad was taking an order from one of their German importers, Meg had her first encounter with a wine snob. Chad had warned her they were out there in the crowd, but hadn't met one until she was accosted by Dr. Dreadful (at least that's what she privately called him), who made it clear that he hated white wine and that any red wine not produced in France was probably unfit for human consumption.

Seriously.

She nearly laughed when he asked if Dark Horse made white wines and whipped out his little notebook to write down her response. They did produce a few whites, she told him, but they weren't featuring them at the fair.

Dinner Wednesday night at the Upstairs Restaurant was a

smaller affair than Tuesday, and most of the people they invited were UK buyers and importers. In the UK, most wine was sold in the supermarket, in between "beans and tea bags," as one of their buyers liked to say, and this was good for the importers who represented the big supermarkets like Tesco, but not so for the smaller outlets, and the dinner conversation was a lively discussion about whether the supermarkets were ruining the UK wine market by pressuring winemakers to make substandard wines.

During the spirited exchange, Chad looked over at Meg and smiled.

He smiled at her all the time, but tonight it was different. Tonight when he smiled, her heart jumped and her body tingled and everything within her felt nervous and sensitive.

Suddenly shy, Meg looked away, not certain what had just happened but aware that *something* had. Chad was different. She felt different. She felt breathless and giddy, as if she were meeting him for the very first time.

Dinner ended with everyone piling into cabs to return to their hotels, but as Chad climbed into the back of the one they were taking and sat pressed to Meg's side to make room for two others, she felt nervous. Her heart was beating a little too fast and her body seemed a little too aware of Chad's. This wasn't good, she thought, drawing in a quick breath even as she smoothed her skirt over her knees. Chad was her boss. She was married. She wasn't interested in anything personal with him.

Chad leaned toward her, voice dropping so that none of the others could hear. "You okay?"

She nodded, swallowed hard. "Yes."

"You've gone all quiet on me."

"Just tired."

"Tomorrow's going to be another long day, but it's the last day."

"Don't worry about me. I'm fine."

"I'm not worried about you. You're fantastic."

Meg flushed with pleasure then was grateful for the dark so that he couldn't see, because she shouldn't be so pleased. Shouldn't need his praise at all. But she did. And that worried her.

The final day of the London International Wine & Spirits Trade Fair was just as hectic as the other two days, and by Thursday night, Meg had had her fill of high heels, late nights, and talking wine, but they still had one last dinner that night for their Russian buyers.

Leaving the conference center, she returned to her hotel room to shower and dress. After showering, she sat on the edge of her bed, wrapped in her towel, and shot Kit a text. *Can't wait to get home.*

She was just finishing her makeup when her phone rang. It was Kit calling to check on her.

"Mags, you okay?" Kit asked when Meg answered.

Meg turned away from the mirror. "Yeah. But I hate that name."

"I know, but I love you."

"I'm glad you do," Meg said, sagging against the counter. "I can't stand myself right now."

"Why? What's happening there?"

"I'm ready to go home. Miss the kids. Haven't heard much from Mom or Jack. Do you think everything is okay there?"

"I talked to Mom just a couple hours ago. She's had a great time at your house. I think she's even reorganized your kitchen and laundry."

"She better not have," Meg retorted testily. "I have a system, and I like it."

"You *are* crabby."

Meg's shoulders slumped. "I know. I can't stand it. Don't even know why I'm grouchy, I just am."

"You're jet-lagged, and probably not sleeping, or getting enough real food to eat."

"The first two are right, but I'm actually eating way more than I should. Every night we have a dinner out somewhere and it goes on for hours."

"Do you have one tonight?"

"Yes. Heading out soon. Fortunately, it's the last one. We fly home tomorrow."

"I know. I'll see you this weekend at Mom and Dad's."

"Will you?"

"You know . . . Sunday's barbecue at Mom and Dad's for Tommy's birthday."

"That's this Sunday?" And suddenly Meg remembered. Not Tommy's birthday. But Jack's. It was the eighteenth. Yesterday. And she hadn't called. Or texted. Or left a card. Or anything. She'd done absolutely nothing for his birthday . . . had failed to remember him in any way. "Oh my God," she whispered.

"What?"

"Jack's birthday."

"It was yesterday. I called him."

"You did?"

"Yes. Didn't you?"

"No. I completely forgot it. I did nothing."

For a second Kit was silent; then she demanded, "How could you not remember your husband's birthday?"

"I don't know. I've never forgotten it before! I have to call him."

"You better call him right now."

The moment Meg hung up she dialed Jack's number. She ended up in his voice mail. Cringing, kicking herself, she left him a cheery message sending belated birthday wishes and love and the hope that they could celebrate Saturday night with the kids. She could make his favorite dinner or they could go out—whatever he wanted. She made a kissing sound into the phone and ended the call.

Dammit, she thought, sitting motionless on the bed. Forgetting Jack's birthday was definitely not good.

Chad was already downstairs in the hotel lobby when Meg stepped from the elevator.

"You look great," he said, briefly touching her arm as they headed outside to grab a cab for dinner.

Meg smiled wanly. "Thanks," she said, still horribly guilty over failing to remember Jack's birthday, especially as she knew he'd had some lonely birthdays during and after his parents' divorce. On his seventeenth birthday neither parent even remembered to call him. No cards or gifts arrived either. He was at a new boarding school, and because he didn't tell anyone it was his birthday, he spent the day trying to pretend it wasn't a big deal and that birthdays weren't special days. But the fact that he shared this story with Meg in Rome meant that it hadn't been an easy thing for him at all.

"You look utterly dejected, Meg. What happened?" Chad asked, holding the cab door open for her.

She stepped into the car, slid across the broad backseat. "I've been a remiss wife."

"Jack upset with you for not staying in touch better?"

Meg pressed her purse to her middle. "I forgot his birthday. It was yesterday."

Chad shot her a surprised look. "You didn't call?"

She shook her head. "Nope. Completely spaced."

"That's not like you."

"I know." Her brow furrowed as she remembered how she and Jack used to celebrate birthdays—one year it was a special dinner at the legendary hundred-year-old Swan Oyster Depot on Polk Street in San Francisco, another year it was their favorite restaurant in San Francisco's Mission District, Delfina, before going to see *Les Misérables*. Some years they went away—like the weekend to Monterey when Jack turned forty—and some years she cooked a special meal for him at home. But it was always a big deal. His birthday was important . . . he was important . . . and she made sure she let him know by showering him with gifts, cards, cake, candles, singing, hugging, loving.

Loving.

Was that the problem? Had she fallen out of love? Meg pressed her purse closer to her middle, chilled at the thought. Couldn't be, she told herself. There was no falling out of love. Not in this marriage.

The dinner at Paradise Pub for their Russian buyers was the most relaxed business meal of the trip. Most of the conversation centered on the recent passage of a new Russian law forbidding the import of popular Georgian and Moldovan wines.

"I'm concerned," one of the importers said frankly. "If the government can forbid the import of Georgian and Moldovan wines, they can forbid the import of French wines or American wines."

"I don't like it," another agreed. "But you have to comply to stay in business, you know?"

Although the discussion was interesting, Meg found it hard to concentrate. It troubled her that Jack hadn't called her back yet. She had her phone on her lap just in case. Maybe he was afraid he'd interrupt a meeting. Beneath the table she sent him a text. *Thinking of you and planning all kinds of ways to spoil you this weekend for your birthday.*

But he didn't answer. Maybe he was in meetings, too.

Dinner broke up at midnight, and after the last buyer left, Meg sat back down in her chair and exhaled. Dinner was over. The show was over. She could finally relax.

Chad reached for the open bottle of red wine sitting on the table between them. "I think that went well."

Meg watched him fill her glass and then his. "I do, too." It was her favorite Dark Horse Shiraz, big, rich, with a hint of cherry and dark chocolate, and while she'd drunk almost nothing during dinner to keep a clear head, she very much wanted a drink now.

He leaned back in his chair, resting his arm across the back of another chair. "Thank you for coming. You were a huge help."

She wasn't sure now that she should have come. She would have been a better wife if she'd stayed home. "I did very little."

"You did exactly what you were supposed to do. You staffed the booth. Talked to buyers and importers while I wrote up orders. That was huge."

Meg took another sip of her wine, focusing on the tang and bite. She loved how a good Shiraz filled her mouth, teasing all of her taste buds. "You worked really hard. Did you get the orders you wanted?"

"For the most part. Sales are a little down again this year, but so is the economy."

"You're not worried?"

He shrugged, smiled. "Can't worry about everything, especially things I can't control."

Silence fell, but it was companionable, comfortable. Meg was just happy to sit and sip her wine. The last four days had been hectic. She'd been stressed all night. She wasn't used to being away from her family and was ready to go home. Thank goodness they were leaving tomorrow.

"I heard someone say that the attendance was down a little bit this year, too. Did you hear any final numbers?" she asked after a moment, thinking of all the different wine regions in the world that had been represented at the fair. South Africa, Australia, New Zealand, Chile, Argentina, Germany, France, the United States . . . and that wasn't everyone.

"Between thirteen and fourteen thousand. Maybe a little less than last year, but I'm happy, and my buyers were happy. They loved you."

Meg stared into her wineglass, watching the way the dark

ruby wine clung in delicate streaks to the glass. This Shiraz had good legs. "They're men on a business trip drinking heavily," she said absently. "With that much liquor inside of them, they'd love anyone."

"They are wine and spirits buyers. They can hold their liquor. The men liked you because you were fun and you're incredibly smart and very sexy—"

"Did you happen to read that blog by the English guy who calls himself the Wine Snob? He spent the entire fair ripping everyone a new one, but was especially awful to Ovation Wines, calling their new labels bloody awful. People were tweeting his latest blog all day."

Chad laughed softly. "You don't think you're sexy?"

"We're talking about the Wine Snob."

"No, we're talking about Mary Margaret Roberts."

Heat rushed to her cheeks. "You know my whole name?"

"Meg, we've worked together for almost five years. I know a staggering amount of things about you."

"Then you should know that this," she said, gesturing down toward her body, "is not sexy. This," and she did another Vanna White gesture, "is practical."

"Do you ever look in the mirror?"

"All the time."

"And what do you see?"

"Mary Margaret. And she's getting old. As well as senile."

"You didn't mean to forget Jack's birthday. You're beating your-self up over nothing. I bet Jack is fine and he probably thought you'd be doing something this weekend after you returned."

She flushed guiltily. It's what they'd planned before she left, but still . . . she should have called. Should have texted. Sent flowers. Balloons. A dancing girl or two . . . "You're not married," she said tartly. "You don't understand."

"I might not have ever married, but I've had girlfriends, and birthdays matter. But you go home tomorrow and you'll make it up to him and he'll be happy. I promise you."

He was right, too. Meg knew Jack would be fine once she got home. But somehow it made her feel better to kick herself . . . why, she didn't know.

"Now enjoy your last night in London," Chad added. "You did a great job here. We did a great job. Let's celebrate the close of the show, and while I have your attention, can we talk about your shoes?"

Meg cracked a smile. "My shoes?"

"They're fuck-me pumps."

"Oh my God, Chad!"

"They are. Four-inch heels, Mary Margaret?"

She blushed furiously and glanced down at her feet. "I thought they looked good with this dress."

"And they do. It's a great dress. A very stylish, silk wrap dress that shows off a great body—"

"How much did *you* drink tonight?"

"—and you have lips to die for."

"You're drunk."

"This is only my second glass of wine, but I'm not opposed to getting drunk now."

"Why?"

"Because you're so clueless, Meg. Clueless about how beautiful you are, and how smart you are, and how good you are at what you do."

She wrinkled her nose. "I actually know that part."

Chad threw his head back and laughed. "That's perfect. Of course you know how good you are at your job. You're you."

Meg sat taller, trying to project some authority. "I'm forty-two, Chad."

"What does that have to do with anything? Age means nothing.

You could be fifty-two, or sixty-two, and you'll still be amazing. But perhaps you know that, too."

Did she?

Did she know she was beautiful and smart? Did she appreciate her gifts? Or was she the uptight, miserable, settled Mags that Brianna had mocked in Capitola?

Which version of her was correct? Which one was real?

Meg secretly feared that Brianna might be right in the end and she took a large gulp of wine, thinking that there were far too many times growing up when she'd hated being the oldest. When she'd longed to be the baby. Being the oldest Brennan sister had been a lot of work. Sometimes too much work. And she felt old already. Crabby.

"I don't feel very amazing," she confessed huskily. "I feel old and cranky." She looked across the table and met Chad's gaze, her lips twisting ruefully. "My sister Bree would tell you the same thing."

"Isn't she the one that loves to torment you?"

Meg smiled reluctantly. "Yes."

"So why would I believe anything she says?"

"Because she's so fierce and in-your-face."

Chad grimaced. "Can't stand people like that. Just because you have a soapbox doesn't make you right."

"But maybe she *is* right. I do worry a lot. And I try to control everything."

"Is that so bad?"

"I don't know. But I would like to enjoy life more."

"You don't?"

Heat crept up her neck, into her cheeks. "No," she said softly. "And I hate that about me. If I could change one thing, I'd change that. I'd try to relax and enjoy what I have. But instead I go through the day worrying about everything that could go wrong. And things do go wrong. I learned early that if you make a mistake, the consequences can be devastating."

He studied her from beneath his lashes, his expression sober. "Did something happen when you were little?"

"I was the oldest of five. Both my parents worked. Bree and Tommy were wild. Every day I worried that something bad would happen."

"But nothing ever did."

On the inside Meg felt a dark wave of helplessness, hopelessness. Nothing she did was ever quite right. Nothing she did was ever enough. And she was tired. Really tired. But she couldn't tell Chad that. She couldn't tell anyone. She was the one who had to help others, make sure things got done, no one was supposed to help her. "What about you?" she asked. "Have you made any mistakes?"

He smiled, his blue eyes even bluer in the candlelit room. "Another nice deflection, Roberts."

Meg smiled crookedly. She liked talking to Chad. He had a way of making her feel better. Lighter. Easier. "Just a little one. But I *am* curious. I don't really know much about you. What have you done that you've regretted? Mistakes? Missed opportunities?"

Chad just looked at her a long moment, his thick lashes lowered over blue eyes, grooves deepening on either side of his mouth. "I was in love with someone a lot like you once. But I didn't appreciate what I had, and wasn't ready to settle down."

"She wanted more?"

"Instead I let her go."

"Why do men do that?"

He shrugged. "We take longer to grow up. Enjoy being Peter Pan."

"So where is she now?"

"Don't know. Do know she's married. Craig saw the announcement in the paper a couple years ago."

"Is that why you're not married?"

"I'm not sure I'll ever get married."

"Because of her?"

"Because all the good girls are already married."

There was something in his expression that made her feel too warm and more than a little bit nervous. "There are millions of amazing single women out there, Chad."

"But there aren't millions that are right for me." He hesitated. "There aren't millions like you."

It was the last thing she'd expected him to say and for a moment she couldn't breathe, the air bottling in her lungs. "You're ridiculous," she said huskily. "I'm nothing special."

"Why would you say that?"

"Because I know what I am. But it's not young or playful or beautiful—"

"It's smart and strong and confident, as well as competent."

"There's a compliment," she mocked.

"It is. I find your competence very sexy."

She rolled her eyes. "I've never heard competence described as sexy."

"Oh, it is. A woman like you . . . a woman who can do anything, manage anything, juggle anything . . . and without complaining? That's pretty hot."

"You're crazy."

"Maybe. But I love your style, your confidence, your smart brown eyes, and your beautiful smile. You're the whole package, Mary Margaret. And Jack is lucky to have you."

Meg's heart turned over. Did Jack feel that way? Did Jack think he was lucky to have her? She wasn't so sure anymore. She and Jack never fought, but they didn't seem to connect either. They existed on the same plane, but that seemed to be all they shared anymore. Well, that, and the kids.

"Are you happy, Meg?"

Her head jerked up. "What?"

"Are you happy at home? With Jack?"

Chad's question threw her. She felt a cold trickle in her middle. "Of course. Why?"

His broad shoulders shifted. "From what you said last night, it sounds as if you're kind of on your own. That you're doing it all. Does Jack help you? Does he try to make your life easier?"

"Of course!"

"Does he?"

"Why would you even ask?"

"I don't know. Just a feeling I had."

"Well, your feeling is wrong. Jack and I have a great marriage. Things between us are really good."

"Good."

"Yeah?"

"Yeah. That's all I wanted to know."

"It's late," she said huskily, looking for her purse even as she slipped her feet back into the high heels, but tears were filling her eyes, making it impossible to see.

"Meg."

Her heart suddenly ached for reasons she didn't understand, and reaching for her wineglass, she swallowed what was left, letting the wine warm her all the way down before getting to her feet. "What?"

"I hate to see you upset."

"I'm not."

"You are." He reached across the table, caught her by the wrist, his fingers sliding up to entwine with hers. "You're crying. And you don't cry."

"I can't explain."

"Try."

She shook her head. "I'm just tired. Need to go home. Get back to my real life."

"This isn't your real life?"

"No." She gently freed herself, and then knocked the tears away with the back of her hand, aware that her life wasn't really about her anymore, but about everyone else. The kids and their dreams. Jack and his needs. Meg came last. But wasn't that true for most women her age?

"Do you want to share a cab back," she asked him, glad her voice was steady, "or do you want to get your own?"

Nine

They shared a cab back to the Crowne Plaza. Neither spoke during the ride, and Meg stared out her window at the lights of London. It was a clear night and the city glittered with light and possibility. The beauty of it made her hurt. She and Jack had been here years before on one of their anniversaries and it'd been a fun trip. A happy trip. But London didn't feel happy right now. London felt lonely. She felt lonely.

But why lonely? Meg didn't understand all these emotions rushing at her, emotions she never let herself feel, and she didn't want them now. She had so much to do, so much to manage, there wasn't time for being teary or needy.

Chad paid the driver on arriving at their hotel and they walked through the glass doors to the lobby together and then to the elevators.

As they waited for the elevator, Meg blurted, "I'm not sad. Sometimes things are just harder than I thought they'd be."

"At work?" he asked.

"At home. I love my kids, but you're right. I don't get a lot of help. Jack doesn't seem to realize that someone has to plan everything and organize everything and make sure things run. For some reason he thinks it just happens on its own. And I know he works long hours—he's really talented—but I work, too. Only I don't think he's ever really got that. I don't think he realizes how tired I get. When I leave work to go home, I run errands and carpool and start dinner and tackle laundry and help kids with homework. I leave work to go home and work some more. But home for Jack is different. Home for him is a comfortable couch and a glass of wine and some peace and quiet."

The elevator doors opened. People got out, and then Chad held the door for her. "You love him," he said.

"He's a great father," she said, entering the elevator and turning to face him as he followed her. "A really brilliant architect. And for seventeen years, one of my best friends."

The elevator doors closed. They were the only two going up.

"But not your best friend?" he asked, punching in their respective floor numbers.

She winced inwardly, remembering the forgotten birthday, as well as the silence on Jack's end. He hadn't once texted her this week, or phoned to see how she was doing. There was so much distance between them. So much space. "Not the way he used to be."

"What changed?"

She thought for a second. "We're just so busy doing different things."

The elevator opened on her floor. Chad's floor was one higher. She stepped out, smiled faintly. "I'll see you tomorrow."

"Things always work out, Meg."

"I know."

But in her hotel room, Meg didn't feel confident. She felt naked. Exposed. She'd told Chad that Jack wasn't her best friend, confessed things about her marriage that she wished she hadn't shared. Marriage was so personal, and difficult, and Chad was a guy. And single. He wouldn't get it.

In bed Meg pressed her cheek into her pillow and groaned. If there was anything she'd learned growing up in a big family, it was that talking too much always led to trouble.

Meg woke up to a text on her phone from Jack. *See you tomorrow. I'll pick you up from SFO. Have your flight info already. Love you.*

She exhaled in a rush, reassured by the message, grateful that everything was fine between them.

The next morning on the plane, Meg buckled her seat belt and tried to get comfortable, not an easy feat as their economy seats were very narrow and Chad's big shoulder kept brushing hers. It was a muscular shoulder and normally she wouldn't pay it much attention, but after last night, after sharing so much—*too much*—Meg wanted, needed, space. Instead she was wedged into the middle seat next to him and suffering from a bad case of regrets.

Why had she talked so much after dinner? Marriage was private, personal . . . intimate. Meg wished she could blame her lack of discretion on the wine, but wasn't sure if it was the wine that had loosened her tongue, or something else . . . something worse. Like genuine loneliness.

Either way, last night was best forgotten. She'd put it behind her and quickly move forward.

"You're fidgeting," Chad said, watching her with a faintly amused smile as she leaned forward to adjust her magazines and headphones in the seat pocket once more.

She had been wiggling around a lot. She was so tense. So frustrated with herself. "The seats are really close together," she said shortly. It was going to be a long flight home if she didn't settle down. Relax. Get some control.

He watched her for another moment as she squared up the magazines and then slipped her water bottle in front. "What's bugging you?"

"Nothing."

"Meg."

"Stop it!" She glared at him, angry. "Stop acting like you know me, Chad. Stop acting like you care—"

"I do care."

"Well, knock it off. It's not right. Or appropriate."

"We're colleagues. We've worked together for five years. I'm allowed to care for you."

"But you're not allowed to make me feel bad."

His blue eyes sparked. "I'm not trying to make you feel bad. I'm trying to boost you up. You've been blue, Meg, I can tell—"

"Did you have an ulterior motive for bringing me along?"

"*What?*"

"Did you?"

"Why would you ask that?"

Because for the first time since she'd gone to work for Dark Horse, for the first time in five years, she was aware of Chad as a man, not merely as her boss. And sitting this close to him, she felt nervous and jumpy . . . skittish. Not skittish as in fearful, but skittish as in *aware*. Aware of him. Chad. She could feel him. He was a man. A very sexy, rugged man, who smelled good and looked gorgeous and made her want touch and love and tenderness.

Made her want heat.

Made her remember desire.

Perhaps that was the worst. Aching for something she couldn't have. Wouldn't have. Maybe not again ever.

"Because you're a man, a dude," she said irritably, hating that they were even having this conversation but determined to get it out into the open. "And perhaps you thought something would happen . . ."

"Happen how?"

"You know . . . business trip, away from home, and things happen . . ."

For a moment he said nothing and then his jaw tightened and his lips thinned. He looked pissed. "Are you implying I made a move on you?"

Meg flushed. "No . . . but when we were talking last night, it did get personal."

"And because it got personal, you think I was trying to get you into my bed?"

Meg scowled at the words *into my bed*. They sounded so intimate, but real. Tangible. As if something like that could have happened. As if something like that could still happen. "No." She took a quick breath. "And we both know I'm not your type," she added, not sure why she said that. It sounded like she was fishing for information, and maybe she was.

His hard blue eyes locked on hers. "What is my type?"

She shivered at the way his voice dropped, hardening, deepening. He didn't sound flirty. He sounded serious. Angry.

"Beautiful young women with sexy young bodies. Women you can control—"

"Bullshit."

Heat rushed through her and her stomach turned inside out. Something was happening between them and it was intense. She knew she needed to back off, turn away, focus on something else, but she couldn't. She needed whatever this was, whatever it meant, needed the emotion and the connection. "What about socialite Alexandra Kincaid? And that Forty-niner cheerleader . . . what's her name? Molly . . . Molly . . . Lydon. And your newest girl, Kari somebody—"

"I stopped seeing Kari a month ago, and yes, I do like beautiful women. I always have. But that's one of the reasons I like you."

There. He said it. He did like her.

She stared at him, taking in his blue eyes and the lean, rugged lines of his face. He was good-looking and physical and sexual and just sitting next to him right now felt dangerous. *He* felt dangerous. Chad had an intense energy, a very sexual energy, and she wasn't used to anything sexual anymore.

She wasn't sexual anymore.

Hand shaking, Meg reached for her Diet Coke and took a quick sip, letting the cold bubbly soda swirl in her mouth and down her throat.

"I also know you're married," he added more quietly. "And I wouldn't do anything to jeopardize your marriage."

Something in his tone sent little shivers through her. Did he mean that? Or were those just words? "Jack and I are having some problems right now, but it's still a good marriage."

He said nothing.

She looked into Chad's face, tried to judge his reaction, but his expression was veiled, blue eyes shuttered. "I know I said some things yesterday that might have given you the wrong impression, but I love him."

"I know you do."

"I'm committed to him."

"I know you are."

She stared hard into his eyes, trying to see past the stunning blue color, but all she could see was her reflection, not him. "You're sure?"

"One hundred percent."

His firm tone indicated that he'd said all he wanted to say and they both turned their attention to the safety briefing. But later, as Meg watched a movie, she couldn't stop playing their conversation over and over in her head.

Last night she'd told him things she shouldn't have and today he'd told her things he shouldn't have. They'd crossed an invisible line and it scared her. It would be different if they were getting off the plane and never seeing each other again. But they were getting off the plane and meeting again on Monday for work.

And Tuesday.

And Wednesday.

And every day except for weekends. That was five days a week, twenty days a month, two-hundred-plus days a year. Far more time with Chad than she spent with Jack, which wouldn't be a problem if she was happy at home, but she wasn't happy at home anymore. She felt adrift. Alone.

And knowing that Chad was attracted to her was almost too much pressure. As well as too much power.

Power to wound, power to destroy. Power to destroy her marriage. Her family. Her friendships.

She didn't want it. Couldn't do it. Nothing—not even this hot, humming sensation rushing through her veins, making her want, making her feel.

It was good to be home, Meg thought much later that evening as she tucked Tessa and Gabi into bed for the night. JJ was going to be up late working on an essay for his sophomore English class, so she kissed him on the top of his head, told him to call her if he needed anything, and then went in search of Jack.

She found him on the couch in front of the TV with an open magazine on his chest and an open book on the arm of the sofa. She glanced at the book. Thomas Jefferson's *Notes on the State of Virginia*. Ever since Meg had met Jack, he'd been fascinated by Jefferson, read his works, and had visited Jefferson's neoclassical mansion, Monticello, numerous times.

"What are you watching?" she asked, squeezing in next to him on the couch.

"I'm flipping back and forth between DIY Network and a rerun of *This Old House* where they're renovating a house in Martha's Vineyard."

Jack the multitasker. She smiled ruefully, thinking she knew no one else who would read two different things *and* watch two different shows at the same time. But that was Jack with his insatiable need to be thinking of something important at all times. She slid her arm through his. "Miss me while I was gone?"

"Yes," he answered, giving her thigh a pat.

But of course he didn't look at her as he gave the pat, pat. Jack wasn't much for eye contact. But then, he didn't need it. There was always so much going on in his head.

"Mom was okay?" she persisted.

"She was great."

"She didn't seem too tired?"

"Not at all. I think she napped a little when the kids were in school, but she was in great spirits."

"I heard Dad came up for a night."

"He went to JJ's game with your mom."

"How did JJ play?"

"I wasn't there, but your dad said he looked good. He went three-for-four, knocked in three runs. Probably his best game this year."

She sat up and pulled back to look at him, disappointment filling her. He hadn't even made JJ's game when she was gone? "Why didn't you go?"

His jaw tensed. He didn't like her tone. "It was the day I went to Virginia."

"Couldn't you have scheduled that meeting for a different day? You haven't been to any of his games in weeks."

"I've been busy with work."

"Well, I'm busy, too, but I still try to make the games."

"It's not as if he didn't have anyone there to see him play. Your parents were there and your dad was really proud of JJ. They talked about the game all dinner. Your dad knows a lot more about baseball than I do."

"You just don't like baseball."

"It's not my favorite sport, no. But I go to JJ's games whenever I can, and JJ knows that, so don't make this a bigger deal than it needs to be."

Meg nodded and rose from the sofa to go back to check on the kids. But as she left the family room she felt angry and terrifyingly empty. Was this all that her life was? Had there ever been more? And would she feel better, happier, if she were with a different man?

The next day was Saturday, and after dropping Tessa at dance, Meg used the morning to shop for presents and buy birthday cards, for Jack as well as something for Tommy Jr. for tomorrow. She ordered a cake from Michelle Marie's Patisserie, Jack's favorite bakery in Santa Rosa, before making dinner reservations for five at John Ash & Co. Meg was still jet-lagged and thought it best to stay in Santa Rosa for dinner, and John Ash & Co. at the Vintners Inn was, in Meg's mind, the best restaurant in Santa Rosa. It was a place you dressed up for, and as the kids had never been there, it would be a special treat for them all to go tonight to celebrate Jack's birthday.

Meg was glad for the errands and the distraction of planning Jack's birthday. Being busy meant she didn't have time to think about Chad, or the trip. She didn't want to think about Chad. And yet, after a week together in London, he'd begun to feel like he was part of her life, important in her life, and that was a problem. Meg vowed to get him out of her system, and fast.

But it wasn't easy to block him from her thoughts. The very act of refusing to think about him made her think about him even more. So frustrating.

Meg picked up Tessa at noon, returned to the bakery to pick up the cake, and then drove home. During the drive Tessa talked about the last week and the grade she got on her math test and the project she was supposed to be working on for social studies. Meg listened and commented at the appropriate times, but felt terribly hypocritical planning this special birthday dinner for Jack while struggling not to think about Chad. Thank God nobody could read her mind. It honestly horrified her that she'd been so physically attracted to him yesterday on the flight home.

It was one thing to be comfortable with him at work. One thing to enjoy his company during a dinner meeting. It was quite another to want him . . . desire him . . .

A siren sounded loudly and red and blue lights flashed in her rearview mirror. Meg's heart fell even as she pulled her foot off the accelerator. But too late. She was being pulled over.

"Mom," Tessa whispered.

"It's all right," Meg answered, braking and signaling that she was moving over to the shoulder. She hadn't been pulled over in years. Couldn't remember when she last got a ticket for anything. She stopped, shifted into park, turned the car off. Hands shaking, she took her wallet from her purse, withdrew her license and insurance, and asked Tessa to get the pink registration paper from the glove compartment.

Meg heard herself answer the officer's questions. No, she hadn't realized she was going that fast. No, she hadn't been drinking. Yes, she knew that it was a reduced speed zone. She'd just been distracted. Hadn't paid attention. Yes, she understood it was dangerous. She'd be more observant. Focus on the road and all signs. The officer ended up letting her go with a warning due to her excellent driving record.

Meg thanked the officer profusely and carefully merged back into traffic and drove away.

Thank God she hadn't gotten a ticket, but she still felt rattled and her hands trembled on the steering wheel the rest of the ride home.

It was Chad's fault she'd gotten pulled over. She'd been thinking about him, not the road, or speed limits, or Tessa's chatter. But why Chad, and why now?

All these years, all this time, there'd been no attraction, no temptation, and yet now, suddenly, she wanted him? It was idiotic. Beyond idiotic. Meg wasn't the type of woman to fantasize about other men. And maybe she did like Chad, but she loved her job. Loved her husband. She was a good mom, cherished her family. She wasn't about to risk all that on a fling. Other women might stray, but not her.

And yet hours later, after dinner at John Ash & Co. and cake and presents back home with the kids, Meg was in her closet stripping off her clothes, getting ready for bed, when she sank to her knees and covered her face and cried.

All night she'd been charming and loving and so very devoted to Jack. She'd been attentive to the kids. She'd made sure tonight was wonderful. She'd made sure Jack felt special. And then Jack and the kids went to bed, and Meg had stayed up tidying the house. She'd put the cake back in the box and in the fridge and the cake plates into the dishwasher. She'd thrown out the crumpled wrapping paper and bows, arranged Jack's new gifts on the kitchen counter so he could admire them in the morning the way he liked to do with new gifts. She'd wiped down counters and turned off lights and set the alarm. And now she was in the closet, half naked and crying because she felt empty.

And hollow. So very hollow. As if she'd misplaced her heart and soul and she didn't know where to find them. Or maybe she'd never had a heart. Hard to remember.

Eventually she pulled herself together and went to bed. She moved close to Jack and just lay there for several moments, absorbing his warmth, listening to him breathe. He'd been so happy tonight, grinning at each of them during dinner. He loved being the center of attention. Loved his moment in the sun.

Meg pressed her face into his back, smelling his skin. She'd always liked his smell. He didn't wear fragrance or aftershave, but he always smelled good. Smelled clean. And just like that, the sadness returned. The terrible need to be held. Comforted.

She kissed his back, slid a hand over his biceps, down his arm. He didn't stir. She stroked his arm a little more firmly. "Honey."

"Mmmph?"

She wiggled closer. "Want to . . . you know . . ."

He didn't respond.

She caressed his arm again, from wrist to shoulder, hoping he'd wake, respond, needing him to respond, needing to become whole and real and permanent. Because lately she felt almost transparent. As if she was dissolving . . . melting away . . . becoming nothing. "It's your birthday . . . we should do it," she said, trying again.

"Too full," he mumbled. "Ate way too much."

She stayed there a moment, absorbing the disappointment, and then she turned onto her back, scooted over a little, and folded her hands on her chest. He wasn't rejecting her, she told herself, fighting panic. He was just tired. It was all right. She was all right. She was fine and the marriage was fine and everything would be fine tomorrow.

Meg woke up at six, remembered it was Sunday, and tried to go back to sleep. But instead of falling asleep, she remembered her dreams.

She'd dreamed of Chad.

Dreamed of making love to Chad. Dreamed she was maybe even in love with him.

Meg shuddered and pulled the pillow over her head. She didn't want to be dreaming about Chad. Didn't like feeling this way . . . out of control. And the dreams had been hot. Intense. She'd woken up aroused and dissatisfied. She needed relief. She needed an orgasm. It'd been weeks—months?—since she'd had one. Maybe it was time to break down and buy a good vibrator. Kit had one. Brianna had several. Perhaps a vibrator would bring some relief.

Ten

"Tomorrow Tommy and Cass find out if she's pregnant," Meg said as they drove to her parents' home in San Francisco's Sunset District that afternoon for her brother's birthday dinner. The Brennans still got together as a family for birthdays and special occasions, usually at Mom and Dad's since that would always be home.

"I imagine they're nervous," Jack said. He was at the wheel of Meg's Lexus SUV, the car they took when with the kids.

"They've got to be nervous," she agreed. "I'm nervous for them."

"If it doesn't work, they do have options."

She nodded, chewing on the inside of her lip, aware that Tommy wasn't interested in most of those options. He didn't want to adopt. Didn't want to use a surrogate. Didn't really want to deal with the whole baby thing anymore. "Can't believe he's thirty-seven."

"Are we bringing a gift?"

"I got him a shirt at Nordstrom. He can always exchange it for something else if he doesn't like it." Meg glanced into the backseat at the kids. They were quiet, all of them engrossed in some form of entertainment. The girls were watching one of the *Twilight* movies on the car's DVD player and JJ was staring out the window, listening to his iPod wearing earbuds. His head was bobbing and the girls' eyes were wide, their expressions rapt. Someone was either going to die or get kissed.

"So Richard's not coming?" Jack asked.

"No. They broke up two weeks ago, just after the girls' weekend in Capitola. That's why I had to help Kit move into her new house," Meg said, suppressing annoyance, aware that Jack had a hard time focusing on anything she told him about her family.

Early in the marriage, Jack had rebelled at the idea of spending holidays with her entire family, but she knew his family wasn't close. He had one brother he didn't see very often, and he saw his parents, who divorced when he was eleven, even less. The divorce and subsequent custody battle (neither parent seemed to really want the boys but, at the same time, didn't want the other parent to have them) decimated holidays and family traditions, and by the time Jack headed off to Cornell, he was glad to escape family.

But then, in graduate school, Jack met Meg while they were both studying in Rome, he on a professional architecture studies program headquartered at the Palazzo Lazzaroni, and she on a semester-long study program earning credits for her communications degree at the University of San Diego. Rome was romantic and they fell in love, continuing their long-distance relationship once they returned to the States to finish their degrees, Jack with his M.A. in historic preservation planning from Cornell and Meg with her B.A. in communications from USD.

Jack hadn't wanted to marry right away. He was a liberal atheist and interested in changing the world one building at a time. He'd hoped Meg would join him on the East Coast and they'd live together, and do some traveling when finances and schedules permitted, but Meg wouldn't—couldn't—move east without a commitment. He was angry that she would force his hand. Couldn't she accept that he loved her without a wedding ring? But Meg held her ground. She'd grown up in the Catholic school system, and had just graduated from a Jesuit university, and was the eldest of five kids. What kind of example would she set if she just moved in with her boyfriend?

Jack reluctantly proposed, Meg moved to New York, and they spent the sweltering, muggy summer job hunting while Meg planned the wedding with her mom. Meg was the first to find a job. It was just an entry-level position with a big advertising agency, but there was a paycheck attached and they needed the money. She started working August 1, but October came and Jack still had nothing.

Meg supported them for another two months on her measly salary while she and Jack made love and fought. He accused her of being too controlling. She said he was aloof and unrealistic. Privately, Meg worried that the two of them weren't truly compatible. He wouldn't go to church. He'd read late into the night instead of going to bed with her. He'd be sleeping when she left for work. Meg called her mom in tears on Thanksgiving Day, missing her family, hating not being home for the holiday. She'd never not been with her family for Thanksgiving. Even during college she came home for the holiday, but there wasn't money for her to fly to San Francisco for the weekend, and her parents hadn't offered.

The fact that they hadn't offered upset her almost as much as Jack's refusal to eat turkey. But Meg got the message. She was an adult now. She had to stand on her own two feet.

One week later Jack got a job offer, a very good offer, and ironically it was from a prominent urban design firm in San Francisco. Maybe God did help those who helped themselves, because she was getting to go home, permanently.

By Christmas they'd moved to San Francisco and settled into an apartment in Cow Hollow. In February they married at St. Cecilia's on Seventeenth Avenue, the parish church Meg had grown up attending, and took a one-week honeymoon to Kauai.

Jack missed the East Coast but grew to like San Francisco. He wasn't as happy with the firm, though, and struck out on his own after a fortuitous meeting with a member of the Getty family. The Getty name opened doors and one job led to another. Within three years he had more work than he could handle, allowing him to be selective regarding projects and giving him the ability to set higher rates. JJ was two years old when they moved from their San Francisco apartment to the "cottage" in Petaluma, putting some needed distance between Jack and his overly involved in-laws. It wasn't that he didn't like the Brennans—he did—but he wasn't accustomed to, or comfortable with, so much group activity.

Once again Meg missed the city and the proximity to her family, especially because Dad loved his grandson, baby Jack Jr., and Mom would babysit once a week so she and Jack could have a date night, but it was important that Jack be happy, too, and he liked Petaluma, where he felt like a big fish in a small pond.

Holidays remained a point of contention, though. Meg knew that Jack didn't delight in all the Brennan family get-togethers—they'd had some terrible rows over Thanksgiving, Christmas, and Easter in those early years—and it had taken tears, negotiation, and compromise, but if she wanted Jack to attend the big "three," then she had to understand he wouldn't make all the family dinners and birthday celebrations.

Thus she'd been surprised that he'd agreed to go to Tommy's birthday dinner tonight, especially after spending five days this last week with her mom. Meg wondered if her mom's cancer had influenced his decision, but didn't ask, just glad he was going.

"I thought they'd gotten back together," Jack said, frowning as he slowed to accommodate traffic, his thoughts still on Kit and Richard's breakup.

"No. He hasn't even talked to her since the night they ended it."

"That's too bad. He was different, but I liked him."

Meg shot him a sharp glance. "He didn't treat Kit very well."

"She seemed happy enough."

"What's happy enough?"

"They were together a long time."

"That doesn't mean they were happy."

"I suppose that's true."

Jack found a parking spot on Fifth Avenue just two houses from Meg's parents' house, an olive, white, and cream house that had been Meg's childhood home. Built in 1910, the three-story house still had the Edwardian exterior charm, the original millwork interior, and forty years of memories.

Meg's children loved Grandma and Grandpa's house, especially the bonus room on the third floor that her parents had converted into a playroom for their grandkids, and after kissing their grandparents hello, they tramped up the stairs to the bonus room and shut the door.

Meg carried the salad makings into the kitchen while Jack took in the wine and birthday present for Tommy. Tommy and Cass hadn't yet arrived, but Kit was there in the kitchen making a pasta salad to go with the tri-tip. Dad loved barbecuing and now that the weather had warmed up, when he wasn't at the fire station, he was usually at the grill.

Meg kissed her mom, hugged her dad. She hadn't seen him in almost a month and she welcomed his bear hug. He was a big guy, a little over six feet, with thick salt-and-pepper hair, blue eyes, and the ruddy complexion of the Irish. "How are you, Dad?" she asked, getting another hug.

"Good," he said, patting her back. "Enjoyed seeing JJ play last Wednesday. He looked good."

"I'm glad you went," she said even as she realized that Wednesday had been Jack's actual birthday. So Jack wasn't even in town for his birthday, but in Virginia for business. Meg wasn't sure if this made her feel better or worse.

"He's fun to watch. Reminds me a lot of Tommy. He was a first baseman, too. Remember?"

"I do," Meg answered, glancing at Jack, who was talking animatedly to Kit. The two of them had always gotten along well. They both liked books. History. Art. Meg suspected they were talking about either Kit's new house or Jack's project in Virginia. "Rumor has it that you're thinking of retiring soon," she said, turning her full attention back to her father. "Is it true?"

"I'm thinking it's time. I'm the oldest guy in the house."

"And probably still the strongest."

He flushed with pleasure. "Nah."

They were still talking about the guys at the station when Tommy and Cass arrived ten minutes later. Tommy, a firefighter for the past ten years, was just over six feet, but solid, too. He'd inherited their mom's darker coloring, Dad's ruddiness and the famous Brennan blue eyes.

Tommy caught sight of Meg and grinned. "Mary Margaret, how are you?"

She grinned back. Tommy was a charmer. Girls had found him irresistible in preschool and he'd built a solid fan base until graduating from Fresno State, where he'd played baseball for four years. Tommy got drafted by the Padres, but after an unsatisfying year in the minor leagues, gave up ball to become a fireman like his father.

It'd been their dad's hope that Tommy would work for the San Francisco Fire Department, too. Tommy would have been the seventh generation to do so, but there were politics involved and the department was intent on hiring and promoting women and minorities—quotas, Dad had said in disgust (and not very politely)—so there was no place for Tommy, at least not immediately.

Dad nearly quit the department, but Tommy convinced him that would be a mistake, and he quickly found a position in the East Bay, which made Cass happy, as she was a nurse at Kaiser in Walnut Creek.

Tommy had been with the Walnut Creek Fire Department ten years and it was a good fit for him. He liked living in the suburbs and shared season tickets with two guys in his station for the A's and Warrior games.

Dad and Tommy immediately launched into sharing stories, and Meg joined Cass, Kit, and Mom at the small island where Mom was buttering a sliced loaf of French bread.

"How are you feeling?" Meg asked Cass, giving her sister-in-law a hug.

"Good." Cass's blue eyes shone. She was wearing a simple cotton dress in a subtle floral turquoise-and-aqua print with chocolate piping, and the color made her eyes pop, and highlighted her blond hair and fair complexion. Cassidy was a natural blonde, the quintessential California blonde with freckles across the bridge of her nose, only she was from Oklahoma, not California, and had grown up on a derelict poultry farm. Cass hated chickens now, didn't even like eating eggs, although she could bake with them. Meg loved her. She was a sweetheart, down-to-earth and funny, and she fit in perfectly with the family.

"You're holding up okay?" Kit asked as she tore off a sheet of foil for Mom to wrap the bread in.

Cass nodded and bit her lip. Her eyes shone even brighter.

She looked so happy, Meg thought, studying her sister-in-law's face; she was almost bursting with happiness.

Kit was thinking the same thing, and her brow furrowed as she looked at Meg and then back at Cass. "You know something," she said under her breath.

Cass's cheeks turned pink and she glanced at Tommy's back and nodded. "You can't tell him," she whispered, pulling her phone out of her sundress pocket. "I'm waiting to tell him tonight when we get home." And then she clicked on a photo she'd taken with her phone and held the picture out for them to see. A pregnancy test with a pink plus sign.

"You're pregnant?" Mom whispered in delight.

Cass nodded, a sheen of tears darkening her eyes. "We still have to take the blood test tomorrow, but I'm pretty sure the home tests are right. I took three tests. They all came out positive."

Meg hugged Cass swiftly, and dropped her voice so her dad and brother wouldn't hear. "Congratulations, Cassidy. I'm so happy for you!"

"I am, too," Cass answered. "And Tommy will be such a great father!"

M eg was still in a buoyant mood when she drove to work the next morning. She was so happy for Tommy and Cass that she'd found it hard to sleep last night, wondering how he'd reacted to the news, wishing she could have been there to see his face.

Now arriving at the winery, Meg parked her car and tried to shift gears, changing into work mode.

She had been at her desk for a couple hours when Craig stopped by her office to let her know that Chad had some friends in town and wasn't planning on working until Wednesday.

Meg had been on pins and needles waiting for him to arrive, and she told herself she could relax now, but she couldn't. She was disappointed, and missed him. Missed his quick smile and the flash of his blue eyes. Missed his low laugh—it was husky and sexy. She missed the way he leaned toward her as he talked, and he talked with his hands—not a lot, just enough—and he had a sexy body. Great body.

And then she caught herself thinking about him and was appalled with herself. She was married. *Married.* And Chad was her boss. As well as a lady-killer. What was she thinking?

But that night Meg could only think of Chad. Even when Jack was on top of her.

It wasn't their best lovemaking. It wasn't even good lovemaking. She felt nothing and had to resort to using lubricant again and Jack came before she did, then gave her a peck and rolled over and went to sleep.

Meg lay awake seething. Not with anger. But with emptiness.

She needed more, ached for more. But why did she need more now? Why was she so dissatisfied with her life?

Craving touch, and warmth, she reached under the covers and covered her breast with her palm. It was full, heavy. Lightly she stroked the nipple once, twice, until it firmed. But she didn't want to be the one touching her. She wanted someone to do it, someone to want her, someone to love her.

Closing her eyes, she could almost imagine Chad's golden head bent over her breast, his lips taking the nipple in his mouth and sucking. She squirmed, thighs rubbing against each other. She loved it when Jack used to suck and lick her nipples, loved it when he paid attention to her breasts. He didn't anymore. Tonight he'd given her body a one-two caress and then entered her. Tonight it'd been two minutes of pumping and then ejaculation.

Tears of frustration filled her eyes. She missed good sex. Missed feeling good with Jack.

Emotion filled her, huge, consuming. What if Jack never really wanted her again? What if fast sex was all there would be? She was already feeling so empty, and she didn't think she could live forever feeling this way.

But then she pictured ten-year-old Gabi with her big brown eyes and crooked smile. And twelve-year-old Tessa in her pink tights, black leotard, and pale pink pointe shoes. The girls were so young still. They knew nothing about the world, or how hard it would be. They needed her. Needed her to guide them, protect them, help them find their way.

Meg turned over onto her stomach, pressed her cheek against the sheets, guilty for even wanting more. She had enough. By all accounts she was blessed. She had a loving husband, a beautiful house, three wonderful kids. How could she need more than that?

Meg called Kit as she drove to work. Kit was in her classroom but wouldn't start teaching for another fifteen minutes. "Do you have a second?" Meg asked her, putting her sister on the car speaker.

"I do. What's up?"

Meg flexed her fingers against the steering wheel. "I think I'm having a nervous breakdown."

"Why would you say that?"

"Because I'm losing my mind."

"You seemed fine at Mom and Dad's."

"That's because you don't know what I'm thinking."

"What are you thinking?"

"I'm thinking about having sex with someone who isn't my husband."

"Meg!"

"*I know.*" She drew a short breath. "This isn't me, Kit. I'm not like this, but I feel almost obsessed."

Meg heard the squeak of Kit's chair as she sat down.

"With who?" Kit asked.

"I don't want to talk about it."

"Someone at work?" Kit guessed. "Craig? Chad?"

Meg cringed. "I shouldn't have gone to London."

Kit sighed. "Chad."

"I'm not going to do anything," Meg said roughly. "I'd never cheat on Jack, but then, in seventeen years of marriage I've never wanted anyone but Jack . . ." Her voice drifted off. She didn't finish the thought. She didn't need to.

"You don't want to do it, Meg. You'd hate yourself."

"I'm not going to do it. I couldn't. I just need my hormones to calm down. They're going crazy right now. You'd think I was sixteen." Meg heard the bell ring in the background. "You've got to go."

"I do." Kit hesitated. "Be careful."

"I will."

Chad had appeared unexpectedly that afternoon. Meg hadn't thought she'd see him until next week and had come to work with her long hair loose, wearing cropped black leggings, black heels, and a taupe knit tunic. It was a little edgier than normal, a little sexier, but she hadn't been dressing for Chad. She'd been dressing for herself, trying to feel good about herself. Confident. She certainly wasn't confident at home.

She was sitting in Craig's office after lunch, talking about the dinners in London and her impressions of the trade fair, when Chad walked in looking very *GQ* and British in a brown herringbone wool suit with a white shirt and a striped tie.

"Afternoon, Craig," Chad said, taking a chair across from his brother's desk. "Hello, Meg. Recovered from the show?"

"Yes," she answered, studying his leather shoes and then his shoulder to avoid meeting his gaze. He wasn't supposed to be working today. He was supposed to be taking the rest of the week off to be with friends. "Where are your friends?"

"Calistoga. Doing the mud baths and spa thing, at Melissa's request."

Meg smiled tightly. She was dismayed by his sudden appearance, not yet ready to contend with these new feelings she had for him. "No golfing?"

"We golfed for the last two days in Pebble Beach, which is why Adam is doing the mud baths with Melissa today."

"And you weren't up for the mud baths?"

Chad laughed softly. "Not big for the mud baths, no. That hot mud gets everywhere.

Meg's cheeks warmed. "Nice visual," she said, getting to her feet. "I'll let you two talk. I've got work to do." And she left before either of them could stop her.

But an hour later, when she got a Google alert about an article in *Wine Salon* regarding the winery's new label, and it wasn't positive, criticizing Dark Horse for trying to do too much and rushing the new red, she left her office to find Chad.

As she walked she reread the review. "Unimpressed," the critic wrote of the new Shiraz. "A lot of sales hype, but no substance. The new Shiraz might be bold, but it lacks concentration and depth."

Chad was in his office on the phone when she knocked on his door. He motioned her in and wrapped up his call.

"You look amazing," he said, after hanging up.

"This isn't amazing, though," she replied, handing him the review.

"What?"

"*Wine Salon.*"

"I heard about this," he said, taking the piece and skimming it. "She's obviously not a fan," he said, when he finished reading.

"Everyone else loved the wine."

He shrugged. "It might be personal. Or she maybe just didn't like it."

"You're not upset?"

"I expected as much when I didn't return her calls." He gave the review back to Meg. "That's why you're not supposed to mix business and pleasure."

"But you did."

"She was single, and available."

"That's all you need."

"No, she was attractive, too."

"Single, attractive female. And you had to have her."

"She chased me."

"So that makes it okay?"

"Doesn't it?"

"Chad!"

"It was just sex."

"That's pathetic."

He leaned back in his chair, folded his arms behind his head. "You're awfully judgmental."

"I just don't know why you'd risk the winery's reputation like that. Theresa Scully is a prominent wine critic. She blogs all over. Tweets nonstop. She could do serious damage if she wanted."

"You want me to whore myself to get good reviews?"

She rolled her eyes. "No, but you didn't have to sleep with her in the first place. You could have been polite, charming, and kept your pants on."

"She knew it was just a one-night thing."

"Obviously she didn't, or she wouldn't be making her bitterness public."

"Or maybe she honestly didn't like the wine."

Meg's eyebrows arched. "Or maybe she didn't like you." Then, with a muffled oath, she stalked out of his office and back to hers. He was making her crazy. He really was.

She was just sitting back down behind her desk and reaching for her phone when he followed her in, and closed the door behind him.

"You're mad at me," he said.

Meg slapped her phone down. "Yes. I am."

"Why?"

Now she was really upset with him. And it wasn't just sleeping with Theresa, or the dozens of women who flocked around him. It was also the trip to London and how it'd changed everything for her. That being with him there had taken a professional relationship, one she valued highly, and made it uncomfortably personal. "What are you wearing? You look like a professor."

"That's why you're upset? *My suit?*"

"No. But . . . why? It's really preppy." Meg shifted some of the piles of paper from the middle of her desk to the corner and then adjusted her laptop. She knew Chad was looking at her, but she'd be damned before she looked back at him. "It's not . . . you. Stick with your jeans and boots. So much better on you."

"You think?"

"Yes. But I'm not complimenting you. Just trying to save you money."

"Wow. Thank you. That's really nice of you but I just came from a meeting."

"Oh." She flushed. "I'm sorry if I was rude about your suit. It just looks like something Jack might wear if he had to dress up."

"Ah."

"And another thing . . ."

His eyebrows shot up. "Yes?"

"I was so comfortable with you," she said roughly. "Happy working for you. But now . . . now . . . it doesn't feel right. It's changed."

She waited for him to argue, or say something flippant, but instead he nodded. "You're right. It has. I feel it, too."

"You do?"

"Yes." And then he held his hand out to her. "Come. Let's go for a walk. We need to talk."

She nodded and got to her feet but didn't take his hand. Instead she followed him through the administrative offices into the cool, pungent barrel room, between the rows of oak casks, where he opened one of the wooden doors into the tasting room. The large Tuscany tasting room was empty, but the lights were on and a row of wineglasses stood on the counter. They continued into the wine shop, where Gina, the shop assistant, was ringing up a purchase for a twentysomething-year-old couple. Gina introduced the couple to Chad, who asked if they'd had a chance to sample any wines. They said they'd visited the day before and were just returning to buy more of their favorite Shiraz.

Chad thanked them and reminded them to get on the winery's mailing list for updates and information about future events, and then he held the door open for Meg and they stepped outside into the sunshine.

It was nearly noon and a gorgeous day. The blue sky stretched overhead without a cloud in sight and the temperature was perfect, warm, without being hot, probably midseventies, and Meg rolled her shoulders and stretched, grateful for the warmth of the sun on her back. They walked across the sweeping drive, their footsteps kicking up gravel, to the employee parking lot. In the parking lot between Chad's Jaguar and Meg's Lexus SUV, was the winery's old work truck.

"Want to check the grapes with me?" he asked her.

"In that suit?"

"I'm never going to wear this suit again. Are you coming?"

She laughed, and he opened the gray truck's passenger door for her. She slid in on the bench seat. The leather was old and cracked and it caught at the knit of her tunic. She drew the garment closer to her body as Chad climbed in on the other side and started the truck. He drove up a dirt road and then along the top of a hill. Rows of grapes spread in every direction, cloaking the hills with dark green. The truck disappeared down the back of the hill before climbing another one, even steeper this time. Meg's breath caught in her throat as they reached the top of the mountain. Sunshine gilded the valley and small farmsteads could be seen tucked between the verdant vineyards.

Chad turned the engine off and faced her. He didn't immediately speak. And then he looked at her, his eyes locking with hers. "I wasn't entirely truthful on the plane on the way home from London."

She simply looked at him and waited.

"I want to respect your marriage," he added. "I'm trying to. And I've done my damnedest to stay away from you because I respect you. But you don't seem happy, Meg."

He stopped talking and waited for her to say something. But she couldn't think of a single thing to say.

What could she say to that?

"Are you happy?" he asked.

This was wrong, Meg thought. Wrong to sit here with Chad, wrong to let him say these things, flirt with her, and yet at the same time she couldn't find her voice to stop him. It'd been a long time since a man looked at her, and stared into her eyes, and called her beautiful. Husbands of seventeen years didn't do that anymore. She wasn't so sure Jack ever had.

"All marriages have ups and downs," she said hoarsely.

"You didn't answer my question."

"I don't have to. You're shameless."

He suddenly leaned forward, closing the distance between them. His face was inches from hers, his blue gaze hot, intent. "If I thought I had a shot with you, Meg, I'd take it."

Heat flared within her and nerves tightened, danced down her back, so that she arched her spine. Could he possibly be serious? Impossible. Her gaze fell from his eyes to his mouth. His lips were just a kiss away. "You shouldn't say such things," she protested, but her voice was husky, unsteady.

"Because you're married?"

"Yes. And you're Catholic, too. You go to Mass. I know you do."

His lips curved at the edges. "To confess my sins, Mary Margaret."

He said her name as if it were something delicious in his mouth and she blushed, dazzled by his energy. He was warm and physical, so very male, and her pulse raced. "And there are many, aren't there?" she retorted, feeling as if she'd embarked on a very dangerous game.

His lips curved up higher. "Debauchery being top of my list."

"You're poking fun at me."

"I am. But only because I love how fierce and feisty you get." He moved toward her, closing the distance between them, so close now she could feel his breath against her lips and the scent of his cologne—very subtle, a hint of warm vanilla and spice—and wave after wave of need rushed through her, overwhelming her. He was seducing her, and she, wanton woman, liked it.

Loved it.

Kit would die if she saw them here, parked in his truck. "This is not a good idea," Meg whispered.

"You're absolutely right."

That made her smile even as her stomach fell. She shouldn't be smiling, though. This was not funny. She shouldn't be here, shouldn't be encouraging him.

His eyes searched hers, and it was so intimate that blood rushed to her cheeks. Jack couldn't look at her and Chad couldn't look away.

Little by little her smile slipped.

And he just kept looking at her, staring into her eyes as if trying to see all the way inside of her, and it felt good. Intense.

Heat rushed up through her, from her middle to the skin of her collarbones and up her neck. The heat burned her cheeks and licked at her nose and jaw, making her skin tingle.

It was then that his head dropped, and his mouth hovered over hers for a fraction of a second before settling against hers. He kissed her slowly, exploring the shape of her lips, the feel of her mouth. She felt as though he were discovering her and it was heady, dazzling. New. After twenty years of kissing the same man it was wildly different kissing someone new. Kissing someone who really wanted to kiss her. Kissing someone who really wanted her. Not Meg the wife, Meg the mom, but Meg the female. Meg the woman.

An aching need rushed through her, twisting and knotting with the pleasure. Desire and an inexplicable hunger for more. More out of life. More sensation. More emotion. More appreciation.

Chad's hand slipped up to cup her face, his palm against her cheek, and then to slide back, fingers burying, tangling in her hair, and she felt like velvet, soft, delicate, pliant.

Meg leaned in toward him, kissing him back, even though part of her mind was shouting at her, reminding her of her values, her morals, her responsibility to Jack and the family, but with Chad's lips moving across hers, with the tip of his tongue stroking the seam of her lips, she couldn't focus on anything but this, and the urgent need to feel, escape, burrow into another. She needed warmth and comfort and goodness. She needed good feelings. She'd felt bad for so long, empty and hollow and frightened of herself, of the monster prowling the perimeter of her mind and heart, whispering she was bad, whispering she was scarred, whispering she'd never get it right.

But right now she felt right. Protected. Alive.

Chad lifted his head, looked down into her eyes. "You are one hell of a kisser, Mary Margaret."

She simply stared up at him, unable to speak.

He caressed her cheek once more, then said regretfully, "And now I have to drive you back."

Eleven

The twilight smelled of summer—warm, earthy, ripe. Meg sat in the bleachers at the high school stadium with Laura and Farrell. The field had been recently mown and the soaring stadium lights turned on, chasing the dusky shadows away.

Meg wrapped her arms around her knees, her gaze fixed on the field, but she couldn't concentrate on JJ's game.

She couldn't believe that just hours ago she'd sat parked in Chad's truck, kissing him in the middle of his vineyard.

Who did that?

Not her, Mary Margaret Brennan Roberts. Mary Margaret was good, responsible, loyal, honest.

Or used to be.

Meg shivered and drew her thin cotton sweater closer to her body as the phrase *stupid things women do to mess up their lives* echoed through her head. The phrase came from the title of a self-help book by Dr. Laura Schlessinger called, appropriately, *Ten Stupid Things Women Do to Mess Up Their Lives*. Meg had found the book at a used bookstore years ago and had given it to Kit because she worried that Kit hadn't set proper boundaries with Richard, and was loving him too much, and herself not enough, and she had marked the chapter called "Stupid Attachment" for Kit to read, in case Kit didn't know which stupid thing she'd done.

Exhaling hard, Meg was confident there had to be a chapter in the book for her. She wasn't sure what it'd be called. "Stupid Midlife Crisis." Or "Stupid Horny Forty-Year-Olds." Or perhaps just plain "Stupid Women."

Because right now she was most definitely a stupid woman. And Meg knew she'd ruin her life if she didn't get her values and priorities sorted out fast.

The fear of fucking everything up should have stopped her from even thinking about Chad, but it hadn't. She was flooded with shame . . . and desire. Completely illogical, and a terrible combination, but there it was.

Meg longed to call Kit but couldn't. How could she tell her sister that she'd kissed Chad? Kit would be horrified. Just like Meg was horrified.

This is why God gave us will, she thought. Will to choose. Will to do good, or bad. She'd always tried to do good, be good, she'd always chosen the right thing.

Today she chose the wrong thing. And she felt different. Scared. But also terribly, frantically alive.

Nervous, unsettled, and jittery as hell, Meg crossed her legs, smoothed her soft knit tunic over her knees, and scanned the stands looking for Jack. He was supposed to come to today's game. Ordinarily she'd be upset that he wasn't here. It was the bottom of the seventh inning. If Jack didn't arrive soon, he'd miss all of the game. Just as he'd missed most of the games this season.

If she hadn't been sitting in Chad's truck kissing him three and a half hours ago, she might be really angry with Jack, resentful, but how could she be angry with Jack when she had been kissing a man who wasn't her husband . . . and loving it?

Maybe it was a good thing that once again Jack had got caught up in a meeting or planning and lost track of time. Maybe it was better without him here. Meg wasn't sure she could face him right now. Wasn't sure what she'd even say to him. *Hey, honey, how was your day? Anything interesting happen?*

Meg exhaled, shifting anxiously on the old wooden bench as JJ stepped into the batter's box, glanced around, his gaze searching the stands for his parents. He spotted Meg, lifted his eyebrows, and Meg knew what he was asking. *Is Dad here?*

She gave her head a slight shake.

His shoulders sagged for just a second as he turned away, and then they straightened as he took a practice swing. It was a hard, clean cut. JJ had a great swing. He could hit the ball. When he got the right pitch, he sent the ball sailing. But then, he was the team's cleanup hitter. He was the guy they counted on to get the job done.

Meg loved that about him. She loved his confidence and his swagger and the way he approached the plate, expecting to hit. She'd never had JJ's talent, or Brianna's. She'd never been gifted, or a star, but she'd tried to go through life with confidence. She'd expected herself to succeed, the same way JJ now expected himself to.

Maybe it was a firstborn thing. Birth order. Or maybe it was genetic. Either way, Meg hoped JJ would never lose that confidence and determination.

Farrell nudged her with her elbow. "Hey, isn't that Jack?" she said, pointing to the edge of the field bordering third base.

Meg looked toward third base and didn't see him. She pressed her lips together as she searched the park. Her lips still tingled. But then everything in her tingled. Maybe the worst thing about the kiss wasn't the kiss itself, but the fact that it made her want more. Made her realize she felt starved for more.

And that was bad.

"Where?" Meg asked, forehead creasing.

"There," Farrell said, "Look toward the visitor dugout."

And then Meg spotted him. Tall, serious, dark tousled hair, rumpled shirt. Her brilliant but self-absorbed architect. It was the top of the eighth, but he was here and he'd made it in time to watch JJ's next at-bat and she was very grateful for that.

And that was good.

Just then, Meg's phone buzzed in her purse with an incoming text. Her eyes suddenly watered. The text was from Cass. *Pregnant!! Due date January 28th!*

And that was wonderful.

JJ talked the whole way home, which was rare these days, as he preferred single-syllable words and grunts to real conversation, but he was stoked that his dad had been there to see his home run in the top of the eighth, a solo home run that won the game for his team.

Meg listened to JJ talk about how good he'd felt at the plate today, and how baseball was his game, and that he wished his uncle Boone had been there to see him play.

"Do you think I'll ever have scouts come watch me play?" he asked her, putting his feet up on the dash.

Meg ignored the feet on the dash. It wasn't something she normally liked, but he was in a great mood and she didn't want to kill it. "Probably college scouts," she answered, "and then if you do well in college, like Uncle Tommy did, you'll have the chance to play minor league ball."

"Yeah, but Uncle Tommy didn't get out of the minors. I want to go to the big leagues."

She glanced at him, eyebrows arching. "And so does every other kid playing high school baseball."

"You don't think I can do it?"

"I didn't say that. I just think you're going to have to work hard. Keep up your conditioning. Get good grades."

"I am."

"Good."

"Jeez." He glared at her, good mood gone.

Meg managed to get through the rest of the week at work by avoiding Chad. She suspected she was successful avoiding him because he seemed to be avoiding her, too. Which was smart, and the right thing to do, but it didn't help her mood. Not seeing him made her grouchy, far crabbier than normal, which was saying something since crabby and her forties seemed to go hand in hand.

Toward the end of the week Meg couldn't even remember when she last felt good. She was so short-tempered Thursday morning that she'd yelled at the kids twice before they'd even gone to school. Dropping them off at school, Meg didn't know if she was PMSing or just losing it. There was no reason for her to be this irritable. Everything was good. Kids were healthy, Jack was employed, Meg had a great job . . . but instead of feeling proud, or pleased, she felt nothing. Absolutely nothing, as if she were hollow. Numb. *Dead.*

Dead wasn't good. Dead was bad.

Impatient with herself, Meg switched on the radio and turned up the volume. She kept the radio set to the local NPR station. Loved listening to NPR—the intelligent news, the uplifting music, the smooth, soothing broadcaster voices. In NPR-Land everything was a little bit smarter, calmer. Just listening, she felt smarter and calmer.

Meg was still driving and being soothed by the morning broadcast when Kit called. Meg muted the radio. "Hey, Kit," she greeted her, glad for the interruption. "How are you?"

"Miserable. Lonely. But otherwise good."

Meg smiled. She'd always liked Kit's sense of humor. "Come up and hang out with us for the weekend. I promise you won't be lonely."

Kit didn't immediately answer, and when she did speak, her voice sounded rough. "Why didn't he love me? How could he just let me go like that?"

Meg's heart fell. She'd wondered if Kit was still hurting from the breakup but hadn't wanted to pry. "Richard loved you, Kit. He wouldn't have spent ten years with you if he didn't."

"But he didn't even fight for me! He just let me go, and other than a few texts those first few days, he hasn't contacted me since. Ten years living with him. Ten years of grocery shopping and cooking and eating dinner together. And then poof—it's all over. As if I was no one. As if I didn't even matter."

"Men grieve differently."

Kit exhaled hard. "Ha! He's not grieving. I can tell you that right now. He's going to work, and meeting friends for drinks, and working out and doing all the things he always did. Except he's able to shut the door on his emotions, pretend I don't exist. And I'm pissed off and jealous that I can't do that, too."

"What are you doing this weekend?"

"Might go to the beach house. Brad's in Germany on business, so I invited Polly to go with me for a few days. But if she can't, I don't think I'll go. I don't want to be alone for Memorial Day weekend."

"Let me know if Polly can't go. Maybe I can drive over with the kids for a day or two."

"You're not doing anything with Jack?"

"Jack's leaving for Virginia this afternoon and will be there all weekend."

"He was just in Virginia last week."

"I know. But he's going to be there a lot in the coming year now that he's renovating and restoring a two-hundred-year-old plantation house."

"That's cool."

"He's excited about the job. It's not far from Mount Vernon, and it's an enormous undertaking, but that's his favorite kind. He even fell asleep last night poring over the plans."

"Well, I'd love your company in Capitola this weekend. I've got to get away. Can't spend a long weekend alone."

At three that afternoon Kit texted Meg that Polly had decided to go with Brad to Germany, so she was free for the weekend. Meg texted back saying she'd come with the kids to Capitola, but would wait to drive down Saturday morning to avoid Friday traffic.

JJ and Gabi were happy about going to the beach for the weekend, but Tessa was worried that she'd be missing classes on Saturday and a mandatory rehearsal.

Meg wasn't sympathetic. "I never get to see you, Tessa, you're always at the dance studio. You can spend a weekend with your family."

Saturday morning Tessa sulked in the car on the way to Capitola, but once they descended Highway 17 and turned south on Highway 1, she spotted the ocean and forgot why she was sulking. Suddenly animated, she began to make plans with her, JJ, and Gabi for what they'd do when they reached the beach house. It was hot enough to hit the beach and they wondered if any of their friends would be in Capitola for the weekend, too.

Meg glanced to her right as she drove, drawn to the peekaboo glimpses of the Pacific Ocean through the dark evergreens and Soquel redwoods. The bright line of blue made her glad she'd decided to come with the kids this weekend. In Capitola the kids ran free. The village was small and safe and everyone knew them. Meg was hoping that once they arrived she'd be able to relax. She'd been wound so tight ever since she returned from London. She couldn't remember when she'd last felt so conflicted.

At the beach house, the kids greeted their aunt Kit with hugs and high fives before racing to the bunk room to drop off their stuff and change.

"Stay together," Meg warned them as they dashed back down the stairs in swimsuits with towels balled under their arms. "Stay near the lifeguard. Listen to what he says. And no one swims alone. Got it?"

"Got it," they chorused, the screen door banging behind them and their rubber flip-flops slapping the front steps.

Kit joined Meg on the porch and watched her nieces and nephew run across the lawn toward the beach. "They're getting so big," she said, shaking her head. "Even Gabi's starting to look like a preteen."

"The idea of Gabi as a teenager terrifies me. Tessa is so focused on her dance that I can't see her getting in a lot of trouble. But Gabi . . . it's going to be boys, partying, and breaking all the rules." Meg shuddered. "I don't know how I'm going to get through it."

Kit's lips pursed, imagining Gabi gone wild. "You'll grin and bear it, just the way you did with the rest of us when we were growing up."

"I didn't grin and bear it," Meg retorted drily. "I think I suffered a great deal."

Kit just laughed.

Kit and Meg were sharing the master bedroom for the weekend and they changed into sundresses they could wear on the beach and around town.

It was almost noon and unusually warm for late May. "It feels like summer," Kit said, tugging a large floppy straw hat into place as she left the house.

It was hot out and Meg welcomed the heat. She'd felt so cold these past five days. "I'm looking forward to summer," she answered, slipping on her sunglasses.

"Have any big news for summer?"

She shook her head. "Not really. Jack's going to be spending a lot of time in Virginia and the kids will be going away to their summer camps once school gets out."

"Are they all going to be away at the same time?"

"For the first time ever, yes. I don't know what Jack and I will do for two weeks without the kids to entertain us."

They left the house and headed to the beach. Meg breathed in the familiar tang of salt and seawater as they walked along the water's edge. Kit was hunting for sea glass to add to her collection and Meg was just glad to walk, to move. She was restless. Anxious.

"How are things at work?" Kit asked ultracasually as she reached down to pick up a big piece of cloudy white glass.

Meg knew her sister well enough to know there was nothing casual about the question. Kit was asking about Chad. "Fine," she said vaguely.

Kit shot her a speculative look. "You're not—"

"No."

Meg's sharp tone made Kit's eyebrows arch. "You sound really defensive, Mags."

"I'm not defensive. There's just nothing to say. Nothing's going to happen with Chad." It was a lie. Meg felt her face burn. This is exactly why she shouldn't have confided in Kit. Kit would hold her accountable. Just as Meg would hold her sisters accountable.

Kit pocketed the white glass and they kept walking. Neither spoke until they reached the pier and turned around.

"I'm sorry," Meg said as Kit reached for a bright blue fragment poking out of the sand. "I'm a grouch. I know it. I hate it."

"What's wrong?" Kit asked, realizing the bright blue fragment was plastic not glass.

"What's right?" Meg retorted, pushing her sunglasses higher on her nose. "I'm stressed and angry and grouchy and resent the hell out of Jack. But why I'm resenting Jack is beyond me. He hasn't changed. He's exactly the same man I married. And yet all of a sudden it bothers me. *He* bothers me. I know Jack has good qualities, but all I see are the bad."

"What are the bad ones?"

"He doesn't see what needs to be done. He doesn't try to help. Doesn't seem to think he really needs to help. He assumes that if he doesn't do it, it's okay because it'll still get done—"

"You mean, you'll do it."

Meg nodded. "But why does he get to sail through life without pitching in? Why does going to work and coming home mean he's done his job? Why is it my job to make money and do everything around the house?"

For a moment Kit said nothing, her memory stirred. She'd heard this before, she thought, a long time ago when she and Meg had been just girls themselves.

She trembled inwardly, flashing to a hysterical scene in their parents' house just hours after little Danielle was fished from their pool and taken to the hospital.

Dad was tearing into Meg, just ripping her apart for turning her back on Danielle, telling Meg that it was her fault that little girl nearly drowned. Meg started screaming. Meg, who never screamed, was hysterical, and her shriek echoed through the house. "*I'm not perfect. I've never been perfect! But you put me in charge of everything, and make me responsible for everything and I'm tired of it. I need help! I need the others to pitch in. Why don't you make Brianna and Kit do their part? They're both fifteen!*"

Kit had never forgotten that moment, or the things Meg had said. They were powerful words, weighted with truth. Meg had had to do too much at too early of an age. And she and Brianna had never done enough.

"You're overwhelmed, huh?" Kit asked huskily, awash in the sick guilt she felt whenever she remembered that incident. If only she'd been home that day, if only she'd been around, she could have helped Meg. She would have watched Danielle properly. She liked kids. She was good with them.

"Yeah."

But Kit hadn't been there. She'd been at the library, curled up in an old squeaky vinyl chair, reading. Growing up, every chance Kit could get, she escaped the house to go somewhere quiet and read. And so that Sunday afternoon while she'd sat lost in Jackie Collins's *Hollywood Wives*, Danielle nearly drowned in their pool.

Danielle's accident was the end of their pool as well. It had only been built for them three years earlier, and it took a year of saving and planning to get the pool in. After Danielle's accident, it took only two days to have the pool torn out.

Kit exhaled slowly, her insides lurching the way they always did when she remembered the accident. Her father had blamed Meg entirely. But it hadn't been just Meg's fault. It'd been all of theirs. They were a family. Sisters. "Not surprised, Meg," she said unevenly. "You've got a full-time job and three kids with full-time activities. I don't know how you do it. I don't have kids and I'm exhausted every day."

Meg picked up a gleaming bit of green sea glass and handed it to Kit. "But the kids aren't really the problem."

Kit frowned, worried. "It's Jack."

Meg nodded. "I'm not happy with him anymore."

"You want a divorce?" Kit whispered, clutching the gleaming green sea glass to her chest. She couldn't bear the idea of Meg getting divorced. She liked Jack. He was a good person, a good man, and he loved Meg. Kit knew he did.

"No. We're not there. Nowhere close to that. But I've got to find a way to get happy. Have to find a way to enjoy him. Not sure how I'm going to do that when I don't even enjoy myself."

Meg started walking, and Kit followed. "Do you think it's hormones?" Kit asked.

Meg glanced at Kit. "You mean menopause?"

"Or perimenopause. Or maybe your system's just out of whack. You said you're tired—"

"All the time."

"And a little depressed."

"More often than not."

"Could be your thyroid. It happens to women. Perhaps you should go see an endocrinologist and get your thyroid checked. Have them do a complete workup. It might be something really small that just needs tweaking."

Meg's lips curved faintly. "Wouldn't it be nice if it were that easy?" she said, tucking her hands into her skirt pockets. "Just take a little pill and suddenly everything is all better. Pop a pill and that voice of discontentment goes away."

"It could be," Kit said halfheartedly, because she didn't think it was Meg's thyroid. She thought there was more to it but didn't want to say so.

They walked in silence, heading back toward the kids, who were playing in the surf. JJ was jumping waves and the girls were splashing each other.

Kit glanced at Meg once and again. Meg looked serene. But then, Meg usually did. Meg was a rock.

Suddenly Meg's lips quivered and Kit's insides did a nervous loop-de-loop. But of course even rocks could crack. "Does Jack know how you feel?" she asked.

Meg shrugged. "I doubt it. When I talk he tunes out." And then she laughed, a low mocking laugh. "Not entirely sure I blame him. I don't think I probably have a lot of interesting things to say anymore. Kids, kids, kids. Bills, bills, bills. Work, work, work. Kind of mind-numbing."

"But isn't that just life?"

"God, I hope not." Meg leaned over to pick up a tiny bit of red glass, the shard shaped almost like a miniature heart. She turned it over in her hand once, twice, before giving it to Kit. "If we only have one life, who wants to live it that way?"

They went to Margaritaville for dinner because the kids loved Mexican food and Meg and Kit could order a drink. Everyone had gotten too much sun and they all looked pink and shiny as they sat down. The kids ordered platters of tacos and enchiladas but then quickly deteriorated into bickering. The combination of being tired, hungry, and sunburned made them surly, and Gabi had done her best to annoy everyone by arguing with Tessa and challenging JJ.

"Whew," Meg said as her kids trooped out of the restaurant, their voices still loud and querulous. "They're not your kids, Kit. How do you stand them?"

"They're not that bad, Mags. In fact, they're pretty darn good. Gabi's just a firecracker. She likes to get them all going."

"And she's good at it."

Kit grinned. "She doesn't lack for confidence."

"No, I know. Her teacher sent me an e-mail a few weeks ago letting me know that Gabi was one of the 'leaders' on the playground, and while that was good, Gabi could also try to work on being a little more sensitive to the needs of others."

"She's a bully?"

"Oh, I'm sure she can be. If she tries to steamroll all of us at home, I imagine she's doing the same thing at school."

Kit's expression turned pensive. "The more things change, the more they stay the same."

Meg studied Kit from across the table. Kit had been quiet all afternoon, and Meg knew why. She was a worrier. The family peacemaker. She couldn't stand it when someone in her family was having a difficult time.

Meg reached across the table, tapped Kit on the arm. "I'm fine, Kit. I really am. You don't have to worry about me."

"I'm not worried," Kit said, her long dark hair with glints of red spilling across one shoulder, her hands circling her mojito glass.

"I know it upset you when I said I wasn't happy—"

"No. I'm glad you told me. Glad you talked to me. Sometimes I think you think you have to be Sister Mary Margaret, all perfect and saintly, but you don't. I admire you so much, Meg. I'd do anything for you."

Meg's eyes burned and she swallowed hard. No one in the family knew her, or understood her, like Kit did. It wasn't Kit's love of books that made her a great teacher. It was her compassion. "Shhh."

Kit pushed her glass in a small circle on the table, leaving a wet trail of condensation. "We're not that far apart in age, less than four years, but I'm always going to be the little sister, aren't I?"

"Because you *are* my little sister."

"But I'm an adult now. You can lean on me."

"I know, and I have, just like I did today. I told you I was having a rough time and you listened and that helped."

"But I haven't done enough to help you. You're the one always helping me. You're always there when I need you, Meg, whether it's giving me a loan, or helping me move, or picking me up when my car breaks down—"

"That's what family is for."

"But I wasn't there for you when you needed me most."

"What?"

"I wasn't there that day Danielle was at the house—"

"I don't want to talk about it."

"But I should have been there. I should have helped you. If I had, nothing bad would have happened—"

"Kit."

"We never talk about it, that day, but I still blame myself for not being there."

"Kit. Honestly. I don't want to do this. Don't want to rehash it. Hate remembering it. Danielle was my responsibility and I blew it, and there's no one to blame but me. End of story."

Kit looked at her, blue eyes wide, somber. "But that isn't the end of the story. I think about it more than you know."

"Well, you shouldn't," Meg said shortly.

Kit smeared the streak of water with the side of her fist. "Did you know I have her daughter in my freshman English class?"

Meg's head jerked up. For a moment she said nothing, her eyes searching Kit's, and then she gave her head the faintest shake. "Impossible. Danielle would only be about thirty now."

"She got pregnant at sixteen, and married her boyfriend. It didn't work out, but she kept the baby. She remarried a few years ago to a really nice man. I met them both at the teacher conference this year."

"You didn't tell me."

"You don't like talking about her."

Meg's brows pulled, and for a moment she couldn't speak, seeing Danielle's long wet hair hanging off the hospital gurney as the paramedics wheeled her toward the ambulance. No one knew if she'd live that day. And if she did survive, they expected her to be brain damaged.

"How is she?" Meg asked, her voice just a whisper of sound.

"She's good. She's had some hard knocks, but she's okay." Kit covered Meg's hand with hers. "When she sees me, she asks about you."

Tears filled Meg's eyes. "Oh God."

"She doesn't blame you, Meg."

"You've talked about this with her?"

Kit nodded. "If anything, she's apologetic. She said she knew she shouldn't have gone into the pool. Said it was her fault—"

"Oh my God," Meg cried, jerking her hands free and leaning back in her chair. "She was just a little girl! Little more than a baby!"

"You were her favorite babysitter, Mags. She hated that she never got to see you after that day. She said she used to ask for you and her parents refused."

Meg knocked away tears. "Why are you doing this? Why are you telling me this?"

"Because I thought it'd help you to know that Danielle's happy and grown up with children of her own."

Blinded by tears, Meg grabbed a bunch of twenty-dollar bills from her wallet and put them on the table. "I gotta get out of here."

Kit double-checked the bill, tucking the twenties into the leather folder, and followed Meg out, catching up to her on the curb. "I'm sorry I upset you," she said, slipping her arm through Meg's.

Meg shook her head and just walked in the opposite direction of the beach house, down Esplanade to the wharf. The original pier was built in 1857, and rebuilt repeatedly over the last hundred and fifty years after heavy storms damaged the wooden structure.

They walked down the wharf, footsteps echoing on the planks. The night was clear and the stars were bright overhead. The weather report said that rain was expected over the weekend, but clouds hadn't moved in yet. Meg was shivering and hoped the rain would stay away. Her kids enjoyed Capitola so much more when they could head to the beach and mess around.

They reached the end of the wharf, and still shivering, Meg gently disentangled herself from Kit, needing space. Maybe, being a twin, Kit liked lots of physical contact, but it sometimes smothered Meg, and it was smothering her now.

"I don't want you worrying about me," she said hoarsely, facing her sister. "Or feeling guilty in any way. I'm a tough cookie, and it's enough that you love me. You're not just my sister, you're my closest friend—"

"Am I really?"

"Most definitely." Meg blinked hard, unwilling to cry. "And if I need something, Kit, you're the first person I'd turn to."

"You mean that?"

"I do. And you know I never say something I don't mean."

Meg woke up to discover that the rain clouds had settled in during the night. It drizzled a little Sunday morning but then cleared somewhat late afternoon, and the kids clamored to go to Pizza My Heart for dinner. Pizza My Heart, a Capitola institution since the early 1980s, was literally just a hole in the wall, without any indoor seating, but the kids loved taking the pizza to the sand dunes just a few feet away, and tonight, with the cool weather, Kit brought a big quilt from the house for them to sit on. JJ carried down sodas and Meg brought a bottle of red from Dark Horse Winery, a corkscrew, and two plastic cups.

They sat on the dark red-and-black patchwork quilt in jeans and sweatshirts munching on pizza and people watching. The cloud cover didn't scare anyone and the beach was dotted with kids and families hanging out.

At Pizza My Heart they ordered pizza by the slice, and Tessa delicately nibbled on her one slice while Gabi inhaled two. JJ ate four before bounding off to play beach volleyball with friends who had a house on Depot Hill, and the girls trailed after, hoping to be included.

"Yum." Kit sighed, wiping a shine of grease from her fingertips. "This is my favorite pizza in the world." She always ordered the Manresa, a white pizza with fresh basil, garlic, Romas, and ricotta. "Remember the summer I ate pizza every day and gained ten pounds? I was huge by the time school started. Didn't fit into any of my clothes."

Meg finished her red wine and lay back on the sand. "You

weren't that big. But you did eat a lot of pizza." She folded her arms behind her head and stared up into the sky with its smattering of stars and banked clouds. "Didn't some guy you liked work there?"

Kit stretched out next to Meg. "Manny." Her lips curved in a mocking smile. "He managed the afternoon shift."

"I don't remember him."

"Yes, you do. Manuel Abrino. Tall, dark, incredibly handsome? Beautiful cheekbones, dark brown eyes, long long black eyelashes? He was unbelievably gorgeous." She sighed. "And tragically, not very bright at all."

Meg laughed softly. "You always did have a thing for the darkly handsome bad boy."

"Except I never actually went out with one." Kit grabbed a handful of sand and let it slide through her fingers. "Too scared."

Meg rolled onto her side to look at Kit. "Scared of what?"

"Of what could happen." Her shoulders shifted. "You know . . . that a bad boy would be . . . bad."

Meg studied Kit's face. "Is that why you stayed with Richard? Better to be safe than sorry?"

Kit reached for another handful of sand. "I've always played it safe." For several moments she focused on the sand. "Hate that about myself."

"You miss Richard?"

"I miss having company. I don't love living on my own. I thought that by buying my own house I wouldn't be as lonely, but I am."

"Maybe you should get a roommate."

"I've thought about that."

"Or a dog."

"I've thought about that, too." Kit rolled over onto her back. Meg did the same. Their heads were almost touching.

"This is nice," Kit said after a minute.

Meg folded her hands on her chest. "We've pretty much done

this our whole life, haven't we? Eat, hang out on the beach, hope a cute guy would notice us."

"Yeah. And didn't all the cute guys notice Brianna?"

"Yep. Even with her freckles and red hair." Meg made a rough sound. "She was such an exhibitionist! Always flashing someone something."

Kit laughed. "I remember the first time she got caught for flashing her boobs. She was in seventh grade. Didn't even have real boobs yet."

"But Mrs. Murphy saw and told Dad. Brianna got a spanking and threatened to call the cops on Dad, saying that he was abusing her."

Kit bent her knees. "I forgot all about that! Didn't Dad hand her the phone and tell her to do it?"

"Yeah. Most of the police officers were his friends and he said once they heard that his twelve-year-old daughter was flashing her titties as if she were a hooker in the Tenderloin District, they'd spank her, too." Meg shook her head. "She makes Gabi look like an angel."

Kit fell silent for several minutes. When she spoke again her voice was quieter. "You know, she's not all bad, Meg. There are lots of good things about her."

Meg sat up, her attention diverted to the kids and their volleyball game. Gabi was shouting and shoving Tessa into the sand while JJ was trying to pull her off. Gabi *was* a little Bree. Hotheaded, emotional, passionate, spirited, opinionated, stubborn. And so very full of life. "I know she's not all bad, Kit. And I don't dislike her. Part of me envies her. I wish I had her courage. Wish I could be that free. It'd be such a different life, you know?"

Twelve

B ack at work on Tuesday Meg got a call from Amy Chin, the producer from the Food Network who'd attended the launch party in May. Amy hoped to set up a meeting with Meg and the Hallahan brothers to pitch an idea for a reality show.

"A reality show?" Meg repeated, picking up her calendar to check for possible meeting dates. "I thought you just wanted to do a segment on the winery."

"I did, but the network has been looking at developing a new series and we were throwing ideas around and the idea everyone liked best was a series about a winery, and Dark Horse Winery immediately came to mind. Craig and Chad Hallahan are really telegenic, and single, and I think our viewers would love them."

Meg thumbed through her calendar. "Craig's taking next week off, so it'd have to be the second week of June. The fourteenth or fifteenth maybe?"

"I was thinking this week. Thursday, the second. We'd fly a

couple of the producers in from New York, tour the winery, introduce them to the Hallahans, then maybe have lunch in Napa or Healdsburg."

"This Thursday?"

"Yes."

Meg flipped her calendar back to the current week. Craig and Chad both had appointments but nothing that couldn't be moved. But the issue wasn't their availability for Thursday. The issue was whether or not Craig and Chad would even be interested in listening to a pitch on a reality series. Craig loathed being in the public eye. He was such a private man. And while Chad was comfortable representing the winery, Meg wasn't sure how he'd feel having his personal life captured on television.

"I have to be honest with you, Amy. This could be a very hard sell. The Hallahans aren't media hounds. They're down-to-earth, salt-of-the-earth people. At heart they're just farmers . . . ranchers . . . who love making wine."

"But that's why I think they're perfect, and why they'll appeal to our audience. The median age of our audience is forty-nine years old, and we're going after young viewers and male viewers and it's working. We think a series about a Napa winery will add to that growth."

Meg pictured trucks and vans and camera crews crawling all over the winery and shuddered. Craig would hate it. He really would. And Chad would probably listen to the pitch if only because it was a marketing gold mine. A reality show about Dark Horse Winery would sell wine. Tons of it.

But at what cost?

"I need to talk to the guys," Meg said.

"We want to meet this Thursday."

"I'll see—"

"I'm going to book the flights."

"Amy, I wouldn't. Not until I can—"

"Convince them to take the meeting, Meg. I know they both listen to you."

Hanging up, Meg found Chad in the tasting room. He'd just finished pouring wine for a group of ten women who were out celebrating one of their birthdays with a day of wine tasting. Meg could hear their laughter in the wine shop as several paid for purchases.

"Sounds like they had fun," she said, peeking into the tasting room to get a glimpse of the women—all young and pretty, fashionably dressed, and happy—before taking one of the stools at the counter.

"They did," he agreed, wiping the counter off. "A thirtieth birthday and loving life."

Meg couldn't even remember what turning thirty had felt like. By the time she was thirty, she had two kids, a job, and when not officially working, she was helping Jack restore the old house they'd bought several years before in Santa Rosa when the Petaluma cottage became too snug after the birth of Tessa. "What I wouldn't give to be younger," Meg said with a sigh as she crossed her legs and made herself comfortable on the stool.

"I think you're perfect the way you are," Chad answered, leaning on the counter. "Don't know why you'd want to change anything."

She blushed, and then hated herself for melting a little from the compliment. Hated that being even this close to him made her think of the kiss, and how good it had felt. "That's because you don't see the grouchy side of me. I'm a bear at home."

"Are you?"

She hesitated, then added, "Especially this last week."

He looked at her, closely, and she knew he knew what she was talking about. They'd never discussed the kiss after, but perhaps they needed to. Obviously they needed to. Meg had been on pins and needles ever since. "I'm sorry," he said.

Her insides turned over and her chest felt tight. "It was a mistake," she said, her voice nearly inaudible. "It's made everything harder."

"I get that."

Her throat hurt when she swallowed. "It's made me want things I can't have."

He didn't move, not even a finger, and yet suddenly he felt close, as if he'd drawn her to him and was holding her against him. "But you can have me."

"Chad."

"If you wanted me."

"I'm not telling you to jump into bed with me, or suggesting that it's the right thing to do. I'm just saying that if you ever need me, you've got me. I'm here for you."

Meg half closed her eyes, overwhelmed. "Is this about sex? Or the chase, Chad? Getting me into bed so you can say you've done it?"

He reached across the counter and pushed her chin up so that he was looking into her eyes. "Is that who I am, Meg? Is that what you think this is about?"

"Maybe. Yeah."

He drew back, said something sharp and short under his breath, and walked out from behind the counter, heading toward the barrel room.

Meg slid off the bar stool and chased after him. "Don't be mad," she said, opening the wooden doors after they'd shut in her face behind Chad's retreating back. She followed him deeper into the barrel room, which was cool and dimly lit, the stone walls lined high with racks of large American oak barrels. The smell of ripe fermenting grapes hung in the air, along with the woody oak.

"Chad, don't be mad," she repeated, feeling desperate. She couldn't bear the idea of him being upset with her. She needed him, needed his kindness and warmth and attention. He made her feel good, and hopeful, and sane. As if she still mattered. As if she, Mary Margaret, were actually important.

He turned to face her, hands on his hips, a lock of blond hair falling forward on his brow. "For your information, I don't lie awake at night thinking about all the ways to seduce you. I don't think about your breasts or your ass—although those are nice. I think about you. About your smile and your laugh, and how much I want to be with you, and what it'd be like to have a winery with you, our own winery, somewhere not here, but on land of our own. I think about going to Paso Robles and getting acreage and making a life there with you." His jaw flexed, hard. "So, no, Meg, this isn't about screwing you and leaving you. It's about having a future with you. Creating something with you. Maybe even kids with you."

She blinked, stunned. "Why?"

"*Why?*" he repeated, his deep voice snapping with anger.

"Yes."

"Because I love you. I've loved you for a long time." He walked away, but paused at the doors, hand on the knob. "We have to figure this out," he said. "I have to figure this out."

"What does that mean?" she asked, a catch in her voice.

He turned around to face her. "It means I can't do this with you, Meg. Can't work with you. Not right now. Maybe we figure out another arrangement, just for a few weeks, and then—"

She crossed the floor, reached up to cup the back of his head and bring his mouth down to hers. She kissed him, kissed him with everything she had, everything she felt, everything she wanted and needed but didn't have. The emotion was huge, wild, raw. His arms moved around her, low on her back, pulling her hard against him. His arms were warm, he was warm, and she welcomed the heat of his body and the way his chest crushed her breasts, his hips pressed to hers, making her aware of the thick ridge of his erection.

She hadn't planned on kissing him, and yet now that she was, she didn't think she could stop.

She wanted him, and needed him, and needed him to make her feel alive. She'd been dead. Dead for so long.

His hand moved up her back, a slow caress she felt all the way through her. She shivered and arched against him as his hand brushed the side of her breast. Pleasure shot through her, and she inhaled sharply. She wanted to feel his hand on her bare skin, wanted more of the electric sensation.

The door to the administrative offices opened and yellow light spilled into the dark barrel room. Craig entered the room talking on his cell.

Chad pushed her back and stepped away. "Is that everything?" he asked, raising his voice so that it was loud enough for Craig to hear.

"I think so." Her heart pounded and yet her voice was clear, steady. How could she sound so calm when she was shaking from head to toe? "But I do need to talk to you about Amy Chin. From the Food Network."

Craig passed them, nodded as he continued his phone conversation. Chad waited for the door to the tasting room to close before he turned and headed for his office. Meg struggled to keep up. She wasn't sure Chad wanted her following him, but she didn't know where else to go or what to do.

Chad sat down behind his desk, leaving his door open. Meg stood awkwardly before him, feeling like a schoolgirl taken to task by the principal. She glanced around the space, simply furnished. Chad liked things clean. Spare. He wasn't one for clutter.

"Sit," he said tersely.

She did, taking the caramel-colored leather chair opposite his desk. She sat tall and yet her legs felt boneless as she crossed them.

For a moment he said nothing and then he shook his head. "That was close," he said, closing his laptop and pushing it onto a corner of his desk.

She nodded. She felt completely undone.

"Too damn close," he added curtly.

She nodded again, unable to speak.

Chad exhaled, features tight. "Craig would have a real problem with this." He paused, considered his words. "Hell, *I* have a problem with this."

She laced her fingers together. "I'm sorry."

"Don't say that."

"But I am."

"And what does sorry mean?" His voice was harsh, almost cruel. "Sorry you're married? Sorry you kissed me? Sorry I fell for you?"

She shook her head, lips pressed tightly, eyes stinging as she blinked the tears away. She wouldn't let them fall. Meg plucked at her coral sweater, pulling at a thread near the bottom button. None of this made sense. There was no reason for any of this to be happening. But it was. And she was allowing it. Not just allowing it, but creating it, fanning the flames. She'd gone after him. She'd kissed him. She'd responded when he touched her.

"Do you want me to quit?" she asked unsteadily.

"No." He didn't even hesitate. "That's ridiculous. I don't hate you. I'm not mad at you. I'm not trying to punish you. We just have to figure this out."

She nodded, watched Jennifer walk briskly down the narrow hall toward the copier with a sheaf of paperwork in her hand, and Jennifer reminded Meg of all the things she herself should be doing right now, like talking to Chad about Amy Chin's proposition.

"I came looking for you in the tasting room because I had an interesting call from Amy Chin."

He just looked at her, waiting.

"She wants to meet you and Craig for lunch on Thursday," Meg said, gathering her thoughts, putting her focus back on the tasks at hand. "She's hoping to fly in with two producers to discuss an idea they have for a show."

"She can't just talk to you?"

"Their show idea is bigger than what she'd initially mentioned to me the night of the launch party. It's not an episode anymore in a different show. Instead they're talking about creating a whole show about you and Craig, and Dark Horse Winery."

"I don't get it."

Meg could hear the anger and frustration in his voice. He wasn't happy. He wanted to lash out at something, and she was the one here. "The Food Network isn't just about cooking shows anymore. They've expanded their programming to include lifestyle shows, reality shows—"

"So what would they be doing here? A lifestyle show?"

"No. A reality show."

"They can forget about it."

"You won't even let them come out and pitch the idea to you?"

"No."

He was in a really bad mood. Meg held her breath, counted to ten. "Their demographics are essentially ours. Many, if not most, of their viewers are probably wine drinkers."

"Don't care."

"You could make Dark Horse Winery a household name."

"Still don't care."

"Why are you so opposed to even listening to a pitch?" Meg asked, hanging on to her temper by a thread. "You and Craig have a dream job. You're interesting people. A reality series about a winery would probably be a big hit."

"I don't want a bunch of people I don't know setting up cameras, taking over the winery, acting as if this place is theirs."

"I agree. But I have a feeling they don't film every day. They couldn't afford it. They'd have a script, some kind of story line, and probably would shoot one or two days a week, and it'd have to be on mutually agreeable dates."

"So they could be here, filming this, us talking," Chad said, gesturing from her to him.

"Possibly."

"Then, no, I don't want my personal life on camera, for millions of people to see. Craig's private. I'm private—"

"But I'd be willing to listen to a pitch," Craig said, cutting Chad short.

Meg turned in her seat to look at Craig, who was standing in the doorway.

"When do they want to meet with us?" Craig added.

"Thursday." Meg glanced from Craig to Chad and back again. "Amy said they'd like to fly some producers out to tour the winery, check out the area, and sit down and talk to you over lunch."

"Where would we eat?" Craig asked.

Meg shrugged. "Probably wherever you wanted."

"Why waste their time?" Chad retorted, putting his feet up on his desk. "You won't do it, Craig—"

"How do you know?"

"Because you're the most introverted guy I know and you avoid talking to people. You wouldn't even go to London this year—"

"That may be, but we didn't get to where we are without considering opportunities. This might not be right for us, but it might not be wrong. Let them come out. Let's hear what they have to say."

Chad shrugged indifferently. "If that's what you want."

Craig frowned down at his brother. "What's wrong with you? You've been in a shitty mood for days."

Meg felt Chad glance at her and she blushed.

"Just stuff," Chad answered.

"Well, figure your stuff out and leave the bad attitude at home.

No one wants to work with a dick." Craig nodded at Meg and walked out.

Meg watched Craig for a second and then looked at Chad. He was staring straight at her. She swallowed around the lump in her throat. "So where should I make the lunch reservation? Bouchon?" she asked, naming Thomas Keller's highly rated bistro-style restaurant in Yountville.

"Craig would hate it. Too pretentious, especially if he's meeting with TV producers. Try Boon Fly Café. Burgers, sandwiches, simple food that Craig will eat."

Meg rose from her chair, anxious to get out of Chad's office and away from the tension. "I'll call Amy and then make the reservation."

Meg had offered to pick up the Food Network executives Thursday morning from the San Francisco airport, but late Wednesday she got word from Amy that they'd be renting an Escalade at the airport and would drive themselves north to Napa so they could have freedom to explore the area on their own.

Meg dressed that morning in impractically high, brown platform bootie heels by Michael Kors. The shoes had been a total splurge last fall but they pulled together her burnt-orange linen skirt and dark teal blouse, making the outfit zing. Meg wasn't sexy, or trendy, and she rarely wore color, but lately she found herself pushing her own fashion comfort zone, going for a bit more style and flare.

Downstairs in the kitchen, Gabi announced that she loved her mom's shoes. JJ wasn't sure about the orange-skirt-and-teal-blouse combination. And Jack, who'd returned the day before from Virginia, glanced up from the morning paper to say he'd forgotten what great legs Meg had. Meg kissed the top of his head, glad he'd noticed.

Meg was driving to Napa when she got a call from Amy that they'd landed and were just picking up the rental car. Meg told her that they couldn't have come on a better day. It was going to be perfect—clear, warm, sunny, with temperatures peaking right around eighty degrees.

The producers used the morning to scout possible locations, arriving at Dark Horse Winery at eleven. Meg and Chad welcomed the three producers—Amy, Patrick, and Evan—to the winery while Craig finished a call. She had been right about the weather. It was a gorgeous, sunny day, not a cloud in the sky, and the hills shimmered with shades of pale gold and green.

Craig emerged outside a few minutes later and had Chad and the New York team pile into his Jeep to take them on a tour of the property. The tour lasted forty minutes and they finished it back at the production facilities, where Craig explained the various steps from grape growing to bottling.

The whole thing took longer than expected and Meg phoned the restaurant to push the lunch reservations back. Tour completed, Craig poured wine in the tasting room for the three producers, wanting them to understand the wines Dark Horse Winery made and what set them apart from other wineries.

The tasting turned lengthy and Meg phoned Boon Fly Café a second time to let them know they'd be even later. Fortunately the restaurant management knew the Hallahans well and were happy to accommodate them for a late lunch.

By the time they were getting into the cars to head to lunch, it was almost two. Craig insisted Meg join them and she agreed, provided she could take her own car so she could leave the restaurant to head straight to JJ's game.

Once everyone was seated, Evan got very serious about pitching their idea for the reality series. Meg had expected Craig to be the one with the objections to a reality series, but it was Chad who presented the most opposition, saying the show sounded like a cheesy version of *Falcon Crest*, the popular prime-time TV show from the 1980s about rival winery families in Northern California. The show aired for nine seasons on CBS and was a hit for a number of years. It was also sexy, salacious, and over-the-top, three things Chad said he and his brother weren't.

"But we don't want salacious, and we're not looking for melodrama," Evan answered.

"And sexy?" Chad retorted.

The producers looked at each other. Evan shrugged. Patrick nodded. And Amy answered, "Sexy is good. Sexy in this case is okay because food can be sexy. Wine is most definitely sexy. And we're here talking to you because the Hallahan brothers are sexy."

Chad groaned. Craig's eyebrows lifted, but he looked amused more than anything.

"We're always looking for formats and talent that could drive our median age down," Patrick said. "You guys have youth, style, charisma. We think you two could be our next network stars."

"Thanks, but no thanks. I have absolutely no desire to be a TV star," Chad said drily.

"Let's not talk about you for a moment. Let's talk about the winery. Let's talk about the economy. You've got great wines, and a beautiful little winery, but it's a competitive business and an expensive business, and at the end of the day, your employees get paid, but as the owners, I don't know how much you get paid. Are you personally pocketing anything right now?" Patrick lifted his hand, stopped Chad from speaking. "You don't need to actually answer that. I don't know your finances, and don't need to know them, but I do know from studying the market and talking to other wineries in the last couple months that the only people really making money right now are the big commercial wine producers."

"You're saying there are financial benefits to doing the series," Craig said.

Evan gestured to the waitress for the bill. "Yes. Definitely."

"I know you don't like the word 'star' but our network stars have been able to capitalize on their 'brand' and have made very lucrative deals in publishing, entertainment, and product placement."

"To hell with product placement," Chad said shortly. "I just want the winery to be solvent."

"It will be," Evan answered.

"We've put everything we have into this winery," Craig said after a moment. "The European grapevine moth nearly took us out of business a couple years ago. We took out a lot of big loans, mortgaged ourselves to the hilt, to stay in the game."

Meg glanced at Craig, surprised. She knew that back in 2009 the European grapevine moth had caused irreparable damage to crops and entire hillsides had to be replanted, but she hadn't realize that the winery was still feeling the fallout.

"It's not just any land either," Chad added. "This was our grandfather's ranch. My father was born here. We were born here. It'd be hard to lose it to the banks."

More than hard, Meg thought. It'd be heartbreaking.

"We're making you a solid offer right now," Patrick said, looking from Chad to Craig and back again. "Can we make this work?"

Craig nodded slowly. "I think we can."

Chad's mouth compressed. "I think we have to."

In the parking lot they said good-bye to the Food Network producers, who were now having to race to the airport to make their return flight to New York. Craig climbed into his Jeep and waited for Chad. Chad gestured that he needed a second as he walked Meg to her car.

"Looks like we're doing a reality series," he said, holding the driver's door open for her.

She climbed behind the wheel. "I was surprised Craig was even interested in the idea, but now I understand why."

He put a hand on top of the doorframe and another on the door itself, and looked down into her face, his blue eyes locking on hers. "We're not about to go belly-up, if that's what you're thinking."

"Not thinking that."

"Just because Craig and I aren't getting rich off the winery, doesn't mean we're poor."

He looked real and rugged and so very appealing, and she reached out and touched his thigh, her fingers brushing across the faded denim of his jeans. "I love that you love what you do."

"Jesus, woman, I'm crazy about you."

Her eyes smarted and her throat threatened to close. "You need to find a young, single version of me."

"No, Meg, I just need you."

She couldn't breathe for a moment, her lips parting but unable to get any air in. Instead she touched his thigh again, lightly, briefly, and tugged on the denim fabric. "If your brother weren't there, I'd make you kiss me."

He bent down, low, and looked her square in the eye. "If my brother weren't there, I'd drive you home and put you in my bed where you belong."

"I don't belong there."

"In my world, you do."

"God, I wish you could kiss me."

Chad straightened abruptly, gestured to Craig, giving him a wave. Craig lifted his hand, waved back, and took off.

Meg's insides did a crazy flip. She watched the Jeep kick up dirt and gravel before glancing wide-eyed at Chad. "He left you," she said huskily.

"He did." Chad leaned into the car, kissed her slowly, and then lifted his head. "Move over. I'm taking you home."

And from the expression on his face, Meg didn't have to ask him what he meant.

Chad lived in a turn-of-the-century farmhouse tucked deep into the winery property. The farmhouse had been built for a great-great-aunt, who never married and needed a place of her own. The farmhouse had sat empty for nearly forty years when Chad claimed it, remodeling it from top to bottom. The exterior of the three-bedroom house hadn't been changed—just freshened and enhanced—with new trim, new energy-efficient windows, and several good coats of paint. But the interior had been gutted and re-imagined, and walls had come down to create a sunlit gourmet kitchen that opened to the great room and a spacious master bedroom suite. The two secondary bedrooms had disappeared, swallowed by the reconfiguration, and everything in the farmhouse was light, bright, clean, and spare. The down-filled couch in the great room had been slipcovered in white, just as the two armchairs flanking the fireplace had been slipcovered in white cotton.

The farmhouse ceiling was now vaulted, but the floor was a wide plank hardwood that looked original to the house. Jack would love it. The dining table was made of antique pine surrounded by slipcovered dining chairs. An antique oil of early California hung above the fireplace, but the fireplace's original wooden mantel had been replaced by a classic, modern limestone surround. A gorgeous grandfather clock stood against one wall. Natural woven blinds were at the window. The countertops in the kitchen were a pale, creamy limestone.

"Gorgeous," Meg said with a sigh. "Can I live here?"

Chad had watched her as she explored his house, and smiled now. "Yes."

"This is really beautifully done."

"Did it before the winged moths decimated the southern vineyards."

Her faint smile faded as she did another slow turn, taking in the sophisticated mix of contemporary and antique pieces, as well as the vases of white roses and lilies on the dining table and entry table. "It's almost too perfect. You really live here?"

"I do live here, and I'm a pretty tidy guy, but it's cleaner than usual. And I don't always have flowers. But I thought it'd be a nice touch if the producers wanted to see the house."

"Did they?"

"We stopped by."

For some reason the thought of everyone trooping into Chad's house and looking around made her heart hurt. But then, the idea of millions of Americans turning on their TV and seeing the inside of Chad's house hurt even worse. "What did they think?" she asked, already knowing the answer.

"That it's ideal for the show."

She walked to the end table next to the couch and set her purse and briefcase down. "I imagine they'll put together some story lines that focus on you dating."

"They did mention something along those lines," he replied, watching her from beneath lowered lashes.

"Of course they did," she murmured, feeling that sharp pain high up in her ribs again.

"Is that sarcasm I hear?"

She faced him, feeling ridiculously close to tears. Chad would be the world's soon. He'd belong to everyone. "No. You're gorgeous. Women are going to go crazy for you."

"I don't need women going crazy for me. I just need one woman." His blue gaze held hers. "Just need you."

In Chad's serene, luxurious limestone bathroom with the waxed pine cabinets, Meg washed and then dried her hands on one of the plush white hand towels hanging on the chrome towel bar. Her eyes were locked on her reflection as she adjusted her dark teal blouse and then smoothed down the front of her burnt-orange linen pencil skirt, her hand lingering briefly over the pooch of her stomach, a pooch that wouldn't go away no matter how much she worked out, or how many Pilates classes she took.

Was she really going to do this?

After seventeen years of being faithful, was she now going to cheat on Jack? It was one thing to kiss Chad, quite another to actually sleep with him . . .

It was so pathetic. Never mind clichéd.

Sneaking off with your boss in the middle of the day . . . hoping you're not going to get caught . . .

This visit to Chad's farmhouse was fodder for *Cosmo* stories, not her life. She'd always been honest, loyal, a straight shooter. A devout Catholic until the last few years when she'd gradually stopped dragging her kids to church, she didn't know how she came to be in this place. In Chad's bathroom preparing to meet Chad in his bed.

Jack was a decent man, and a good father. She'd made vows to him, promised to be faithful to him for better and worse.

Things weren't so bad that she needed to break those vows, were they?

Yes, their marriage had gone stale. True, there'd been no sparks for years. And worse, their sex life had dwindled from infrequent to pretty much nonexistent, while her needs hadn't dwindled and faded. Her needs were stronger than ever. Since turning forty, Meg fantasized about sex almost daily.

How weird.

She felt like JJ, who thought about two things—sports and girls. Or more accurately, girls and sports. Except she didn't think about sports. She thought about her responsibilities, the endless responsibilities, and sex.

How much she missed it. How much she wanted it. How much

she feared never being made love to again. And not the *thump, thump, thump* intercourse, but the slow, maddening make-out sessions of her teens and twenties, where you kissed for hours and touched and explored and got worked up to a feverish pitch.

The black and wooden bangles on Meg's wrist clanked as she pushed dark hair back from her forehead, watching it fall across her shoulders. She looked so calm. One wouldn't know she craved feverish. One wouldn't know she craved passion and exploration and sexual tension.

How many other women fantasized about sex? Or was she a freak, thinking about being tied up, held down, and licked as if she were an ice-cream cone?

Only it would kill Jack to go down on her. He loved her, but performing oral sex wasn't his thing. Of course he wanted it done to him. But she was supposed to be fine without any.

Meg didn't realize how angry she was about the inequality of their sex life until lately, when all she could think about was what Jack wanted for himself but wouldn't give.

Once during a fight she'd shouted at him, "You should have told me this when we were dating. You shouldn't have pretended you liked it back then."

"Why? You wouldn't have married me if I'd told you I didn't?" he'd answered.

Yes, she'd wanted to tell him then. She wouldn't have married someone who had such a narrow definition of sex, but the truth was, she probably would have. She'd wanted to get married. Wanted kids. Jack was smart and ambitious and a good provider. All the necessary requirements for husband material.

Instead Jack climbed on and off as if she were part of the mattress, with no more needs than the quilted top layer, before he rushed off to his books and plans and relationship with historical accuracy.

And so here she was.

Her stomach churned. She felt almost sick. But the fear wouldn't let her turn around and retreat.

What if there wasn't more? Could she spend the rest of her life feeling flat? Numb? Dead?

Could she march through another forty years of nothingness?

But Meg was sure there was more. There had to be more than kids and bills and dishes and headaches.

There had to be beauty. There had to be joy. God forgive her, there had to be pleasure, touch, sensation . . . great sex.

Meg drew a slow breath and reached for the doorknob, and even as the door swung open, she knew that once she did this, there was no going back. Once she did this, she'd forever be the cheating spouse, one of those ugly statistics that were bandied about.

Her conscience begged her to stop. Her body refused to obey.

Door open, she looked across the bedroom to the king-size bed, expecting to see Chad in it, naked.

But he wasn't there.

"Second thoughts?" he asked from the bedroom doorway.

She turned her head and looked at him where he stood barefoot but otherwise dressed in jeans and his button-down shirt, although the shirt was now untucked from the waistband and partially unbuttoned.

She nodded slowly, tears stinging her eyes. "I'm scared."

His brow lowered, his expression troubled. "That's the last thing I want you to feel, baby."

Heat rushed through her, and she blushed, her cheeks burning. "What do you want me to feel?"

He looked at her for an endless moment, before his lips struggled to curve. "Good."

And so did she.

Meg swallowed hard and walked from the bathroom door to

the edge of the bed and sat down, hands folding in her lap. "I'm afraid you'll be disappointed."

"Nothing about you has ever disappointed me."

Her heart turned over. "You're sure?"

He nodded. "Are you?"

No. Not at all. But now that she was here, in his room, on his bed, she couldn't see herself leaving. Not without finding out what he felt like, naked, against her.

She nodded.

"I'm not convinced that's a yes, baby, and I'm not about to force you."

For a moment she did nothing and then she reached for the tiny buttons on her teal silk blouse and began to undo them one by one until the blouse gaped open, revealing her black lace bra.

She heard Chad hiss a breath and blood rushed to her cheeks, but he hadn't moved from his position against the doorframe, so she stood, and peeled the blouse off before she unzipped her pencil skirt and stepped from the puddle of burnt-orange fabric, leaving her in nothing but her high heels and black lace underwear,

"You dress like this every day, Mary Margaret?" he drawled, his voice dropping, deepening even as his hand moved to his fly and covered his bulge.

"Now I do," she whispered, watching in fascination as he palmed the jeans covering his erection.

"Why?"

She exhaled in a rush, her skin so hot she thought it would burst any second and peel off. "I pretend I'm dressing for you."

"Good," he said, pushing off the wall and walking across the room toward her, his gaze never leaving her face. "And don't you stop."

Thirteen

She never got to JJ's baseball game. Didn't get home until seven-thirty. She'd called at five, though, stretched out naked on her stomach in Chad's bed to tell the babysitter that important people were in town and she was needed at the winery.

Even as she made excuses to Linnea, the Tuesday and Thursday sitter, Meg tried to tell herself it wasn't a total lie. There were important people at the winery earlier in the day. And she had been needed there. Then.

But as Meg never had emergency meetings crop up, Linnea was happy to stay and take care of things until Jack got home. Meg texted Jack next, told him the same. He replied that he'd see her when she was done.

When she was *done*.

That had given Meg pause.

She turned off her phone feeling rather sick. What had she done?

And then Chad swept his hand down her back, from her shoulders to the small of her spine, before caressing the swell of her ass.

He liked her ass. Liked looking at it, touching it, holding it as he'd thrust into her. Chad, she'd discovered, was a butt man. Jack hadn't been. He liked legs.

"Everything all right?" Chad asked, his palm warm against her hip.

She nodded, still feeling sick. "I'm going to hell," she said quietly, thoughtfully.

"You're not going to go to hell."

She looked at him, expression grave. "This is a sin, Chad."

He stretched out next to her, smoothed hair back from her ear, his thumb brushing her earlobe to her cheek. "Is it less of a sin if I love you?"

"Not if I'm married to someone else—"

"*If* you're married—"

"Which I am."

"But maybe you shouldn't be."

Meg said nothing.

"At least not to him," he added.

She pushed up on her elbow to look at Chad more closely. His dark blond hair was rumpled, and his jaw was shadowed with a hint of stubble. There were deep grooves bracketing his mouth and his blue eyes were sleepy and sexy. In short, he looked better than she'd ever seen him look before. It turned out he was one of those men who needed to be naked to be best appreciated because his body was amazing, muscles in all the right places, not to mention handsomely hung. "I'm not going to get a divorce. I can't. The kids—"

"That's fine," he interrupted, closing the distance between them to kiss her lips.

She loved the feel of his mouth against hers, and the warmth of his breath and the long hard feel of his body. She felt delicate and fragile and feminine against him. "Let's not talk about any of that," she whispered against his mouth. "I can't. I can't think about them and be here."

* * *

Meg drove home in a daze. Her body hummed and throbbed and her lips felt tingly and sensitive from hours of kissing and making love.

If she let herself think about what had just happened, she wanted to throw up. She'd missed JJ's game . . . something she hated doing, and for some reason she thought of Laura and how Laura was counting every baseball game that Meg had missed so far this year. Well, add another to that scorecard.

She'd lied to Linnea.

Lied to Jack.

Worse, she knew they'd both accepted her story because they trusted her. But then, she'd never given them reason not to trust her.

Until now.

Her hands suddenly shook on the steering wheel. Her body felt warm and languid, touched, pleasured, and deeply satisfied. Her heart felt cold. Her chest felt hollow. Guilt and remorse pummeled her, and yet . . . if she pushed thoughts of Jack and kids and home out of her mind, if she thought about today, and what had happened today, she was happy. She'd been happy with Chad, happy to be in his arms, held close to him. She'd felt good there. Right. Strangely safe, considering it wasn't safe at all.

And the sex . . . the sex had been mind-blowing, if not some-what exhausting. Three orgasms in one afternoon was a lot, and the third O had taken some doing, but Chad loved sex, including oral sex, and had been determined to explore, and enjoy, all of her.

She was alone in the car, but remembering made her blush.

She'd forgotten just how . . . personal . . . oral sex was. When you're young it seems like everyone's doing it, and you're doing it, but after seventeen years of marriage and three kids and a husband who wouldn't do it, she kind of freaked when Chad went down on her.

It probably didn't help that she was in nothing but one of his shirts and they'd just showered (together . . . another nerve-racking situation, but the day seemed to be full of them) and were hanging out in his kitchen sipping chilled white wine and nibbling cheese and crackers when Chad scooped her up, put her on the edge of the pine table, and kissed her senseless. And then, when her head was spinning and she was struggling to catch her breath, he put his hand between her thighs and then he was kissing her there and it all got very confusing fast.

Did she mention that it felt really good? A warm hand, a cool mouth, a slip of a tongue, and little lights were exploding in her head and she hadn't even come yet.

The pleasure was so intense, so much more focused than during intercourse, but she'd had serious reservations about doing it there and then. She was lying on the dinner table. The farmhouse was brightly lit. She probably needed a proper wax. And she'd already come twice.

But Chad had serious expertise and knew exactly what he was doing, and so while she tried to yelp "no, no thank you," he was hitting all the right nerve endings at exactly the right time, making her terribly conflicted, and then hugely aroused. If it hadn't been for his patience and talent, she couldn't have come, but she did, and screamed—screamed—from the intensity of it.

And that was when she knew she had to go.

Meg didn't scream during sex. Or cry after. And she did both.

He carried her back to bed after she came and she cried in his arms. His room was dark. The moon peeped in the sky. And her heart felt broken.

She loved what Chad did to her body. She loved how Chad made her feel so alive. But Chad would destroy her life.

She knew this without a doubt, knew this with all the conviction one can know something, and so she cried because she'd forgotten how good it felt to be wanted and needed and desired, but she'd made commitments that had nothing to do with need and desire. She'd made commitments that were about fidelity and sacrifice. Being a mom and wife required devotion and a selflessness she obviously lacked.

Tears filled her eyes now as she turned off the highway onto the road she took to her house.

She was screwed.

Chad had sent Meg a text late that night to see if everything at the house was okay. Meg texted back, yes, and then turned off her phone.

Even though she was exhausted, she slept badly, dreaming of Chad, dreaming of Chad making love to her, and the dreams were so real they felt surreal. At first in the dreams he was a generous, skillful lover, and then he became physically demanding, wanting sex in positions she wasn't comfortable with, before turning aggressive and emotionally demanding. He loved her and she would do what he wanted. He loved her and she would listen to him. He loved her and she would do what he said.

In the morning Meg dressed for work in dark straight-legged jeans and a severe, fitted gray blazer. The tight fit of jeans and blazer was to bind her, control her, keep her emotions under wrap, since she'd woken up jittery. Teary. She dreaded going to work. Could hardly eat anything for breakfast. Cried during the drive.

She was wrong. What she'd done was wrong. She'd become someone she didn't like.

At the winery, Craig had scheduled a morning meeting with Chad, Meg, and Jennifer to discuss the show for the Food Network. Jennifer was excited and delighted by the news. Craig told her that logistics were still being worked out, and he had no idea when the series would air—if it really happened—but if it did happen,

Jennifer needed to be prepared. She also needed to be comfortable with the idea of being filmed.

"Let's face it, the cameras will be invasive," he added, "and while the network has said they'll try to minimize the disruption in our work, the show is going to impact our lives. It will probably complicate our lives. And I think we have to be really clear about that. Reality-TV shows can be damaging and the last thing I want to do is hurt anyone here . . . or our families. So please take the weekend to think about whether you want to be part of this show. You can opt out—well, everyone but Chad can."

Meeting over, Craig returned to his office for a couple hours before taking off for the weekend. Jennifer was also working a shorter day because Mike was taking her camping for the first time that weekend.

At noon, Meg and Jennifer went outside to the flagstone patio to eat their sandwiches in the dazzling sunshine. It was so warm on the patio that Meg had to remove her blazer and roll up the sleeves of her blouse.

Jennifer picked at her sandwich as she chattered nonstop about being on a reality show for the Food Network. "It's crazy," she said yet again, repeating herself as she shredded the crust from the bread. "I love the Food Network. I pretty much only watch the Food Network and am addicted to the *Next Iron Chef*. And you know I have all the Barefoot Contessa's cookbooks. I think she's amazing. But they're all amazing over there. And to think we're going to be on a show. We're going to get so much exposure. People will come here just to say they've come here."

Meg simply nodded, grateful that the young woman didn't need much of a response. But eventually Jennifer paused, glanced at her watch, and commented that she only had another hour of work before she was to go.

"I don't really want to go, though," she confessed to Meg. "But

Mike went to San Francisco with me, so I feel like I've got to do this with him." She sighed heavily. "Mike *loves* the outdoors."

Meg felt like hell on the inside, but she hid it with a quick smile. "You don't?"

"A picnic is fine. But for a whole weekend?" Jen's nose wrinkled. "Why?"

"Why what?" Chad asked, appearing on the patio and overhearing only the last little bit of Jennifer and Meg's conversation.

Meg straightened and sucked in a nervous breath as Chad took a seat next to her at the picnic table. And just like that, she remembered every detail about yesterday. His kiss. His smell. The texture of his skin. The way his tongue felt on the inside of her thigh.

"I don't know why people have to camp," Jennifer said plaintively, toying with her water bottle. "Can't we just look at the woods? Do we have to sleep in them?"

Chad's lips quirked. "You don't like camping."

"I've never been before."

"So how do you know you won't like it?"

Jennifer's nose wrinkled. "You sleep outside. On the ground . . . with the bugs." Her eyes widened. "And *spiders*."

"You'll be fine," Chad said soothingly. "Just wear a long-sleeved shirt to bed and check your shoes in the morning—"

"Why my shoes?" Jennifer interrupted.

"Something may have crawled into them in the night—"

"Oh my God! Are you serious?"

Meg's eyes burned and she choked on a muffled laugh. How could she laugh when her heart hurt so much? "Jennifer," she said hoarsely, wanting desperately to be anywhere but here, sitting next to Chad, "nothing will crawl into your shoes."

"You can't tell her that, Meg. It's not true. Things crawl into people's shoes all the time. Lizards, beetles, spiders, snakes—"

Jennifer shot to her feet. "I'm not going!" Her voice was shrill and her hands were shaking as she rolled up what was left of her sandwich in the plastic bag. "Mike will be so upset, but I can't go. I'm deathly afraid of snakes—"

"Jennifer, Chad is just scaring you," Meg said firmly, before turning to Chad. "Chad, knock it off. I've camped for years and never had anything crawl into my shoes, or my sleeping bag."

"Then you were very lucky, Mary Margaret," he answered, lips twitching as Jennifer rushed away into the tasting room.

Meg eyed him reprovingly. "Have you ever been camping?"

"Yes. Have you?"

"Of course. We didn't do hotels in our family. I grew up camping with my family on the Russian River. Where did you camp?"

"Mostly with Boy Scouts—"

"I can't picture you as a Boy Scout."

"I didn't earn a lot of badges."

Meg studied him a moment, and it was very hard not to smile. He looked roguish and charming and his cornflower-blue button-down intensified the blue of his eyes and made his teeth look even whiter. "Somehow that's not a big surprise."

He laughed, and the sound was low and husky, and Meg flashed back to his bedroom yesterday afternoon and how it had felt to lie in his arms, his chest pressed to her back, his long legs tangled with hers.

She'd felt so good yesterday. Warm and safe and loved. So different from how she felt today.

"You look so sad today," Chad said abruptly, suddenly serious. "What's wrong?"

"Everything."

She had to concentrate very hard on a splotch of sunshine on the picnic table to keep from crying. "I am not who I thought I am. I am not who I want to be."

"You regret what happened yesterday?"

She nodded.

"I don't," he said quietly. "I'm glad. I loved being with you. It felt right. You feel right. You belong with me."

"*Chad.*"

"Let me ask you one thing: If you weren't with Jack, would you feel this way now? Be honest."

A lump filled her throat. "I can't answer that."

"Of course you can."

"Fine. No. I wouldn't feel bad right now. I'd feel good. Yesterday with you I felt good. But it was wrong."

"If you weren't married, would you want to be with me? Could you see yourself with me?"

"Chad, I . . ." Meg's voice faded as she rubbed a restless hand across her forehead, rubbing at the heaviness and the ache. "I *am* married, though."

"Not happily."

She closed her eyes, overwhelmed by emotion because he was right. She wasn't happy. Hadn't been happy for a long time. And suddenly she was feeling things again and it was scary. Overwhelming. But also overwhelming in a good way.

To feel . . . to feel alive . . .

"You are too young to settle for less," he said quietly, almost fiercely. "And maybe you don't see it, but I do. You should be happy. You deserve to be happy. You deserve to be loved, and if Jack won't give you what you need . . . then let me."

For a long minute she couldn't speak. Her thoughts spun wildly in different directions. Hope. Fear. Gratitude. Guilt. Back to fear. Because what if . . . what if she did leave Jack, what if she turned to Chad, and Chad changed his mind? What if this was just about the chase? Getting her in bed?

"Meg?" he prompted.

Her shoulders shifted. She mustered a breezy tone. "I know how these things work, Mr. Hallahan, and the clock's ticking."

"What does that mean?"

"Now that you've had me, you'll soon tire of me. It's human nature."

"That's a joke, right?" he retorted grimly.

She forced a smile, feeling stupidly needy. Stupidly vulnerable. And again Dr. Laura Schlessinger's book flashed to mind. Stupid passion. Stupid emotion. Stupid Meg.

He reached under the table and put his hand high on her thigh, his fingertips just brushing the zipper of her jeans. She inhaled sharply as he stroked over highly sensitive nerves.

"I've been hard all day thinking about you," he added under his breath. "Had to go home and jack off—"

"Don't need to hear that."

"Why not? It's real. I want you. And not just in my bed, but in my home. In my life." The entire time he talked, the side of his pinkie finger caressed her, running up and down across the sensitive spot hidden by her jeans.

She couldn't focus on what he was saying when he touched her like that and she batted his hand away. "Not appropriate," she choked.

Undeterred, he rubbed his hand against her once more. "As soon as Jennifer's gone, we are, too." And then he stood up and headed into his office.

She wasn't going to go home with him. Not today. Not ever again. There wasn't going to be another time.

But then, after Jen left, Chad stopped by her office under the pretext of needing her signature, and while she bent her head he kissed the back of her neck, and it was all over for her. His kiss sent shivers of sensation through her. Her traitorous senses overwhelmed her judgment. She left with him.

Sex was even better than yesterday. Satiated, Meg felt warm and lazy and the wine they'd drunk made her pleasantly buzzed. And now, lounging in Chad's sun-drenched bed at three o'clock in the afternoon, she felt so very decadent. Who did this?

Certainly not her. And yet here she was, an open wine bottle on one bedside table and two empty goblets on the other.

She'd needed this. Needed to feel loved, physically loved, grounded to life and earth and her own skin. And maybe Jack loved her, but he didn't love her like this—with hunger, passion, intensity. He didn't crave her. Didn't kiss her everywhere. Didn't hold back his orgasm to drive her to the brink and beyond.

The sex with Jack was quick, basic, over before it'd even begun. And yes, there were times fast and proficient was good, but more times than not she longed to feel his hand sweep over her slowly, head to toe and back again, waking her skin, stirring her senses, making her feel.

Chad's hand was sweeping over her now. Slowly, so very slowly, and she tried sucking in her stomach so he wouldn't feel how thick she was in her middle, but his fingers brushed her belly again and then once more as if he didn't mind.

It was on the tip of her tongue to ask him if he minded that she wasn't skinny, but she stopped herself, knowing without asking that he didn't want to hear that. Maybe husbands would answer questions about weight and poochy stomachs, but lovers had other things on their minds.

Like sex.

Pleasure.

Escape.

Meg tipped her head back to look into Chad's face. He looked down at her, his blue eyes locking with hers. "What?"

He was so handsome. And seven years younger. But mostly handsome. She swallowed hard. "Nothing."

"You're thinking something."

The corner of her mouth curled. He'd worked with her for almost five years. He knew her. She picked up his hand, kissed his palm. "Just not sure what you see in me, Mr. Hallahan."

"Why don't women have more confidence?"

"Because we know you love *Penthouse* vixens and *Playboy* centerfolds, and most of us women are ordinary women with ordinary bodies."

"And you think we men don't know those models are airbrushed?"

"The *Penthouse* centerfolds aren't."

Chad laughed softly. "And how do you know that?"

"My brother. And father."

"They talk about that sort of thing in front of you?"

"No. You can just tell that they're not."

"You've seen them?"

"Of course!"

He dropped his head, his lips teasing hers. "And you're sure you didn't masturbate when you looked at them?"

She punched his arm, laughing against his mouth. "Looking at naked girl bodies doesn't turn me on."

"That's weird. Because it turns me on." And then he was moving over her, his knees pushing hers open to settle between her thighs. His head dipped, his mouth inches above hers. "You turn me on."

For one week Meg lived a strange, maddening, disorienting double life. With Craig gone the following week, she and Chad used every moment during the day to be together. And Jennifer was so accustomed to them working closely that she didn't think twice when they came and went.

Jen had no idea that the two of them were making lunch in Chad's farmhouse kitchen and then love in his bed. She was oblivious to the sexual tension crackling around her and Chad's almost insatiable need.

He wanted Meg. And not just for an afternoon of illicit sex, or an extended secret affair. He wanted Meg for keeps, and he told her so on Thursday as he watched her dress and get ready to head home.

Meg didn't know how to answer him. She loved the woman she was with him—fiercely alive, stunningly physical and emotional—but she had responsibilities. A husband. Children. "I have a family," she told him in response, standing next to the bed, half dressed. "They need me."

"And you think I don't?" he asked quietly. His tone wasn't plaintive. There was no self-pity in his voice. He simply wanted an honest answer.

"I think different people could meet your needs," she said after a slight hesitation. "Whereas I'm the only one who can meet my family's needs."

"Your kids, you mean," Chad corrected her, sitting all the way up, smashing a pillow between him and the headboard. "Because you're right. Mom is always Mom. You don't replace your mom. But men replace wives. They do it all the time."

She stiffened. "I don't think Jack wants another wife."

"Then maybe he should take better care of the one he has."

She didn't know how to answer that. Part of her agreed with him, but another part thought he didn't understand marriage. When you first married, you thought it would be like glorified dating. You thought there would be romance and good feelings and that little fizz of happiness whenever you saw your significant other. But over time, with bills and kids and work and problems, that significant other became one of the problems. But you didn't just leave the problem. You lived with it. Or tried to learn to live with it.

Chad was studying her face. "Could you be happy with me?"

Unease filled her. She didn't like this talk. Divorcing Jack wasn't part of the equation. He was the kids' father. Her husband. They were a family. "This is crazy."

"Not that crazy."

Meg leaned over the bed, kissed him. It was a brief kiss, but he deepened it, melting her so that she allowed him to pull her down onto his lap. His hand slid beneath her blouse to cup her heavy breast, her nipple hardening immediately at his touch.

"We could make this work," he said, kissing the side of her neck. "Think about it."

And Meg did. The drive home she thought of nothing else, and then once home, she felt torn, adrift, her heart back with Chad in the farmhouse while her body moved through duties in her house.

And the schism was beginning to make her feel insane.

How did something so innocent turn into something so intense?

How did one kiss become sex? How did sex become love? How did love become so consuming that she felt like fire being whipped by wind?

Everything inside of her was getting bigger, crazier, wilder, needier.

Everything inside of her was threatening to explode . . . break free.

Making dinner, Meg smiled tightly, listening to the kids chatter as she sautéed the pasta for a Mediterranean pilaf. She smiled even more tightly when Jack asked about her day, and then wrapped an arm around her waist and kissed her.

How could she love Jack and yet crave Chad?

How could she love Jack and yet risk everything for thirty or sixty stolen minutes in Chad's arms?

It was stupid. She was stupid. But she couldn't help herself. She was feeling so much she felt fat, full, glowing . . . infused with emotions and sensation and light. An affair was wrong, and the wages of sin were death, and yet she'd never felt more alive in all her life . . .

"Everything all right?" Jack asked her over dinner as she stared off into space.

Meg jumped guiltily. "Fine. Why?"

"You just seem so preoccupied."

"Just winery stuff. The usual."

And that was another lie, she thought, chewing the lamb with difficulty. There was nothing usual about anything she was doing these days. She'd changed. Had walked down a forbidden path. And now that she'd started down this path, she wasn't sure how she'd ever get off.

Meg woke up to the sound of rain drumming just above the sloped ceiling of the master bedroom. It was still dark and she looked at the clock: 3:53. Still the middle of the night. She turned on her side and drew the duvet closer to her chin and listened to the rain pelt the shingled roof. Usually she liked the sound of rain, but now it sounded lonely. Forlorn. Meg's eyes suddenly stung and she blinked hard to keep from crying.

She should be scared. Should be worried. She was playing with fire, and if she wasn't careful, she was going to get burned.

And just like that, she wished she was with Chad, his arms around her, holding her close. She felt safe with him, safe and warm against his chest, with his heart thudding beneath her ear.

Was it wrong to want more love? Wrong to want a new love?

And then Jack rolled over and reached out to her, his fingers grazing her bare back. "Awake?"

"The rain woke me."

"It's nice, isn't it?"

Her eyes burned. Her chest ached. Jack was a good man. He

loved her, loved their kids, how could she leave him just because she wanted more?

Meg turned in bed to face him and laced her fingers through his and they fell back to sleep holding hands.

Later that morning Meg sat with her coffee and her laptop at the kitchen island paying bills. Tessa was the first to wake up and come downstairs, already a bundle of nerves about that evening's performance.

"You should eat now while you can," Meg said, looking up from the computer screen. Tonight's recital was the biggest of the year and the last dress rehearsal was scheduled for nine this morning at the theater. "I can make you some eggs if you'd like."

Tessa shook her head. "Don't think I could eat them."

"Do you want oatmeal?"

"I'll just eat this now," Tessa said, taking a box of Honey Nut Cheerios from the cupboard and wandering out of the kitchen with it.

At nine Meg dropped Tessa at the Wells Fargo Center for the Arts before driving Gabi to the stables on the outskirts of town.

They were early and sat in the car talking for ten minutes about school and life and Grandma and Grandpa and Aunt Kit coming up tonight for Tessa's performance. Gabi wanted to know why they never came to see her do anything and Meg had to gently remind her that they all had, many times, just not in the past few months.

At a quarter to ten, Gabi grabbed her helmet and ran from the parked car to the stables. Meg stayed behind, knowing that it'd be a while before Gabi and her horse entered the ring.

She was glad for the extra few minutes and leaned against the hood of her car and breathed in deeply. It was such a beautiful morning. The sun had risen high enough to gild the hills and gnarled oak trees, and Meg tipped her head back to look up high. The sky was a pale wispy blue, but beneath the blue everything else was cloaked in gold. So pretty. A perfect June day.

And just like that, Meg thought of Chad, thinking he'd appreciate the massive oaks and sky and the pea gravel beneath her feet. Chad loved rolling hills and grapes the way Jack loved buildings . . .

Impulsively she grabbed her phone, sent Chad a quick text, *Thinking of you*, before tucking the phone in her jeans pocket and leaving the car to go watch Gabi's lesson.

Meg propped her elbows on the wooden railing of the outdoor ring and watched the instructor work with Gabi on keeping a secure seat. From Gabi's expression, Meg could tell that she was bored. Clearly Gabi didn't think she needed to be covering old lessons again, but Meg liked the instructor's thoroughness, appreciating that this riding school didn't rush through lessons. Riding could be dangerous. Jumping was dangerous. Gabi needed to know how to stay on a horse if he should decide to buck.

Meg was trying to hear what the instructor was telling Gabi when her phone buzzed in her pocket. Her heart jumped a little, and fishing her phone out, she hoped it was Chad. It was her sister Sarah instead. "Hi, Sarah," she answered.

"You have a second?"

"Yeah. I'm just at the stables with Gabi. How are you?"

Sarah didn't immediately reply. And then she drew a swift breath. "I found a text."

Meg felt a cold prickle in her middle followed by a flood of guilt. "A . . . text?"

"On Boone's phone."

"When?"

"Last night." Sarah took a quick, sharp breath. "I couldn't sleep and so I got up and checked his phone. He had it locked, but I figured out his combination and was able to look at his messages." She drew another quick breath. "Someone's texting him. Said she misses him." She made a choking sound. "Who does that sort of thing?"

Meg turned away from the ring, her legs suddenly weak, a sick knot in the pit of her stomach. "I don't know."

"I don't know either, because she has to know he's married. It's common knowledge. It's in his profile on the team Web site. It says he has two kids, too. It says he has a family. Why go after a man with a family?" Anger and pain deepened her voice. "Why go after my man? If she wants a man so bad, why doesn't she go get her own? Because Boone isn't up for grabs. Boone is married to me!"

"I'm sorry, Sarah."

"Just when I get comfortable . . . just when I think everything is going to be okay—" She broke off on a strangled cry. "Fuck. Fuck him, fuck her, fuck them all!"

Meg sank onto a nearby bench, her legs unable to support her. "Did you tell Boone?"

"No."

"Why not?"

"Because he'll just give me excuses . . . explanations . . . and I can't deal with another story. Not right now."

"But maybe it's not what you think it is . . . maybe it's entirely innocent. A high school friend, or relative . . ." Meg's voice faded away as she realized how pathetic that sounded. Sarah just cried quietly into the other end of the line. "I'm sorry, Sarah. I really am."

"It's not your fault."

"I just wish I could do something to help."

"I just wish women would leave my husband alone."

Sarah hung up and Meg's hand trembled as she went to her text messages and deleted the text she'd just sent to Chad.

But deleting the text wasn't enough. Meg couldn't keep seeing him. There was nothing remotely right about the situation. Meg wasn't a single woman. She had a family. And for better or worse, she was married to Jack.

Back home after the riding lesson, Meg browned the ground sausage, turkey, and beef for the red sauce that she'd use later to make the lasagnas for dinner that night. She was making a huge batch of red sauce since she intended to make two pans for dinner tonight, plus a small one for Cass to take home to Tommy. Tommy loved lasagna, especially their mother's version, and that was the same version Meg made.

As she drained the fat off the browned meat, she couldn't stop thinking about Sarah's call.

The call had hit home. Hard.

Chad was like the woman texting Boone. He was poaching. Chad had to know he was poaching. And maybe Meg had sent out signals that she was available, but she was wrong. She wasn't available. She needed to remember that, too. She needed to make Chad back off. She needed to let him know that what had happened between them was wrong, and that it was over, and that there could be nothing more between them again.

But a half hour later, when she finished layering the hot noodles with cheese and sauce, she felt absolutely bereft. Life had felt different lately . . .

Strange and wonderful and frightening and new.

She felt strange but new.

For the first time in a long time, Meg felt young, and full of possibility. She no longer felt as if she knew everything, had done everything, but instead life beckoned, new experiences were within her grasp, making her eager to wake and start each day.

If she ended it with Chad, she'd be back to what she had, and yet with less. With loss. Because now she knew that there was someone who wanted her, someone who enjoyed her, someone who would pay attention to her.

Lasagna finished, Meg made a quick lunch for Jack and Gabi before Jack headed into town to pick up Tessa from the theater.

Chad sent Meg a text while Jack was gone. *Miss you.*

The text thrilled her. Terrified her. In the garden cutting roses for a centerpiece, she read the text again. And again.

She put the phone back into her pocket, but it felt heavy and dangerous, as if it were alive. Meg tried to calm her thoughts. She was feeling really anxious and guilty and she hated that she craved these texts from Chad. Hated that just two little words from him—*miss you*—could make her feel so alive. So valuable.

She was crazy.

In the kitchen she trimmed the stems of the roses and put them in a Waterford vase she and Jack had been given for a wedding present seventeen years ago. Her roses weren't white, but a riot of pinks and yellows and deep corals. Her house wasn't open and airy and devoid of clutter either. Shoes littered one end of the house to the other. Kids' backpacks lay in the hall. Books and magazines spilled on coffee tables and end tables. Water glasses were on every surface.

Chad would hate her house, she thought. Chad would hate the clutter. The chaos. The lack of organization.

Chad, she thought, would hate the reality of her.

And then, knowing Jack would be back soon, she shot Chad a text. *You wouldn't miss me if you saw my house . . . knew my life. Messy. Noisy. Crazy. Cluttered.*

He responded immediately. *I'm not a neat freak. I just have a housekeeper.*

She smiled faintly and texted him back. *My kids aren't easy.*

I wasn't easy either, he answered.

Her heart turned over. It was a good answer. She'd hate to think she'd fallen for someone who wouldn't like her children. She stared at his text for a moment, thinking, and then typed, *If we got serious, could you handle three kids?*

He didn't reply for a second and she chewed on her thumb, nervous all over again.

She waited, and waited, and was beginning to think he wasn't going to respond. And then the text came. *I thought we were serious.*

Meg exhaled in a rush. Nervous. Excited. Horrified.

What in God's name was she doing?

Her parents were the first to arrive that evening for dinner, with Cass and Kit walking in ten minutes later, having driven up from the East Bay together since Tommy Jr. had to work tonight.

Jack opened bottles of wine and everyone filled the kitchen while Tessa flitted nervously in and out, her hair already drawn back in a tight bun high on the back of her head. She wasn't going to eat, said she'd eat after the performance, but accepted hugs from her aunts and grandparents.

Meg saw her mom take a seat in the family room and wondered if she should go to her, but then Gabi stepped into view and Mom put an arm around her granddaughter, drawing her down onto the couch next to her. Marilyn's salt-and-pepper head tipped close to Gabi's and they sat there talking quietly together, and Meg's chest ached. Mom.

Jack left the dinner table early to drive Tessa to the auditorium. Meg and Gabi would catch a ride with Meg's family. JJ had elected not to go and Jack had sided with him that he shouldn't have to attend a ballet recital if he didn't want to. It's not as if the girls went to his games.

Meg gave Tessa a hug and kiss, telling her she'd be wonderful, and Jack and Tessa left to a chorus of good lucks and break a leg. Dinner ended not long after Jack and Tessa had gone. Meg headed to the kitchen to load the dishwasher and was rinsing the dinner plates when Kit came up behind her with the water goblets from the dining table.

"Have you heard from Sarah?" she asked, leaning past Meg to empty the glasses into the sink. "I got a cryptic text from her, texted her back, but never heard from her again."

Meg just kept scraping plates. "What did the text say?"

"'Leopards never change their spots.'" Kit placed the glasses in the dishwasher. "I figured it was about Boone. I was hoping I was wrong. I love that guy. I know you've been down on him ever since he cheated, but that was years ago and he's so wonderful, so loving with Sarah and the kids."

"I did talk to her this morning," Meg said reluctantly, not wanting to discuss this at all. "She found a text on his phone. It was from a girl. Sarah was pretty upset."

"Oh no."

"Yeah, I know." Meg paused at the sink. "I told her to talk to Boone about it. There might be an explanation for it."

"And what did she say?"

"That she didn't need any more stories and lies. That things were hard enough as it was." Meg placed two rinsed china plates in the bottom rack of the dishwasher. "I don't think they're going to make it."

"You don't want them to make it," Kit countered stiffly.

"That's not true."

"You've never forgiven him for cheating—"

"That's not true, and honestly, it's none of my business." Meg straightened swiftly, color sweeping her cheekbones. "I'm not the one married to him."

"But you think Sarah should have divorced him."

"I *never* said that—"

"You did!"

"I didn't."

"Meg, I love you to death, but you weighed in pretty heavily on this topic a couple years ago."

"Then I miscommunicated because I'm not a proponent of divorce. If they can make their marriage work, I think they should."

Cass entered the kitchen through the swinging dining room door, arms filled with a platter, bread plates, and cutlery. "We can hear you," she said quietly, setting everything on the wet counter. "And Gabi is taking it all in with great relish."

Meg clamped her jaw tight and Kit looked away, biting her lip.

Cass reached out to her sisters-in-law and wrapped an arm around each of them, drawing them toward her. "You two never fight."

"We're not fighting," Meg said tightly.

"Just talking," Kit added.

"About Sarah and Boone," Cass said. "I know. We all know. But it's not going to help Mom. She's not feeling very good."

Kit pulled from the embrace. "She's not?" she whispered.

Cass shook her head. "Dad said she's been running a fever all week. She's not eating properly. Doesn't seem to have much of an appetite."

"Did she eat tonight?"

"Picked at her food."

Meg dried her hands on the nearest towel. "Is she in pain?"

"Her joints hurt. Her body aches." Cass glanced from Meg to Kit and struggled to smile. "Your dad say's she's taking Advil or something, an over-the-counter pain reliever, nothing prescription strength. But she probably needs something stronger." She frowned, hesitated. "I'm thinking we need to get more involved. Understand what's happening. Mom's going to need us. Need our help."

"I thought she had six months to a year," Meg murmured, shaken by the thought that maybe Mom didn't have as long as they'd thought.

"She just might need better pain medicine," Cass comforted.

"Either way, she's going to hurt." Kit's eyes were wide, her expression troubled. "She's going to be scared. And she's going to try to hide it from us to try to protect us."

"That's Mom," Meg said softly, closing the dishwasher door. Mom hated to be vulnerable. She wouldn't want any of them to see her in pain. "But I don't want to be a burden. I want to help. I just don't know what to do."

"I think we need to get educated," Kit said. "Learn about the advanced stages of cancer, and how we can help Mom through it."

For a second Meg couldn't breathe and then she choked on a strangled laugh. "You sound so matter-of-fact. As if Mom dying is going to be easy."

Kit's eyes filled with tears. "There's nothing easy about it. But we have to be there for her. She can't worry about us now. She did her part. Now it's our turn."

Tessa was spectacular that evening, absolutely gorgeous onstage. Meg hadn't realized how much her daughter had grown as a dancer. Her technique was beautiful. Her lines exquisite, her extension impressive. Maybe she did have a chance at being selected for the prestigious San Francisco Ballet School. She certainly had promise, and ambition.

After the program ended, they greeted Tessa with applause. Jack had an armful of roses for her and she blushed and giggled as she accepted them.

"You were the best one up there," Meg's father told her.

Tessa blushed and giggled again, both happy and relieved that the performance had gone as well as it had.

Everyone said their good-byes at the auditorium. They'd planned on going out for dessert afterward, but Mom was fatigued and Cass said she had a headache, so Meg and Gabi drove home with Jack and Tessa, stopping en route for ice cream.

At home Meg told Tessa yet again how wonderful she'd been and how proud she was of her, and Tessa did a little pirouette. "So you think the San Francisco Ballet School will pick me?"

"I would hope so. I think you deserve the opportunity."

Tessa hugged her mother tightly, happily. "I love you, Mom."

"I love you, too, honey."

"You're the best mom."

Meg squeezed her, gave and received a rare butterfly kiss, something they used to do when Tessa was just a little girl, and then headed to bed. But in the privacy of her room, her smile faded. Her heart was too heavy. It had felt good to get a big hug from Tessa tonight. It felt even better to know that her daughter loved her. But Tessa was wrong. Meg wasn't the best mom. Meg was actually a very selfish mom. Because good moms didn't have affairs. Good moms put their families first.

Fourteen

Meg woke early and decided she needed to go to Mass. She hadn't been since Easter and it was time. Tessa wanted to go with her to the nine A.M. service at the Cathedral of St. Eugene in downtown Santa Rosa, but Gabi and JJ opted to stay home with Jack.

Meg was glad for Tessa's company. She hadn't slept well. The argument she'd had with Kit in the kitchen last night had haunted her for the rest of the night. Kit was right, too. Meg had been very disappointed in Boone after they'd all learned of the affair. Beyond disappointed. And she'd told Sarah that she supported whatever decision Sarah made, including leaving Boone.

Meg felt like such a hypocrite.

The car windows were down and she drummed her fingers against the door. "Can't believe school is out on Friday," she said to Tessa as she drove, trying to take her mind off Kit and Sarah and Boone and Chad and how tangled it had all become. "What are your plans for the summer?"

Tessa's hand was out the window, playing with the air as it rushed through her fingers. "Dance, I guess."

"Is there anything you want to do? Anyplace you want to go?"

Tessa thought for a moment, then shook her head. "No. I just want to dance."

Meg's lips curved reluctantly. "Okay."

Reaching St. Eugene's, Meg parked on a side street since the parking lot was already full. They arrived in the middle of the opening hymn and found a pew toward the back of the cathedral. Even though everyone was standing singing, Meg drew out the kneeler and prayed.

Meg knew she was a sinner in God's house. She hadn't been to confession. She was still living a life of sin, and yet she was here today because she needed to quiet her mind. Life was spinning out of control—she was out of control—and she didn't want to live this way. Didn't like feeling this way.

And still kneeling, praying, Meg wondered why after forty years of trying so hard to do what was right, she'd knowingly, willingly chosen that which was wrong. What happened to good intentions? Where did they go and why? And why now, when Meg had children she loved more than anything?

An hour later, service over, Meg and Tessa made their way out through the back of the cathedral. The bishop was there, shaking hands with the parishioners. He knew Meg and asked where the rest of the family was. She stifled her embarrassment as she answered, "Home."

"Awkward," Tessa muttered as they walked back to their car.

"Totally," Meg agreed.

They drove to their favorite doughnut shop to buy doughnuts to take home to the family and split a raised glazed doughnut on the way out of the warm, fragrant store.

They were just returning to the car when Meg's phone vibrated where she'd left it charging in the middle console. Licking the sugar off her fingers, Tessa leaned over, picked the phone up. "A text," she said, pausing a little before adding, "from Chad."

Meg saw Tessa's expression and, wiping her own fingers off on a paper napkin, took the iPhone from her daughter. The text was prominently displayed. *Can't wait to see you tomorrow.* Meg clicked on the text, deleting it.

"That's weird," Tessa said, closing her door. "Why would he say that?"

"Say what?" Meg asked, shoving the key in the ignition. She hadn't even thought about an incoming text being seen by someone else and she silently kicked herself for her stupidity. She wasn't cut out for a life of duplicity. She'd never needed to guard her e-mails or phone before.

"I think it's weird that he said he can't wait to see you." Tessa eyed her mother, her dark auburn hair held back with a headband. She had the same thick loose curls as her aunt Kit. In fact, she had a lot of Kit's coloring—hair, eyes, complexion—but had fortunately inherited Aunt Brianna's slender frame, which was good considering she wanted to be a professional ballerina. "He's your boss."

Meg felt swamped by sick waves of guilt. It would kill her if Tessa discovered that her mother was having an affair. "There's something big going on at work," Meg said, stumbling for words. "He's just eager to talk about it."

"What?"

"Oh, it's . . . uh, nothing."

"But you just said it was something big."

Meg couldn't breathe. "Yes, it's big, but it's nothing I can talk about yet."

"That's stupid. Why can't you tell me? I'm your daughter."

"We're not supposed to tell anyone—"

"I *won't*."

"Okay." Meg took a quick breath. "The Food Network is going to create a series around the winery."

"What kind of series?"

"You know, a reality-TV show."

Tessa's mouth dropped open. *"Seriously?"*

Meg nodded.

"Would you be in it?"

Meg nodded again, hating herself.

Tessa's eyes grew even wider. "Does Dad know?"

"Not yet. I'm waiting to tell him until the contract is signed and we can share the news with everyone."

"Will I be on TV?"

"I'm not sure what the story lines will be."

"Well, make sure we're part of the show. That way the San Francisco Ballet can see how good I am, and then they'll want me for their school."

"I'll let the show producers know your thoughts," Meg said faintly, knowing she'd averted the crisis but disgusted with herself for lying to her own daughter.

But Tessa was oblivious to any tension and happily clicked her seat belt into place. "We're going to be famous!"

Meg shuddered inwardly. God, she hoped not.

It felt like summer, that juicy ripe summer of tangy orange Popsicles and sunshine and coconut-scented sunscreen. Maybe it was because Meg was outside with the kids at the pool, and they were racing off the diving board, doing flips, and cannonballs to see who could get the most air and create the biggest splash. Of course it was Gabi who succeeded in drenching Meg. She'd howled with laughter and Meg reluctantly smiled.

She loved summer. And yet the hot afternoon with the glaze of sun made her chest ache. Summer was about youth and innocence and she'd lost both a long time ago.

Tessa slipped from the pool into the hot tub and her brother and sister followed. Meg picked up her book. It was the same novel she'd been trying to read five weeks ago during the Brennan Girls' Getaway in Capitola. How sad to think she'd only progressed by twenty pages since then, and she wasn't making much progress today either. It was hard to read, hard to concentrate. The words seemed to blur and slide off the page, mocking her lack of control.

God gave people free will so they would use it, a little voice said in her head.

Maybe it was time she used hers. Time she turned things around.

Jack's Saab sounded in the driveway and moments later he entered the pool area. He'd just returned from town, and stopped on the way home to buy chicken breasts for dinner.

He handed her the plastic grocery bag, and leaned over to give her a kiss on the forehead. "Feel like marinating them? I'll throw them on the grill later."

She rose from her chair. "Of course."

In the house while the chicken marinated in fresh lemon juice and seasoning salt, Meg peeled and boiled potatoes for potato salad and Jack took a wire brush to the barbecue outside, cleaning the wire racks.

She paused while peeling the potatoes, her gaze going to Jack and then the kids, who'd climbed from the pool and sat down on the lounge chairs wrapped in towels. *This,* she thought, *is my life. This is what it's about. Feeding them. Loving them. Making sure they're all okay.*

And yet . . .

And yet . . .

A part of her wanted more. A part of her whispered she'd go mad if she was merely a pair of hands . . . kitchen help . . .

With Chad she was more.

With Chad she was beautiful and sexy and alive . . .

And that was wonderful, but she also had to be practical. Could he fit into their lives? Could he handle three kids, two of them teenagers? Her children already knew him. They liked him. But what if he was no longer Chad Hallahan, Mom's boss, but Chad Hallahan, Mom's lover?

Meg cringed and returned to her potatoes, peeling the last two with quick, aggressive strokes.

The afternoon's warmth lingered into evening and they ate dinner outside on the patio. Candles flickered on the table and the heady fragrance of wisteria filled the air. Grilled veggies, wisteria, freshly mown grass, and chlorine . . . summer had indeed arrived.

Jack was in a great mood at dinner, talking about the house he was working on in Virginia. "When so many older homes are renovated, the millwork is lost in demolition or replaced with cheap millwork, but the Kendalls want all the original millwork preserved. They see the renovation as a gift to the house, and the community."

Only Tessa appeared to be listening to her father. JJ stared off across the patio toward the pool, lost in his own thoughts, Gabi chewed a fingernail, and Meg's lips pursed. The kids had grown up listening to Jack talk about his work. He was so passionate about design, wanting to share his love of architecture with everyone.

It was one of the things she'd loved about him when they'd met in Rome. So many guys her age either didn't know what they wanted out of life or wanted to make a ton of money, which both seemed so soulless to her. Jack was different. He was so excited about studying in Italy, and its history, and when they weren't with their respective colleges, studying, he took her around Rome, gave her personal tours of the ruins, explaining how the buildings would have looked, and how they were used, and his passion had been contagious. He made Rome come alive for her. He made life come alive. She fell for him so hard.

If only they had that passion now. She missed it. Missed that intensity and energy and connection.

That night after the kids were in bed she reached for him and he kissed her. They made love, and Meg tried desperately to feel something other than platonic affection. She tried to respond, she did, but it felt like she was just going through the motions. Jack's touch was just as perfunctory. He touched her only enough to get the job done. But Meg wasn't a job and she didn't get done. After he came, he rolled off her, kissed her cheek, and went to sleep.

Meg couldn't sleep.

She lay on her back, seething. Feeling as if she were suffocating. The night was warm, the comforter too heavy. Jack's snoring was making her crazy. Angry.

Turning on her side, Meg pulled the sheet up to her chest and stared out the open window at the moon.

She felt so empty. Empty and numb.

Sex with Jack was terrible. Sex with Chad was unbelievable. But Chad wasn't her husband. Jack was. And her husband seemed completely oblivious that she might need anything, never mind an orgasm. Somehow sex had evolved into being about his release, not hers.

But that didn't make sleeping with Chad okay. It wasn't okay. There was nothing okay about having an affair. She didn't want to be doing this. Didn't like doing this. Didn't like the person she'd become.

A liar. A deceiver. A cheat.

Pressure filled her chest, bearing down, making it hard to breathe. She wanted—needed—her old life back. The uncomplicated life. The one where Meg had been good and true. The one where Meg had been herself.

*   *   *

Meg slept badly, tossing and turning much of the night, and wasn't feeling rested when the alarm went off at six. For a moment she considered staying in bed and calling in sick, but if she stayed in bed, who would get the kids up and dressed and off to school?

Bleary-eyed, she dragged herself out of bed and headed down-stairs to make a strong pot of coffee. How funny to think that she used to wake up early, earlier than six, and go to the garage to the recumbent bike or treadmill to exercise. Maybe she needed to get back to exercising. Maybe it would help her find her discipline. God knew she needed some.

Downstairs, Meg kept an eye on the clock as she sat with her coffee, reading the morning paper. In a few minutes she'd need to wake up JJ and then the girls. JJ always had to be woken up first. He took twice as long as Gabi and Tessa to get ready for school. Meg made a point of *not* thinking about what he did during his twenty-minute showers.

Her cell phone rang. Meg glanced at the kitchen clock. Just quarter to seven. She suspected it was Kit, who loved to call early, but instead it was Sarah.

"Can the kids and I come stay with you awhile?" Sarah asked, after Meg had answered. "They're out of school and they'd love to spend some time with their cousins and I'd really love to come hang out with you and Kit—" Her voice cracked. "Feeling kind of trapped here at the moment."

"Of course you can. You're always welcome," Meg said.

"I don't know how long we'd stay."

"Doesn't matter. Stay for a day, stay for a week, stay for ten weeks. My house is yours."

"Thank you. I knew I could count on you." Sarah struggled to regain control. "Oh, Meg, we had our worst fight ever. So bad. I cried all night. Can't stop crying now. He acts like none of this is his fault. That I'm just digging into things, looking for trouble."

"Are you?"

"No." Sarah hiccuped. "Yes. I don't trust him. I don't. And I can't live without trust, but I love him. I can't imagine life without him. I can't imagine taking the kids from him."

"Then don't. Don't go there right now. There's no need. Come here. Get some rest. You'll get a different perspective. Things will work out. They always do."

"I don't know what I'd do without you, Meg."

"I don't either," Meg teased gently. "So book your air and let me know when to expect you."

The drive to the winery in Napa was longer than usual due to an accident on Highway 12 that brought traffic to a standstill. Meg could see the big black plume of smoke in the distance. Police, fire trucks, ambulances raced past her car. She was going to be here awhile and she texted Chad to let him know. He texted back that he and Craig were going to Yountville for a meeting and would see her later.

For one hour Meg sat in her car in the same spot, browsing the Internet and answering e-mail, and then at last traffic started to move again. She shuddered as she crept by the scene of the accident, one car burned out, another flattened in on itself. Yellow crime-scene tape closed the area off for the investigation. The cars were normal cars, family cars, and Meg prayed there were no kids in them.

She reached the winery feeling subdued. She talked to Jennifer for a little bit about the accident and then went to her desk to prepare some press releases to be e-mailed out about a charity fundraiser that they were hosting in August before the big harvest. But the entire time she worked she kept thinking about the accident and the ambulances, three of them, and she hoped everyone would be okay.

She was just leaving for lunch when she bumped into Chad and Craig in the parking lot.

"Heard about the accident," Craig said, greeting her in the parking lot. "Pretty damn awful. Two fatalities so far. Just teenagers. And two more kids in intensive care."

Meg sagged against the side of her car. "Teenagers?"

Chad nodded. "Four of them in one car. On their way to school."

"Do you know what happened?" she asked, knowing they were someone's kids, knowing that hearts were forever broken.

"Sounds like the kids tried to pass a slower car but couldn't get back over in time. Hit the oncoming car head-on."

Meg went to lunch in town but couldn't eat. She wandered up and down Main Street, stopping here and there to look in a boutique, but she was shaken, and very blue, and she kept picturing the kids at home showering and dressing and getting ready for school. Boys like JJ who took endless showers and girls who fussed over their hair. Kids with normal worries like tests and teachers, parents, grades, and sex.

Sex.

And suddenly she was standing outside Zinsvalley Restaurant and crying for the kids who'd just died, and the two in intensive care, and the four families whose lives would never be the same.

Life was so precious and fragile and there were no guarantees. No amount of insurance could protect you from fate. There was no escaping one's mortality. There was no escaping reality.

Back at the winery Meg knocked lightly on Chad's door. "I'm not feeling so good," she said. "You all right if I head home?"

He looked like he'd just tramped through the vineyards. Sweat darkened the front of his chest and his boots were still caked with mud. "Of course." He looked at her more closely. Her face was swollen and puffy from crying. "You okay?"

She nodded, folded her arms across her chest, suppressed a shiver. "Can't stop thinking about the accident, and those kids."

"It's a terrible way to start the day."

"A terrible way to end a life." Fresh tears filled her eyes and she drew a shallow, hiccuping breath. "Chad, I'm worried."

"About JJ?" he asked, leaning back in his chair.

"No. I mean, I always worry about him, boys are so reckless." She held her breath, the air bottled in her lungs, before blurting, "I'm worried about us."

"Do you think Jack knows?" he asked.

She shook her head. "No. But I know, and this isn't right. It's tearing me up on the inside. The guilt's beginning to eat me alive."

His blue gaze searched her face. "What do you want to do?"

Meg felt her chest seize, the tightness and tension overwhelming. "We have to end this."

"Is that the answer?"

The guilt and fear had become consuming, oppressive. She wiped away tears. "Isn't it?"

"No." He left his desk, moved toward her, put his hands on her shoulders. His thumbs stroked her collarbones, a light caress. "I think you should leave Jack and move in with me."

At home, Meg heated up tomato soup, made a grilled cheese sandwich, and carried both to bed, where she watched three recorded episodes of *Dance Moms* and then two of *Project Runway* and finally started to feel better.

But once she turned the TV off and carried the dishes downstairs, she felt sick again. Sick with fear, and guilt.

Would leaving Jack be the right thing to do? Would making her relationship with Chad official make it right? Was living with Chad the answer?

She searched her heart and didn't think so. But how to tell him that? And how did one end something like this?

C had and Meg went out the next day for a fast lunch at Taqueria Rosita. Chad was craving burritos and Meg picked at her favorite taco salad, and then they were done and looking at each other from across the small table.

"I thought about what you said yesterday," Meg told him, folding her paper napkin into little squares. "But if I left Jack—" She broke off, glanced around, making sure no one was listening. "I couldn't move in with you. Not right away." She folded the napkin yet again. "It'd be like jumping out of the frying pan into the fire."

Chad pushed his platter away. "You'd want your own place?"

"I'd have to."

"Are you seriously thinking about leaving Jack?"

She shrugged uneasily, thinking of Sarah and her children, and all the people who looked to her, expecting her to do the right thing. "We can't continue as we are."

"I agree."

M eg drove home that evening so tense and jittery she could barely sit still. This was all getting out of hand. She was in so dee— She'd never meant for things to go this far. But then, she'd never meant to sleep with Chad either.

Her heart raced. Her thoughts were tangled, fatigue and guilt adding to her mental confusion. Could she actually leave Jack? Could she start over with Chad?

All evening she mulled over her options. She thought of little else as she made dinner and did dishes, and then oversaw the last few homework assignments of the year and glanced through a few pages of JJ's yearbook before he snatched it away from her, afraid she'd read something someone wrote in it. Meg wanted to be honest, needed to be realistic, and she forced herself to imagine life with Chad. She pictured finding a bigger version of his farmhouse, pictured waking up in another sunlit bedroom and having coffee together on a white, slipcovered couch.

She pictured using his heavy ivory ceramic mugs for her morning coffee, the ceramic glaze crackled, the mugs handmade by an artist friend of Chad's. Chad knew lots of local artists and chefs, and she pictured them having small dinner parties in his house, entertaining in a way she never did with Jack since Jack didn't need people. Chad did, though.

Living with Chad, there would always be white roses and lilies on the counter, or maybe a vase of white tulips. And in this world the sun would always be shining, or if it rained, there would be a fire crackling in the hearth.

And picturing this life, she realized it was pure fantasy.

Nothing about these pictures in her head were real. Nothing about this life with Chad would be real either.

Because her life wasn't about white dishes and couches and fresh flowers on hall tables. Her life wasn't serene and pale and gilded with sunlight. It was hectic and filled with rushing about, and frustration over dinner, and carpooling, and dirty clothes heaped in endless mounds in the laundry room.

And maybe initially the life with Chad would be about sparkling wineglasses, and clean sheets she didn't have to put in the bed. But after a while she wouldn't see the sparkling wineglasses or appreciate the clean sheets because real life would get in the way. And maybe Chad would be loving and tender, but eventually the love and tenderness would fade, buried by the weight of reality.

Eventually she'd have cramps and the kids would get the flu and Chad would come home moody.

And that part was real. That was life. Not white flowers and couches and a crisp, cold Chardonnay in the middle of the afternoon.

Meg left her bed to go downstairs. She made a cup of tea and curled up in Jack's leather recliner in the family room. They'd bought the chair the year they'd married and the dark brown leather was cracked and scratched and beat up to the point of disrepair, but Jack loved it and she could smell Jack on the chair. She started to cry.

What had she done?

What had happened to the life she'd so carefully made?

Meg cried so hard she had to wrap one arm around her middle, and the other across the top of her head, to keep from shattering, disintegrating, into a thousand pieces.

She'd poured herself into this life, into this family, lovingly, fiercely creating, crafting every tradition, every celebration, making this family hug by hug, tear by tear, making it real. Making it hers.

For what?

To tear it apart? To take a hammer and destroy it? To destroy the people she loved best?

And she did love them best. She liked Chad, maybe loved Chad, but he wasn't her home. He was exciting. New. Unknown. He represented skin and excitement and sex and possibility, and with him she felt more alive than she'd felt since Jack Jr. arrived. But she couldn't trade Chad for Jack and the kids. She couldn't. It'd kill her. Break her. Destroy her.

Closing her eyes, Meg drew her knees even closer to her chest and began to pray. First the Our Father and then Hail Mary.

Meg's resolve wavered as she dressed for work in the morning. Was she really going to quit work today?

As she climbed into her car and waited for the kids to join her, she couldn't imagine not ever going to Dark Horse Winery again, couldn't imagine what it would feel like tomorrow to wake up with nowhere to go. With nothing to do.

She loved her job. It had been a perfect job for her, too, but how could she break things off with Chad and continue at the winery? It would be too painful being in close proximity to him. She knew too much about him now.

She knew his smell, his touch, the warmth of his skin, the curve of his biceps, the hard plane of muscle in his chest. She knew how his mouth felt against hers as his body pressed into hers. She knew that hitch in his breath just before he came. She knew he could make her feel amazing things . . .

But he wasn't the one who was supposed to make her feel amazing things and she shouldn't know how he tasted or smelled. Those were things another woman should know, not her. She wasn't his. And he wasn't hers.

As she drove to work her stomach hurt. Her coffee wasn't sitting well on an empty stomach. Her heart felt as if it would shatter at any moment. She was a mess. Definitely wasn't going to be able to get another job right away. She'd need time to put her heart and life back together.

Still driving, she sent Chad a text letting him know it was over between them. She added that she was also giving notice. She was only coming in to pick up her stuff.

Chad didn't respond.

Meg greeted Jennifer with a tight smile and nod before heading straight to her office. She was emptying her desk when Chad entered her office and closed the door behind him.

"What's going on?" he demanded.

She couldn't look at him, couldn't allow herself to feel anything, and just shook her head.

Chad moved around the desk, caught her hands in his. "Talk to me, Meg. You're killing me. What's going on?"

She kept her gaze fixed on the back of his hands. His skin was tan from working outdoors. He was a man, like Jack, who loved his work. "I love you," she said softly, "but I also still love Jack, and I made a commitment to him and I have to honor that commitment. It's the right thing to do. It's the only thing I can do."

"Don't quit. We'll cool things between us. It doesn't have to be physical—"

"I can't do that," she interrupted. "I care too much about you to be around you but not be with you. Because when I see you, I want to be with you. When I see you, I want to touch you and kiss you, and I can't. Not anymore." She finally looked up at him, eyes swimming with tears. "Chad, I'm losing my mind. It's bad. I feel bad. I honestly feel like I'm going crazy."

He stared down into her eyes for an endless moment and then lifted her hands to his mouth and kissed them. "Can't have that," he said quietly.

"I don't want to quit. Don't want to say good-bye to you. But I don't have a choice. "

He took her hands, pressed them to his chest, over his heart. "How do you want to do this? What shall we tell Craig?"

She could feel his heart thudding through his chambray shirt. His chest was warm and hard. He felt so solid and real, more real than Jack, but that was beside the point. She'd come to work today to do the right thing—finally—and that's what she would do. "That there's a crisis at home and I need to give notice today."

"When do you want to tell him?"

"Soon. Immediately." Fresh tears filled her eyes. "He'll be upset."

"It'll be all right. I'll smooth things over with Craig. Don't worry about that."

"Thank you," she choked.

"It's going to be okay, Meg."

She nodded, squeezing his hands as if her life depended on it. "I'm going to miss you, though. So much."

He kissed the top of her head. "I'll miss you, too, baby."

Tears rained down on her skirt. "Do you hate me?"

"Could never hate you. Love you too much, Mary Margaret."

Craig called her into his office an hour later, just a little bit after she'd turned in her letter of resignation. His door was open and she stepped in. "You wanted to see me, Craig?"

"Yes. Sit, please."

Meg turned to find a chair and that's when she discovered Chad seated just behind her. Her eyes met his for a split second and she nearly started crying again, and it took considerable effort to clamp down on her emotions so that she could sit and face Craig calmly.

"I got your letter," Craig said once she was seated. "I have to say I'm surprised, and disappointed. You've been a big part of our operations, Meg."

Meg could feel Chad's gaze on her and she stared straight ahead, telling herself that soon she'd be out of here, soon she'd be gone, and once she was in her car, she could cry. But not here. Not now. Now she had to keep it together, be professional. "My mom's not well," she said unsteadily. "Her cancer's returned. I need to be available to help her."

"I really don't want to lose you, Meg. Would it help if you worked from home once or twice a week? Or would you want to cut your hours back and work part-time?"

Meg swallowed hard to hold back the rush of emotion. She would miss the winery. She'd loved working here, loved working with Craig and Chad, but she didn't think she could ever be around Chad without wanting him. Without remembering how he felt and tasted and kissed. And how when he kissed her, she felt so unbelievably beautiful. "Maybe one day down the road, I could think about work, but I can't now."

"I'm sorry to hear about your mom," Craig answered.

She nodded, eyes burning. "I'm sorry to leave on such short notice. I realize it puts you in a difficult position."

"Chad has said he's got it covered. Don't worry about us. Take care of you."

She nodded again as a lump filled her throat. "I've loved working here, Craig. I'm going to miss it. You." She heard Chad shift in his chair and she almost broke down. "Chad. Jennifer. All of you."

"If you ever want to come back," Craig said, "you always have a home here with us."

Meg almost began crying then. She turned her head away, struggling to keep control. "Thank you."

He stood up, held his arms open. "Can I give you a hug good-bye?"

She nodded, and hugged him, and then stepped out of the office before either of them could see her cry.

Meg spent the next couple hours packing her things, sorting through files, copying folders and e-mails to Jennifer's computer, organizing notes for Jennifer and Chad, and then she was done.

Chad wasn't around when she was ready to go. She sent him a text letting him know she was leaving but didn't get a response, and so after hugging Jennifer, she carried her box of things out to her Lexus, stashed it in the back, and was just about to get in the car when Chad's voice stopped her.

"Meg."

She turned around, spotted him walking across the parking lot from the wine shop. "Hey."

"You're leaving," he said, frustration sharpening his voice. "Just like that?"

"I sent you a text."

"A text is no way to say good-bye."

Meg slowly closed the car door, the keys still clutched in her hand. "I don't want to say good-bye."

He stopped several feet from her. His brow was creased, his lips compressed. "I don't understand this. Not any of this. Two days ago we were talking about getting a place together and now you're leaving here, telling me it's over."

"It was a fantasy, Chad."

"Don't ever say that again. Maybe to you it was, but not to me. Not ever to me."

"I told you in the beginning that I wouldn't divorce Jack. I told you—"

"You did. I should have listened. Would have saved me a hell of a lot of heartache."

Her chest squeezed, aching. "I didn't want to hurt you. Why would I want to hurt you? You've been nothing but kind to me—"

"Kind? Is that all I was to you?"

She shook her head, overwhelmed by his anger and hurt and pain. This had all gone so terribly wrong. "No," she answered, going to him, and standing close to him, soaking up his warmth one last time. "But it was your kindness that won me over. It was your kindness that made me yours. Too many of us women don't get enough kindness, so you must see that your kindness meant everything to me."

He smoothed her hair back from her face. "Your man should always be kind to you."

She loved the feel of his hand against her face, his fingertips lightly caressing. Even now he made her feel beautiful. "I wish things were different," she whispered. "I wish you could be that man."

"I wish that, too."

Meg pressed herself against him, held tightly on to him. She didn't care who saw. Didn't care what anyone thought. It would be so hard—impossible?—to let him go. It would be so hard to forget how he made her feel. "I love you," she whispered.

"I love you, too, baby."

She didn't know who stepped away first—him or her—but she supposed it didn't matter. They couldn't stand there in the parking lot hanging on to each other forever. She was Meg Roberts, a former employee. He was Chad Hallahan, the owner. It was time for her to go. Time for both of them to move on with their lives.

"Call me anytime," he said, reaching out to wipe away the tears from beneath her eyes. "I'll always be here for you."

She caught his hand in hers, kissed it, feeling the wetness of her tears on his skin. "Don't say that."

"Why not?"

"Because you can't give me those options. You can't leave the door open for me. I'm not that strong, not when it comes to you."

His eyes narrowed, expression darkening. "So what do you want me to do? Refuse your calls? Block your number?"

"Yes." She tried to smile but failed. "Don't take my calls. Don't answer my texts. Don't let me come running back to you when I'm lonely. You deserve better than that, Chad. And Jack does, too."

And then with a last quick kiss on his cheek, she slid behind the steering wheel and drove away.

It was brutal leaving. Brutal watching Chad fade in the rearview mirror. Driving away from Chad and the winery made her heart feel as if it was breaking. After almost five years at Dark Horse, she was finished. Done. Gone.

Meg told Jack economic issues at work meant they were downsizing at the winery. He didn't question her. The economy was bad everywhere, especially in Napa.

By the end of the week the kids were out of school for the summer, baseball was over for the year, and Tessa had a week break before the summer session of dance started.

Gabi, though, still had her weekly riding lesson, and on Saturday morning Meg drove her to the stables. While Gabi ran in to saddle her pony, Meg sat in the car.

Was it just a week ago that Meg was talking to Sarah about the text she found on Boone's phone? Was it just a week ago that Meg was still seeing Chad?

Hard to believe only seven days had passed. It seemed so much longer. Meg felt so much older.

Older and broken.

And now the Fourth of July was just a little over two weeks away and Sarah would soon be coming out with the kids. Meg shot her sister a quick text asking her what day she'd be flying in with the kids. She was really looking forward to all of them being at the beach house this summer. Meg hadn't seen Ella and Brennan in a long time, and she worried if she didn't see them soon, her niece and nephew would grow up without knowing how much Aunt Meg loved them.

There were also purely selfish reasons for wanting to head to the coast. Meg needed out of Santa Rosa for a while. Santa Rosa was too close to Napa. And Chad was in Napa. And Meg still wanted Chad.

Meg climbed out of the car, shut the door behind her, wondering how she could miss Chad so much. She'd known that she'd cared about him, but hadn't thought it had been love. Now she was sure it was love. She thought she'd do just about anything to see him. But that would be a mistake. If she saw him, she'd want to kiss him. Want to love him. Want him to love her. Because right now she felt so empty and hollow she might as well be dead.

Standing outside the ring, Meg watched Gabi's lesson. Her phone suddenly vibrated. Her heart jumped. What if it was Chad?

She dug her phone out of her purse. It wasn't Chad. It was Jack. Her heart fell, a wild free fall that jangled her nerves, made her twitchy, teary. If only she could see Chad, just for a little bit, she knew she'd feel better.

Quickly suppressing her emotions, Meg took Jack's call. He was calling to ask her to pick up toner for the printer at home. She agreed. They said good-bye and Meg hung up, eyes burning, throat aching.

Now that she'd thought about Chad, all she wanted was to hear his voice. Get a text. Just a little contact to make her feel okay.

She didn't feel okay. She was so lonely.

Blinking back tears, Meg watched Gabi in the ring in yet another longeing exercise. Gabi's hands were no longer on her hips but extended as she slowly rotated to the right, and left, forcing her to be totally dependent on her legs for balance and control.

She was doing great until she panicked and her hands went flying for the pommel.

"Gabriela!" her instructor reprimanded swiftly.

"I was going to fall off!" Gabi exclaimed, still clutching the pommel.

"Not if you stay focused! Now let's try again."

Meg buried her phone in her purse, thinking that the instructor was right. Gabi wasn't the only one who had to stay focused. Meg did, too. Because if she didn't, she'd fall, get hurt, make everything worse.

Fifteen

Removing Chad from her life was supposed to fix it. It was supposed to allow her to heal it. Instead Meg discovered she couldn't function without him.

He was company and friendship, sex and excitement, touch, comfort, and pleasure. Without him, there was no pleasure.

Without him, she didn't know what she was doing.

And so two weeks after walking away from the winery and Chad, Meg called him. She didn't know if he'd pick up. She'd told him not to take her calls. She'd told him to pretend she didn't exist. But when she phoned him, he answered right away.

"Chad, I can't do this. I'm losing it. I have to see you." Her voice cracked, broke. "Please meet me."

"You made me promise—"

"I know. But I'm losing it. I can't function. Can't get out of bed. Can't stop crying." She drew a swift breath. "I stopped seeing you so I could focus and take care of my family, but not seeing you is even worse."

"This isn't good, baby."

"I know." Her voice broke and she covered her face with her hand. "I know."

He was silent for several seconds, as if trying to make a decision. "When are you free?" he asked.

"Now. Anytime. Whenever you can see me."

"What about the kids?"

"I'll make arrangements."

"Where do you want to meet?"

"Anywhere."

"How about two at Petaluma Coffee and Tea Company on Second Street in Petaluma?"

Meg glanced at her watch. It was just noon now. It would take her almost a half hour to drive there. But that still gave her time to pull herself together. Make herself look presentable. Beautiful. She needed to be beautiful for Chad, even if it was just for a few minutes. "I'll see you there," she said.

But in the shower Meg cried again, feeling like a drug addict about to get a fix. Because just like an addict, there was no real relief. The "fix" of seeing Chad would be temporary. She would have thirty minutes, maybe an hour with him, but then she'd be saying good-bye again. Walking away from him again. This time forever.

Meg's pulse quickened when she spotted Chad's gray Jaguar in the coffeehouse parking lot. It jumped again when she entered the coffeehouse and saw him at one of the tables in the corner. Meg went directly to his table, drinking him in as if she were desperate for water. He looked good. Tan, fit, handsome as always. "Hi," she said nervously, breathlessly, as she sat down in the chair opposite his.

He smiled at her, but it was a different smile. It was distant, reserved. He was distant and reserved. "Not doing so good?" he said as she sat down.

She shook her head, tried to smile, but she felt his distance, and coolness, and understood it. She'd walked away from him. She'd chosen her family over him. He had to be hurt, had to feel rejected. And now she was here, seeing him, but just for a bit. She was a tease. He should hate her.

"I miss you," she said simply.

His blue gaze met hers and held. "I've missed you, too," he answered, but there was no smile in his eyes, no encouraging warmth.

She rubbed her hands together beneath the table. "Everything okay at the winery?"

"Yes."

"Have you found a new PR person?"

"Promoted Jennifer and have hired a new receptionist."

"That's good," Meg replied, nodding, smiling, feeling stupid for calling Chad and asking him to meet her. What did she think would happen here? How did she think this would go? "Craig okay?"

"Yes. Everything's fine, Meg. We're working and life at the winery is continuing on. Nothing's really changed, except for the fact that you're no longer part of it."

She realized belatedly she'd come here for purely selfish reasons. She'd come hoping Chad would do what he always did—turn on his charm and warmth and comfort her. Make her feel good. That's what their relationship had always been about. Her. What she wanted, needed. If she were honest, she'd admit that it had never been about him.

Chad seemed to be thinking the same thing. "You were never going to leave Jack, were you?"

She shook her head. "No. I couldn't. I can't. Not with the kids."

"If you didn't have the kids?"

"It'd be different. But I do have the kids. And they need their dad."

"If you and Jack weren't together, they'd still have their dad."

"Yes, but not in the same house. And I think kids need their parents together, raising them together."

Chad said nothing for a long time and then he smiled crookedly. "I could have almost any woman in the world, but I have to fall for you."

"I never understood that either."

He laughed briefly, shook his head. "I do miss you, baby, but am happy if you're happy. Are you happy?"

She looked into his eyes, glad to find that some of the ice had thawed. "It's hard getting over you."

"You will. Just like I'll get over you. Step-by-step. Day by day. That's how these things work."

He walked her to her car, gave her a hug, and then a brief, bittersweet kiss good-bye. His lips felt so good. He smelled so good. He was warm and real and she'd miss him. Terribly.

"Take care of yourself, Mary Margaret."

She blinked back tears. "You, too, Chad Hallahan."

Jack was waiting for her when she got home. He was never home early. And if he came home early, he called her, let her know he was on the way. But today he was there and the kids weren't.

And Meg knew immediately that something was wrong. She knew it by the way he just looked at her when she entered the kitchen, his expression closed, his gaze narrow, looking at her as if she were someone else.

"Jack?" she said uncertainly, setting her purse and keys on the island counter.

"Where were you?" he asked quietly, flatly, and it wasn't an innocent question. She knew from his voice that something had happened.

"Out. Running errands."

He smiled but it was cold, very, very cold. "Having coffee?"

Her heart jumped and her fingers curled around the edge of the marble counter. He knew, she thought, panic surging through her. He knew. "Yes."

"With who?"

"Why?" she bluffed, hoping against hope she got it wrong. Hoping against hope this was about something else.

"Barbara Rankin saw you at the Petaluma Coffee Company."

Ah. So he did know. Barbara had worked as a bookkeeper for Jack years ago when they first moved to Petaluma, and she was about as moral and righteous as they came.

Meg pushed her purse toward the middle of the counter, trying to think of something to say, anything, but nothing came to mind. "She called you," she said, amazed she could sound so calm when she could hardly breathe.

"Yes."

"What did she say?"

"She wondered if I knew that my wife was having an affair."

Meg blanched, pulled out a stool at the island, and sat down heavily. "She said that?"

"No. She wondered if I knew that my wife was kissing a man in the parking lot, but I can put two and two together. If you're kissing a man in a parking lot, you're probably having an affair." He hesitated, his dark gaze hard. "I wondered. Every now and then something seemed off . . . you'd smell different, look different, acted different . . . and I wondered. But every time I dismissed that little voice of doubt, telling myself that Meg wouldn't cheat. Meg wasn't like that."

Meg drew a slow breath, dizzy, dazed. She hadn't seen this coming. She should have.

"Who is he, Meg?"

"What are you going to do?"

"I just want to know who my wife is fucking while I'm at work."

Her eyes stung, watered. "I'm not fucking anyone."

"You didn't ever sleep with him? Today was just an innocent kiss at a Petaluma coffeehouse?" He walked toward her, leaned on the counter, forced her to make eye contact. "Who is he? I want his name. You owe me that much, Meg."

She closed her eyes, icy cold and trembling now from head to foot. "Chad."

"Chad Hallahan?"

She nodded once.

"So Tessa was right."

Meg stiffened, looked at him, and he nodded. "Yes," he said, "Tessa told me you'd gotten a strange text from Chad, a text that was overly personal. She was upset and came to me. But I told her it was nothing. That she didn't need to worry. That her mother was honest to a fault." He swore softly, walked away from her to stand at the sink. "I was wrong. Completely wrong about you. Seventeen years of marriage and I realize I don't even know you."

Meg hung her head.

"Who are you?" he asked softly.

She didn't answer, couldn't.

"Who are you?" he repeated.

She struggled to speak. "I don't know."

"Who does this? *You?*"

"No."

"But you did. You, of all people, Meg."

"I'm sorry. I . . . don't know what happened." He said nothing and she swallowed hard, around the lump in her throat. "I guess I needed more—"

"Then you ask me. You tell me you need more, instead of some guy you work with."

Meg bowed her head, knowing he was right, knowing she deserved his anger.

"How long has this been going on, Meg?"

"Not long."

"How long? Days, weeks, months, years?"

"Weeks." He just looked at her and she laced her fingers together. "We saw each other for a couple weeks, and then I ended it."

"When? Today?"

"No. Two weeks ago. That's why I left the winery. Didn't think we should work together anymore."

"So what was today?"

"I—" She looked at him, hurting, scared, feeling completely naked and broken. "I needed to see him. Talk to him. Closure."

"Closure."

"I'm sorry."

He made a hoarse sound. "Me, too."

He asked her to move out. Actually, he told her to move out, told her he wanted her gone before the kids came home. Dazed, drowning in guilt and heartbreak, Meg couldn't think, couldn't defend herself, couldn't do anything but gather a few things from her closet, and then get a hairbrush and toothbrush and toothpaste from the bathroom before Jack escorted her down the stairs to the garage.

Somehow the kids, who'd been gone all afternoon, had returned. Linnea was somewhere in the background, but the kids were on the stairs.

As Jack marched her past them, Meg felt as if she were being walked to her execution.

"What's happening?" Tessa cried.

"Mom's leaving," Jack said, his hand on Meg's elbow as if she'd try to make a run for it.

Meg could hardly see through the tears. She didn't even have her things in a suitcase but bundled beneath her arm.

"Where is she going?" JJ demanded.

"Ask her," Jack retorted.

Meg shook her head, unable to speak. Where was she going?
What was happening?

"Mom," Tessa cried, racing down the stairs after her parents.
"Where are you going?"

"Meg, you're upsetting the kids," Jack said as they headed for
the kitchen. "Tell them. Tell them so they understand."

But she said nothing. What could she say? She hadn't just betrayed Jack, she'd betrayed her family and herself and everything
she held dear.

Jack opened the mudroom door that led to the garage and
pushed Meg through it.

As the door shut behind her, she heard him say, "Your mom has
a boyfriend and she's going to go live with him now."

Meg was crying as she backed her car out of the garage and
clipped the mirror on the driver side. She struggled to correct
her angle and ended up ripping the mirror off completely.

Shit! Shit, shit, shit.

She hadn't had an accident in years. Didn't make these kinds of
mistakes. Wasn't normally reckless, but nothing was normal now.

Blinking away tears, she reached for her phone and called Kit
but went straight to voice mail. She tried again a few minutes later.
Same thing. Meg left a message this time. "I need you to call me,
Kit. Please."

She hung up and tried to focus on her driving as she got on
the freeway because she was shaking so much. She drove to her
parents' house in San Francisco, crying off and on, sometimes
hysterically.

"Can I stay here for a few days?" Meg choked, when Mom
opened the door.

Marilyn looked closely into her swollen face and nodded, es-
corting Meg to what had once been Tommy's bedroom on the third

floor without asking any questions. Tommy's room had a balcony and a private bathroom and had been converted into a guest room with a queen-size bed.

"Would you like some water or a cup of tea?" Marilyn asked as Meg set her bundle of clothes, toothbrush, and hairbrush on the bed.

Meg sat down next to her bundle and then lay down. She shook her head.

Marilyn stood silently next to the bed, her brown gaze troubled. "It must have been a pretty bad fight," she said at last. "You've never come home before."

Meg closed her eyes and balled her hands against her chest, trying to keep the pain in. It was so huge and sharp and overwhelming that she wasn't sure she'd survive it.

"Does he know where you are?" Marilyn asked, her voice quiet.

Meg slowly shook her head.

"He has the kids?" her mom persisted.

Meg nodded once.

"Meg, are the kids okay—"

"He kicked me out, Mom." Meg opened her eyes, looked at her mother, no expression in her face. She felt dead. Absolutely destroyed. "Threw me out in front of the kids."

Marilyn's lips parted, but before she could speak, Meg wearily added, "I had an affair. He found out."

For the rest of the day Meg stayed in Tommy's old bedroom. She closed the wooden shutters, darkening the room, and climbed into bed, only leaving it to use the bathroom. Her mom knocked on the bedroom door at six, letting Meg know dinner was ready. Meg answered she wasn't hungry and would prefer to sleep, and her mom walked away.

A few minutes later her father opened the door and turned on the overhead light. "Your mother called you to dinner, Mary

Margaret." His voice boomed as if he was in the firehouse issuing orders. "Get out of bed and come down and eat."

Meg covered her face with her arm. "Dad," she protested.

"Your mother worked hard to make a nice meal. Don't keep her waiting." He walked out.

Meg sat up and watched him go. He was pissed off. He knew about her affair. Groaning, she climbed from bed and pulled herself together, aware that dinner would be miserable.

She could smell the curry and spices wafting from the kitchen and knew Mom had made one of her famous dinners. Five years ago, after Mom's first bout of breast cancer, she'd celebrated beating cancer by taking Thai cooking lessons in Berkeley. She'd loved her lessons and had made meal after meal of chicken pad thai, *tom yum gai,* fish coconut curry, coconut lime prawns, *satay* and cucumber salad, and had become impressively proficient.

Food was the last thing Meg wanted, though, and as she headed downstairs she wondered what the kids were doing right now, and what Jack was giving them for dinner. She wanted to talk to them, but didn't know what to say. It had been such a horrific scene at the house this afternoon.

Meg took her place at the dining room table. Both her parents were already seated. The atmosphere wasn't easy. Meg wished she hadn't come here. Wished she'd gotten hold of Kit and gone to her house instead.

Meg bowed her head as Dad said the blessing but heard none of the words, just sound. Afterward Mom passed rice and noodles and her clay-pot ginger chicken and Meg took a spoonful of each, but the fragrant spices on the ginger chicken made her stomach rise up in revolt. It killed her that the kids knew she'd had an affair, and she fought tears, her throat aching, chest burning, body heavy with shame. How could she have done it? What had she been thinking?

Blinking hard, Meg focused on her plate, on pushing the grains of rice around, listening to the clink of everyone's cutlery against the dinner plates. Any moment her father would say something. Any moment—

"Mom said you had an affair," he said bluntly, breaking the silence.

She looked up at him, swallowing with difficulty, realizing there would be no sympathy card here. Marriage was sacred. She couldn't imagine her father ever cheating on her mom for any reason. "Yes."

He was silent and she felt the full weight of his disapproval. It was almost like being eighteen again and seeing her dad standing dripping wet on the pool deck.

"I thought we raised you better than that," he said lowly, flatly, and fresh shame rushed through her. Shame and a horrifying sense of failure. She'd fucked up bad. Again.

Meg pressed her knees tightly together, her shoulders hunching. "I'm sorry."

"Why would you do that to Jack? He's a good man. A good husband."

Her eyes stung. She bit the inside of her lip.

"I asked you a question, Mary Margaret."

"I don't know, Dad." Her voice was but a whisper of sound. She wanted to die in that minute. Felt like the worst person alive.

"Did he sleep with someone else?"

"No."

"Was he treating you badly?"

She shook her head. "No."

"Then what?"

She looked away as a tear fell. "I just got caught up in . . . wanting . . . more." Her father said nothing and she looked at him, and then her mother. "I just felt empty and needed more."

Marilyn's eyes were dark, the brown irises shadowed, but she didn't look angry. She looked sad. "More what, Meg?"

"Love. Affection. Attention." Meg knew it sounded so shallow and pathetic when said like that. But it was true. It's what she'd felt.

It's what she felt now. Jack hadn't even given her a chance to explain. He'd just hustled her out of the house. Throwing her out in front of their children. He could have done it in a way that would have been less painful for the kids. Less painful for all of them.

"Are you having a midlife crisis?" Tommy Sr. demanded, dragging her attention back to him.

She looked at her dad, at his cool blue gaze and thin, unsmiling mouth. "I don't know. Maybe. I just know I screwed up. Bad."

Back in bed after doing the dinner dishes, she could hear her father's voice and her mother's muted response. They were talking about her. Discussing her. She was sure it wasn't good. She was glad she couldn't hear. She didn't want to hear. Didn't want to think or feel anything more tonight.

The next morning Meg was woken by her father opening the blinds in the bedroom. Blinking at the sting of light, she covered her face with her arm.

"Mary Margaret, you can't lie in bed all day. You have a family and a job—"

"I don't have a job," Meg interrupted, sitting up and pushing heavy tangled hair from her face.

"What happened to your job?"

"I quit. Two weeks ago." She couldn't look her dad in the eye. He didn't quit anything, but he didn't question her on why, since he'd probably figured that part out.

He folded his arms across his big chest and looked at her through narrowed eyes. "So who is taking care of the family now?"

She drew her knees up to her chest. "Jack, I guess."

"You guess?"

She bit her lip and he sighed, frustrated. "Well, you can't hide here, Meg. You need to go home and fix this. You're a mom, and a wife, and your family comes first. Do you understand?"

She squeezed her eyes closed and nodded her head.

"Your mom's made you coffee and cinnamon toast. Come eat something and then head home."

Her mom smiled at her as Meg entered the kitchen. Marilyn was sitting at one of the counter stools sipping tea. "I remember how much you liked cinnamon toast when you were a little girl," she said. "Whenever you were sick or sad, I'd make it for you."

Hot tears filled Meg's eyes and she had to turn away and press a knuckled fist to her mouth to keep from crying out loud.

"Don't cry, my big girl." Marilyn's voice was patient, quiet. "Come sit down next to me."

Meg took the stool next to her mother's and wiped away tears with the back of her hand. "Why are you being so nice to me?"

"Because I love you."

"You're not disappointed in me?"

"Of course I'm disappointed, Meg. Your father and I are both disappointed. We might have expected this from one of your sisters, but not from you. And we can't help worrying about Jack. We love Jack. He's been part of this family for seventeen years now and is like a son to us. But you're our daughter and you'll always be our daughter."

"Even when I screw up bad?"

"Even then."

Meg added milk and sweetener to her coffee and stirred it. "I have to call him. Try to apologize."

"You do."

"He's not going to be happy."

"No, he won't be."

Meg nibbled on her toast and sipped her coffee, grateful for her parents, but most of all for her mom, who was a rock. She really was the heart and soul of the family. And the last thing she needed was to worry about Meg. Mom had enough on her plate as it was. "I love you, Mom."

"I love you, too, Meg. And I know you can make things right. If anyone can fix this, it's you."

Meg left her childhood home on Fifth Avenue with her little bundle after giving her mom a hug and kiss good-bye. It was a cold, damp, foggy morning, and she shivered as she walked down the street to her car. She'd left home without a jacket and one needed a jacket for summers in San Francisco.

Reaching her car, Meg discovered a parking ticket on the window. Today was street-cleaning day and she should have moved her car at eight. Shit, she thought, grabbing the ticket and stuffing it and her things into the backseat of her Lexus.

Her iPhone was also dead, since she'd left the charger at home and her car charger was nowhere to be found.

Meg drove to Chestnut Street, where she bought another coffee, a strong latte, and a new charger for her car and house. She sat with her coffee in her car, the morning fog cloaking the street, letting her phone charge.

After a few minutes, she touched Jack's number on her favorites list. Her stomach hurt, sharp with nerves. She waited for him to answer. But the phone rang four times before going to voice mail. She almost never went to Jack's voice mail, so she knew it was deliberate.

Meg called him again. And again she went to voice mail. This time on the second ring.

Heart heavy, she sent him a text. *I am so sorry. Please forgive me.*

He answered with a text. *I do not want to talk to you. Do not call me again.*

I understand you're mad, she replied. *And I understand you don't want to see me, but I need to see the kids.*

The kids don't want to see you. They know what you did.

Meg read the text over and over again. Her eyes filled with tears. *That might be true,* she texted back, *but I am still their mom.*

You should have thought of that before you slept with Chad.

Her hands shook. Her heart hammered sickeningly hard as she texted, *Do I need to get a lawyer?*

Jack replied, *I need time to figure out what I want to do.*

He didn't know what he wanted to do. That was both good and bad. It also put the ball firmly in his court.

Meg sat in her car for another few minutes staring out the window at the soupy fog, not sure what to do or where to go. She called Kit. Went to Kit's voice mail. Then she hung up and checked her messages and discovered a voice mail from Kit. She was calling from Miami. She'd flown with Polly on Tuesday to see the June 29 U2 concert at Land Shark Stadium since they'd missed the Oakland show due to high school graduation ceremonies. Kit and Polly were going to meet Sarah and the kids and then fly back with them for Fourth of July in Capitola. After the Fourth Sarah, Ella, and Brennan would be joining Meg and her family in Santa Rosa.

Meg's stomach cramped. It crossed her mind that Sarah and the kids wouldn't be coming to Santa Rosa now. Not unless she could patch things up with Jack fast.

Meg shot Jack another text. *I love you. I do. And I made a terrible mistake. Forgive me. Please.*

He didn't respond. She waited five minutes. Ten. And then realized no text would be coming. Finally she started the car and headed for the only other place she could think to go. Capitola.

Sixteen

The first couple days in Capitola Meg stayed in bed all day, either crying or sleeping, sometimes both. It was easy staying in bed, too, with the June gloom wrapping everything in misty gray and her heart broken. She had no one to blame but herself. No one to rage against either. There were no excuses. She knew right from wrong. She'd known better.

And knowing that she knew better made her cry harder. She understood Jack's anger and shame. Of course he was disappointed in her. She was disappointed in herself, too.

But Meg wasn't the type to take to bed and stay there. She was too practical, too disciplined. On her third morning in Capitola the sun broke through the clouds and the brisk breeze chased away any lingering tendrils of fog, and Meg felt foolish lying in bed with the sun shining and the beach just beyond her door.

After showering and dressing, she put on a baseball cap and sunglasses to hide her puffy eyes and headed out for coffee. The barista at Mr. Toots remembered her and asked about the family.

Meg suppressed a pang and answered with a smile that everyone was doing well.

Coffee in hand, she headed outside and took a seat on the wall overlooking the pale sand, numbly sipping her coffee as teenagers started a game of beach volleyball in front of her while young children built sand castles at the water's edge, their mothers standing protectively nearby. Everything this morning looked normal and familiar. The air smelled of salt and fruity-sweet sunscreen, and hummed with sound. The sounds were heartbreakingly familiar— the crashing surf, the harsh squawking of seagulls, the high-pitched squeals of children playing.

How could everything be so normal when her life had been turned inside out?

And why had she turned her life inside out?

What in God's name had prompted her to do it?

She had everything any woman could want—a lovely home, a smart, successful husband, three beautiful, healthy children, a thriving career. How could she be dissatisfied with that? It was everything . . . wasn't it?

But if it was everything, and she had everything, why had she reached for Chad? What had she wanted from Chad? What had she imagined he could give her?

Someone on the beach shouted "heads up," and then a volleyball slammed into the side of Meg's head. She jerked, yelped, spilling hot coffee on her thigh. One of the teenage boys ran up to get the ball. He apologized for the accident and she forced a smile. "It's okay," she said, rubbing at her head, thinking she felt far from okay. But then, it had been a long, long time since she felt okay. If she were honest, it had been years since she felt okay.

God forgive her, but underneath the smiles and the good job and the great family, she was tired. Desperately tired. Tired to the point of breaking. In the last few years the exhaustion had grown, rising up like a specter to knock on her door. No one knew, she hadn't told even Kit, but in the past year she'd begun to question her entire existence. Why was she even here? What was life? Was she even necessary?

Maybe all women had these thoughts. Maybe all women felt tired. But the thoughts confused her. Good women weren't supposed to have doubts. Good women were supposed to be strong and selfless. Instead Meg felt needy and afraid. What if there was no reward for all the hard work? What if life was just one sacrifice after another?

Meg realized now that she knew the answer to those questions. She just hadn't liked the answer.

I t was going to be a long summer if Jack didn't let her see the kids more often, Meg thought, sitting on the porch of the beach house in Capitola, legs stretched out in front of her as she impatiently waited for them to arrive.

It had been twenty-two days since Jack kicked her out of the house and she'd only seen them once—for two days—in the past month, and that was eleven days ago when she drove up to Santa Rosa to stay at the house for two days while Jack was in Virginia on business.

Jack hadn't wanted her to stay at their big shingle house, had booked Linnea to stay with the kids, but at the last second Linnea couldn't stay, and he couldn't find a replacement for her, so he reluctantly called Meg and told her she could come for the weekend, but she'd have to sleep at a hotel, not at the house. Meg pointed out to him that this defeated the purpose of her staying with the kids, so he relented on the condition that she not sleep in the master bedroom because it wasn't her room anymore and she wasn't welcome there.

It'd been painful being back in the house as a "guest." The kids were aloof, as if she were a stranger instead of their mother. She'd tried to ask them about their summer camps, the trip to Virginia, but they gave her brusque one-syllable answers. Fine, fine, everything was fine.

Meg had expected them to be upset, but had imagined they'd have questions, or want to vent. The silence, hostility, and reserve were harder. She wasn't sure how to reach them, and knew time was short. She only had the two days. Only two days to try to begin fixing things before she'd be gone again. Shut out once more.

And so she focused on being cheerful, calm, and patient even when they acted aloof and insolent. Meg thought she was handling their attitude and anger well. Thought she was doing well. And then she went upstairs in the afternoon to her room, to put on her swimsuit to swim with the kids, and discovered her side of the closet empty. Her dresser drawers had been emptied. Her drawers and cabinet in the master bath were empty, too.

Everything that belonged to her—even the photos of her holding the babies as newborns—had disappeared. Everything she owned was gone. Jack had erased her from their room. And then she went through the house, looking for some sign of her, and there was nothing to be found.

She returned upstairs, and cracked. Completely broke down. And once she started crying, she couldn't stop.

Meg rarely cried in front of the kids, and Tessa panicked when she saw her mother prostrate on the master bedroom floor. She called Aunt Kit, telling her that Mom was having a nervous breakdown. Good Kit jumped in her car and raced up to Santa Rosa to play Mary Poppins and make everything all right.

And Kit had done a good job. She shoved Meg into the shower, told her to pull herself together, and then drove the kids to a movie, handed them a twenty-dollar bill for snacks, and told them to call her when it was over. And then she was back at the house, dragging Meg with her wet hair and puffy face out to the pool to get some sun.

Kit, the rare redhead who could tan, plopped down on the side of the pool with her feet in the water. Meg followed more slowly, carrying a tray with two glasses and sliced lemons.

Meg didn't know why she'd brought the glasses out on a silver tray. Didn't know why she'd brought a plate of sliced lemons either. Apparently some part of her was screaming for civility, so there they were, having iced tea by the pool in Meg's best Waterford crystal glasses.

"I can't believe you actually did it, Mags," Kit said, breaking the silence as Meg took a seat on the side of the pool next to her. "I know you were tempted . . . but doing it?"

"I know."

"It's something Brianna would do. Not you."

Meg made a hoarse sound. Mom and Dad had said pretty much the same thing. "Yeah," she said huskily, putting her feet in the pool. The water was warm, but not as warm as her shower. She'd made that scalding hot. Boiled the tears and anguish away.

"I wish you'd called me. Talked to me. Given me a chance to talk some sense into you."

"Me, too." Meg blinked hard and stared at her toes in the water. She needed a pedicure. Needed to shave her legs. Needed serious help. "I don't know why I did it, Kit. It wasn't planned. It wasn't what I even wanted. It just . . . happened."

Kit drew her mustard-yellow skirt higher on her thighs and flexed her feet, the muscles in her quads tightening. She'd joined a gym in early June, had started working out every day on her way home from school, and had dropped almost ten pounds. She was rather impressed with her newly hard body. "But that's not who you are," she said after a moment of watching her quads and calves contract. "Nothing happens to you by chance. You plan everything."

Meg sighed and drew her damp hair off her shoulders into a pile on her head. "I've had this conversation with myself a thousand times. I honestly don't know why I fell for Chad. I don't know what I was thinking."

Kit shot her a swift side glance. "I know why you feel for him. He's insanely good-looking. I've seen his chest. The man has abs."

Meg's insides did a painful little flip at the mention of Chad's body. He did have an amazing body, and he made her feel amazing with that body. But he and that body also destroyed her, and her world. "But that wasn't it. He's always been good-looking and I didn't care before."

"What changed?"

Meg made a soft strangled sound as she lifted her foot and watched the water drip off. "I wish I knew."

"You really don't?"

"No, I do. I was lonely. Thought I needed attention."

"And you didn't?"

Meg laughed hollowly and looked past the sparkling blue pool to the green-and-gold hill rising up behind the house. She lived in paradise, and she, like Eve, had ruined it. All for the taste of something forbidden. Something that had promised to be delicious.

And sin was delicious. But of course there were consequences.

Even if Jack hadn't found out about the affair, there would still be consequences. Like the damage to her relationship. The damage to her heart. The damage to her self-respect.

"No," she said quietly, "I did. I needed something . . . but it shouldn't have been from him."

Kit took a sip from her tea and the ice clinked together. "Now what?"

Meg glanced around her. This was her home but not her home. Her pool but not her pool. Her life but not her life. It was crazy. She felt crazy. "I'm hoping Jack will forgive me. Hoping he'll calm down and talk to me. But he isn't talking to me yet. So I'm trying to be patient. Trying not to pressure him. Just giving him time to sort out his thoughts and feelings."

"Has he hired a lawyer?"

"I hope not. I don't want to get divorced."

"But what would he do? His parents went through a bitter divorce. I remember talking to him once about it."

Meg cringed. Jack had been terribly scarred by his parents' divorce. She could only imagine the hell he was going through now. "Knowing Jack, he's probably consulted a lawyer. He'd be stupid not to."

"Why do you say that?"

"We have a lot of assets now. He's been quite successful. So I think he'd be proactive. Do what he could to make sure I didn't destroy him financially like his mom did to his dad."

"Did she really?"

Meg shrugged. "It's what Jack told me. But who knows what really happened. Who knows what will happen now."

"You're so calm, Meg."

Meg shot her a mocking glance. "I wasn't earlier. Remember?"

Kit grimaced. "That's true. You looked like you were in need of Nurse Ratched."

Meg was still exhausted from crying so hard. "I'm all cried out. For now."

"It's hard being back?"

"First time back in two weeks. And then I return and all my stuff is gone. Clothes. Jewelry. Makeup. Everything."

"I doubt Jack got rid of any of it. He probably just boxed everything up and put it in the attic or the garage for storage." Kit reached into the pool with one hand, cupped her fingers together to catch the water in her palm. For several moments she just played with the water, cupping it, shaking it. "So has he really not talked to you at all?"

Meg looked at the water shimmering in Kit's hand. "No. Not once since he found out. We just e-mail and text . . . well, I e-mail and text him, but he generally doesn't answer."

Kit spread her fingers open and the water fell through. "That's how Richard was when it ended between us. He just cut the cord and moved on. Weird."

"But Jack can't just move on. We have the kids. We have to try to make it work for them."

"I would hope so, but Jack's a Taurus. And Tauruses are bulls. Hardheaded. Stubborn. Placid until pissed off and then watch out."

That was Jack to a tee, Meg thought. "He can hold a grudge."

"And he probably will." Kit's expression was sympathetic. "So it's up to you now to keep it together. Be strong. Get your family through this."

"I can do that." Because she'd have to do it. Meg had no other choice. Divorce wasn't an option.

Silence fell, and the sun shone hot, bright. Heat shimmered around them and Kit lay back on the pool deck, covered her face with her hands, shielding her eyes from the sun's glare. "I finally heard from Richard," she said casually, conversationally, as if it wasn't big news. "He called me when I was in Miami. Said he wants to see me."

"*What?*"

"I told him I'd think about it."

Meg turned to face Kit. "You didn't!"

Kit uncovered one eye and smiled crookedly. "I did. After waiting five days before calling him back. Wasn't going to be too anxious. He waited two months after breaking up with me to call me. He could wait five days to find out if I'd see him." She looked quite satisfied with herself. "Felt good making him wait, too."

"So are you going to see him?"

"We're supposed to go out tonight."

"Tonight? And you're here?"

Kit shrugged. "So I have to cancel. No biggie." But she was smiling. She clearly enjoyed having the upper hand. "I don't know if it's because I made him wait for an answer, but he texts me all the time. 'Hey, babe, just thinking about you.' 'Hi, babe, can't wait to see you.' ' Hi, babe, hope you're having a good day.'"

"Sounds like he wants to get back together."

"Sarah thinks so, too."

The mention of Sarah made Meg's stomach knot. Kit was still in Florida with Sarah when Sarah learned about Meg's affair. Brianna had e-mailed Sarah with the news, after hearing of it from Mom. Kit was surprised by the news, but Sarah flipped out. Sarah, making a statement, canceled her plans to go to California for the summer. Didn't want to be anywhere Meg would be, didn't want her kids around Meg either. Mom got upset that Sarah found out through Brianna, and sent a short, sharp reprimand to Brianna before deciding to fly out with Dad to spend the Fourth of July in Tampa Bay with Kit, Sarah, and Sarah's family.

Before Mom left for Florida, she called Meg and asked her to reach out to Sarah. She wanted Meg to try to make amends. Meg told her that Sarah would probably still be too angry to listen to anything she would have to say. Mom said that she could at least try. So Meg phoned. And Sarah took Meg's call, but only to tell her how disgusted she was with her. How sickened she was by the news. Appalled that her sister—a paragon of virtue—would stoop to sleeping around, with her boss no less. It was a short, brutal call that ended with Sarah hanging up on her.

Meg ended up spending the Fourth of July in Capitola alone. Jack took the kids to Virginia with him, promising them a visit to historic Williamsburg.

It was the first time in over twenty years that the Brennans hadn't gathered in Capitola for their traditional Fourth at the beach house.

It had been a lonely holiday for Meg, but she didn't complain. Nor did she feel sorry for herself. She got what she had coming.

"How is Sarah?" she asked carefully now.

Kit sat up, reached into the pool to splash water on her knees and lower thighs. "Still mad at you."

Meg swallowed around the lump in her throat. Jack might be a Taurus, but Sarah was a Scorpio, and when provoked, she could sting. She might be the baby of the family, but she was no pushover. "I didn't have an affair to hurt her."

"I know. But given the situation, you can see why she felt betrayed. She'd confided in you all this stuff about her marriage and her fears about Boone, and the texts she found, and there you were, acting sympathetic and indignant on her behalf, even while you were doing the very same thing."

Meg looked away. Her affair had hurt everyone. "Jack will probably forgive me before Sarah," she said with a low, bitter laugh, still remembering every harsh criticism Sarah had leveled at her, calling her fake, false, dishonest, deceitful, a master manipulator . . .

"You should go home and get ready for your date," Meg said, rising to her feet and picking up her iced tea glass. She'd had enough sun. Had enough confessions and apologies and sorrow and girl talk. She just wanted to come back home. Wanted to be a full-time mom again. Wife again. Wanted the life she'd foolishly taken for granted.

Two weeks had passed since then, and now Meg sat on the front porch waiting for Kit to arrive with the kids. It was the middle of the third week of July. August would be here soon. And then September and the start of school. Meg idly wondered where she'd be when the school year started. She hoped to be home. She intended to be home. The house wasn't just Jack's. It was in her name, too.

And now the kids were about to arrive. Finally. She was sick of her own company. Sick of missing her children. Thank God she'd have them with her for the next several weeks, until early August. She'd been sprucing up the house all week. Had swapped out the ancient metal bunk beds for new wooden ones from PBteen. She hoped the kids would like them. She'd even painted the room, a fresh light grassy green, and bought new sheets and comforter covers so it would be fresh and fun. Beachy. Happy.

Please let it be happy, she prayed, fighting back the despair that had threatened to engulf her all summer. She wouldn't let herself fall apart. She would stay strong, and she could. That was her job now. To be there for the kids. To help the kids heal. And hopefully Jack would see that she was trying, and was sorry, and he would relent and forgive her.

M eg needed him to forgive her, too. She wouldn't be able to forgive herself until he did. Which is why she didn't push him, or press him, or demand equal time with the children.

If she lost her marriage over a two-week affair with Chad . . .

Her stomach cramped. She couldn't even complete the thought. She liked Chad, had imagined that maybe she even loved him, but two weeks of hot sex couldn't replace sixteen months of dating and seventeen years of marriage.

But for a few weeks it had. For a few weeks she'd been living in a fantasy world, being someone else, someone daring, someone exciting, someone sexual, powerful, full of possibilities . . .

Agitated, Meg stood up, walked down the steps, hot and nervous and uncomfortable with the direction her thoughts had taken.

She couldn't let herself think about Chad. Normally she didn't. Wouldn't say his name, or picture his face. She wouldn't even think about the winery. It was all too painful. Not just because she missed him. But because he was now a villain in her family. He'd never be part of her life again, or welcome in her home again. What a horrible way to end their friendship.

Meg's cotton T-shirt clung to her damp, warm skin as she paced the sidewalk, impatient for the kids to arrive. She'd baked chocolate-chip and snickerdoodle cookies that morning and was planning on making homemade ice cream with them tonight. She'd been scouring the paper for fun things to do, from seeing movies to visiting the Santa Cruz boardwalk.

And then suddenly they were there, bounding up the sidewalk. JJ, Tessa, Gabi. Meg hugged each of them, doing her best to ignore Tessa and JJ's resistance. They didn't want her to hug them. They just wanted to rush past her and into the house. Fortunately, Gabi wasn't as tough. She lingered for an extra hug.

"Where's Aunt Kit?" Meg asked, squeezing Gabi tightly and breathing in the scent of her shampoo—Suave Green Apple. Gabi's favorite.

"She didn't come," Gabi answered.

Meg smoothed her daughter's dark brown hair back from her forehead, seeing how tan Gabi was already and relishing the warm softness of her skin. She'd missed her kids. She had. "How did you get here?"

"Daddy," Gabi said, pointing to the street.

Meg straightened quickly, saw Jack on the pavement just standing there, waiting. Watching. She couldn't read his expression and she felt completely caught off guard. "Hi," she said, aware that she hadn't seen him in weeks. Not since June 29. The day the shit hit the fan.

"Hi," he said brusquely, remaining where he was, car keys dangling from two fingers.

He was taller than she remembered, thinner, too. Meg couldn't imagine he was eating very well. "Kit was going to bring them," she said, painfully self-conscious, aware that she looked plain, even sloppy, in her oversize khaki shorts and favorite red GAP T-shirt.

"I know. But it seemed silly for her to do it. They're my kids."

She flushed at the way he said "my kids." He sounded so territorial. As if she had nothing to do with their existence. "Thanks for bringing them to me," she said, glancing at Gabi as she headed inside with her suitcase and backpack, wishing that Gabi had stayed, wanting and needing a buffer.

"My pleasure."

But it didn't sound like his pleasure, she thought. He sounded icy. Combative. But maybe Meg was reading too much into it. She struggled to feel less defensive and gestured to the porch. "Would you like something cold to drink? A Coke? Lemonade? Iced tea?"

"You have all that?"

"I wasn't sure what the kids would want."

He opened his mouth as if to say something and then seemed to think better of it. Meg watched his face, his profile hard, expression shuttered. "Water would be great, Meg. If you don't mind."

His excessive politeness made her ache. He, too, had become a stranger in a matter of weeks. "I don't mind," she said with a quick smile before disappearing into the house, glad to move, glad for something to do.

In the kitchen Meg opened the old fridge and stared blindly at the shelves, forgetting what she was doing. Why had he come? He didn't seem happy being here. Was there an ulterior motive for the visit?

The blast of cold air reminded her that he was waiting. She was supposed to get him a water. She grabbed two chilled water bottles and headed back outside, heart racing.

She saw that Jack had taken a seat on the porch in one of the big wicker chairs. She handed him one bottle. He thanked her and added that she looked tan.

Meg held out an arm, inspected it as she took the rocking chair two seats away from him. "I have nothing to do all day but walk on the beach or run."

"I would say lucky you—"

"Please don't." She tried to smile but couldn't. "This is the worst summer of my life."

"Am I supposed to feel sorry for you?"

"No."

"Good. Because I don't." He tipped the bottle, draining half of it. "The kids are pretty upset with you."

Her insides hurt. She felt as if she'd been swallowing glass. "I've noticed."

Jack's eyes met hers. "JJ didn't want to come. I had to force him into the car. And I mean that literally."

"What?"

"I physically put him in the car," he said, his tone acidic. "I never want to do that again. The girls were both hysterical. It was a bad scene."

Meg exhaled slowly, sickened at the thought of Jack having to force JJ to come see her. "They seem okay now."

"It was a three-hour drive today. Lots of traffic. They settled down."

"I'm sorry."

He gave her an incredulous look. "You have no idea what you've done to them, Meg, do you? No idea what you've done to all of us. We—I—the kids and me. We trusted you. I trusted you. And you just hung us out to dry."

Meg got up from her chair, moved down the porch, her insides sharp, her emotions brittle. "This wasn't about them, Jack. This was about you and me. Problems we were having, but you made it about them. You forced them to be part of this—"

"I didn't have the affair!"

"But if you had, I wouldn't have dragged you through mud in front of our children. I would have protected your relationship with them. I would have protected you—"

"Like you protected me while you were sleeping with Hallahan?"

Her chest burned and her throat ached and she felt the suffocating shame in every cell of her body. "That was wrong. I am so sorry."

"You're just sorry you were caught."

"No. I'm sorry it happened. It shouldn't have happened. I wish I could undo what I did. I wish I could go back and make different choices, because I would. But I can't go back. I can't undo what I've done, all we can do is try to move forward with compassion and—"

"Compassion?" He was on his feet. "Is that what I'm to do? Offer you forgiveness and compassion?"

"Yes!"

"And why would I do that?"

Everything in her tensed, tightened, vibrating with pain. "Because we have children. And we're a family."

He shook his head, once, and again. "Not anymore."

"*What?*"

"That's why I'm here. I thought it best to tell you personally." He drew a breath, blurted. "It's over."

She didn't speak. Couldn't believe he meant it.

"I'm filing for divorce and moving to Virginia," he added. "I've already looked into enrolling the kids in school in McLean. The schools are great, the area has tons of culture and history, and it'd be good for them. I also think after they got used to the change, they'd like it." His hands gestured out. "I grew up on the East Coast. I know they'd like it."

"No. Absolutely not," Meg choked.

"I'm filing for sole custody."

Meg stared at him, unable to believe what she was hearing. Was he serious? Did he honestly think he could take the kids—her kids—and move them across the country? Move them away from her? "No judge will allow it."

"My lawyer says I have a good case."

"Your lawyer is wrong."

He shrugged. "Think about it. You abandoned them this summer—"

"I didn't abandon them. You kicked me out!"

"You're unemployed, living off your family, and the kids have already stated that their preference is to live with me, not you."

Meg's legs gave out and she sank onto the top step of the porch. "Who are you?"

Dark red color suffused his cheekbones. "I have to protect myself. Protect the children."

"And who are you protecting the children from?" She demanded. "Me?"

He nodded.

"Wow," she said softly, rubbing her palms across each other, struggling to take it all in. "Can't believe it's come to this." She looked at him, numb, horrified, exhausted. "Can't believe you won't give me a chance."

"You honestly think you deserve a chance?"

She pressed her hands against her stomach. "We spent seventeen years together, and I love you—"

"So what was Chad to you? A fling?"

At the time she was seeing Chad, the relationship had felt like so much more, but now, in hindsight, knowing what that two-week affair had done to her life, she could see that he was just a blip in the screen. A speck in the rearview mirror. "Yes."

He crumpled the empty plastic bottle, flattening it. "You threw away our marriage for a fling?"

"I didn't want to throw away our marriage. I was trying to save it."

"By sleeping with another man?"

"I thought if I could just feel more . . . if I could just feel needed . . ." Her voice drifted off and she looked out toward the beach and the blue horizon. "We'd be okay. I'd be okay. I was wrong."

"Yeah," Jack said beneath his breath, whizzing the flattened bottle across the porch so that it ended in the bushes. "You were."

Meg watched him walk past her, down the walkway toward his car. Anger and pain bubbled up, burning her insides.

She could accept her part in the story. She could play the sinner, the adulteress. But her fall from grace had happened over time. It's not as if she'd jumped from a happy marriage bed into her lover's bed. She'd jumped from a cold, lonely bed into another bed, seeking warmth. Connection.

"I am so sorry that I hurt you," she said, chasing after him. "I regret it more than you know. And I understand that you're still hurt and angry and want to punish me, but moving to Virginia, taking the kids away from me, that's not the answer. It hurts them. Punishes them for something they didn't do."

"I didn't want this, Meg. I love our kids. I loved our family—"

"Then work with me to protect what's left of our family. Don't move to Virginia. Go to counseling with me. Give us a chance—"

"Meg—"

"The kids can't fix this. Only you and I can. And I need your help to make it right. Please."

He looked away, a small muscle pulling in his jaw. "I loved you, Meg."

Her eyes burned and she swallowed hard. "I know. And it probably doesn't help, but I love you. I have always loved you."

"Even when you were sleeping with Chad?"

Her jaw tightened. He wouldn't understand, didn't want to understand. She'd found pleasure with Chad, but Jack was more than pleasure. Jack was family. Jack was home. At least he had been home.

Meg stood on the sidewalk for several long minutes after he drove away. She kept her arms bundled across her chest to contain her anger. It blew her mind that after seventeen years of marriage he wouldn't give her a chance . . . that he'd rather divorce her and take the kids away from her than attempt to work things out. She knew he was proud. Knew his ego had been damaged. Knew he was scarred by his parents' protracted, acrimonious divorce. But they, Meg and Jack, didn't have to become Jack's parents. They could work out their differences. They could work through the pain. They could . . .

Meg was still on the sidewalk when the girls came out of the house, screen door slamming behind them. They'd changed into swimsuits and had huge bright beach towels hanging from their shoulders.

"We have new beds!" Gabi cried, tugging her bikini top down over her still-flat chest.

"They are soooo comfortable," Tessa enthused. "Finally I won't wake up with an aching back."

Meg forced her anger back, unwilling to let Jack ruin a moment of her time with the kids. "They were pretty bad, weren't they?"

"Terrible. But Grandma's going to have a fit," Tessa said. "Does she know you've gotten rid of them?"

"No. Not looking forward to telling her either."

"Then don't," Gabi said with an air of practicality. "No need getting her upset. Daddy says she's not feeling well. We have to be extra nice to her right now."

Meg's brows pulled. "When did Daddy say that?"

"Right before we went to summer camp. Told us to write her and send postcards and stuff so she'd know we loved her."

Meg didn't know whether to be angry or grateful that Jack had said something to the kids. "And did you?"

The girls both nodded. "She wrote us, too," Gabi answered.

Tessa looked troubled. "She's sick again, isn't she? Her cancer's back."

This wasn't how Meg had planned on telling them. It was sooner than she wanted to tell them, too. "Yes," she said reluctantly.

"When will she start her chemo?" Tessa asked.

Gabi glanced from Tessa to her mother. "Is that when her hair falls out?"

"Yes. And I don't know about the chemo," Meg answered, unwilling to tell them that the cancer was terminal, and because of that, their grandmother had elected not to get treatment.

"Poor Grandma," Gabi said, giving her mom a hug. "Makes me sad for her."

Meg hugged Gabi back. "Me, too."

And then they were off, heading to the beach, dashing across the street.

"Be careful!" Meg shouted after them as they dodged between cars.

"We are," Gabi shouted back, running through traffic, not watching for anything.

Tessa and Gabi spent the first few days in Capitola on the beach, catching up on tans and socializing with the kids who came there every summer. JJ was more aloof, and he was either "out" or in the bunk room, listening to music on his iPod.

Meg opened the door to the bedroom late one afternoon to let him know she was going with the girls down to Esplanade Park for the Twilight Concerts. The Twilight Concerts ran every Wednesday evening, June through September. Meg had packed a picnic of fried chicken, watermelon, and potato salad, and she was hoping that JJ would want to go.

The blinds in the room were half drawn. JJ was lying on one of the bottom beds, earbuds in his ears, his hand drumming a rhythm on the mattress.

She hesitated in the doorway, watching him. He looked so big in the narrow bunk, as if he were Gulliver in a Lilliputian bed.

She entered the room, moving closer to his bed. He saw her and pulled out one earbud. "Yeah?"

Meg tried to smile, hoping she looked approachable, friendly, like the mom she'd once been. "Can we talk?"

Expressions flitted over his face—anger, disdain, pain—and then he slid the orange earbud back in. "No."

For a moment she just stood there, looking at the boy who was becoming a man. "We need to talk."

"There's nothing to say."

"You've never been so distant with me before."

"That's because I didn't know you before."

"JJ!"

He propped himself up on his elbow. "It's true. And now that I know who you are, I'm embarrassed you're my mom."

Meg inhaled sharply, feeling sucker punched. Jack was right. JJ was angry with her and she scrambled to think of the right words. "I know you're upset with me, JJ, but you don't need to be rude."

"Rude?" He laughed. "I wasn't rude. Rude would be calling you a whore. But I didn't say that." And then he lay back down, and slid the earbud back into place.

M eg took the girls to the Twilight Concert in the park, and the girls had fun, although Gabi did express some disappointment that there were no *Twilight* stars there. And so while no *Twilight* film saga actors appeared, Gabi did spot a boy she'd met last year and, deciding that she liked him, wandered off to talk to him.

Tessa was still sitting next to Meg on the blanket on the sand as she watched Gabi approach the boy and his friends. "I couldn't do that," she confessed. "Couldn't ever just walk up and start talking to a guy like that. I'd be too scared."

"Gabi is fearless, isn't she?" Meg said, keeping a close eye on her younger daughter and the circle of boys, waiting to see if Gabi would be rebuffed. But the boy Gabi liked was smiling, perhaps a little bit self-consciously, and he looked friendly. Flattered. He said something to Gabi and she laughed and sat down on the sand next to him.

Tessa was still watching, too, and she sighed. "She's younger than me and yet she gets all the guys."

"He's probably eleven, Tess. A sixth grader. You wouldn't want him."

Tessa flushed. "You know what I mean, Mom."

Meg did. And she understood. When she was growing up, the boys always went crazy for Bree. She was like honey. Horny boys buzzed around her like little bees. Of course she couldn't quite say that to her daughter. Tessa admired Bree.

Meg reached out to smooth Tessa's dark red hair. It was so thick with lovely soft curls that Tessa absolutely hated. "Aunt Brianna was very popular, too," Meg said. "I'd be sitting home on weekends dying for something to do, and your aunt Brianna was always heading out . . . parties and dances and dates."

"So what did you do?"

"Joined more clubs. Became more active in student government."

"That sounds terrible."

Meg grimaced. "It was."

Tessa's brow furrowed as she plucked at the threads of her dark purple sweater.

"Mom?"

"Yes, Tess?"

Tessa bent her head, hiding her face. "Why did you . . . with Chad?"

Meg's heart slowed, stopped. She'd known the subject would eventually come up. Had wondered how it would come up. And now it had. And she still wasn't prepared. How did one explain infidelity to one's thirteen-year-old daughter? "I let my guard down."

Tessa turned her head, looked at her. "What does that mean?"

"It means that I got lazy, and distracted, and I forgot to be vigilant about protecting the family." Meg's gaze met Tessa's. "I forgot that my job is to protect you kids—"

"Not Daddy?"

"No, it's to protect Daddy, too. To protect all of you. All of us. But I got caught up in me, and thinking about me, and what I thought I needed, and I was wrong. I was selfish and I hurt Daddy badly."

"Are you going to get divorced?"

"I hope not."

"Does Daddy want a divorce?"

"I'm not sure he knows what he wants. He's really mad at me right now. And I don't blame him."

Tessa's gaze dropped. She smoothed her skirt over her knees and then her sweater over the skirt. "I was really mad at you, too."

"I know."

She put her head down, touched her forehead to her bent knees. "I told Daddy I didn't want to live with you anymore. Said if you got divorced, I'd rather be with him."

Meg's lips parted but she made no sound. That hurt. But it wasn't a total shock. Jack had said Tessa had come to him . . . and Tessa had seen that text from Chad.

Tessa turned her head to look anxiously at her mom. "I don't really want to go to Virginia, though. I don't want Daddy sad, but I don't want to live so far away from you either."

"You won't have to. Daddy and I can figure this out."

Tessa turned away again, pressed her face to her knees. She was quiet. Her shoulders shook. She was crying.

Meg put her hand on her daughter's back, rubbed it. "Tess?"

"Why did you do that to Daddy? Why did you have to make him so sad? He's never done anything mean to you!"

For a moment Meg couldn't speak. A lump filled her throat. "I wish I hadn't. I wish I could take it all back, undo all the bad, sad things—"

"Is it because of Grandma?"

"What? No. Oh, no, baby."

Tessa lifted her head. "But Aunt Kit said it was. She said that the you-know with you-know-who happened 'cause Grandma's sick and you're worried and lonely—"

"No! That's not true, and Aunt Kit should be ashamed of herself for saying such a thing. I can't believe she'd say that. Why would she say that?"

"Don't get mad at Aunt Kit! She was just trying to explain to JJ why you . . . you know . . . so he wouldn't hate you anymore."

Meg balled her hands in her lap thinking she didn't know what was worse . . . Kit trying to help and blaming Mom's cancer, Tessa trying to empathize, or being told that JJ hated her.

Tessa hung her head. "Please don't be mad at Aunt Kit. She loves you so much—"

"And I love her, but there are some things you don't say, especially to children, and that was one of them."

Tessa's lips pressed thin, her expression suddenly imperious. "At least Aunt Kit doesn't treat me like a baby. She talks to me like I'm an adult. Like she respects me. You should respect me, too. I'm smart. And I'm not a little girl anymore."

And with that, Tessa jumped up and stalked off, heading back to the beach house.

Late that evening, after the concert had ended and everyone had gone to bed, Meg stayed up late reading in her room. Reading was better than lying awake thinking. Reading kept her mind occupied. She didn't want to think anymore tonight. Didn't want to feel. Didn't want to replay the conversation she'd had with Tessa on the beach one more time, or the scene in the kids' bunk room when JJ called her a whore.

Correction: when he said he *didn't* call her a whore.

God, that had been brutal. He was brutal. The conversation with Tessa was brutal. The only one who hadn't unleashed on her yet was Gabi, but Meg suspected that was coming.

She gave up trying to read and, leaning over, turned out the light.

The ringing of her cell phone jarred Meg awake. Opening her eyes, she saw it was light. Morning. But she wasn't ready to wake up and she groped on the bedside table for her phone to mute it. But once she saw it was a restricted number, she answered. "Hello?" she said, sitting up and getting a glimpse of gray outside the window. Yuck. Fog had rolled in during the night.

"Meg?"

The voice was scratchy and sounded far away. "Yes?"

"It's Bree."

Meg blinked. "Bree?"

"Brianna. Your sister. Ring a bell?"

"Vaguely," Meg said, sitting up, stunned. Brianna had never once phoned her in the ten years she'd lived overseas. "How's the Congo?"

"Full of natural beauty, political instability, death, and disease."

"Sounds nice. I should visit sometime."

"You'd hate it."

"Yes, I would."

Brianna laughed, the sound low and mocking. "So, Sister Mary Margaret, you really fucked up this time, didn't you?"

For a second all Meg could feel was pain, and humiliation. Jack divorcing her. JJ hating her. Her sister Sarah wouldn't speak to her. Her parents were avoiding her. "Yes, I did."

"Sarah's pretty freaked out."

"Well, she's not the only one."

"Heard Jack is filing for divorce."

Meg closed her eyes, pressed a hand to her temple. "Yeah."

"Your life is shit," Bree said, laughing.

Laughing.

Meg's throat squeezed closed. Only Brianna would call to gloat about something like this. "I'm glad you find my pain so entertaining. At least my suffering and shame can amuse you."

Brianna laughed again. "Oh my God, this is good. I should have called sooner. You're hilarious. I love the 'shame and suffering' part. So very biblical."

Meg gritted her teeth, loathing Brianna with all her heart. "Well, thanks for calling. It was great hearing from you—"

"Knock off the woe is me, Sister Mary Margaret. You fucked up. So what? Everyone fucks up."

"My fuckup cost me my marriage, and my family." Her voice suddenly broke. "Even my son thinks I'm a whore. But I'm sure you'll find that funny. Uptight, miserable, righteous Mags had it coming."

"Now you're being a little hard on yourself," Bree soothed. "And you're not a whore. You got laid a couple times. Big fucking deal."

"It is a big fucking deal," Meg cried, unable to hold the tears back any longer. "I've worked so hard to provide for my family. I've been a really good mom. And until this thing with Chad, I was a really good wife."

"That's right. You have worked hard, and you've been a great mom, and you're an incredible wife, too. You've put up with boring Jack for seventeen years. My God, Meg, you have my full respect. You're a saint."

Meg snorted with laughter as she wiped away tears. "That is so sacrilegious, Bree. You will go to hell if you're not careful."

"That's okay," Bree retorted cheerfully. "I don't mind since it looks like you'll be there with me."

Meg stretched out on the bed, hugged a pillow to her. "This is so not funny, Bree, and you're making me laugh."

"Good. I figured you'd need a laugh. There is only so much flagellation one can do before you're nothing but a bloody pulp and useless to the world."

Meg used her shoulder to dry her wet cheek. "Why?" she asked hoarsely.

"Why what, Mary Margaret?"

"Why are you being nice? You hate me. You should be cheering my fall."

"I should be. I fully expected I would be. But when Sarah told me what was happening, I couldn't celebrate. In fact, I was pretty bummed. Turns out I actually care about you a little bit. Now, *that* freaked me out." Bree fell silent for a moment. "Now get up off your ass, girl, and stop feeling sorry for yourself. You can fix this. You can."

"And what if I can't? What if it's too late? What if my stupid curiosity has destroyed everything?"

"Then you forge ahead, knowing that whatever comes is going to be okay. With or without Jack, you'll be okay."

"I don't want it to be without Jack."

"Then don't give up. Be tough. And remember that the only person who can take Mary Margaret Brennan out of the game is Mary Margaret."

For a moment Meg couldn't say anything. Her throat ached. "Bree—"

"Don't. No need to get mushy. Just keep your chin up and take care of those kids."

Hanging up, Meg lay back on her bed and held the pillow to her chest.

Bree called. Crazy, impossible, improbable Bree called and offered support. Wow. Pigs did fly.

Still struggling to process the call, Meg dressed and left the quiet house to get a coffee.

The coastal fog obscured the village buildings and hid the ocean behind a veil of gray. Town was quiet. People weren't out yet. The fog had a way of keeping people inside.

At Mr. Toots Meg ordered a latte to go. With seagulls squawking overhead, she carried her coffee down the wharf, but it was cold and damp and she shivered at the chill. Instead of lingering on the pier, she walked back into town, up Capitola Avenue, down Bay Avenue, and the entire time she walked, her heart ached.

It burned. It throbbed. She felt every little beat.

Bree, Bree, Bree, Bree.

Meg's throat swelled closed and she fought tears. Stupid Bree. Stupid, stupid Bree for caring.

She knocked away tears as she reached the top of Depot Hill. Bree was supposed to hate her. But she didn't.

And somehow that changed everything. Well, not everything. Jack still wanted a divorce, and JJ still thought she was a hooker, and Sarah still wanted nothing to do with her, but Bree's call gave Meg hope.

And Brianna was right. Mary Margaret was not a quitter. Mary Margaret did not give up.

Back home Meg made the kids breakfast, waffles and bacon, and while they ate she sat down with her laptop and sent Jack an e-mail.

Jack,

I'm so sorry I hurt you. I am sorry for the affair, and I will always be sorry that I caused you pain. But you are not taking the kids to Virginia. And no judge or court would allow you to take the children from me. So let's sit down and sort this out. It's time.

Meg

She reread what she'd written, edited a few words, read it again, and then finally pushed send.

Meg didn't hear back from Jack. She hadn't really expected to, but she'd hoped. Hoped that he'd feel a little something . . . remorse, regret, fear, loss . . . something.

She did get a text late that day, from her mother. Her parents were thinking of coming down the first of August for a few days if Meg's kids would still be there. They hoped the kids would still be there.

Meg studied the text. The word *hoped* popped out at her.

Hoped. Hope. Such a small word, but so powerful.

She answered her mother's text. *Kids will be here until August 3. I hope you and Dad will come. We'd love to have you join us.*

Her dad called that evening to confirm that they would drive down next Thursday for a long weekend. It was the first time Meg had talked to him since she'd stayed at her parents' house. He asked about the weather, the tourists, the surf conditions just as he always did, continuing the fantasy that he'd been a surfer in his youth.

He mentioned that Cass had been hit hard with morning sickness and had taken a few days off work.

He said that the Fourth of July in Tampa had been a lot of fun. Boone had hit well. He and Sarah seemed really happy.

He said he'd just helped Kit install some new light fixtures in her house.

But in all the conversation and updates, he never once asked about *her.* And she knew why. He couldn't go there. Didn't want to hear that she either hurt or was doing well, because either way, her life was still a mess and he was still disappointed. She knew he hadn't forgiven her yet either. Not because he liked to hold grudges, but because he had high standards. He wanted her to save her marriage. He expected her to do it. He was old school. Catholic. Irish. A man who still believed in miracles.

Ending the call, Meg walked outside to the front porch, air bottled in her lungs. She didn't want to disappoint her dad. She didn't like disappointing anyone, but there was only so much she could do.

And so she looked up, refusing to think or feel, determined to clear her mind of everything but the dark sky above. She studied the sky, and the way the clouds obscured the stars, hiding the moon. The only light above was in the pinpricks of stars at the edge of the clouds where the moon fought to shine through.

Fight moon, she prayed. *Fight hard.*

Her eyes suddenly stung. She swallowed around the lump in her throat. She hated that her father was so disappointed in her. Hated that Sarah wouldn't speak to her. Hated that Jack wanted to take the kids to the other side of the country. But it was what it was, and she didn't have to please Sarah or her father or even Jack anymore. Jack could think what he wanted. He could say what he wanted. But he wouldn't be able to take the kids from her and she wasn't going to be intimidated. Wasn't going to grovel or break either. Yes, she'd messed up—and messed up bad—but wallowing in shame and self-pity would help no one.

K it arrived in Capitola Saturday at noon with Polly in tow. After two days of fog the sun had returned and the sky was a clear, lucid blue with just a few puffy white clouds sailing serenely overhead. Polly and Kit had come to the coast to run Sunday's wharf-to-wharf race.

Meg couldn't believe that Kit was actually planning on running it. Kit didn't run. Had never been a runner. But she was going to do it because Polly, who entered races all the time, said it would be fun.

Fun.

The race, limited to the first fifteen thousand people, sold out months in advance, so apparently Kit was using Brad's registration form, since Brad hadn't come. Meg wasn't sure how Kit would pass for Brad, but she left that issue alone, as there were other more pressing issues, like getting the living room's sofa sleeper to unfold. The forty-year-old pullout couch seemed to have finally decided after many years of use that it would not pull out.

Meg and Kit took turns beating the old white vinyl couch to no avail. It would not budge. Polly thought it was hilarious. Kit only started laughing after Meg fell off the arm of the couch. Meg wasn't amused.

That evening Kit ended up sleeping with Meg in the master bedroom and Polly took the last bunk in the kids' room. JJ, uncomfortable about having a teacher in his room, slept on the couch in the living room.

And now, Sunday morning, Meg was outside with her coffee watching Kit stretch. The race started in Santa Cruz and ended in Capitola. Capitola would be a zoo soon.

"It's six miles, Kit," Meg said, sipping her coffee.

Kit looked up from her runner's stretch. "I know. About three miles more than I'd like, but I can do this. It's for a good cause."

"What's the cause?"

"Supporting Polly. She just broke up with Brad."

Meg frowned. Polly didn't look like she was taking the breakup hard at all. "Were they together a long time?"

"Eighteen months. Two years. Something like that."

"I envy Polly. If I didn't have kids, I almost think I'd start over. I'd love a fresh start. A chance to do things differently."

"You'd miss Jack," Kit said, lunging forward on the other leg. "Maybe not right away, but eventually."

"I don't know. He's being such an ass."

"He's hurt, so he's trying to hurt you."

"That's mature." Meg caught Kit's arched eyebrow and mumbled, "Yeah, I know. Having an affair wasn't mature either. But I regret it. And I want to move on. Only Jack won't let me."

"Not yet. But it's only been what? Five weeks since he found out?"

"A little less."

"So give him time."

"And what if I give him time, and he still wants the divorce?"

"Then you get divorced and you'll share the kids with him, and you'll still be a family . . . just a different kind of family." Kit reached up to adjust her ponytail. "And maybe . . . maybe a divorce is what you want. Maybe you had an affair because you did want out. So maybe instead of rushing into reconciling, you use this time to figure out what you really want. And maybe it's Jack. Maybe it's not. Maybe it's Chad. Maybe it's someone new. You owe it to yourself—and Jack—to figure that out."

"But you like Jack. You liked me with him."

"I did. I do. But you're my sister. I want you to be happy. And if you're not happy with Jack, then don't stay. Don't be like me . . . afraid to take risks, afraid to offend, afraid to disappoint, afraid afraid afraid, because it gets you nowhere. Just leaves you stuck. Look at me. Almost forty and single and pissed off that I wasted the past ten years on a dick!"

Meg smiled faintly at Kit's vehemence. "And now you're free to choose a different path. And a different kind of man."

"I hope so. Can't do what I've been doing. Doesn't work." She hesitated. "Do you think you'd be happier divorcing Jack?"

Meg's smile faded. She rolled her coffee cup between her hands, chewed the inside of her lip. It was an interesting question.

Meg had spent so much time fearing Jack wouldn't take her back that she hadn't even asked herself if she really, truly wanted to spend the rest of her life with him. It was obviously the best thing for the kids. But what about for her . . . Meg? Was Jack the right man? The right partner? The right lover?

How odd to ask this now.

How odd to think she'd never stopped to think about what she wanted in the future . . .

Meg frowned, her brow creasing. "I can't separate what I need from what the kids need. And the kids need their dad. They need their family—"

"Yes, but can you be happy? Really happy, Meg? Or are you just going to go through the motions?"

Kit was asking some hard questions, questions that made Meg uncomfortable. "I don't really know," she said at last. "I'd like to work things out with Jack. I think it's the best thing for the kids, and we were happy together once. I think we could be happy together again."

The screen door squeaked open and Polly stepped out of the house in nylon shorts and a snug running top. Meg was glad to see her, glad for the diversion. Talking to Kit was beginning to depress her. She didn't have answers. She didn't know what would happen in the future. She didn't have control.

She could only hope. And be strong. And not give up.

"Am I interrupting?" Polly asked, bounding down the steps. In her early thirties, she was still slim, sleek, and built for speed. Even her long straight blond hair was pulled back this morning in a skinny ponytail.

"Nope," Kit answered. "I was just about to go get you."

"Good." Polly took a spot on the grass and started stretching next to Kit. "Morning, Meg."

"Morning. How did you sleep?" Meg asked.

Polly flashed a wide, white smile. "Awesome! Your girls are so cute. I felt like I was at summer camp."

Meg took another sip of her coffee. It had gone cold. And Polly might have broken up with Brad, but she looked light and bubbly. Disgustingly happy. The breakup was obviously good for her.

"Wish you could go with us," Polly added, sitting on the grass and shifting into a yogalike pose. "But the race is sold out."

"It's unfortunate," Meg said, feigning disappointment. "But that's okay. I'll stay here with the kids. Eat some more cinnamon rolls."

Kit laughed. "Easy on the carbs, Meg. They'll just make your butt bigger."

"Wow, Kit. Thanks. That was a real pick-me-up."

Kit laughed again, blew her a kiss as she and Polly headed for the car. "What are sisters for?"

The kids hung out in town watching the race and listening to the bands, and then later that evening, along with Meg, Kit, and Polly, they bought hot dogs and burgers from one of the food vendors and ate on the beach. After a while, the kids drifted away to hang out with other kids and Meg sipped a beer that had gone flat a half hour earlier, while Kit and Polly shared a bottle of red wine.

Meg wistfully eyed their plastic cups of wine. "I miss wine. Haven't had it in weeks."

"Why not?" Polly asked.

"Didn't seem right. Reminded me of Dark Horse." And Chad. But Meg didn't add that. She couldn't bring herself to say Chad's name out loud anymore.

"You live in Sonoma County. You can't avoid wine forever. Might as well get over your hang-up now," Polly answered, thrusting her cup into Meg's hand. "Drink. Enjoy. It's delicious."

Meg took the cup from an insistent Polly and had a sip. "Delicious," she agreed. "And you're right. I can't avoid wine, or Santa Rosa, or going home." She wrinkled her nose. "I want to go home. Hiding out here in Capitola is getting old."

"When the kids go home, why don't you come stay with me in Oakland for a few days?" Kit said. "You can help me paint the dining room. I'd like to paint it red. I think it'd look really good with the white wainscoting."

"How could I refuse such an appealing offer?" Meg teased.

"I thought Richard was going to help you paint the dining room," Polly added.

"He was a big talker. He just wanted to come over." Kit rolled her eyes. "Have sex. What a loser."

Meg's lips twitched. Hard to believe this was the same Kit who was so shattered a couple months ago. "Whatever happened with Richard? Did you have that date a couple weeks ago?"

"Yes."

"And?"

Kit made a face. "It was fine."

Meg glanced at Polly and then back at Kit. "It doesn't sound fine."

Kit stretched her arms up over her head. "We went out, had dinner. He wanted some action. I said no. He got all huffy and indignant, which seriously annoyed me." She looked at Meg, completely matter-of-fact. "It'd been months since I last saw him. And just because he bought me a forty-dollar steak doesn't mean he gets pussy."

"Oh my God, Kit!" Meg cried, laughing and blushing at the same time. Did her little Miss Catholic Schoolteacher sister just say that? "I can't believe you used the word 'pussy.'"

Kit's small straight nose tilted. "But it's true. I'm not a free lunch. If a man wants me, he's going to have to work for me."

"Which is why Kit was going to have him paint her dining

room," Polly said, struggling not to laugh. "He had to earn his way back into her good graces."

Kit nodded. "Yes, he did. But then I thought it over and realized he could paint the whole house and it wouldn't be enough. He had his chance. Ten years of chances. Now I'm saving myself for someone special."

Seventeen

The next week passed with family coming and going and frequent trips to the Santa Cruz Beach Boardwalk. And then on August 3, her parents drove the kids back to Jack, and Meg was alone again.

And she was fed up with being alone again.

A day passed before she called Kit to see if her sister still wanted help painting the dining room. Kit gave her an enthusiastic yes, and told Meg to jump in the car and head on over. By evening Kit's dining room was the color of tomato soup. It wasn't the shade Kit had envisioned, but she liked it.

They got Indian takeout and crawled into Kit's queen-size bed with their chicken tikka masala (the choice inspired by the newly painted dining room) to watch taped episodes of *Downton Abbey*. Meg had heard of the show but hadn't seen it yet, and so Kit started her at the beginning. They stayed up until one watching back-to-back episodes, and then finished the first season in the morning over coffee and French toast.

"Amazing," Meg said, unable to believe that she'd have to wait months for the new season to air. She opened a section of the paper, unfolded it, but couldn't make herself read. "But I do feel like an addict. We watched an entire season."

"But you enjoyed it."

"I did. I loved it."

Kit smiled smugly and curled up on the opposite end of the couch with the paper. "I told you it was a good show."

They chatted about the characters, and casting, and how no character was better cast than Maggie Smith. They were discussing the way she delivered the dowager's lines when Kit suddenly shoved the newspaper's food section in front of Meg.

"Look," she said, gesturing at an article in the middle of the page with the heading NAPA VINTNERS NEXT FOOD NETWORK STARS. "It's about the Hallahans."

Meg skimmed the article about the new Food Network series now filming in Napa. *The shows' stars, Craig and Chad Hallahan, are incredibly charismatic and viewers will really identify with them. Successful vintners, both brothers are bachelors, and the season is dramatic, with episodes focusing on the winery's new export opportunities in China, as well as the personal lives of the brothers as they both embark on new relationships. The series is set to air late September.*

Meg lowered the paper, looked at Kit. "So the show is definitely happening."

"You knew about this?" Kit asked, seizing the paper from her sister's hand to skim the article again.

"Yeah. Wow." Meg's hand shook as she reached for her coffee and took a quick gulp. "Not that I'm going to watch it or anything."

Kit studied her sister. "Still have feelings for him?"

Meg wiggled into a more comfortable position. "I have feelings for all of them. I loved working there. Craig was amazing and smart and real. Jennifer was a sweetheart. And Chad . . ." Her voice drifted off as she pictured Chad, and then she couldn't. It hurt remembering him. He had such a great personality, so much warmth, and emotion, and he'd made her feel so much . . .

"And Chad?" Kit prompted.

"He was a good guy. And he'll make a great husband for the right woman one day."

"But not you?"

Meg felt blood rush to her cheeks. "Kit, I'm married."

"But if Jack doesn't want to be married . . . ?"

"Can't go there."

Meg drove back to Capitola at noon. Summer traffic snarled Highway 17 and she was miserable trapped in her car with her thoughts as they inched along toward the beach. She should have waited until later tonight to drive. Should have waited until traffic was light.

But she hadn't. And so she was stuck in bumper-to-bumper traffic going nowhere.

Her thoughts had nowhere to go either, and she found herself thinking about the newspaper article, and then about Chad. But she didn't want to think about Chad. She wished she'd never gone to London. Wished she'd never talked to him, kissed him, opened herself to different emotions and possibilities. Those emotions and possibilities haunted her. Mocked her. Mocked her reality.

She'd screwed up and she was paying the price. Paying, and paying, and paying. And maybe Bree could say enough with the flagellation, but Meg couldn't stop. She couldn't stop hating herself until she was home, back with her family.

If only she hadn't climbed into that truck that day . . .

If only she hadn't leaned in for the kiss . . .

If only . . .

But she had.

*   *   *

Meg reached the beach house a little after three. Her mood was sour. She was angry and itching for a fight.

She was mad at herself, but she was also mad as hell at Jack. How could he give up on their marriage so easily? How could he walk away from her like that? If Jack cheated, she'd give him a chance. She'd be angry, but she wouldn't throw away seventeen years because he had sex . . .

Would she?

She didn't know. She didn't know anything. And that was the problem. She couldn't do this anymore. She was done waiting. Done hoping. Done giving Jack all the control. It was time to call his bluff. Find out if he ever intended to take her back, or if he just planned to leave her there, hanging at the edge of his universe.

It was late afternoon, but Jack would still be at the office. She picked up the phone and called him. Not on his cell, but his office number. He answered. "Jack Roberts," he said crisply.

She was surprised he picked up. "It's Meg," she said. "Hi. How are you?"

He didn't speak. She'd caught him off guard. He hadn't meant to take her call. "Doing well," he said, recovering. "Can I help with something?"

"I'm coming home, Jack."

"No."

"It's time—"

"I don't want you there, Meg."

Her hands balled into fists. She would have punched him if she could have. "You don't own the town. You can't keep me out."

"Then rent a house. Get an apartment. But you can't come home."

"Oh yes I can—" He cut her off by hanging up.

Asshole!

Meg softly swore. She wanted to call him back but knew he wouldn't pick up this time. And so she sat down at her computer and wrote an e-mail. This time she didn't reread and rewrite. This time she just wrote what she felt, and it would have to be enough.

Jack,

I'm sorry I hurt you, but you don't get the kids, and you can't kick me out of the house. It's not just yours. It's ours. I own half. And I'm taking my half. California is a community property state. I get fifty percent of all assets acquired during our marriage, which means I get not just half the house and furniture, but fifty percent of your business, and fifty percent of your income. So go ahead, tell your lawyer to draft the papers, and let's get this going because I'm done waiting, done hoping. I'm ready to move forward . . . without you.

And pressing send, she wondered if this e-mail would get a response.

It did.

Jack answered almost immediately, sending a very brief response. His reply consisted of just one word: *Great.*

Meg stared at the single word, repeated it to herself, and then smiled crookedly, ruefully. She'd done it now. And sitting there, thinking about it some more, she was relieved.

After sitting a little longer, digesting the fact that her marriage indeed was over, she called one of her college friends who was a lawyer in the city and asked for the name of a top divorce lawyer. If there was going to be a fight for survival, Meg was going to survive. Her friend gave her three names, all really good, and wished her luck.

Meg felt lucky when the first name on the list was able to see her a week from Tuesday and assured her that she'd come to the right law office, that she would be back home soon and Jack wouldn't know what hit him. Meg hung up slightly dazed. She was finally doing something. It seemed a little harsh, and more than a little scary, but if Jack wanted to play hardball, then she was game.

Meg took advantage of her last week at the beach by reading, walking, and swimming. The summer would soon wind down and she'd miss the beach with its squawking seagulls and tangy salt air. But she'd return with her family—whether it was her children, her mother, or her sisters—and it would all still be here. The soft sand, the watery blue horizon, the surf crashing on the shore.

On Friday, perhaps the last Friday she'd spend in Capitola that summer, Meg took a folding chair down to the Esplanade for Friday night's Movies at the Beach. They always served free popcorn for a half hour before the movie played, and tonight she sat in her chair, bundled up in a sweatshirt and blanket, and watched *Raiders of the Lost Ark* while munching popcorn with one hundred strangers who soon felt like friends.

She was going to be okay. She'd have to be okay. There weren't any other options.

Meg went to bed knowing she'd turned the corner. Things would be better. Not necessarily easier. But better because she was moving forward.

The phone rang, jarring Meg awake. It took her a moment to find it on her nightstand. She glanced at the alarm clock as she answered. The yellow neon numbers glowed 1:30. Something had happened. No one called this late. It was either the hospital or the police. "Hello?" she said.

"Mary Margaret Roberts?"

"Yes."

"Are you the mother of Jack Henry Roberts?"

Jack Jr. JJ. Oh God. "Yes."

"This is Officer Perkins with the Santa Rosa Police. He's been arrested—"

Not the hospital. The police. "Arrested?"

"For violation of 25662, Minor in Possession of Alcohol; 25658, Furnishing Alcohol to a Minor; 10-28030 Hosting Party Where Minors Are Drinking—"

"Where is he?"

"Sonoma County Jail."

"I'm on my way."

Meg hung up and called Jack. Her call went straight to voice mail. "Jack, it's me. JJ's been arrested. They're charging him with an MIP. He's being held at the jail in Santa Rosa. I'll meet you there."

She yanked jeans and a sweatshirt over the T-shirt she'd been sleeping in. In the car she tried Jack again. Straight to voice mail a second time. Then she tried the house phone, but that went to voice mail, too. Christ. Christ. He probably had turned the phone off for the night. He did stupid shit like that.

Tears burned in her eyes and she wiped at her nose, and blinked hard so she could focus on the road.

JJ arrested. Charged. He'd never get a baseball scholarship now. He'd never get any scholarship now. Might not even get to go to the school of his choice.

Jesus.

She clenched the steering wheel, fighting anger, and then panic. She was so overwhelmed it was hard to breathe. Her fingers curled tighter around the steering wheel and Highway 17 appeared before her, steep, winding, and treacherous.

She grabbed her phone, called her father's cell. He answered.

"Dad, it's me."

"What's happened?" His deep voice was as steady as a rock. Bless her father for his cool head and fortysomething years as a fireman.

"It's JJ. He's been arrested. Charged with at least three different violations related to alcohol."

"Minor in possession?"

"Yeah, among other things." She broke off, took a quick breath. "I can't reach Jack and I'm just leaving Capitola, two and a half hours away."

"Where is JJ?"

"They took him to the Sonoma County Jail."

"I'm on my way." He hesitated, voice softening. "Be careful. Stop for coffee. And drive safe."

Fortunately, at two in the morning, windy Highway 17 was virtually deserted. Ignoring her father's advice, Meg drove fast, making use of both lanes on the steepest curves, grateful there was little oncoming traffic to blind her.

She was in shock, couldn't believe the call. JJ drinking? JJ providing alcohol to minors? JJ arrested? How? Why? *Where?* Where did he get the liquor, and where had this party been? And where was Jack—the supervising parent?

She shook her head, fingers tightening on the steering wheel. How could Jack not keep closer tabs on their son? JJ was just sixteen. Old enough to take stupid risks without understanding the consequences.

Meg shot up 101 to the Bay Bridge, and then up and around to Santa Rosa. Thankfully it was a clear night, no soupy fog to obscure visibility on the roads, and she arrived at the Sonoma County Jail just a little after four.

Her father was there as promised, his thick salt-and-pepper hair immaculately combed, his polo shirt tucked into khakis. He looked calm and strong and steady, so very steady. Meg hugged him tightly, knowing she'd lucked out in the parent department. "Thank you, Dad."

"It's going to be all right," he said.

She nodded and took a breath to calm herself. "Where is he?"

"In a holding cell."

"A holding cell?"

"They have to put him somewhere. He broke the law. But it's his own cell. He's okay."

"Have you see him?"

"The guys let me go back, talk with him a little bit."

Her father must have mentioned that he was a San Francisco firefighter. "How is he?"

"Still pretty intoxicated."

She winced. "Oh, Dad. Why?"

"Because he's sixteen and this is what kids do."

Meg shook her head. "Not me. I never drank in high school."

"Oh, I know," he said drily.

Even with her father's assistance, it took another forty-five minutes to get her son released. The problem wasn't just getting JJ out of jail. The problem was what put JJ in jail.

The big party hadn't just been anywhere. The big party had been at their house. *Her* house. Meg's legs buckled when she heard that. It made no sense. Where was Jack? "Was my husband there?" she asked the officer.

"There were no adults there," he answered. "But a lot of kids. Close to one hundred."

"One hundred kids? At my house?"

"Drunk as a skunk. The arresting officer couldn't believe the amount of liquor on the premises. Gallon-size bottles everywhere."

Finally JJ was brought to the desk from his holding cell. He looked pale but composed. He shot her a worried look. "Sorry, Mom."

She didn't know whether to hug him or beat him. He was in so much trouble. But at least he was out of the holding cell. She hated the idea of him locked up.

Paperwork finished, they headed outside. Her dad held the door for them. "What were you thinking?" she whispered to JJ as they left the building.

He hung his head. "I don't know."

"Where is Dad?" she asked.

"Virginia."

"He left you home alone while he went to the East Coast?"

JJ shook his head. "I'm supposed to be at Cole's house. At least Dad thinks I'm there."

"And the girls?"

"They are at friends' for the weekend. Gabi's at Haley's, and Tessa is with Dina."

"When is Dad coming back?"

JJ rubbed his head slowly, as if he had a headache. "Sunday night. I think. What is today?"

Meg bit her tongue to keep from saying something she might regret. She couldn't believe JJ would lie to his father, throw a huge party, and serve alcohol to fifty-plus minors.

Unbelievable. When the kid screwed up, he screwed up big.

The sun was just starting to rise, and tiny fingers of light lit the horizon, illuminating the hills. Meg's dad headed to get his car in order to follow them back to the house. In the car Meg shot JJ a hard glance. "One hundred kids at the house, JJ?"

"There were more like a hundred and fifty. It was a rager—"

"A *what*?"

"A rager. A crazy huge party—

"I heard enough about that from the police. How did everyone find out about the party?"

"Facebook."

She squeezed the steering wheel as if throttling it. "Nice."

They arrived back at the house with JJ close to dawn. JJ stumbled up to bed to sleep off the rest of the hangover while Meg wandered around the house inspecting the mess. It had been quite a party. Looked like everyone had had a lot of fun. Red Jell-O shots stained the limestone floor of the mudroom. More Jell-O shots dappled the drive. Every surface was sticky from spilled sodas, mixers, and lemonade. And then there was the broken glass. Liquor bottles, glasses from the kitchen, even the glass window in the downstairs bathroom.

Meg hadn't been in the house since early July and it was hard coming back to this.

She was still sweeping up glass when her cell phone rang. It was five-thirty. Jack had finally woken up and turned his phone on.

"Where is he?" he said when she answered.

"Home. Dad helped me get him out. He goes to court on Wednesday."

"Will he serve jail time?"

"Dad doesn't think so. But he'll probably pay fines, have to do community service, and get probation."

Jack swore softly under his breath. "He told me he was staying with friends."

"They need supervision," she said, trying to keep from sounding accusatory. She didn't want to fight with him, not now, not after the night she'd just had. "Someone has to be at the house with them."

Jack didn't say anything.

Meg took a deep breath. "I'm staying, Jack. I'm moving back in."

Jack was changing his flight to return home that night but wouldn't be back until late. Her dad stayed with her through the morning, helping get the house cleaned up, although he said JJ should be the one cleaning, not sleeping. He, of course, was right. But she couldn't stand the mess. The chaos of the house was far too symbolic of the chaos of her life.

At noon they took a break to have lunch outside by the pool. Tuna sandwiches on wheat bread Meg pulled from the freezer. Dad liked his tuna with chopped dill pickles and olives and Meg had both on the pantry shelf.

It was nice just sitting and eating a sandwich with Dad. Growing up, she'd been close to him. While his job was dangerous, it also had a lot of flexibility. His shifts were twenty-four hours long, but then he'd be off for forty-eight. The twenty-four on, forty-eight off meant growing up she'd had a lot of quality time with him, and he'd been a very hands-on dad, coaching most of their sports.

"Did I hear you right when you were talking to Jack? You're moving back home?" he asked.

She nodded. "I have to. JJ's running wild."

"About time," he answered.

He'd put up the canvas umbrella so they could eat in the shade and she studied his weathered face closely, wondering if her sisters ever compared men to their dad. Meg couldn't help but compare when she was dating in college. It wasn't easy for guys to measure up to Tommy Brennan. He'd grown up in the inner Sunset District, the same neighborhood he lived in now. His parish church, St. Cecelia, was predominantly Irish, like his neighborhood. He was a working-class man whose mission was to make sure everybody was safe—his family, community, and firefighter brotherhood.

"Jack still wants a divorce," she said.

"I disagree. He just wants all this stuff to go away."

"You think so?"

"He can't cope with the kids without you. He's not a ladies' man. He needs you, and you need to be here to remind him of the fact. That's why I told you to come back here and sort things out. Instead you decamped to Capitola."

"Jack was so mad."

"As he would be. But you just gave up, crawled away, when you should have come home and fought for your marriage. Let Jack know he and this marriage and these kids meant something to you."

This conversation wasn't comfortable. "I was ashamed."

"Fine. But sitting around feeling bad, feeling guilty, it accomplishes nothing. You think it does, but it doesn't."

"It's hard to forgive yourself when you do something like that."

"Sure it is. Especially if you're a perfectionist, and you are. You've been one your whole life. Even as a little girl."

He looked at her, his big jaw set, brows pulled over intensely blue eyes. "Of all the kids you were the most independent. You wanted to do everything yourself. No one could help you. Used to make your mother crazy because she had stuff to do, but you wouldn't let her help dress you. Or put your shoes on. Or help brush your teeth. You had to do it all. And I remember this time, you were two and a half, maybe three, and your mother was trying to get you to preschool, but you told her to go away. You were going to get dressed all by yourself. And we could hear you in your room, banging drawers and looking for clothes, and your mom and I kept looking at each other, wanting to go to you, but your mom said no. Let her do it. It's what Meg wants. And then finally you came downstairs. Fully dressed. Pants, skirt, shirt, socks, and shoes—"

"Pants and skirt?"

"Yes. Both. And you were so proud of yourself. Your mom and I were proud of you, too. You said you were ready to go to school, and I said fine, but first, Maggie, let's switch your shoes, because you'd put them on backward. Got the right foot and left foot mixed up. But when I bent down to try to change them, you started crying and you went up to your room and wouldn't go to school that day."

Meg had been watching his face as he told the story. "Why?"

"Why were you upset?" he asked.

She nodded.

"You kept saying you were sure you'd done it right." His big hands lifted, he shrugged. "Your mom and I weren't mad at you. We were proud of you. Thought you'd done a great job getting dressed. But you, you were mad at yourself. You expected more of yourself. Even at two and a half." He looked across the table at her, shook his head. "No one has ever expected you to be perfect, Meg. No one, that is, but you."

Dad left after lunch, and Meg went to her room to take a brief nap because the long night was catching up with her. But she couldn't sleep, thinking of what her dad had said, remembering picking JJ up from jail, wondering what would happen when Jack came home.

She woke at four, went to JJ's room, and knocked on the door. He was still asleep. She crossed the floor, opened the blinds, and shook his shoulder. "You need to take a shower and come downstairs. We need to talk before your father gets here."

He was downstairs in less than ten minutes. Record time for JJ.

"Sit," she said, pointing to one of the stools at the kitchen island.

He sat down, looking a little pasty.

"How do you feel?" she asked.

He swallowed, shrugged. "Rough."

Good. She hoped he'd feel sick for a few more days. Teach him a lesson for drinking, and throwing parties at the house. "Do you want anything?"

"Do we have any Gatorade?"

Her eyebrows arched but she said nothing, and went to the refrigerator and then the pantry to check. "No. And no soda water, or ginger ale, or sodas of any kind. Looks like your friends drank it all last night."

"Can I have some crackers?"

She grabbed a box of Ritz Crackers and handed it to him.

"Dad's on his way home," she said after a moment of watching him munch on a cracker. "He and I are going to talk later, but I've already told him, and so I'll tell you: I'm staying. I'm not leaving. I'm moving back in and I'm not going away."

"Okay."

"I'm back," she added. "And I'm still your mom even if you are ashamed of me."

He flushed bright red. "Sorry I said that. It was mean. I was mad."

"And the comment about being a whore?"

His flush deepened. "I said *if* I called you a whore . . . which I didn't."

"But to even use the word in the same conversation with me?"

He looked away, wiggled his foot. Silence stretched in the kitchen. Finally he said, "Dad says you're getting divorced."

"That's what he told me, too."

"Are you?"

"I don't want to."

"Does he know that?"

"He should. I've been telling him that over and over for the past six weeks."

"Have you really?"

She nodded and pulled out a stool at the island and sat down next to him. "But I don't think it matters to him. He's ready to move forward . . . and so I'm going to get a lawyer. I'm going to let him file for divorce—"

"You can't!"

"I'm sorry, JJ. Sorry for all of this . . . sorry to have hurt you, and your dad, and your sisters. It's been bad. I know it has. But we'll get through this—"

"You don't need a lawyer. You're not going to get divorced—"

"JJ."

"I'm going to tell Dad to let you stay. I'm going to tell him we want you here."

"Honey, I don't think that will help—"

"Yes, it will. I think he misses you, but he thinks we're mad at you. We *were* mad at you. And we felt really bad for Dad. He was so sad. He'd cry when he thought we were in bed."

Meg had no idea. All she'd seen from Jack was anger. "Dad doesn't cry, does he?"

"That's why Tessa and I told him we didn't want to live with you anymore. We thought he'd feel better. We thought he needed us." JJ looked up at her, tears in his gray-green eyes. "And he probably does, but he needs you even more."

Jack's flight landed at San Francisco at ten-forty, which meant the earliest he'd get home would be midnight. The kids were in bed. The house was clean. Meg had cut some of the coral roses from the garden and put them in a pottery jar on the kitchen counter.

Now she paced the house, glancing at the clock. It was only eleven now. She still had another hour to kill. She wasn't sure how this . . . meeting . . . would go with Jack. Wasn't sure if he'd be angry, sad, quiet, nonresponsive. She had no idea and the not knowing was the worst.

Kit texted her while she paced. *Is Jack back yet?*

Meg called Kit instead of texting her. "Glad you're still up," she said when Kit answered. "And no. He should be here in the next hour, though."

"Nervous?"

"You could say that." Meg could feel Kit's smile. "And don't smile. This is serious."

"Jack's putty in your hand, Meg."

"Not anymore."

"Just be patient, and sweet, and he'll realize what a treasure he has in you."

"Oh, shut up. You're becoming insufferable. I think it's all the running. It's ruined you. You feel too damn good about yourself."

Kit laughed. "Heard there was some excitement last night in Santa Rosa."

"How do you know? I've told no one."

"The police scanner."

"Seriously?"

Kit laughed again. "No, Meg, get a grip. How do you think I found out? Dad told Tommy, Tommy told Cass, and Cass called me."

"I swear, you guys are the biggest gossips," Meg muttered, throwing herself down on the couch and putting her feet up on the ottoman. "Dad must be pretty disappointed in JJ."

"Not too badly. I think he expects this kind of stuff to happen. It's part of growing up."

"A hundred drunk kids stumbling around my house. Someone could have died—"

"Now, Meg—"

"Think about it. Someone could have fallen down the stairs and broken his neck, or tripped and gone through a window. Or God help us, fallen into the pool."

"But no one did."

"The laundry room door is broken."

"Anything else?"

"Half my water glasses from the kitchen." Meg took a deep breath, exhaled hard. "But you're right, at least no one was hurt and glasses and doors can be replaced." She was silent a moment, thinking. "He said it was a rager. Do you know what that means?"

"'A large gathering usually of high school or college students where massive amounts of alcohol are consumed.' Or in other words, a very cool party."

"Did you just use quote marks?"

"It's from *Urban Dictionary*. Sadly, it's my students' favorite dictionary."

"Never heard of that dictionary."

"Ask JJ, he'd know."

"JJ's in bed," Meg said tartly, before remembering something she'd wanted to ask Kit ever since she helped paint her sister's dining room. "Will you have Danielle Jones's daughter in your class again?"

"I'm sure I will," Kit answered carefully. "She'll be a sophomore this year.

Meg hesitated, trying to imagine Danielle as a mother. "What's her name? The daughter?"

"Kacie."

Meg silently repeated the name. "That's pretty."

"Kacie's really sweet. She's a nice girl."

"Is she smart?"

"She works hard."

Not the same thing, Meg knew, but it was good. Important. One didn't succeed without effort. "And Danielle is okay?"

"Yes."

Meg chewed her lip. "Will you . . . will you tell her hello from me? Give her my love? Tell her I think about her a lot, and wish her and her daughter well."

"I will."

And then suddenly there were lights shining in the driveway, approaching the house. Meg stiffened. "He's here, Kit. Jack's back."

"So hang up, stay calm, and no matter what he says, be soft, sweet, and agreeable."

"That's not easy for me, Kit."

"No, I know. But you can do it."

Meg waited in the kitchen for Jack to enter the house. Nervous, anxious, she heard the door open and then Jack drop his briefcase and suitcase in the mudroom. She held her breath as his footsteps echoed on the limestone tiles as he headed for the kitchen.

And then he was there. Tall and shockingly thin, his broad shoulders looked almost bony in the blue chambray shirt. There were shadows under his eyes and hollows beneath his cheekbones. He looked like hell. Like he'd been through hell.

He stopped walking as soon as he spotted her at the marble-topped island. "How's JJ?" he asked roughly.

"He's fine," she said quietly, calmly. "Wanted to play Xbox but I wouldn't let him. I've taken his Xbox away for the next couple weeks, told him he'd learn the rest of his punishment when you got home."

Jack seemed to be picking his words. "What are you thinking his punishment should be?"

Meg was surprised that he'd asked for her opinion. Surprised that he'd even care what she thought. Her shoulders shrugged as she struggled for a nonchalance she didn't feel. "I think he should be grounded for the next month. He can go to school, sports, but that's it."

"I also think the Xbox needs to be gone for a month, too. Otherwise he'll just sit around and play all day."

"Fine." Meg hesitated, wondering how to segue into what she really wanted to say. The things about her coming home, her right to be in her own home, her need to be home—with the children. And hopefully with Jack. They were a family, for better or worse. "I know I've hurt you. I know I've betrayed you and your trust, and I am sorry. Very, very sorry—"

"I don't want to do this now."

"But it's time for me to come home. The kids need me here. I'm their mom. This is my house, too. And hopefully with me home, we can work through this—"

"'This' being a euphemism for your affair."

She lifted her chin, unable, unwilling, to be intimidated or shamed any longer. She'd made a mistake. A dreadful, terrible mistake. And she recognized it. "Yes. And yes, I cheated. And yes, I broke our marriage vows, but I've begged for your forgiveness, begged for you to give me a second chance, but I'm not begging anymore. I can't beg anymore. I'm exhausted and broken and it's time for us, and this family, to start healing, one way or another. With you or without you. But hopefully with you. Preferably with you."

He said nothing. It was on the tip of her tongue to mention the appointment with the lawyer on Tuesday. He should know she had options. He should know she wasn't broken. But she held her tongue. Waited. And waited some more.

Finally he spoke. "I'm so mad at you, Meg."

His eyes met hers. She could see the anger in them. He'd still be angry for a long time. "I know," she said gently.

"Really, really mad. And hurt. And disappointed."

"I understand. I'm disappointed, too. I'm disappointed in me as well. Disappointed in my choices, and my selfishness. I know I was selfish. And all I can do now is try to repair the damage and hope we can save our marriage."

"I don't know if we can."

Again she thought of the appointment on Tuesday, and it comforted her to know there were options. That she didn't have to be here. That she was choosing to be here. She was choosing to face Jack and all the messy, intense, uncomfortable emotions in hopes of saving her marriage. It wouldn't be fun, or pleasant, but her family was worth it. Jack was worth it. But she could only do so much. Jack would have to meet her partway. He'd have to choose to forgive her. He'd have to choose the messy, intense, uncomfortable emotions, too.

Could he?

Would he?

She didn't know. They'd have to find out.

Eighteen

On Monday, Meg quietly canceled her appointment with the divorce attorney, knowing she could always reschedule if need be. But Jack didn't pursue filing divorce papers.

She didn't know if it was because JJ told his dad that he wanted Mom home with them, or because Gabi burst into tears and said Mom had to stay, but Jack agreed that maybe it was time for Meg to be in the house, taking care of the kids. "They need you," he said to Meg repeatedly in those first few days of them being back together.

Meg sometimes wondered if that meant Jack needed her, too, but she never asked. Instead they settled into a routine, which quickly felt like the old routine, especially once school started.

She took the kids shopping for back-to-school clothes and purchased the necessary supplies. She made dinners and baked, kept the house spotless, and made sure there was never more than one basket of laundry waiting to be washed.

She missed working, though, and had begun to look at the want ads, wondering if she could find a part-time position somewhere. As much as she loved being mom and wife, she needed work, too, and liked having the income.

Meg told Jack she was thinking about getting a job. He didn't discourage her. But he didn't encourage her either. He didn't say much, which was typical of their relationship.

Privately Meg wondered if their marriage would ever recover. Jack seemed so awkward and uncomfortable with her that she found herself avoiding being in the same room with him.

Around the kids they tried to put on happy faces, but when the kids weren't there, Jack still looked at her with hurt and surprise.

She told herself that it was natural for him to be hurt, and that he might be hurt for a long time. She told herself she'd have to be okay with it. That was the price she paid for losing Jack's trust.

Every now and then, when Meg was falling asleep in the guest room bed, which was now her room, she wondered if the shoe were on the other foot, if he'd been the one to have an affair, if he'd be as patient with her as she tried to be with him. Somehow she doubted it. Meg had a feeling that Jack would expect her to get over "it," but because the shoe wasn't on the other foot, she tried to stay focused on the goal—healing the family—rather than the process.

The process sucked.

Some nights Meg would be woken by Gabi crawling into bed with her. Gabi never remembered coming to her mother's room, but Meg didn't mind. She was happy for the company.

JJ once asked her at breakfast when she'd return to her old room, the master bedroom. Meg teasingly answered that the guest room over the garage had the nicest view of all the bedrooms in the house.

The truth was, Meg wasn't ready to sleep in the bedroom with Jack. It had been three months since they'd shared a room, never mind a bed, and it seemed like such a huge, intimate step. It didn't help that whenever Meg started to feel comfortable, Jack would stagger past her, looking dazed and confused, like a big bear that had been wounded.

Two weeks into the new school year Meg was on her knees, cleaning the girls' bathroom shower with a scrub brush, trying to get the white grout whiter, when her phone rang. It was Jennifer from the winery. Surprised, pleased, she quickly rinsed off her hands to take the call. "Jennifer! How are you?"

"Good. Miss you, Meg. Wish you'd come back."

"I bet you're doing an amazing job," Meg said, pushing hair behind her ear.

"I don't know. I'm not totally sure what I'm doing, but I'm trying."

"You'll get it. And if you ever have questions, feel free to call."

"I will. Thanks."

Meg caught a glimpse of her reflection in the mirror. Messy ponytail. Bare face, no makeup. Massive circles beneath the eyes. Hideous bleach-stained navy T-shirt. Yuck. She turned away, took a seat on the edge of the tub. "So how are things there? Good? Heard that they've been filming."

"All summer. The series premieres end of September. Exciting, but scary. Not sure how they're going to portray us, you know?"

"I know."

"Lots of extra visitors, though, this summer, people drawn by the publicity about the show."

"Tourists hoping to get on television?" Meg asked, laughing and crossing one knee over the other. The show would be good for business. Visitors streaming into the tasting room and gift shop. Increased online orders. All good things for Dark Horse.

"Pretty much." Jennifer paused, and her voice changed. "Hey, I've got someone here who wanted to say hello."

There was another pause and Meg's stomach tightened, knotting, knowing. Chad. Jennifer was handing the phone to Chad.

And then he was there. "Mrs. Roberts?" he said, his deep male voice drawling, sending a little buzz of sensation through Meg's middle and limbs.

She smiled faintly, reluctantly, horrified he'd still have this effect on her. "Chad."

"How are you?"

Her heart turned over. She felt tender, and still so very bruised. "I'm all right."

"Heard you're back home. How was Capitola?"

"You knew I was gone?"

"Yeah. Mr. Roberts stopped by the winery last June. Let me know in no uncertain terms that I wasn't wanted or needed in your lives."

Meg had no idea Jack had confronted Chad. "Can Jennifer hear this?"

He made a rough sound. "She was there when Jack came by."

Oh God. Meg exhaled slowly. "Anyone else there?"

"Everyone."

"Craig?"

"Craig, and everyone."

She cringed, shoulders rising up to her ears. "Who is everyone?"

"The tourists, the film crew."

"Oh no. They got this on film?"

"They did."

"Shit."

"Don't worry. I got you covered. It's not going to be part of the show."

"How do you know?" Meg would die if all of California—no, make that the United States—knew that winery publicist Meg

Roberts cheated on her husband, Santa Rosa architect Jack Roberts, with the younger Hallahan brother.

"Craig went to bat for you. Threatened to pull the plug on the entire production."

"Did that work?"

"Pretty much.

"*Pretty* much? That's not totally reassuring."

She could feel him smile at the other end of the line. "The producers loved the drama of Jack's visit," he admitted. "They were very attached to your husband storming the winery tasting room and threatening to do bodily harm—"

"He didn't."

"He did. And since it was such great television, they knew it'd be killer for ratings."

"None of this is reassuring."

"Big brother Craig might not love people, but he's one hell of a negotiator. He hung tough and managed to convince the producers to take out Jack and all references to you, and substitute a similar story line instead. So that's what we did. We reshot the scenes with a different husband."

"So you're still the bad guy?"

"I *am* the bad guy."

"Your reputation will be ruined."

Chad laughed softly, and the sound sent a tingle down Meg's spine. "It's already in tatters, Meg. I'm not worried."

"Who is this other husband?"

"A professional actor, flown up from Los Angeles just to play the cuckold husband—"

"*Chad.*" She blushed hotly, embarrassed.

He laughed again and Meg suddenly understood why she'd fallen for him. He laughed. He smiled. He was warm.

And she'd needed the warmth. She'd been cold. She was still really cold.

And for a second she couldn't breathe, for a second she couldn't think, for a second she could only feel, and it was so much. So very, very much.

Love and loss and need. Loneliness and pain. And need.

And then she got a grip on her emotions, and battled through the intense longing for the life she didn't have, and the life she wouldn't have. "So what happened?" she asked, her voice steady, even.

"They shot it a dozen different times and he got better with every take. By the time we were done, I'd been punched a good seven times."

"Tell me you're joking."

"I think it's funny. And I'm a big boy. But that's not why I had Jennifer call you. I called you to give you the name of a really good lawyer—"

"I'm not divorcing Jack."

"Not for you, baby, for your son. Call Lyle Nielsen. Have him represent JJ in court. He'll get the minor-in-possession charges off JJ's record. He's good. He'll take care of everything."

"How did you know about JJ?"

Chad hesitated. "I keep tabs on you. Make sure you're okay."

Meg closed her eyes, held her breath, overwhelmed.

"Tell me you're okay, and I'll go away," he added more quietly, all laughter gone from his voice. "Let me know you're good, and I won't bother you again."

Silence stretched.

She couldn't speak.

Not when her chest burned and her eyes burned and she pressed her lips to keep from making a sound. One tear fell, and then another. Meg wiped them away swiftly. "I'm good," she whispered, adding, "I'm fine."

"That's all I need to know." And then he hung up.

Call ended, Meg slowly sank to her knees on the bathroom floor. It was a long time before she was able to start scrubbing the grout between the tiles again.

Days turned into weeks and September was almost over. The mornings were cooler and crisper and the leaves were starting to change, greens turning to yellow and the odd pop of red. Gabi had begun to talk about this year's Halloween costume and was already stressing over school being so much harder than last year. Tessa continued to just live and breathe ballet. JJ, a junior in high school, passed his driver's test on the second try and was now beginning to drive himself places, which terrified Meg. Each time he walked out the door, she cautioned him to drive slowly, safely, reminding him that there was no hurry.

He'd roll his eyes at her and sometimes get irritated with her lack of confidence. And then sometimes he'd return to her and hug her and tell her he loved her.

One Friday night after JJ had gone out, having borrowed the car to attend the high school harvest dance, Gabi was at a friend's, and Tessa at rehearsal for a performance next month. Tessa would need to be picked up at eight, and so Jack and Meg stayed in, waiting to get her, and then the three of them would go out for a late dinner in town.

But dinner was still several hours away and Meg caught Jack opening and closing cupboards and the fridge, looking for something to eat.

"Can I make you something?" she offered. "I can put together some tapas . . . hummus, olives, crackers, cheese . . . little appetizers to tide us over until dinnertime?"

He looked surprised, but also shyly pleased. "You don't mind?"

She bit into her lower lip, suddenly aching with bittersweet emotion. Poor Jack. She'd really done a number on him, hadn't she? "Not at all," she said briskly. "I'll organize the food if you can pour us something to drink."

Jack returned from their small wine cellar with a bottle of red. "This sound good?" he asked, showing her the dusty label.

It was an older wine, a very good wine, a very expensive wine they'd bought at one of the kids' school auctions several years ago. "Sounds fantastic," she said, arranging the crackers and cheese on a platter.

He opened the wine, grabbed some big goblets, but didn't pour the wine immediately in order to give it a few minutes to breathe. "This is nice," he said, taking one of the stools at the island. "Haven't done this in a long time."

She glanced at him, seeing his erect posture and wistful expression. Her heart turned over and she flashed back to their first date in Rome. Jack had been so idealistic, so romantic, so full of hope and beauty and ambition. And now look at him . . . bruised and battered and so very tentative. It made her feel suddenly protective. Her Jack. Dear Jack. Her absentminded architect.

She placed the cheese and crackers, and the tray with sliced vegetables and hummus, before him. "We used to love tapas," she said self-consciously.

Jack watched her get plates, forks, and napkins. She then wiped down the counter. Straightened the stools. Adjusted the lights, dimming them slightly.

"Sit," he said at last. "You're making me nervous."

She smiled quickly. She was feeling nervous. It was strange being here, alone together, like this. Strange and overwhelming and it made her heart ache. For him. For them. But she took a stool, and sat, and watched him pour the wine. It was a Cab, a beautiful deep red, and it splashed into the glass like a liquid jewel.

Working at the winery, she'd poured wine for tastings, talked wine to buyers, pitched wine to media. And it had become a business. A job. But suddenly watching the wine hit the glass, it seemed intimate again.

Jack handed her a glass. They lightly clinked the rims. She felt exhausted. Frightened. Sad. Maybe things would eventually be fine. But they certainly weren't there yet.

"Why did you do it?" Jack asked abruptly.

No, she thought, things most definitely weren't fine. "I was lonely."

He ducked his head, stared hard at his plate. "How could you be lonely? Yes, I travel, but not that often. I'm here, usually all the time."

A lump filled her throat. "But when you're here, you're not always here."

"Explain that to me."

"You don't have the same needs for touch and conversation that others do. That I do." Meg noticed that neither of them had tasted the food. But then, how did you nibble on hummus and crackers when discussing infidelity?

"Why didn't you tell me?"

"Because it felt weird—"

"Weird?"

"Wrong." She licked her lips. They were so dry. Her heart was so very sad. "As if I was complaining."

"So?"

"I wasn't raised to complain. It's not something you're praised for as a little girl. We're supposed to be happy and content, and find ways to make ourselves happy and content without causing trouble."

"Well, you did cause a lot of trouble. It would have been a hell of a lot easier if you'd said, 'Jack, feeling kind of neglected, pay me some attention.'"

"You really think it would have been as easy as that?"

"I think it would have given us a fighting chance."

Meg bowed her head. He was right. Absolutely right. "I'm sorry. I'm sorry I didn't go to you. I'm sorry I've hurt you. I was wrong."

"I just didn't *know*." His tone was sharp. "I've lived with you seventeen years, and I had no idea you were so unhappy."

She nudged her glass forward an inch. "It wasn't all the time. Just sometimes." She took a breath. "Like when I reached out to you, but felt shut down."

"I never shut you down."

"Every time I reached out to you, you turned away."

He looked at her baffled. "When?"

She flushed. "At night. In bed. You were never interested."

His confusion grew. He frowned. "That's not how I remember it. I remember us making love." He paused, still thinking. "Maybe not as often as we used to, but we're older . . . I'm heading toward fifty . . . I think what we have—had—was good."

She knew that now. Their lives together were good. And their relationship was good, except for one area. Intimacy. She'd craved more intimacy. Physical and emotional closeness. She still craved it. "But sex is different now. It's changed, it's . . . rushed . . . and"— she gulped—"one-sided."

"What?"

This was really really difficult. "Do you realize I don't even have an orgasm during sex?"

He stirred uneasily. "I didn't think you cared . . ."

"Not care about an O? Jack, I'm in my forties. Horny as hell."

He looked even more uncomfortable. "But you . . . don't . . . come."

"Because it's over so fast." She saw his face and rushed on. "I know you can last. Staying power hasn't ever been your issue. I think you don't necessarily try to last." She shrugged. "But maybe I'm wrong."

"So you can come?"

Meg nearly rolled her eyes. "I used to have multiple orgasms

when we were first dating! Rome was just one orgasm after another! But then . . . there was less time, and you were in a hurry,
and I was tired, and I'd let you come just to get it over with, and
after a while . . . you stopped caring that I didn't come."

"And that's what this is about? You not having orgasms anymore?"

She flushed. My God, this was excruciating. "It's about feeling
close. Being a couple. So yes, it's about sex, but also affection.
Hugs. Knowing I have someone who will talk to me, and listen to
me—" She broke off, aware that he was thinking she was always
on the phone with one of her sisters. "And yes, I do have my family,
and they do talk to me. But you're my partner. My husband. I need
you to listen, too."

"And I don't?"

She hesitated. "It seems like you listen with half an ear, your
attention always divided between your work and me." She exhaled.
Maybe they should have just focused on eating the hummus. It
would have been a hell of a lot easier. "And most of the time your
work gets the bigger share."

He took a long sip. Swallowed. And another sip. Finally he
turned his head and looked at her. "I feel stupid. I do. I feel like I'm
meeting an all-new you."

"Why?"

"I just had no idea you were lonely. Or dissatisfied. You're so
contained, and efficient, with a thousand places to go and a million
things to do. I didn't think you needed me."

"Of course I need you, Jack. I need you to keep me sane. And
feeling loved so that I can do all those errands on that million-thing
to-do list."

"Did you love him, Meg?"

The abruptness of the question knocked her off balance. She
touched the tip of her tongue to the inside of her lip, thinking there
was no good answer.

It was a yes-but-no answer. Yes, part of her would always love Chad, but no, she'd never act on that desire again. She was committed to Jack. Fully committed to Jack and their marriage. Period.

"No." She exhaled and looked at him, hoping he couldn't see any of the pain she was feeling, because being with Chad had been like opening Pandora's box. She'd created something, unleashed something into her life, that was never meant to exist. "I love you. I really do love you. I just need you to love me, too."

He studied her for a long second. "I do." Then he reached over and took her hand. "I'm sorry. I'm sorry I didn't pay attention to you in bed. I'm sorry if I didn't appear interested. But most of all, I'm sorry if you didn't feel loved. Because I do love you. I love you very much."

Her eyes stung, smarting with tears. "I'm glad."

"This has been hard, Meg."

She nodded. "I know."

"I still can't believe that this happened."

"I understand."

"But I accept responsibility for not being there for you. I need to be there for you. And if you should ever feel neglected again, get my attention."

"Yes. I will."

"Good. And if you can't get my attention, grab a rock. Throw it at my head."

She laughed. "That would hurt."

His eyes searched hers. "Not half as much as losing you." He held her hand tighter. "Don't want to lose you, Meg. I know I'm lucky to have you."

It was late that evening by the time Tessa finally went to bed. Meg knocked lightly on her door before entering to say good night. "Ready to be tucked in?" she asked, standing in the doorway.

"Yes," Tessa answered, still a little cool with her mother.

Meg knew her older daughter hadn't forgiven her completely yet, wasn't sure when she would, and that was another relationship that needed work. And patience.

She crossed to her daughter's bed, smoothed the covers over her shoulders. "Good night, Tessa. Sweet dreams." She leaned over, kissed the top of Tessa's head, before stepping away. "I'll see you tomorrow."

Tessa hesitated. "Mom?"

"Yes?"

"Can you come back?" she asked, reaching for her hand and tugging her mother toward her. "Here," she added, pulling Meg closer.

And then, with Meg just a breath away, Tessa tipped her head and gave her mother a butterfly kiss. "Remember?" she whispered.

Meg nodded.

"Now you," Tessa said softly.

Meg crouched next to Tessa, and gently blinked, making her eyelashes brush her daughter's cheek.

"Butterfly kisses," Tessa whispered.

Meg's heart ached. She smoothed Tessa's dark red hair back from her oval face. "My favorite kind."

Tessa smiled unsteadily. "I love you, Momma."

"I love you, too, my oldest, biggest girl." And then Meg turned out the light, closed the door, and leaned against the hallway wall, overwhelmed by emotion.

She needed her girls, her boy, her husband. She needed this family so very much.

Jack rounded the corner and discovered Meg in the hall.

"What's wrong?" he asked. "What happened? Was it Tessa?"

She looked up at him, tears swimming in her eyes. "Butterfly kiss."

"What?"

"Tessa gave me a butterfly kiss." Meg dashed away the tears before they could fall. "I forgot how much I loved them."

Jack straightened, and studied her. "You're tired."

"Maybe a little," she agreed, realizing how close she'd come to losing all this . . . butterfly kisses and weepy hugs . . . teenage sons who didn't think they needed Mom anymore. But this was her life. These were the things that mattered most to her. There was nowhere else she'd rather be.

Jack seemed unsure what to do next. He opened his mouth to speak, thought better of it, and then ran a hand through his dark wavy hair, tousling it further. "Do you want to come watch TV with me?"

It was such a simple thing, and yet it was such a huge step. To watch a show together. To sit in the same room and view the same program.

"What show?" she asked, not caring what it was but trying to make conversation, wanting to ease that awkwardness that shadowed them always.

"Doesn't matter," he answered. "You choose."

So they sat on the family room couch, not close, but not on opposite ends either, and watched HGTV's *House Hunters International*. It was a show they'd once both enjoyed—if they had the money to buy a vacation home, where would they go?—and one more step in the right direction.

The next day was the last Saturday of September and Sonoma's Valley of the Moon Festival celebrating the annual harvest of grapes and the yearly crush. Jack offered to take Meg and the kids to the plaza, reminding the girls that two years ago they'd nearly won their division of the Grape Stomp.

JJ didn't want to go, but the girls were eager to compete as a team again in the kid division. In the past, Tessa had been the "stomper." She'd been the one inside the small barrel mashing up the grapes, while Gabi was the "swabber," kneeling on the outside of the barrel, trying to catch the juice as it dripped through the drain spout.

But this year Gabi wanted to stomp, and Tessa agreed.

The girls had a clear goal, to make the finals for their division, and discussed their strategy so seriously during the drive to downtown Sonoma—Gabi had to keep her knees high, come down hard; Tessa had to use quick hands and not spill or drip a precious drop—that Jack and Meg exchanged amused glances. They'd raised two very competitive daughters.

The old plaza was already packed by the time they got there, crowds still milling about after the annual Blessing of the Grapes and waiting for the start of the Grape Stomp.

It was warm and sunny and dry, perfect Indian summer weather, and the girls had come dressed for the stomp in T-shirts and short shorts.

Realizing that he'd inadvertently left his "real" camera in the car, Jack dashed back to Meg's Lexus, saying he'd only be a second. He was only gone a few seconds when the announcer called for the girls to take their places.

"Where's Daddy?" Gabi asked.

"He went to get his camera," Meg answered, thinking this was so Jack. He was never quite where he was needed when he was needed there, but fortunately she usually was. It's what had made them such a good team all those years. Jack created. Meg organized. Jack dreamed. Meg implemented. And it worked. They worked.

The girls went to their assigned barrel. Gabi hiked up her shorts even higher and Tessa crouched in front.

"Stomp!" the announcer shouted.

Gabi began stomping. Her feet flew, pounding up and down, while Tessa shouted encouragement.

"Come on, come on," Tessa cried to Gabi as she swirled her hand in the wet grapes, trying to help extract juice. "You can do it!"

Gabi's knees flew up to her chest, a vigorous, relentless one, two, three, and juice went flying, splashing Tessa with purple.

"That's it," Tessa cried. "Faster!"

Meg glanced around for Jack, wanting him to capture this with the camera—the sunlight streaming over the girls, the open barrel, their daughters laughing, happy—but she didn't see him, couldn't find him.

Instead she saw Chad and a big camera crew. Looked like they were filming a segment for the reality series here today.

Meg sneaked one more peek in his direction. She hadn't seen him in over three months, not since that last day at the winery, and he looked good. Still tall and ruggedly handsome, still that blond sexy vintner in jeans and boots and a chambray shirt rolled back on his tan forearms.

Wow.

Her breath caught in her throat. It hurt to see him. He was still golden Chad—lovely but oh so very dangerous—and Meg didn't want or need any more pain in her life. She'd had enough. She'd inflicted enough. Time to move on.

And so she deliberately turned away, turning her back on Chad and the film crew to focus exclusively on the girls. These children were her life. They were the important people.

And apparently from the sound of it, her important people were becoming unhinged.

"We're losing!" Tessa screamed, burying her slim arm in the fruit to clear the little screen. "Jump, jump, jump!"

"I'm jumping!" Gabi screamed back.

"Not fast enough."

"Then you do it!" Gabi cried, grabbing a handful of mashed-up grapes and smashing it on Tessa's face, staining her sister burgundy and purple.

Tessa shrieked with rage. She reached up and shoved Gabi's hips. Gabi toppled over, dragging Tessa into the barrel.

Meg watched the grape fight unfurl in horror. Some spectators were cheering. Some were protesting. One person was whistling. And Meg was wondering where the hell Jack was.

"Do something," one of the stomp organizers cried, rushing over to Meg.

"What?" Meg asked as her girls took grape wrestling to a whole new level. Tessa was shoving grapes down Gabi's pants while Gabi was shoving grapes into Tessa's shirt. They were like mad men. They were out of control. Reckless. Crazy. And absolutely bursting with life.

"Do something," the stomp organizer cried.

Meg really wished Jack was there. Surely he'd know what to do. And so she did the only thing she could think of.

She laughed. Hard.

It had been a long, difficult summer, and a bumpy start to fall, but maybe the worst was behind them. Maybe they were finally moving forward, together. Stressed, strained, but still intact.

"Mom!" Gabi cried.

Meg looked at her daughter just in time to be pelted by a mushy, juicy grape.

"Gotcha!" Gabi crowed.

Tessa snorted indelicately.

And Meg just laughed harder.

So what if the kids were out of control? So what if she'd lost control?

Life would go on, and with a little faith, and a whole lot of love, they'd be fine. They would. Children were resilient and they'd heal. One day they'd be strong again.

Sister Mary Margaret Brennan Roberts would make sure of that.

If you enjoyed *The Good Woman*,
keep reading for a special excerpt from
the next novel in the Brennan Sisters trilogy

The Good Daughter

Coming in February 2013 from Berkley Books!

One

Make a wish.

That's how it had all started. The idea. The hope. The sense of possibility.

It wasn't Kit who was supposed to be making wishes, though. It was Cass as it was her night. The Brennan family had gathered to celebrate Cass's thirty-sixth birthday at Kit's childhood home in San Francisco's inner Sunset District.

They were gathered now in the Edwardian period dining room with its high ceiling and formal wainscoting, the lights still out, the last of the happy birthday song dying away.

There were ten at the table. Kit Brennan. Her parents. Her sister Meg and her family. Her brother, Tommy, and his wife, Cass, whose birthday they were celebrating.

"Make a wish, Cass," Mom said from her seat at the head of the table. She was smiling but looked tired. But then, Mom always looked tired now.

"Make a wish, Aunt Cass," eleven-year-old Gabi Roberts

echoed, crowding in close to Cass, unable to contain herself, the flickering candlelight reflected in her shining brown eyes.

"Make a wish, babe," Tommy Jr. said, patting his wife's back. "Before your cake catches fire."

Cass Brennan crinkled her nose and tucked a long blond curl behind her ear. She'd married into this family eleven years ago and they'd immediately made her one of them. "Not too worried," she said lightly, even with her candles ablaze. "I've got two of the city's finest firefighters here."

Dad lifted his hands. "I've retired, hon, and we don't know how good Tommy is. Better make a wish and blow out those candles."

"Come on, Aunt Cass," Gabi shouted, trying to be heard above the good-natured laughter. "Wish for a baby. Wish hard!"

The laughter immediately died.

Cass froze.

Tommy's shoulders squared aggressively. "We don't need a baby. But we could use some money. Maybe a vacation. Wish for something useful, like winning the lottery."

Cass flinched, as if struck. Tears slowly filled her eyes.

All pretense of happiness was gone. Kit could feel Cass's grief, was sure everyone else felt it, too. The endless sorrow hung in the dining room, heavy, aching, a tragic specter weighting the room.

Tommy reacted first, his strong jaw—Dad's jaw—tightening, his blue eyes snapping. He didn't do this. Didn't break, grieve, mourn. Not in public. Not even in front of his family. He clapped his hand impatiently on Cass's slender back, between her shoulder blades. "Come on, babe. Blow out the candles."

The edge in his voice, brought Cass to life. She gulped a breath, leaned toward the tall coconut cake with the fluffy icing, staring at what was left of the candles and formulating the wish, then blew out the flames in a broken rush of air.

Everyone clapped, smiled. The kids cheered. Meg rose and rushed to get the knife and delicate porcelain dessert plates. Jack asked if anyone wanted coffee or tea. Mom wanted tea and Jack headed to the kitchen to make the tea and all the while, Dad was talking loudly, carrying the small stack of presents from the sideboard to the table, making a big deal about which present Cass would open first. Everyone was talking, busy doing something, but Tommy.

Tommy sat stiff and silent and grim in his chair at the corner of the table. Kit refilled water glasses but kept an eye on her brother. She knew Tommy well, could tell from his expression that he was angry, resenting Cass, maybe everyone, for making him into the bad guy. Because that's what he was thinking, feeling, that they'd all turned him into the villain in the story, and he wasn't the villain. He was just being honest. Practical. After six years of trying unsuccessfully to have a baby, Tommy was done. He didn't need a baby. He wanted peace. He needed to stay sane.

As Cass cut the cake and Meg assisted by passing the plates around, Kit wondered what Cass had wished for. Was it a baby? Or was it for Tommy to want a baby again? Because their marriage was suffering. Both of them were suffering. Kit wasn't even sure a baby would solve everything anymore.

Kit suddenly ached with wishes of her own . . .

For Mom's cancer to go into remission.

For Cass to have her baby.

For Tommy to be happy with Cass again . . .

Later, after cake and presents, Meg's three kids cleared the dishes from the table, taking them to the kitchen to scrape and stack, while Jack and Dad headed outside with Tommy to look at Tommy's new car, which was really an old car, a 1960 Cadillac he bought on Craigslist for next to nothing and was determined to restore himself.

"Just us now," Meg said, sitting back in her chair with a soft, appreciative sigh. "The girls."

Kit was glad, too. She was tight with her sisters, and they were all close with Mom, so close that for the past ten years the five of them had taken an annual girls-only trip together, calling it the Brennan Girls' Getaway, spending a long weekend or week at the family beach house in Capitola.

On their getaway they'd eat and drink, talk, read, sleep. It was a time to let their hair down, a time to celebrate family, and hopefully a time to feel safe, although the last couple getaways had been tense due to friction between Brianna, Kit's fraternal twin, and Meg. Cass had missed the last getaway, too, back in May, as she'd been in the middle of an IVF cycle and her doctor wouldn't let her travel so close to the egg retrieval.

Mom shifted in her high-back chair and focused on Cass. "How *are* you?"

Mom wasn't making polite conversation. She was genuinely concerned about Cass, and now that Tommy was gone this was a chance for Cass to open up . . . if she could. No one was sure that she could, or would. It'd been almost three and a half months since she'd miscarried and this miscarriage had been the worst . . . not just for her, but the whole family. It was her fourth miscarriage, and it'd happened later than the others, this time at twenty-four weeks, just when Cass had let her guard down. Just when she'd started to get excited about the baby.

The entire family had grieved with Cass. All of them had been so happy about the baby, and then their hearts were broken. But this time Tommy didn't want their meals or phone calls or visits. This time Tommy announced that he and Cass wanted to be alone, and he asked that the family give them space and privacy to deal with the loss their way, in their time.

Kit's baby sister, Sarah, who lived with her husband and children in Tampa Bay, had been on the phone immediately with Kit and then Meg, hurt, even outraged that Tommy would push them away, but Mom and Dad backed Tommy, insisting that his sisters respect Tommy and Cass's need for space. As Mom reminded them repeatedly, having children, or not having children, was part of marriage and no one's business but Tommy and Cass's.

Of course the Brennan sisters couldn't ignore Cass, not when they knew she was hurting so much. Without consulting each other, each of them quietly sent Cass private e-mails and text messages, letting her know she was loved. Tommy could refuse meals and visitors, but he couldn't expect his sisters not to reach out to Cass. They loved Cass, and they told her so, repeatedly. Cass didn't answer all, or even most, of the messages, but later in December, just before Christmas she sent her sisters-in-law a group message thanking them for their amazing support and constant love. She hadn't had sisters, only two younger brothers, and she told them that she felt incredibly lucky to be one of the Brennan girls.

"I'm good," Cass said softly now, two spots of color in her cheeks. "Well, better than I was in October." She paused, studying the blue, white, and gold pattern on her dessert plate with the half-eaten slice of birthday cake. "October was bad. And November." Her full mouth quirked and one of her deep dimples appeared. "To be honest, December wasn't much better either."

Kit knew Cass had been in a very dark place and yet there had been nothing any of them could do for her then. There was really nothing they could do now. Kit hated feeling helpless. "We've been worried about you."

"I know. And I was kind of worried about me, too," Cass admitted on a strangled laugh, pushing back the same wayward curl that had slipped out of her ponytail. She had long, loose curls and big blue eyes like a pink-cheeked shepherdess from a Mother Goose nursery rhyme. In reality she was a labor and delivery nurse at a hospital in Walnut Creek specializing in high-risk deliveries.

"Are you doing better?" Mom asked, a deep furrow between her eyebrows. Mom had been a nurse, too, before she earned her master's degree and became a hospital administrator.

Cass toyed with the lace edging her white linen napkin. "I don't know. This last time broke something inside me. Here I had this beautiful, perfect little boy . . . and my body rejected him. Killed him—"

"Cass!" Meg interrupted, horrified. "Don't say that. You're not responsible. You can't blame yourself."

"But I do." Cass looked up, the grief clouding her eyes. "How can I not? He was twenty-four weeks old. Thirty-six percent of babies can survive premature birth at twenty-four weeks. Instead, my body—" She didn't finish, pressing a hand to her mouth to keep the words in, but her eyes were enormous with sorrow and pain.

Kit slid out of her chair to wrap her arms around Cass's shoulders. "I'm so sorry," she whispered. "So very, very sorry."

Cass covered Kit's hands with hers. "I want him back. I want to save him."

"It shouldn't be this hard to make a baby, should it?" Meg said. "Doesn't seem fair that people who shouldn't have kids pop them out, and those who should have them, struggle."

"I think about that all the time," Cass answered.

"Did you have a name for him?" Mom asked.

Cass nodded. "Thomas. After Dad. Thomas Joseph Brennan."

"Your own baby Tommy," Mom said, understanding.

For a moment no one said anything and then Gabi ran into the dining room with a plastic plate from the kitchen, asking if she could please have another slice of cake since her piece had been small. Meg cut her a sliver. Kit asked if she could have another sliver, too. It was good cake. Meg was an excellent baker.

After Gabi left, Mom circled her teacup with her hands. "You won't ever forget your Tommy," she said quietly. "I know I've told you this before, but I've never forgotten the babies I lost. There were three between Meg and the twins. I never knew if they were boys or girls. Back then they didn't tell you those things. I wondered, though."

"What did Dad do when you lost them?" Cass asked, brow furrowing.

"Told me he was sorry. That he loved me." Marilyn paused, looking back, remembering the years of being a young wife and mother. "That I would conceive again. And then he'd go to work. Escape to his beloved fire house. To his boys." Her voice held the barest hint of bitterness. "He was lucky. He had somewhere else to go. I was here alone with a toddler."

The clock in the living room suddenly chimed nine. It caught them by surprise. No one knew when it'd gotten so late, and it was Sunday night, a school night, too. Meg said she'd need to get the kids home soon. They lived in Santa Rosa, and once Meg and Jack left, everyone else would go, too. Tommy and Cass to Walnut Creek. Kit to her small house in Oakland.

"I'd try again," Cass said in a rush when the clock stopped chiming. "I've met with a new specialist, a doctor who thinks he can help me, but Tommy has said no. Says he can't go through that again."

Kit opened her mouth to speak but then thought better of it. She wasn't married. Had never been married. Wasn't her place.

Instead Mom said carefully, "Maybe he just needs more time—"

"It's our tenth wedding anniversary this year. I want a baby." Cass's voice dropped, deepening with emotion. "I don't want to wait. I can't wait. I'm ready to be a mom now."

"Have you two considered using a surrogate?" Kit asked, feeling Cass's desperation and aware that her brother didn't want to adopt. He'd wanted a son to follow in his footsteps, just the way he'd followed in his father's. The Brennan men had been San Francisco firefighters for six generations, all the way back before the Great Earthquake and Fire of 1906, and Tommy Jr. was proud of this legacy. Maybe too proud.

"Tommy says the Church is against it."

"The Church doesn't support IVF either," Meg pointed out.

This was greeted by an uncomfortable silence, which stretched until Meg added, "Maybe it's time you and Tommy revisited the idea of adopting—"

"He won't," Cass said shortly. "It's our baby or nothing."

Meg gestured impatiently. "But when you adopt, that baby becomes your baby."

"I know, but Tommy won't even discuss it. He wants—" Cass broke off as the front door opened and the men's voices could be heard in the hall. She pressed her lips together, frustration and resentment in her tense expression. "Let's just let this go. Okay?"

They did.

But in the car, driving home, Kit played the evening over in her head. The cheerful dinner conversation, where everyone made an effort to be light, kind, and funny, and where even Meg and Jack seemed to put their differences aside for the night. The fluffy coconut cake on the heirloom sideboard. The dimmed lights. The golden glow of the birthday candles. Her dad's big baritone singing "Happy Birthday." The bittersweet chorus of *make a wish* . . .

Hands flexing against the steering wheel, Kit thought of the wishes that had come to her. Wishes she'd make if it were her birthday . . .

For Mom to live.

For Cass to have her baby.

For Jack and Meg's marriage to survive this rocky transition.

And for Kit, herself? What did she want personally? What was her heart's desire? That was easy. She was selfish. Wasn't wishing for world peace or clean water for developing nations? No, she wanted love. Marriage. Babies. She wanted to have her own family. She'd be forty in a couple weeks. It was time. The clock was ticking.

And yet, if she only had one wish . . . and if the wish could come true . . . what would she do? She'd save Mom, of course.

The oncologist was astonished that Marilyn Brennan had lasted this long, but couldn't imagine her making it through the spring. It was January 8 now. That meant Mom had what? February? March? Maybe Easter? Easter came late this year, mid-April. Would Mom be with them then?

The thought made Kit's insides churn. She wished she hadn't had that second sliver of birthday cake. Wished she was already home in bed instead of still driving at ten o'clock at night.

Kit's phone rang. It was Meg, her oldest sister. "Home safe?" Kit asked, answering.

"Just got back a few minutes ago. Sorry we left you with all the dishes."

"Not a big deal. Dad helped. Gave us a chance to talk."

"He's okay?"

"Seemed like it. But it's hard to tell with Dad. He doesn't like to burden us."

"I'm not okay. I've been upset ever since leaving the house."

"Cass and the baby thing," Kit guessed.

"Yes. I'm worried about them, Tommy and Cass. I can understand why he doesn't want to do the IVF anymore, but his stand on adoption is ridiculous."

Kit changed lanes to let a faster car pass her. "I agree."

"He'll lose Cass if he's not careful."

"I know."

"Now's the time for them to explore all their options if they want to become parents. But I don't think Tommy wants to be a parent at this point. I think he's decided that he's okay without kids."

Dad had said something similar to Kit while they washed dishes. Apparently Tommy had told Dad tonight that he was ready to move forward and just get on with things. That he had come to terms with the infertility thing and that he was good without kids. Cass wasn't, though. "He's worn out," Kit said. "He needs a break from the focus on making babies."

"Which is great, but Cass is a labor and delivery nurse. She wants a baby of her own. Needs to be a mom."

Kit understood. She loved kids. That's why she'd become a teacher. She'd taught for seventeen years now, the last sixteen at Memorial High, a Catholic school in east Oakland, not far from San Leandro. She'd recently been promoted to head of the English department, which would look great on a resume, but wasn't such an honor if you knew there were only three English teachers at Memorial. "What do you think about them using a surrogate?"

"I don't have a problem with it. Do you?"

"No."

"I don't think anyone in the family does. I wish they'd look into it. It's expensive, but Cass and Tommy already have the frozen embryos."

Remembering her conversation with Dad, Kit rubbed at her brow, easing the tension headache. "I just can't see Tommy ever agreeing to it. I don't know if it's a control thing, or a society thing, but Tommy's against taking any more extreme measures to make a baby."

"Adopting isn't extreme. I'd adopt, if I couldn't have kids."

"I would, too. Let's just hope Cass can convince Tommy to reconsider all their options."

Monday was Kit's least favorite day of the week. It was hard to rally Monday morning after a weekend away from school. She knew her students felt the same way, too, so she made a point of making each Monday morning's lessons interesting, trying to hook her students' attention quickly, painlessly. Or as painlessly as possible considering that most of her students were sleep-deprived and school started early.

Fortunately, as the head of her very small department, Kit was able to pick the classes she wanted to teach and she chose to teach everything—from basic, freshman English to the very advanced AP British lit. It meant she had six different preps but she liked it that way, as the varied curriculum held her interest and allowed her to teach far more novels, poetry, and plays every year than she'd be able to teach otherwise.

Kit loved her books. Reading was her thing. But being a teacher wasn't just about sharing great books with young, bright minds. It was also about managing, controlling, organizing, disciplining, advising, as well as assuming extra duties to keep the school's overhead down. At Memorial, the faculty all had duties outside their classroom. Yard duty, cafeteria duty, extracurricular jobs, advisor jobs, coaching positions. Teachers wore many hats. Kit was spending her lunch hour in her classroom wearing her Drama Club advisor hat now.

Kit had founded the Drama Club her first year at Memorial High and for the past fifteen years it'd been one of the school's most prestigious clubs, putting on wonderful, if not extravagant and exhausting, productions every spring.

But this year she was beginning to think there wouldn't be a production. The club was small, with less than a dozen students. Her die-hard thespians, the most talented kids she'd probably ever worked with, had graduated in June, and she—and the club— missed those nine kids. The seven students that remained in the club had only managed to recruit one new freshman, and the eight club members couldn't agree on anything.

"You're running out of time," Kit said from her desk, raising her voice to be heard over the rustle of paper bags and crumpling plastic and conversation taking place at the student desks. "You don't meet again until next month, and then it's auditions. So you really need to discuss what kind of production interests you, and get some consensus. If you can't agree, then I think it's time you accepted that there won't be a spring show."

"What kind of show can we do again?" one of the sophomore girls asked.

Irritation beat at Kit. She hadn't slept well last night, had woken late, and had dashed to school without breakfast and was starving right now. Her gaze fell on her sandwich. Although it was looking bruised inside its plastic bag it made her mouth water. But she couldn't eat it here, in front of them. She might get grape jelly on her white blouse. She might need to answer a question. She might choke . . . And these kids, helpless as they were, might let her die. Or worse, they might try the Heimlich maneuver on her.

Better to go hungry.

"You can do virtually anything," Kit said, hiding her exasperation with a wry smile. They were just teenagers after all. Fourteen-, fifteen-, and sixteen-year-olds searching for identity, meaning, and clear skin. "Remember the list you brainstormed last month? You could choose a comedy, musical, drama, a series of one-act plays . . . It's up to you. Perhaps you'd like to take a vote?"

Alison Humphrey, the current president of the Drama Club, and the only senior in the club this year, came to life. "We're going to vote now," she said decisively. "It'll be anonymous. Write down on a slip of paper what you'd like to do for the spring production, fold the paper up, and pass it to the front and then we'll tally the votes. Okay?"

The classroom door opened while the students were scribbling down their preferences. It was Polly Powers, one of Memorial's math teachers and Kit's closest friend, in the doorway and she gestured to Kit.

Kit left her desk and stepped out into the hall with Polly.

"Are you going to be stuck in there all lunch?" Polly asked.

"Looks like it. They can't agree on anything."

"Which club?"

"My little thespians."

Polly rolled her eyes. "No wonder." She didn't get theater, or theater kids. Thought they were weird.

And perhaps they were, Kit thought, but she liked that. "How was lunch? Anything interesting happen in the staff room?"

"No. Lunch was boring. Fiona stayed in her room, too."

Fiona Hughes was one of the science teachers, and Polly's and Kit's close friend. The three of them hung out together a lot. "Why?"

"Chase is being a dick. She was crying. Didn't want anyone to see her."

Kit frowned. Fiona and Chase had only been married for eighteen months but it'd been difficult from the start. "What's he doing now?"

"I don't know. The usual. But she needs some cheering up. Think we need to take her out after work. Have a drink. Are you free?"

"Yes." Kit peeked into the class, saw that Alison was now recording the votes and turned back to Polly. "Let's head out as soon as the staff meeting's over."